# THE ONE

## T.A. CALDWELL

INKUBATOR
BOOKS

Published by Inkubator Books
www.inkubatorbooks.com

ISBN (eBook): 978-1-83756-622-8
ISBN (Paperback): 978-1-83756-624-2
ISBN (Hardback): 978-1-83756-625-9

# NOTE FROM THE AUTHOR

Dear Readers,

First and foremost, I want to say thank you!

Marcus and Emily have a twisted love story. The One explores the dark depths of power, obsession and possession. Be prepared. Marcus Sterling is not for the faint of heart.

I adore you all and your mental health matters. Here is a list of content warnings for this book. Take care of yourself because there are some graphic and triggering scenes.

- Violence Physical and emotional abuse
- Domestic violence
- Consensual sex and dubious consent
- Age gap
- Manipulative main male character

Now that you've been warned, enjoy the story. You can help other readers find this book by leaving a review.

Love to all of you,

T. A. Caldwell

# 1

## MARCUS

It's a beautiful afternoon. The sky is blue and the sun is high, sparkling off the water that a few fluffy clouds floating overhead shadow. Rocky cliffs on both sides create a private cove, providing a breakwater that softens the surf.

This is a favorite spot on my island, and Karyn and I have spent a lot of time here since we met. The water is warm as we wade in, crystal-clear and shallow enough that we can see the colorful fish dart around our feet. I take her hand and pull her toward the sand. "We'll swim later. Let's have our lunch."

Her dark hair is loose and tousles around her face with the gentle sea breeze. I paste on a smile as we spread our blanket out on the powder-soft sand and start to prepare our picnic. She fixes me a plate filled with tea sandwiches and crab cakes while I pop the cork on the champagne.

The sun gets higher as we enjoy our food, sip the champagne, and enjoy the sound of the waves rolling in. Karyn gives me a coy look as she stretches out on her side. Her lacy cover-up opens enough for me to see her black bikini top that enhances the swell of her breasts. It wasn't her beauty or her body alone that attracted me. It was her personality, but the truth is in her lies.

For two years, I gave her everything. Comfort, wealth, the notoriety of my name. I only asked one thing from her. Honesty.

I force a smile and feed her a plump grape from the basket. She gives me a small smile back as she chews, then wipes the juices from her full red lips.

"Are you enjoying this day?" I ask, leaning back on the blanket.

"So much," she tells me, lying out beside me. "I missed you while you were away."

I hold her hand and a gentle breeze cools our sun-heated skin. "It's not a bad life, is it? Living on an island in paradise."

"No." She squeezes my hand, but now I know that's another lie.

"On our last trip to New York, I got the feeling you missed the city."

She sighs. "It gets lonely here without you. I wish we could travel together more often."

Perhaps there was still a place inside me that knew she couldn't be trusted, or we would have done that. If you give a woman an inch, she'll take a mile. In Karyn's case, she looked for a way out of our relationship. Thankfully, my employees are faithful and I was alerted to the situation. "I have a phone meeting this afternoon," I redirect the conversation in a lazy tone.

"You always have something," Karyn replies.

I briefly wonder if that's why she did this. "Does that bother you? The work I do to afford a place like this?"

"No." She props up on an elbow. "I didn't mean anything by that. I'm sorry."

"Don't be sorry." I run a finger over the smooth skin of her shoulder. "Just be honest. Are you happy?"

"Yes."

Her bottom lip quivers and her eyes tell me that's another lie.

"Good." I cup her chin. "Let's go for a swim before I have to go to this meeting."

I get up and she pulls off her cover-up, revealing her seductive body. Busty with a small waist that flares into wide hips that narrow into supple legs. She's lovely, but she isn't perfect. Karyn has been a waste of my time.

Together, we wade into the surf, warm today in the shallows. She wraps her arms around my neck, and her legs grip my hips as I walk us into deeper waters.

She laughs as I dip her back, wetting her hair, and her brown eyes sparkle. A guy could almost believe she's in love. I capture her smiling lips in a kiss and she sighs as I pull us out farther. With my tall frame, I can still feel the sand under my feet, but Karyn couldn't if she let go of me. We look like the lovers I believed we were, but I taste the lies in her kiss. I'm not so angry; more disappointed. I believed she was the one.

She breaks our kiss, laughing and leaning back in my arms to dip her head in the water. I get a view of her little black bikini top and a firm, tan tummy. I wonder if I'll miss her.

She pulls herself back up, wrapping her arms around my neck, and I let go of her ass, dropping her. She sputters in surprise and starts to tread water.

I swim a few feet away from her and hold out a hand to

her with a playful grin. Her face lights up with a new smile and she joins me. I pull her into my arms, kissing her deeply. She holds me to her and our tongues swirl together. Leaning back, I search her eyes as she gazes at me, and I tuck a wet strand of hair behind her ear, memorizing her face.

"Karyn, tell me why?"

She tilts her head as her brows knit together. "Tell you why?" Confusion mixed with concern darkens her eyes.

My arms tighten around her. "I know what you did in New York."

Her eyes grow wider as the fear sinks in. That's right, baby. I'm always watching.

How many times have we had this conversation? Not often enough lately, apparently.

I believed she had accepted this, us. How could she not know this would end us?

The tears start. "Don't hurt my mother."

I snort. "Your mother? This is between you and me. I trusted you."

She palms my cheek. "No. Marcus, I love you."

More lies. How did I not see it before? I place my hands on her face and kiss her again, our goodbye, and she knows it too as she shivers under my touch. I draw out this kiss, my last taste, knowing we've shared some good memories. She won't be forgotten.

Dropping my arms, I pin hers to her sides with my embrace. She tries to pull away and I let her go, enough for her to turn and try to swim away. I pull her back against my chest and wrap my legs around hers. Securing her with one arm, I place my hand on the back of her head.

"Marcus," she begs. "Please..." But her pleas are drowned out when I shove her head under the water. Karyn struggles, but my grip is firm in her hair. The water churns as she thrashes with her arms and kicks her legs. Bubbles surround my face as she claws at me and I take in some water too. I let the buoyant waves keep me afloat as I hold her under, and it doesn't last long. The fight wanes as her life slips away.

I'm not sure how long we float like this, letting the current take us out farther. I could let her go here, and no one may ever see her again, but I'm not that kind of guy. She'll have a proper burial after we announce her tragic and accidental drowning.

With an arm supporting her head, I swim back and drag her onto the sand.

I notice we're a ways down the beach from where we had our picnic, and I'll have a decent walk back to the house.

I catch my breath, sitting by her lifeless body, her legs still in the surf, but I know she won't wash out here in the shallows. I'll send someone to look for her soon.

Studying her profile, I see her eyes are open but sightless. She's certainly not as pretty in death as she was in life. I pick up her left hand, touch the ring I gave her, and feel the loss. I'm right back at square one again.

I've tried, and Karyn isn't my first failure, but it doesn't dim the disappointment. Finding the perfect wife isn't as easy as I imagined. I brush the wet strands off her face and swallow hard. "I'm sorry you did this to yourself," I tell her lifeless body. "I'd hoped for more."

I'd stay with her longer, but I have an appointment, and I pull myself up from the sand.

I don't look back at her as I start my hike home. I keep close to the tide line, letting the waves wash away my footprints until I reach our picnic site. I don't look back. I'm not a man who revels in the past. I face the future.

I climb the steps to my home, the one I built to live my life with my perfect wife, and stop at the outdoor shower. Peeling off my trunks, I take a quick rinse and dry off. My mind is already on my upcoming meeting as I pull on a dry shirt and a pair of loose shorts. I cross the pool deck and enter the house through the glass doors. Carmen, my housekeeper, catches me right away.

"Where is Mrs. Sterling?" she inquires.

"She stayed to sun herself a little longer. I'm sure she'll be back shortly," I reply with a quick glance at my watch. I pass her and hurry to my study, where the phone is already ringing. I cut that one close, and I answer the call, placing it on speaker. With a deep breath, I plaster on a smile. "Good afternoon, Heath. How is the weather in New York?"

He snorts. "Freezing rain. You?"

"Sunshine and blue skies."

"Some days I hate you," he teases. "Let me patch in the others."

Heath and I met in college and we started Sterling Enterprises together. He's the genius behind the renewable energy technology we sell. I excel on the business side and together we're building an empire. Neither of us could have done this without the other.

Our call lasts thirty minutes as he covers everything I need to know, including the agendas for the next few weeks. James, our CFO, informs me I'll need to be back in the home office next week to finalize some contracts. We'll see how that goes since I need time to lay Karyn to rest.

As the others drop off the call, Heath stays on. "Don't

forget next month we have that skiing trip in Aspen. Is Karyn joining us?"

I did forget. It feels like that happens more often these days. I do enjoy the sport of skiing, but this is more of a business trip with potential clients. "I doubt it. Karyn isn't a fan of the cold. I think she'd prefer to stay here."

"Who wouldn't," he chuckles.

Who indeed. I chose to build on this island around the time I started getting antsy to settle down. It's the ideal place to keep a wife. I just haven't found the perfect woman yet. "I'll see you next week."

As I head upstairs for a proper shower, Carmen catches me. "Mrs. Sterling hasn't returned yet," she informs me.

I turn on the stairs, pulling up a concerned look. "Hmm. Have Lucas go fetch her. Perhaps she fell asleep. We wouldn't want her to burn," I add with a smirk.

She retreats with a nod to find Lucas, my security guard who travels with me everywhere. I'm grateful for the staff I've employed and their loyalty to me. Lucas won't ask questions. I check my watch again. Dinner is always served at six. I'll make my normal preparations, but I'm sure tonight's drama is going to fuck up that schedule.

# 2

## EMILY

The ice cream is already starting to melt in the New York summer heat. I shift the bag on my arm and push open the door to my apartment building. I make a quick stop at my mailbox, and my phone rings. Balancing the phone between my shoulder and my ear, I dig out my keys. "Hi, Gia."

She starts talking a mile a minute as I shuffle through the mail. Bills, more bills, and a letter from my mother, which is probably another request for money. I stuff all the envelopes in my purse and take the stairs down to my garden-level apartment.

"Gia, slow down," I mutter as I unlock my door. "Now, what did you say?"

"I said I have two VIP passes to Ecstasy for tonight and you're going with me."

"No." I chuckle, dropping my keys on the counter, and then get my ice cream in the freezer. My cat, Bella, rubs against my legs, demanding dinner. "I already have plans tonight."

"Emily!" she yells into the phone. "You have to go. I have

VIP passes! They're priceless. It's a once-in-a-lifetime opportunity!"

I hold the phone away from my ear and roll my eyes. The last place I want to be tonight is a noisy dance club.

"What are your plans anyway?" Gia continues. "Sweatpants and watching some dumb movie with your cat?"

Ah, she knows me well. I do have an old movie in the queue, full of crime and drama along with a heartbreaking romance. Cuddling with my cat on a Friday night sounds way better than hitting the town. "I wouldn't have anything to wear to a fancy nightclub." I take a can of wet food out of the cupboard and open it as Bella mews.

"Come over. I'll loan you a dress and do your makeup."

I sigh at her bubbling excitement and dump the can in Bella's bowl. Gia and I met in college, although she dropped out two years ago to pursue a modeling career. That decision paid off for her, and today she's working all the time, living in a nice one-bedroom apartment and getting perks like VIP passes to the hottest new nightclubs' opening nights.

I, on the other hand, graduated this spring, live in a studio apartment, stressed about my student loans and how my entry-level job will pay for anything.

Gia, however, is an artist at Emily makeovers. "I can't afford a cab or drinks." Or anything really.

"Emily! Why do you always assume you have to pay for anything? I'll pay your cab fare. I'm not letting you get out of this with your lame excuses, so get your ass over here."

Oh Lord, help me. Gia and I do not have the same bodies and cannot pull off the same clothes. We do, however, share a shoe size, which can be awesome. Gia has amazing shoes.

"Are you on your way?" she asks.

I give up. How many nights does she come over to curl

up on the couch and watch old movies with me with a bucket of ice cream? I accept this is happening. "Fine, just don't dress me like a hooker."

She laughs. "I'll dress you like something other than a twenty-two-year-old virgin cat lady."

That's fair and all true. It's sad that I'm so reluctant to go. I'm too young to feel so old.

I tell her I'm on my way and hang up. There's no need to look in my fridge to know dinner options are scarce. Meanwhile, Bella licks the bottom of her bowl.

I sigh and look around my apartment. I love this city. It screams opportunity. I just haven't exactly found mine yet. Gia discovered a fast track while I'm climbing a mountain, but I still believe I can do this. I crouch down and scratch Bella's ears. "Sorry, girl. It's Friday night in New York City, and it looks like I'm going out."

---

GIA RUNS the blush brush over my cheek and smiles with a nod. "Perfect."

I look in the mirror, always impressed by Gia's skill with makeup. I don't look overdone. She just highlights my features so my hazel eyes look bigger, my lips fuller, and my skin brighter.

She goes to work on my hair, another thing I normally fail at, usually settling for a ponytail. Gia pulls out the hot iron and bobby pins, creating a perfect updo with curly wisps that frame my face.

Satisfied with my look, Gia ducks into her closet and returns with a jewel-green dress. "It's pretty," I admit, but I can see it will leave little to the imagination. The plunging neckline might show off Gia's cleavage but will more than likely point out my total lack thereof.

"Okay, shoes." She taps her lips as she looks over her selection and chooses a pair of strappy sandals. Her phone dings as I'm putting them on. "The car is here," she alerts me, and I grab my wine, draining what's left in the glass.

We giggle like schoolgirls as we head outside and climb in the back of the car. I've loosened up considerably, a mixture of Gia's enthusiasm and alcohol. The city feels alive, lit up with the streetlamps and glowing lights from the restaurants, bars, and shops. Pedestrians crowd the sidewalks while traffic clogs the streets in this trendy part of town. We pull up to the newly renovated, two-story building and my heart drops at the sight of the line in front that disappears around the corner. "Gia?"

"Don't worry." She grabs my hand as we exit the car and leads me to the front of the line. The bouncer gives her a long, appraising look before she presents our passes. "Ms. Cincetti, welcome." He steps aside to let us in. As usual, he barely gives me a look. I'm a ghost in Gia's presence.

Loud music immediately assaults us. The bass thumps my insides and the atmosphere is electric. I'm swept up in the crowd's excitement as we take the stairs to the second floor.

The VIP lounge is less crowded, with a long bar on one wall, intimate tables in the center, and more conversational seating areas in the corners. Gia and I stop to look down at the dance floor, and my hips grow a life of their own as they start to sway. Gia giggles. "Let's get a drink first."

I glance over at Gia, refusing to be jealous of her amazing, tiny, metallic gold dress that shimmers with every movement. It shows off her incredible legs, and well, let's just say it shows off everything! Gia is beautiful. She knows it, and knows how to use it. She flips her long black hair over her shoulder. Her light green eyes land on her target, and immediately a man is up and offering his seat at the bar.

"Can I buy you a drink?" he asks.

Gia slides onto the stool, crossing her legs and batting her lashes. "Yes. Two apple martinis, please."

Taking the open spot next to her, I sip my drink while Gia chats up our new friend. A minute later, she's off to the dance floor. Personally, I need another drink before I make a fool of myself out there.

She disappears into the crowd and I turn, setting my drink down. It's not unusual for me to find myself alone in situations like this. Gia is a magnet for attention, where I possibly repel it. It's not just because I'm shy, but I have no desire for a meaningless hookup with a guy at a bar.

Mike, our friendly bartender, kindly keeps me company between serving others. He sets a fresh drink in front of me and I shake my head. "I didn't order anything."

He nods to someone behind me and I turn to see a man taking Gia's empty stool. He looks at my drink and smiles. "You looked lonely."

My lips part, but no words come out. I simply stare into the most striking blue eyes I've ever seen. He's dressed in dark slacks and a blue button-down shirt with the sleeves rolled up, and his scent invades my space but not in a bad way. His cologne is not drugstore-cheap or overdone but subtle, warm, and herby.

He holds out his hand and smiles. "My name is Marcus."

I ignore the hand, focused on his full, kissable lips set in a square jaw with a dark shadow of afternoon stubble. His eyes twinkle with amusement, perhaps at my failure to react to the outstretched hand. My manners manage to kick in, but not my ability to speak as I shake his hand. His skin is warm, and suddenly I'm hot everywhere.

"Um. Hi," I choke out. I'm full-on blushing now, totally wishing the ground would open up and swallow me right here. This man is gorgeous, and it's not just his gorgeous face or broad shoulders and sexy smile. There's an air to him that's both confident and smooth, and I'm neither. He needs a Gia. Where the hell is Gia?

As if I've mentally summoned her, Gia bounces up behind me. "Hey, Emily! Who's your friend?" Her hands land on my shoulders. It's then I realize I've never taken my hand back. Oh my God! How long have I been holding onto his hand? I jerk mine away in the most awkward way imaginable. Gia rubs my shoulders. It'll be fine. His eyes are on her now. I'll be completely forgotten in three, two, one.

"Emily." My name rolls off his lips with the sexiest accent. "It's so nice to meet you."

I've just died. The sex god is in the presence of the goddess and is still talking to me. This is a dream because it completely cannot be real.

Another handsome man joins us at the bar. His dark blond hair is a little too long, his brown eyes a bit mischievous, and he fills out a suit rather nicely. Where do these kinds of men come from? I'm never saying no to another 'invite only' premiere opening of anything Gia comes up with!

"Hey, Marcus, I found you. I thought you bailed," the newcomer says, then lands a megawatt smile on me and Gia. This time, predictably, his eyes stay on her. "Hi, I'm Heath."

"Hello, Heath," Gia purrs from behind me, no social awkwardness at all from her. She leans over me to shake his hand. "I'm Gia. This is Emily." Her sultry introduction will probably have him sealed to her for the night. Damn, why can't I have her skills, just this one time?

Heath looks at my fresh drink and Gia's empty hands. "What are you drinking, beautiful?"

"An appletini." They exchange smiles before he pats the bar.

"One appletini and two Macallans neat, please."

Mike gets to work on his order, and I look back at Marcus. He gives me a subtle grin as though he's apologizing for his friend, who is asking Gia if she'd like to dance. As the beverages are served, they take their drinks and I'm left alone—no, not alone, on my own—with Marcus. With his drink in hand, he nods at mine and taps it in a toast when I pick it up. My eyes follow the glass to his mouth and stare as he licks a drop from his lip. He grins at me and I take a generous swallow of my own drink.

He leans closer. I lean away and his brow furrows.

"I apologize. Do I make you nervous?" he asks.

"No." I try for a laugh, but it comes out like a snort, and now I know my face is on fire.

"Good," he says, "it's not my intention." He grins, revealing his dimpled cheeks. "These types of clubs aren't really my thing. I saw you over here avoiding eye contact with everyone and thought perhaps we are like-minded."

Like-minded? Obviously, this man isn't feeling as out of place as I am right now. I go for a chuckle that comes out like a nervous giggle. "No. I mean, my friend invited me, but yes, nightclubs are not my usual thing."

"Hmm." He takes another sip from his drink. "I like a more peaceful environment where I can focus. The bloody lights and the noise here tend to make my head hurt."

Geez, that accent. I think I could seriously orgasm just from listening to him talk.

"Your accent is...?"

"British," he finishes for me. "I'm from the UK."

"Oh." I'm sure my blush is a permanent feature tonight. I just need to accept that.

"And you? You don't sound like a New Yorker. Where are you from, Emily?" he asks.

My lips tip up, but my eyes drop. "I was born in California." I glance back up, and he's watching me intently. I lift a shoulder. "Since then, I've lived in fifteen other states. My mother had a hard time settling in one place."

He cocks his head as he studies me. "Where was your father?"

I'm not sure how to answer. It's not a frequently asked question. "He, um..." Screw it, I choose to be honest. "I never met him."

He doesn't say anything, and I toy with my cocktail glass. "What about you? Are your parents still in the UK?"

"My parents are deceased," he states with a frown and finishes his drink while motioning to Mike for another.

I have no idea how to respond to that. "I'm so sorry."

"Don't be." Those stunning eyes are back on me. "I'm not. What brought you to New York?"

I blink at his response. Maybe he wasn't close to them. It's not my business. "Um, college, but Gia is probably what keeps me here."

"Gia?" he asks, leaning back a little. "The girl you're here with? She's a good friend to you, then?"

"She is. The best." The truth is, with my gypsy lifestyle growing up, I never had the opportunity to attach myself to one person. Finding this friendship with Gia has grounded me in ways I've never known.

"Hmm. Good friends make your life richer," he muses. "I met Heath in college. Those were good times." His eyes roam over my face and down my body, then back up. "Gia is a model?"

I nod, and he asks, "Do you model as well?"

That causes a laugh to escape me. "No. I just graduated. I work for a property management company."

"Oh?" He lifts a brow. "What did you major in?"

My cheeks heat again. "History and political science," I admit. "This is just my first job out of school."

"Ah." He takes a drink and focuses on the shelves of bottles behind the bar.

My gaze narrows in on his throat as he swallows, and I quickly look away. "What do you do?"

He smiles without looking at me. "My company has interests in many areas, but we focus on green energy."

His company? Like, did he mean the one he works for or *his* company? I take in the quality of his clothes and assume whichever it is, he's paid well.

A new song starts, and it's one I actually like. My head bobs to the beat, and I'm mouthing the first part of the lyrics before picking up my drink and wrapping my lips around the straw.

He turns to me now. "Do you like this song?"

I realize I'm doing a little wiggle dance on my stool and quickly get control of myself. "Um, yes."

"Would you like to dance?"

I choke on the liquid and start to cough. Holy flippen what!? He asked me to dance?

He takes in my expression and shakes his head. "It's fine. I'm not really good at this type of dancing."

"No!" I blurt out. "I mean, yes." God, I sound like an idiot. "I can't dance either, but who would notice?"

We both look down at the crowded dance floor, and a grin forms on those too sexy lips. He stands, extending his hand. "Miss Emily?"

My heart stutters at how I love the way he says my name. "Sir Marcus." I take his hand.

"I'm no knight." He grins and twirls me as I stand, which makes me giggle. "Let's see what we can do on the dance floor."

# 3

## MARCUS

There are times when it's better to be lucky than good. I study Emily's hand in mine and note no rings. I was dreading this invite tonight. I've been staying out of the limelight since Karyn's passing, playing the dutiful widower in mourning. Now, as I return Emily's pretty smile, I'm so glad I forced myself to show up.

The music becomes louder as we take the stairs down, and our opportunity for quiet conversation is completely lost. The throngs of writhing bodies encase us, and the scent of pheromones and sweat is strong, but as I pull Emily into my arms, her subtle perfume floods my senses. It's sweet, like fresh berries, and I dip my head to take a whiff. Placing my hands on her lower back, I start to move us in a suggestive dance that fits the beat. She glances up at me with those wide, innocent eyes.

They weren't the first thing I noticed about her, but I do believe they are such a lovely color. Shades of greens and golds. No, it was her posture that caught my eye. She was attempting to look brave and invisible at the same time. Her body is lean, her face still rounded with youth. Age has not yet started to sharpen her features. Her hair, not quite blond or brown, is piled on top of her head and showing off a long, slender neck. She was sitting alone, avoiding eye contact with everyone but the bartender. I could almost taste her vulnerability.

I'm delighted with the way her cheeks flush a pretty shade of rose as I roll my hips into her, and she matches my movements as we dance in sync. It's sensual, sexual even, and I can't wait to experience her more fully. I take advantage of the crowded dance floor and turn her back to me, pulling her in close to where I can feel her ass against my groin. Unlike her girlfriend, who is nearly begging for Heath to fuck her as she grinds against him, Emily rests her hands on my arms and attempts to relax against my body.

We're immersed in the heat of the dance floor for several songs, but when she licks her lips with a shy smile, my eyes drop to the dewy skin of her exposed chest, and I ask if she'd like another drink.

"Yes, please."

I adore her manners, so sweet and compliant. I believe she'll be easy to train with her basic submissive nature. I take her back to the VIP lounge, keeping her hand in mine the whole time. Not only because I enjoy the contact, but I'm staking my claim on her for anyone else whose eye she might catch.

Upstairs, I order us two more drinks, but Emily requests water. "Are you driving?" I ask.

She laughs. "In this city? No."

Hmm. I like that too. My mother was a loud, opinionated drunk who was basically insane. I prefer women who do not resemble her at all. I glance at my watch and know I need to be outside for the photoshoot soon. I'm reluctant to end this time with Emily, but I've already arranged to leave when we're through. I'll stick to my plans, but I believe I have her on the hook. Now it's time to reel her in.

"I'm so glad we had the opportunity to meet tonight. Unfortunately, I must go."

Her cheeks fall with her pout, and her disappointment pleases me. "I was wondering if there was any possibility you'd have dinner with me tomorrow night?"

Her whole face changes with my request. From pouty to surprised, and it's probably wrong how much I'm enjoying this. Her honest nature makes her an easy read, which is perfect for a man who was recently duped by his wife.

"Please," I add with a smile.

Her lips part, and she pulls in a breath. "I—okay? Sure. Where?"

We'll need to work on her ability to articulate, but I'm already in love with her mouth, and I can't wait for the opportunity to explore all the ways I can use it. I hand her my phone. "Enter your number. I'll make reservations and call you with the details."

She enters her number with shaky fingers and gives me a little smile. "I enjoyed meeting you too." She gives the phone back to me, and I clasp her hand, leaning in to brush my lips over her knuckles. "I'll see you tomorrow."

I don't give her the opportunity to react or respond as I step back and turn away, but I can hardly contain my grin. After this six-month dry spell, I was becoming convinced the perfect woman didn't exist for me, but everything is looking up now.

I jog down the stairs and see Heath is already at the entrance with the owner of this establishment.

"Mr. Sterling, thank you so much for making an appearance tonight." He greets me with a handshake.

"Mr. McGrady, it was my pleasure," I assure him. "I'm impressed. It looks like this club is going to be a hit."

"Well, the publicity I'll get from both of you showing up will help make that a reality." He gestures with his hand toward the door.

I smile as we step into the balmy night air. "We're happy to help. Your success only benefits us."

The paparazzi start snapping photos right away as we exit the building. McGrady gets us lined up under his glowing sign and we do our part, smiling for the photographers. Heath and I are not the rock stars or movie actors who may show up tonight, but we do have some notoriety and a personal interest, as our company owns this property.

I shake hands with Mr. McGrady as my car arrives, and I glance at Heath. "I'm heading home. You?"

"Are you kidding? Did you see the girl I landed tonight?"

I did, and I knew at first glance she wasn't my type. "The underwear model?"

He laughs. "Lingerie model, yes, and I'm hoping for a private showing later." He wiggles his brows and I shake my head with an amused smile. I have no doubt his wish will come true. Heath loves women, and when he focuses on one, they feel loved. Unlike me, he has no desire to settle down at this point in his life, so he mows through them whilst sowing his wild oats. For me, my work is finished here tonight. It's time for me to start planning for the future.

MY FINGERS DRUM on the desk as I listen to the phone ring. Gary Thompson is a private investigator who I keep on the payroll for various reasons. It is early, and a Saturday, but I'm at work. He should show up too.

"Hello?" his gruff voice finally answers.

"Good morning, Mr. Thompson. Marcus Sterling here. I need a background check done."

He attempts to muffle a morning smoker's cough before he responds, "On the record or off?"

"Off record. It's a woman I met. Her name is Emily, and I don't know her last name, but I have a phone number."

"Sure. Send me what you know."

I hit send on the already compiled email. "Already done."

Finished with my call, I look around my corner office lit with the sunlight that pours in through two walls of windows. Today, only the janitors on this floor join me, but I have business in London next week, and I want everything cleared off my desk before I leave. But first things first. I pick up the phone and dial the restaurant to set our reservations for tonight. I'm a part-owner of Marseilles, so it's not as if they won't make room, but I have some specific ideas for this evening.

I request a private rooftop table as it should be a lovely night. These late summer days are brutally hot, but the evenings are pleasant. I also arrange for a violinist to serenade us, candle lighting, and flowers for the atmosphere. It's important not to overlook details with these first impressions.

I smile with thoughts of Emily as the first information starts to dribble in from Thompson. He's located a copy of her driver's license and birth certificate. She does not have a passport, I note. We'll have to arrange for that.

Her picture on my screen holds my attention for a moment before I read on. She's only twenty-two, and as she stated, a recent graduate of NYU. Currently, she's employed as an assistant for Gordon Property Management Co., and I'm a little shocked by the lack of zeros in her annual income.

I realize her presence in the VIP lounge was due to her friendship with the model she was with last night. Pinching my lower lip between my fingers, I wonder how those two ever met up and what I'll need to do regarding that relationship.

I glance back at her photo and relax a little. I should be fine. If she turns out to be everything I hope she is, we'll get her life straightened out. An obvious improvement for her. Women like Emily are a rare species that should be obtained, controlled, and nurtured, and I believe I'm the man who can do all that for her.

4

_____

# EMILY

Gia is rummaging through her closet, and I pick up one of her dress selections and look it over.

"You know, Marseilles is like a five-star gourmet restaurant," she informs me as she turns with a huge smile and another dress option. "He's obviously pulling out all the stops for you."

"Did you sleep with Heath?" I know from her red eyes and her pale face that she partied long after I said my good-byes last night.

"I don't kiss and tell." She smirks.

"Yes, you do." Setting the dress on the bed, I strip off my clothes in front of her full-length mirror.

She laughs. "Okay. Let's say I left him with some sweet memories that should have him calling me back."

She frowns in the reflection of the mirror as I drop my jeans. "Emily, don't you have better underwear than that?"

I take a look at my tattered panties and roll my eyes. "It's not like he'll see my underwear tonight."

"Maybe." She scoops up the thin, silky, cream-colored

sheath dress. "But everyone will see them in this dress." She hangs it back in the closet.

I shrug and try the first outfit she picked out for me as she plops on the bed and opens her laptop. "What are you doing?" I smooth out the A-line skirt.

"Some online stalking. We should know more about this guy you're seeing tonight."

"Gia!" I turn to her with a little laugh. "Stop. Why?"

"In today's world, you want some information before meeting someone alone on a date. What did you say his last name was?" She types on the keyboard.

"Sterling." I look back at the mirror. The dress is pretty, but I don't feel I'm pulling off the Jackie-O look. I reach back to undo the zipper.

"Em." Gia drags out my shortened name. "Look at this."

I join her on the bed, getting close to see her screen.

"He has a fricken Wikipedia page!" She points at his picture. "This is him, right?"

"Yeah." I tip my head and start reading. Marcus Sterling is the only offspring of Sir Matthew Sterling and his wife, Gale Madison. "Wow. He's thirty-five?"

"Don't worry about that. Men in their twenties don't know how to please a woman."

Maybe, but still...

"It says his parents were murdered during a home invasion while he was away at university," Gia says.

My heart takes a little hit for him, and I continue to read the bio. A graduate of Cambridge University, he moved to the United States and launched Sterling Enterprises with his fellow classmate, Heath Carrington. More words catch my eye, like innovative technology, vast real estate, and varied business ventures.

"Gia, did you know Heath was his business partner?"

"No. I didn't even get his last name." She runs her thumb over her bottom lip as she continues to read. "Emily, do you see this? His estimated worth is in the billions."

I stare at that number and my stomach sinks. "I can't do this." I place a shaky hand on my chest and climb off the bed. "I have to cancel."

"Why?"

"Because girls like me don't date men like that. What would I say? How would I act?"

"How did you act at the club? Just be yourself." She keeps scrolling.

That isn't the only problem. "He's part of the one percent. The people I politically advocate against. There's no possible way I can go on a date with some royal billionaire."

I turn when she doesn't respond and see she's still reading.

"Em," she looks up at me. "He was married."

"Was?" I sit down on the bed. "Divorced?"

"Widowed." She turns the computer so I can see the screen. There's a picture of a beautiful brunette with a birth date listed that shows she was three years older than me, and a death date that was early this year.

"That's so sad," I murmur.

"I don't know." Gia takes back the laptop. "She hasn't even been dead a year." She clicks out of the website and starts to scroll through other information that's popped up. "Try on the black one." She points at the dress without looking up.

"You think I should still go?"

That gets her eyes on me. "Honey, this isn't fatal information. But we need to be deadly serious about your outfit and makeup."

———————

HOURS LATER, I'm stepping out of a cab, dressed to the nines in one of Gia's reliable little black dresses. I declined Marcus's offer to pick me up since I hardly know this man. The smart thing to do on any first date is meet them at the location.

I grasp the clutch that barely holds my ID and phone as I open the door to the restaurant. A pretty hostess greets me, and I inquire about a reservation made under the name Sterling.

"Ms. Hanson?" Her smile grows.

My eyes narrow. Did I give Marcus my last name? "Yes?"

"Mr. Sterling is waiting for you." She gestures for me to follow. We walk through a dining room filled with customers seated at various-sized tables draped in white linens. Their conversations are a blurred murmur, highlighted by the clinking of china and crystal as we pass through.

We ascend a dimly lit stairwell near the back, and my nerves amp up when she presses the bar on a metal door, opening it and waving a hand for me to step out. I walk through but immediately halt, seeing the twinkling fairy lights strung over a table for two.

Several candles further light the space. A white linen tablecloth adorns our table, with a bottle of champagne chilling on a serving cart next to it.

Marcus stands and rounds the table to pull out my chair. I move robotically, smoothing my dress as I take my seat.

"You look lovely." He smiles at me. "I hope you don't mind. I took the liberty of ordering champagne." He shows me the label, and I have no idea if I should be impressed or not, but damn if that smile doesn't make him ten times more handsome. Tonight, he's dressed in a dark suit, obviously tailored and that probably costs as much as my college tuition. I press out a grin as he hands me the glass. "Thank you."

Taking the seat across from me, he looks perfectly natural in this environment, and I'm feeling completely out of place.

I take a tentative sip. The bubbles tickle my tongue and I notice my hand is shaking slightly. He watches me as he tastes his champagne and sets down his glass. "Have I done something to make you nervous, Emily?"

"No." I wet my lips and think about how to respond. It's not anything he's done. It's who he is. "I'm not sure why I'm here," I blurt out.

He tips his head and waits for me to explain. I rub my damp hands on my thighs with a nervous giggle. "This isn't even my dress." I wave a hand at our table. "My last date was with a delivery guy from Queens. I don't think I fit in with a British aristocrat who's probably dined with *the* Queen."

That has his eyes growing round. "Did you Google me, Emily?"

My cheeks heat up, but I nod. "I did look you up."

He relaxes a notch. "I'm sure whatever you read was far more colorful than my actual life. Yes, I did meet the Queen, briefly, at a holiday function. She seemed lovely. I personally don't have a title, and I didn't ask you to dine with me tonight because I was attracted to your sense of fashion."

I'm not sure how to respond to that, and I stare down at my hands.

He leans forward. "I know very little about you, but I prefer to learn about people the old-fashioned way. Through conversation."

I glance up at him, feeling slightly guilty. "I apologize, but I admit I was surprised to learn who you are."

"And you feel intimidated by what you learned?" he asks, and when I don't answer him, he continues. "Do you have some prejudice against people born into wealth and then further blessed to be lucky in business?"

"No." Maybe. "It's just..." I focus on the flute in front of me. "Do you have any prejudice against a girl born to a single mother who probably didn't even know her father's last name?"

"No. I do not." Leaning back in his chair, he studies me for a moment. "Emily, I'm just a regular guy who met a nice girl and wanted to get to know her better." He chuckles. "It was probably foolish to attempt to impress her. How about I promise, should you agree to dine with me again, I'll take you to wherever makes you more comfortable."

"Like a burger and fries joint?" I tease.

"If you'd like."

I hear the humor in his voice, and it eases my nerves. Enough that a small smile tips my lips as I look back at him. The waiter interrupts us, delivering appetizers, and he gives us a brief description of each dish. The lack of menus surprises me a little, but I'm impressed with his selection. I skip over the escargot but enjoy the cheese-stuffed pastry and make a daring attempt with the oyster fork. This amuses Marcus, and he shows me how to free the meat from the shell. He actually entices a laugh from me as he demonstrates the correct way to eat an oyster by tipping his head back and swallowing it whole.

I imitate him. "It's good," I admit.

He smiles, washing his bite down with the wine. "Tell me more about you, Emily. You mentioned you moved a lot. Where was your favorite home?"

"Oh." I twist my lips. "I never really called a place home." Perhaps it's his natural confidence that has me opening up. "Utah was the worst. My mother joined a cult and we lived in a commune." I shrug. "Colorado was pretty, and we lived in a cabin there, rather than some of the scary trailer parks we were at in other states."

Marcus listens to me quietly, and I glance out at the lit-up skyline. "New York is the only place I've called home, and it's the only state I've lived in without my mother."

He raises a brow. "Did you put yourself through college?"

"I earned an academic scholarship, but yes, I also worked. I was a waitress and a lifeguard during summers."

"You like to swim?"

I look down, remembering his wife died of an accidental drowning. "Yes." He hasn't brought it up, but I ask about her anyway. "I was sorry to read about what happened to your wife."

We're interrupted again with the main course and a new bottle of wine. The name of the dish is French, but it's described as veal in a creamy wine sauce. I don't mention that I have a personal aversion to eating veal as Marcus thanks the waiter. He focuses back on me. "Try it. It's delicious."

I wonder if speaking about his wife is an uncomfortable

topic, but he comes back to it as he cuts into his meat. "Did it bother you to learn I was married before?"

"No." In fact, now it feels intrusive that we looked him up. "There wasn't much information about her in your bio."

"Hmm." He swirls a piece of veal in the sauce. "What can I tell you about Karyn? We met when I was visiting the Hamptons. She was a waitress at a café, and she intrigued me right away. She was beautiful and full of life. We married shortly after and were together for two years." A wistful smile tips his lips. "She was so young. Her death was tragic."

My heart pinches for him and I look down at my plate. "It must be hard to lose someone like that."

"Saying that final goodbye is never easy." Marcus picks up his wineglass. "I do believe she'd want me to move on, be happy, and have a fulfilling life." He takes a sip, keeping his eyes on me, and nods at my plate. "Do you dislike veal?"

"No, it's..." I turn as the door opens again. A violinist joins us and starts to play. The heartfelt music surrounds our space and he serenades us in a language I don't know, but his voice is rich and full. I pick up my wine, looking at Marcus as a warm evening breeze flutters my hair. He takes my hand and gives me a little smile. I glance around at this rooftop wonderland, this romantic setting, this man, and wonder how in the world I ended up here.

# 5

## MARCUS

People always have questions. Whether it's about my parents' murders or Karyn's untimely death. I've become so accustomed to providing answers that they hardly sound sincere anymore. The best thing to do is redirect the conversation. "You did not enjoy the main course."

Her cheeks pink up. "No. It's just... I can't get past the fact veal is made from slaughtering calves."

"Oh. Yet cows are acceptable?"

She squirms in her seat. "Calves are cute."

I'll let her go for this one and enjoy the light in her eyes as she tucks a lock of hair behind her ear. Our dessert plates are set out. I thank the waiter and look back at her. "Do you like creme brûlée?"

"Yes."

Damn, she is so pretty with that shy smile.

Emily picks up her dessert fork. "Tell me how you met Heath."

That's a safe topic. "We roomed together at Cambridge. He was always looking for trouble and somehow roped me into some of his antics." I chuckle. "We have very different personalities, but it's benefited our partnership."

Emily's eyes sparkle as her smile grows. "Gia was the only person I stayed in touch with since college. We are also very different, but I love her."

I agree because I noticed the differences right off. "What about other friends you made growing up?"

Her smile falters, and her gaze drops to her cake. "My life didn't allow me to make real friends growing up."

"That's something we have in common."

She glances back up, questioning that, and I elaborate. "My life growing up didn't allow me to make true friends either. University was the first time I was free enough from my family to really find myself."

Her smile fades as she runs her finger over the stem of her wineglass. "You said something last night that gave me the impression you weren't close to your parents."

I huff through a bitter laugh. "My parents were very self-centered and more focused on their own lives than their son. The only time they noticed me was when I disappointed them. My childhood was filled with more discipline than love." In part, that is all true. The whole picture would be that my mother was crazy and my father was weak, but it's not the conversation I want to have with Emily.

"I'm sorry to hear that."

The compassion looks lovely on her. "Yes, well, that was my past. Today, I've learned to live the life I want and not let others' expectations dictate what I do."

That has her lips twitching up. "Maybe that's something else we have in common. I'm trying to live my life like that too."

At a glance, I doubt that, but it doesn't matter. The only

expectations she'll learn to meet are mine. "That sounds like a good outlook."

I've enjoyed Emily tonight and as our dessert plates are cleared, I raise my glass. "To new beginnings."

Her cheeks pink up, but she clicks her glass to mine. "To new experiences."

An appropriate toast. Emily will be enjoying many new experiences now that I've found her. We seal it with a sip. "Did you take a cab?" I ask.

"Yes."

"I'll have my driver take you home."

"No." She brushes that off. "That's not necessary. I—"

"I insist," I cut her off. She has no reason to be embarrassed about where she lives. I've already seen pictures of the neighborhood and the front of her garden-level apartment. Everything is about to start looking up for Ms. Hanson because I believe I've found the next Mrs. Sterling.

"Emily, I have to leave for London on Monday, but I'm hopeful you'll let me call you and see me again when I return."

"Oh. I, umm... yes, of course."

I smile, reminding myself our early lessons will be in her ability to speak confidently. As much as I adore the rattled, nervous young lady seated across from me, if she's to be my wife, the public will expect more. The transformation is the part of the journey I love the most. You take a fresh canvas and create the perfect picture. Emily is young, soft clay that I'll be able to easily mold.

Nothing she told me tonight was news. I had a rather full report by the end of the day. Hearing it from her perspective sealed the deal. She's estranged from her mother, never had a father figure, she's alone in this world, and what she needs is a firm guiding hand to show her all her potential.

Her girlfriend may be an issue, but after speaking with Heath this afternoon, I believe it's a containable one. Gia is leaving for France in a few weeks for a European tour to grow her modeling career. She'll be distracted while Emily and I are getting started.

"Are you ready?" I stand and offer her a hand.

"Marcus." She stands with me. "Thank you. I really had fun tonight."

"I did too." And I take this last opportunity, under the soft lighting, to appreciate this girl who stands before me. She looks up at me with glittering eyes, and I tuck a lock of hair behind her ear. My finger lingers there, and I trail it over her jaw and down her neck before cupping her head and lowering mine to claim our first kiss.

Her lips are warm, soft, and incredibly pliable. It solidifies my belief she was meant for me, and I taste her as I deepen our kiss. She's sweet with the flavor of wine, her arms come around me, and she melts into my body. It takes everything inside me to break this kiss and step back. We aren't ready to be where I hope to go, and I take her hand again. "I'm so happy that we met. I'm looking forward to more time with you."

She picks up her little purse and clutches it to her chest. "Me too."

We descend the stairs together with my hand resting on the small of her back. It itches to slip lower and clutch that tight ass. A swimmer. It explains this toned, lean body. Emily's hair is loose tonight, hanging in soft waves past her shoulders, and I don't think she has any idea of what a beautiful vision she is. She reminds me so much of Sara, and I wonder if it would brighten her up if we added some blond highlights, or if she simply needs more time in the sun.

I'm aware it has nothing to do with hair color. It's all in the personality. Emily has a backbone, but it's not the oak that will break in the wind but flexible to bend and thrive. I believe she has what it takes to survive me.

My car is waiting out front, the driver standing with the back door open. Emily seems impressed with this rather unimpressive town car, but I don't need a limo to drive me everywhere. She slides into the back seat, and I climb in next to her. The driver closes the door and takes his place behind the wheel.

"Please take us to Ms. Hanson's residence." I gesture for her to give him the address.

She complies, then looks at me. "Did I tell you my last name?"

"How else would I know it?" I read her eyes to see how well she digests that lie.

Holding Emily's hand, I rub my thumb over the back of hers as we leave Manhattan. The city becomes darker, uglier, and Emily attempts to hide her embarrassment when we pull into her neighborhood. "It's not as bad as it looks," she comments.

It's worse than the photos my PI sent me. I've already seen a few bums slumped up against the wall they've claimed for the night. This is no place for my future wife to live. "I appreciate the diversity in the neighborhoods of New York," I say, rather than show my real thoughts.

She smiles at me. "I do too. I mean, some of these buildings are over a century old."

I'm sure. The United States is basically an infant when it comes to history.

"You don't own a car?"

"No." She laughs. "It's too expensive, and public transport is easily accessible."

We pull up outside her apartment, and she blinks, looking up at me through her lashes. "Thank you. Dinner was wonderful."

"It was," I agree. "Tomorrow, I'll be preparing for my trip, but I promise, I will call."

"Okay," she whispers.

The driver opens her door, and I slide out behind her to walk her to her door. I keep my hand on her back as we take the steps up to the building's entrance. I know it's too soon to ask her to see her home. Actually, I don't even care if I'll ever see it. This won't be her home for long.

She turns to me, her face lit up in the dim light of the street lamp, and I dip my head to touch my lips to hers again. Her eyes open as I lean back, my thumb brushing over her cheek. "Good night, Emily."

I wait to see she's safe before returning to my car. In a way, I do wish this business trip weren't on my agenda, but I'll use the time wisely. By the time I return, I'll have her primed to fall into the relationship I envision for us. I smile to myself as I pull out my phone and type an email to Carmen, letting her know it's time to reopen my island home.

# 6

## EMILY

Stretched out on my bed, I grin as I look at the phone. Bella rubs her head on me, obviously preferring I give her my attention, but I reread the text.

> I'm sorry I missed you earlier. Did you enjoy my gift?

I glance over at the dozen red roses that were delivered and my smile grows as I reply.

> They are beautiful.

Bella nudges me again, and I reach up to scratch her furry white chin. She meows and rolls to her back. Marcus's return message appears, and I quickly read it.

> I'm trying to focus on these meetings, but my mind keeps wandering to this amazing woman I met last week. It's been very distracting.

I bite my lip as I type back.

> I've met someone too.

Bella, now completely annoyed, sits up and shakes her head, causing her long white coat to fluff up, her round green eyes glaring at me. I refocus on my phone, but no new message comes back. I sigh, laying my arm over my forehead and closing my eyes. It's only been a few days since Marcus left for London, but he has called me every day. This morning, the flowers arrived, and I haven't been able to wipe this smile off my face.

My phone rings and my heart leaps, but I frown when I see it's Gia and not Marcus. I press accept. "Hi, Gia."

"Hey, girl! How was your day?"

My gaze returns to the flowers, and the smile is back. "Good. I got a delivery of roses today."

"Oh? From Mr. Sterling?"

"Yes." Of course I told Gia every detail of our first date. Despite my initial trepidation, I'm so glad I didn't cancel. Marcus in real life is nothing like he is on paper. He's attentive, charming, and way more down-to-earth than I'd imagined. He opens up to me in our evening conversations, giving me little details of his past, showing me glimpses of his vulnerabilities. He even laughed at himself about his blunder when he spilled coffee on a prominent Japanese businessman.

"Well, that's romantic. Did he ask you out again?"

"He did." I roll to my side, and Bella jumps off the bed. "He's flying home on Friday, but said he'd need a day. He asked me to spend time with him on Sunday."

"Hey, wait. What about our standing brunch date?"

"Oh, God. I completely forgot!"

She laughs. "It's okay. Heath asked me to go out with him Saturday night. Maybe I'll make that a late night."

I can almost hear her brows wagging. "Sure, Gia." It's kind of fun that we're having a little romance with these men at the same time, but Gia never sticks with one guy for any length of time. She swears she isn't ready to settle down and always has a string of men begging for her attention.

One of the main differences between her and me is that I want the perfect guy. I haven't found him yet. Every man I meet only wants in my pants. It seems like Marcus really wants to get to know me.

Other than that amazing kiss on the rooftop, Marcus didn't press me for anything. He wasn't even disappointed when I didn't invite him in. On top of that, I don't spend our conversations listening to him boast about himself, rather he likes to put the spotlight on me, and he listens. We have an ocean between us and somehow he makes me feel special with every interaction.

My phone vibrates with an incoming call. It's from Marcus and I practically float off my bed with glee. "Gia, I gotta go."

I answer his call and I barely say hello when he asks, "What do you mean? Who did you meet?"

Oh. My. God. Is he jealous? "Just a guy. He's cute."

"Cute?"

"Yes." I suppress a giggle. "Smart too."

There's a pause on the line before he says, "I've only been gone a couple of days. I should remind you that I eat *cute* for dinner."

I laugh, rolling to my back and holding my stomach. He's

teasing me about the veal. "I know you do, but I was talking about you."

"Oh." There's another beat of silence. "I've never been called cute. You are, though."

My smile will be a permanent fixture tonight. I glance at the time. "It must be getting late there."

"It is. I'm back at the hotel and getting ready for bed, but I'm thinking about you."

"I'm thinking about you too."

"Good. Continue to do that. And no other cute guys for you. Understand?"

I snort through a giggle. "Understood. I'll see you Sunday."

"I'll call you tomorrow. Good night, Emily."

My whole body heats when he says my name. "Good night, Marcus."

My eyes drift back to the roses. Maybe this time I did find the perfect guy.

---

I TAKE one last look in the mirror. Marcus will be here any minute and, without Gia's consultation, I'm still uncertain of the outfit I chose. Skinny jeans with a pink summer blouse and a simple pair of flats. I have no idea where he's taking me today, but he did mention to dress casually.

Bella rubs herself against me as she maneuvers through my legs. I give her a gentle nudge with my foot. "Bell, you're getting hair on my pants."

A knock on the door has me sucking in a deep breath. I've replaced all my discarded clothing choices back in the closet and tidied up the room, but there's no hiding that it's a simple studio apartment.

I open the door to Marcus's handsome face, and he's holding a small bouquet of flowers. He keeps those blue eyes on mine as he smiles and offers them to me.

"Thank you." My cheeks heat as I take them, and I step back to let him in.

"You look very pretty today," he comments, and my face grows warmer.

"Let me just put these in some water." I clutch the flowers and curse myself, knowing the only vase I have still holds the roses he got me. Taking a glass out of the cupboard, I then fill it with water and glance over my shoulder. Marcus isn't looking at me; rather he has a raised brow and wide eyes on Bella, who is greeting him by rubbing against his black slacks.

"Oh!" I set down the glass and quickly rush over to save him. "I'm sorry." I scoop her up. "This is my cat, Bella."

He's looking down at the white hair she left on his pants, and I die a little inside. "I, um. I have a lint brush."

I set Bell on the daybed and locate the sticky roller from my side table. Hurrying back to him, I drop to my knees and attempt to remove the hair.

Marcus chuckles, and I look up at him, realizing I'm being a complete idiot. He reaches down and strokes my hair. "Emily, it's fine." His eyes are warm as he gazes down at me. "Put your flowers in water."

I climb to my feet with shaky knees. I've been so comfortable all week with our phone conversations and text chats, but having him here, in my extremely humble home, and Bella defiling his pants, my nerves are amping up. "I'm sorry," I say again.

Suddenly, his arms come around my waist, and he hugs me, lifting me off my feet. "I missed you while I was away," he whispers in my hair before setting me back down. I stare up at him, with my hands on his arms and my heart beating wildly in my chest. I missed him too.

He nods at my kitchen counter. "Take care of the flowers."

I back out of his arms and turn to finish the task. Arranging them in the glass, I look back and see Marcus using the roller to remove the last of the hair from his slacks. He grins. "I think I arranged a lovely surprise for you today. I hope you enjoy it."

I hope at some point I relax so I can. "Where are we going?"

"I said it's a surprise." He tosses the roller on my bed and holds out a hand for me.

After grabbing my purse, I take his hand. "I'm sorry about my cat."

He shakes his head. "It's all right. I apologize for my reaction. I've never lived with an animal in my home." He opens the door and allows me to step out first.

"I never did either until I got this place," I admit as we take the stairs up to the ground level. "I adopted her from the Humane Society."

We step out into the sunlight and I see his car right away, looking very out of place on my street. "Do you always use a driver?" I ask as the chauffeur steps out to open the back door.

"Honestly, I learned to drive on the other side of the road." He gestures for me to get in. "It's probably safer for everyone if I do."

The humor in his voice makes me smile, and I relax a

little as he slides into the seat next to me. Today, he's wearing a blue, button-down shirt that makes his eyes seem brighter. The sleeves are rolled up, displaying his muscled forearms, and his chin is covered in day-old scruff. Perhaps this is his version of casual, but he still looks incredibly put together. I catch a whiff of his cologne, which I love, and smooth out my jeans, trying to let go of my insecurities. "How was your flight home?"

He chuckles. "It was uneventful, but jet lag is real. I got you a present."

I blink and look back at him. He pulls out a box from the seat pocket in front of him and hands it to me.

"You didn't have to do that," I say as I take it, recognizing immediately that it's from a jewelry store.

"I was thinking of you. Open it."

I lift the lid, and inside is a necklace with a butterfly pendant on a gold chain. I run my finger over the sparkly butterfly that's fitted with glittering diamond chips. "It's beautiful."

He brushes a thumb over my cheek. "Butterflies represent transformation. I thought it was fitting. Here,"—he takes the box from me—"let's put it on."

I shift in my seat and pull up my hair as he clasps the chain, trailing his fingers over the sensitive skin at the base of my neck. I turn back to him, and he taps the pendant. "It looks lovely on you."

My hand flutters up to touch it. "Thank you."

It feels like too much too soon. Flowers are one thing. Still, my heart seems to have grown hummingbird wings.

Marcus gets a phone call, which he takes. I watch the city go by out the window and listen to his rich voice as he discusses business that I don't understand. My curiosity grows as we near what appears to be a small airport. "What are we doing today?" I ask again as he ends his call.

"I wanted to take you out to lunch," he says, pocketing his phone.

"On a plane?" I look around as we are waved through a tall metal gate in a fenced-off area. Did I mention to him I'm afraid of flying?

"No." He smiles. "On a boat."

## 7

## MARCUS

Emily's face is priceless when we pull up to the helicopter. She stares at it with wide eyes before turning back to me with her mouth agape. The butterfly pendant winks in the sunlight, and yes, maybe I'm going a little overboard, but Emily should understand the perks of the lifestyle I'm introducing her to.

"I thought you said a boat."

I chuckle. "Yes, and the helicopter will take us to it."

"I've never been on a helicopter," she whispers.

"Don't worry. It's perfectly safe," I assure her as my driver opens the door and I offer her a hand. She glances at the chopper, then back at the car before looking at me. With her hand in mine, she reluctantly follows me as we approach the craft.

I help her get up and inside, then briefly introduce her to Lucas, my pilot today, and guide her back to her seat. I help her buckle in and place the headphones over her head before getting myself settled in the seat next to her. She remains speechless as the blades start to rotate, and with our fingers entwined, her nails dig into the back of my hand and dig deeper as we take off.

The harbor comes into view below us. "Relax, Emily. It will be a short flight."

I did miss her last week when I was away. I spent my evenings envisioning what our life will look like together and I was impressed with my ability to sound interested in the mundane details of her life.

My self-control was evident when I didn't simply scoop her up and haul her off the minute I saw her again. Which brings me back to the cat. I wonder how attached she is to it. I glance at her and think it could be a good bargaining chip in the future if she is.

She catches my look, and her lips twitch, but her eyes are still terrified. She looks beautiful with the sunlight high-lighting the angle of her cheek and brightening the greens in her eyes.

We move over deeper water. I point down as my yacht comes into view. "Our destination."

She follows my gaze and her jaw drops. "Is it yours?"

I revel in her awe. "She'll be heading south for winter tomorrow. This was my last weekend with her for a while."

Emily looks back down, watching as we draw closer. Lucas lowers and lands with only a small bump on the heli-pad. I'm amused as Emily releases a relieved breath through pursed lips.

I wink at her. "We survived."

Her eyes are wide, taking in the top deck, and we wait for the rotors to slow to a soft whir before Lucas gets up to open the door. I step down first and offer my hand to Emily, who appears physically relieved to have her feet on solid ground.

"Welcome aboard *The Temptress*." I grin at her raised brow. "She came with that name." I think it's fitting as she tempted me to spend a pretty penny for her.

My captain greets us with a smile and a handshake. I introduce Emily, and he takes her hand before informing me everything is prepared for our lunch.

"Thank you." I nod to him and, with a hand on Emily's back, I guide her to the stairs that will take us to the lounge. We step through the doors at the bottom, and Emily pauses. "Wow. It's beautiful."

The room is filled with soft, sectional seating in cream. The smoked glass tabletops accent the space while giving an air of openness, and the sunlight shines through the windows lining the walls. "It's a little dated," I muse. "Perhaps she'll get a face lift next year."

I escort Emily through the open sliding doors to the outdoor seating area overlooking the sparkling pool. Emily walks to the railing and looks down at it. "I didn't bring a swimsuit," she teases.

I grin, taking her hand again. "Come, our table is down there."

Down another set of stairs is the pool deck. The doors open to a large dining room, and a bar top lined with stools separates it from outdoor seating. We pass the comfortable lounges and stop at the edge of the pool. Our table has been set up here with a lovely view of the city beyond.

"I can honestly admit I've never seen the city from this angle," Emily says, taking it all in with wonder in her eyes.

"It's beautiful at night," I tell her. "I host several summer parties on this boat. You'll enjoy them."

She turns to me with a raised brow.

I smile. "If you continue to put up with me, that is."

"Marcus, this is... I don't even know what to say."

I gesture toward our table. "I know it isn't the greasy burger joint I promised. I did, however, order hamburgers as well as fish and chips for lunch."

She blushes as I pull out her chair. I met Emily in a dance club and dined with her under the starlight, but I haven't had the opportunity to see her in the sun. I admit it's a lovely view. Golden highlights enhance her hair that flows past her shoulders, and I wonder if they're natural. I would assume so as I don't believe she'd spend a small fortune on a hairstyle. Her sleeveless blouse shows off toned arms, but her skin is too pale to indicate she spent time outdoors this summer. What I like most is her eyes, not dramatically shaped, or made up to appear so, and they sparkle in the light.

She blushes. "You're staring."

"You're very pretty," I admit.

Our waiter approaches, delivering two mimosas in champagne flutes. I raise my glass, and she gently taps hers to mine.

"Cheers." I try for my most charming smile.

Emily sets down her glass and looks back at the land. "We're moving?"

"Yes. We'll have a little tour of the coast. Then our flight back will be shorter."

"I thought it had to go south for winter." Emily gives me a questioning look.

"Tomorrow. She doesn't mind a short jaunt north to entertain us." I wonder if now is the time to bring this up. Our dinner sealed my decision, and I'm not a patient man, but I've done my best to hold her interest so far. I want to move our relationship forward. "Emily, next weekend I need to fly to the Caribbean. I have an island home there I'm opening up for the winter months. I'd love for you to join me."

Her eyes pop and her jaw drops, but I've prepared many responses to her reactions.

"I realize it's soon to ask you on a holiday, but it's no pressure. We'll enjoy the beach, relax by the sea, and of course, you'll have your own room." I shrug. "It's just a plot to spend some more time with you, while I get done what I need to."

She closes her mouth, takes a sip of her drink, then looks back at me. "You have a home in the Caribbean?"

"I do. It was part of my inheritance, and my family didn't utilize it, but I have since I moved to the States."

A shy smile lights her face and she shakes her head, looking down. "I don't know. I mean, I haven't really earned vacation time yet."

I'm ready for that too. "Next weekend is Labor Day. Surely they aren't asking you to work on Monday. You'd only need to ask for Friday off."

She glances back up, uncertainty still swirling in her eyes.

"Look, it would only be a couple of days. My staff resides there, so it's not like we'd be completely alone. When was the last time you took a real vacation?"

I can see in her eyes the answer would be never. They dart back and forth, weighing the possibilities before she gives me an uncertain grin. "It sounds amazing, but..."

"But?" I prompt.

"I've never been in a plane," she admits.

Totally not surprising. "You managed the helicopter." I point out.

"I don't have a passport."

"I have ways to expedite that for you."

"And I've never spent a weekend with a man."

That has me taking a drink, completely pleased by that information. "I understand. But think of it as an innocent vacation. I promise I'm a gentleman. I'd never pressure you into something you don't want." I pause for effect. "I only want more time with you, Emily. I'm a busy man. I'm just trying to blend this budding relationship into my life."

Our waiter saves me, delivering baskets of cheeseburger sliders and fried fish and chips. "I hoped to give you options," I tell her as she eyes the display of food.

She tinkles out a little laugh. "Fish and chips are British?"

"Yes. A guilty pleasure."

"Hamburgers?" She raises a brow.

"Sure. We have those too. Did you know the name was derived from the German town of Hamburg?"

She shakes her head, and I pick up a chip. "You call these french fries?"

Emily bites her lip and nods.

I grin. "Chips are better."

The atmosphere becomes more relaxed as we work through our meal. Emily hates discussing her past, which is fine. I don't love discussing mine either. I do learn a lot of information regarding the woman my business partner is currently involved with. Emily seems to adore Gia, which leads to more information regarding the cat.

I pocket all the intel because while it's good for your girl to have fewer attachments, one or two can be useful pieces for negotiation when they're getting uppity.

As our table is cleared, Emily is watching the shoreline. "These are the only islands I've been on." She gets up and goes to the railing, grabs it and leans back, inhaling deeply. "I love the smell of the sea."

I step up behind her, caging her with my hands on either side of hers. "Then you'll love my island," I tell her as the wind blows her hair back to tickle my nose.

"Your island?"

"Yes, where my home is."

"I'm sure I will." She turns in my arms with a smile. "I'll see if I can get the time off. I'd like to go."

Then I'll make sure it happens. I return her smile before dropping my head to brush a light kiss on her lips. She leans back, her lashes flutter open, and I cup her cheek. "Emily, I don't know what magic you have, but I admit, I'm becoming very smitten with you."

Her eyes fill with humor. "Smitten?"

I take her face with both my hands, my thumbs brushing her cheeks. "Yes. Smitten. With your eyes, your lips"—I run my thumb over her bottom lip—"and your heart. You're a good girl, Emily Hanson. I feel so lucky that we met."

My hands drop as she rests her elbows on the railing. The wind flutters her hair around her face as she regards me. "I saw an article about you and that nightclub."

"You'll see lots of articles about me if you look. Heath and I invested in that club. We own the building it's in." Placing my hands on the railing on either side of her, I lean in. "I almost didn't attend that night. I only showed up for the photo op, but imagine what I'd have missed out on if I hadn't..." I shake my head with a chuckle. "I'm so glad I changed my mind."

"I almost didn't go out that night either," she confesses. "My Friday nights usually include ice cream and an old movie."

That makes me grin. "To another thing we have in common, except for the ice cream, and I prefer to read."

Emily smiles. "I love to read as well."

She turns back to look at the ocean. I rest my cheek on her head and breathe her in. With my arms tight around her, I close my eyes and imagine our future. There's a lot to do, but as soon as we're home, our future can start.

# 8

---

## EMILY

Discarding the next dress on the bed, and with my phone stuck to my ear, I sigh. "Gia, my clothes are just boring."

"True," she agrees.

"Gia!"

"What? You're going to an island. All you need is a bikini and flip-flops."

My heart sinks as I survey my options. "I only have one-piece suits I use for the gym, not to seduce a man on the beach."

"Ooh. Seduction?" Gia purrs. "Are we planning on turning in your V-card this weekend?"

Heat creeps up my neck all the way to my hairline as I sit on the bed. "I didn't say that." I have no idea what I'll do, but I do know that no man has made me feel like Marcus does. It's not just the kisses, but the rich sound of his voice, the way his cheeks dimple when he grins, and how he smells—so good—when he holds me close. Every time he touches me, a tingling sensation lights up between my legs, and for the first time in my life—yes—I'm thinking about it. "He said I'd have my own room. He's never tried to press for more than a kiss. I don't think he's the kind of man to rush into that."

Gia snorts. "Right. You've known him for two minutes and he's whisking you away to a Caribbean Island."

"Because he can." I lie back on the bed and cover my eyes with my free hand.

She sighs. "I still can't believe you said yes."

I wasn't going to at first, but then the thought of him leaving again had me reconsidering. Marcus is right. He is a busy man. Plus, he was so polite, thoughtfully offering me my own room and assuring me we wouldn't be alone. He dropped me off that day at my front door with a slow, long kiss that had me believing that I'd made the right decision.

"Gia, why would you say that? You went to Mexico with Julian after one date."

"Because I like sex on the beach and Julian was hot," she defends. "I'm not looking for Mr. Perfect. I just want a good time."

"Speaking of that, have you and Heath... you know?"

She laughs. "Say the words, Em. Have I swallowed his cock? Let him lick my pussy? Rode him like a cowgirl?"

Oh. My. God! I press my fingers to my cheek. "Gia?"

"Don't read too much into that. Sex for everyone is not the pathway to a meaningful relationship. Anyway, I'm leaving for Europe soon. Hey, do you want to borrow a bikini?"

Is that like sharing underwear? "Maybe?"

"I have one I've never worn. I think it will look perfect on you. When do you leave?"

"Friday morning." That's a whole other layer of anxiety that mixes in with everything. The helicopter was terrifying. What will a plane ride be like?

"Great. Come over tomorrow after work. We'll fill out your wardrobe."

I love Gia and her clothes. I agree to her plan and hang up, staring at my ceiling. I can't imagine what this weekend is going to look like, but nervous anticipation bubbles in my belly. Maybe Gia is right, this is too much too soon, but Marcus is smitten with me. I press a hand to my stomach and smile. Honestly, I'm a little smitten too.

———

"IT'S NOT REALLY BIG." I ponder as I look at the jet.

"It's not really small." Marcus sounds offended. I look back at him, and the humor is dancing in his eyes as the driver opens his car door. "Come. Trust me, it's comfortable. I didn't feel we needed the full-sized jet for a quick trip to the Caribbean."

I hesitate, staring at the plane.

He holds out a hand for me. "Emily, do you trust me?"

I nod slowly, and he grins.

"Good girl. Come on."

With a hand on my back, he urges me to go up the steps, and he nearly runs into my back when I come to an abrupt halt at the top. This doesn't look like any plane I've imagined, but more like a luxury suite. Marcus chuckles at my reaction, then introduces me to the flight crew standing near the cockpit door. There's only one pilot and a solo flight attendant.

"What if something happens to the pilot?" I whisper to Marcus as he leads me to a seat.

"I'm certified to fly if anything goes wrong, but it won't," he replies, and now my brain is wrapping around that and not the luxurious leather chair I've lowered into.

"You can fly?"

"My most enduring hobby." He takes the seat next to me. "Do you like my plane?"

I nod several times. "It's amazing."

We are seated in a row for two, facing a wall that forms a cozy cubby with plenty of legroom, and Marcus shows me how to adjust my seat into several comfortable positions. Behind us is more conversational seating dotted with small round tables.

"There's the galley and restroom in the back."

I glance behind us and notice the flight attendant ducking through one of the doors.

"Okay," I whisper as the engines roar to life. One more passenger joins us, and I recognize Lucas from last weekend, the man who flew the helicopter. Perhaps he can fly planes too.

"Sir." He addresses Marcus, then focuses on me. "Ms. Hanson." His eyes are unnaturally blue, not like Marcus, who has more of an indigo color. Lucas's are pale and icy, and they linger on me for longer than seems appropriate. I can't quite read his expression. It's a mixture of curiosity and maybe disappointment?

Lucas takes a seat across the aisle and Marcus asks him if everything is in order for our arrival.

"Yes, sir," Lucas replies and takes out some earbuds, avoiding any more eye contact. "Enjoy the flight," he adds before placing them in.

My eyes are planted on the window as we start to move. It seems to me most plane crashes you read about are small planes, and this is no commercial flight. My stomach drops as we leave the ground, and I continue to watch in awe as the city below gets smaller and smaller. We pass through a blanket of clouds, and now I only get peek-a-boo moments of the land below.

"Emily, would you like some champagne?" Marcus asks. I realize I'm crushing his hand and the flight attendant is standing by our seats.

"Oh, umm, sure."

She smiles at me. "We have some turbulence reported for the next hour, so we're asking you to stay buckled up until we're past that."

I swallow hard. "Okay."

"It's fine." Marcus squeezes my hand. "It's just pockets of air, like bouncing over waves."

My mind immediately goes to a small boat, being tossed and whipped about in a tempest storm before suddenly capsizing completely.

The champagne helps marginally, but when the clouds clear, there's nothing but ocean below us, and my anxiety increases.

We hit those pockets of air and I stiffen in my seat. Marcus strokes the hair off my shoulder, asking me to relax. I close my eyes, praying for it to stop until God finally listens and the flight becomes smoother.

"Sir, the captain has given the okay to move around the cabin," our flight attendant informs Marcus.

He looks at me with a raised brow. "Would you like to move to more comfortable chairs?"

I shake my head. "I'm fine."

He glances at the flight attendant. "How about another glass of champagne and a cheese platter?"

She heads toward the back, and Marcus unbuckles me. I

grab his hand. He smirks and hauls me up, taking me to the sofa behind us. I slowly lower myself into the buttery soft seat and look around. "There are no seat belts here."

"But there are." He sits down and shows me the seat belt tucked between the cushions. "Relax, Emily." He takes in my tense posture and rubs my knee. "What did you end up doing with the cat?"

"Oh, Bella. My neighbor said she'll take care of her and watch my apartment."

"Oh?" He raises a brow. "Are you close with her?"

"No, not really." I shrug. "I haven't lived there long enough to really know my neighbors well. But she's always been nice to me."

"Ah. Well, that was kind of her then. Is she on the same floor as you or...?"

I blow out a breath. "Yes." I'm sure he's just trying to help me feel better. Our food and drinks are set out for us. I glance at Lucas, who seems comfortable dozing in his seat. "Can Lucas fly planes too?"

Marcus follows my gaze. "Yes. He was a pilot in the military."

Hmm. He looks slightly militant with his buzzed blond hair and muscular build. I pick up my champagne, attempting to look as cool as possible, and take a shaky sip. "Tell me more about your island home."

"Ah." He stretches out his long legs and leans back. "It's my favorite house. There were no structures on it before I moved to the States, and I designed it myself. It's not large, but the beach is pristine and the views are spectacular."

"Wait." I set down my glass. "When you said *my island,* you meant you inherited an island?"

He chuckles. "Yes. As I said, it's been in my family for generations."

I chew my lip as I digest that. "It sounds so remote. Do you have electricity?"

"We have solar and backup generators. Trust me, it has all the luxuries of home."

"Hmm. It sounds lovely."

It sounds overboard! Who owns a fricken island!

He tells me more about the house. Our flight attendant tops off our glasses and I let the second glass of champagne relax me more as I settle back in my seat, convincing myself if I live, this will be fun.

---

MY TRIP ISN'T over when this plane gratefully lands. I was just thinking that wasn't so bad, but I'm questioning everything, staring at the even smaller plane we're about to board.

"What is this?" The plane looks like it's on large water skis.

He puts a reassuring arm around me. "It's my seaplane."

Lucas loads our luggage as we stand on the dock. He turns to Marcus. "Where would you like me?"

"Perhaps Emily will be more comfortable up front with me."

Perhaps Emily absolutely would not.

"No. That's fine, I'm comfortable in the back."

Marcus smirks at me, then climbs aboard, turning to offer me a hand. With shaky legs, I follow his movements, and he pulls me inside. This little plane has four seats, and I fall into the one behind the pilot's chair.

"You're driving?" I choke out when Marcus takes that seat.

"I told you, I love flying. Trust me, I've taken this trip to the island many times. I've never killed anyone yet."

I chew my lip as I fumble with the belt buckle. Lucas takes the seat next to Marcus, and I close my eyes at the roar of the engine. Lucas nudges my arm, and I peek up as he hands me a headset.

"It's noisier than the other plane," he yells, and I place the headset over my ears.

It's like nothing I've ever experienced as we turn toward the open sea, pick up speed, and lift into the air. I'm white-knuckling the sides of my seat, but the scenery below us transfixes me. The dark blues blend into light greens, broken up occasionally by white-capped waves.

"The colors are so different," I murmur.

"It changes with the depth of the water," Marcus responds, his voice clear in my ears, and I stare at the back of his head as he focuses forward.

I can feel every movement of this plane, which doesn't lower my anxiety. We haven't gained the same altitude either, and I'm not sure if it's a relief or not. We aren't in the air that long when Marcus tells me to look to the left.

I see the strip of land as we approach, and my fears are momentarily forgotten. An emerald island sits alone in the ocean with a white sand beach that seems stark in contrast and, as we draw nearer, I can make out the structure of his home. It sits on higher ground, perched on a rocky cliff that protects the crescent-shaped bay below it.

I'm clutching my armrests again as we descend, and I close my eyes before we hit the water. They pop open as we slow, and then we're gently rocking our way to a pier.

A boat is docked here as well. "Is that yours?" It's smaller than the yacht but bigger than a speed boat.

"It's for supplies," Marcus responds as he navigates the plane closer.

A young man with bronze skin and dark hair runs down the dock as we approach. The plane floats close to the pier, and Lucas opens the door before tossing a rope to the man who's greeting us.

Oh, thank God. Our travels are over. I survived, and I don't have to do this again for two more days.

Marcus helps me down and my feet welcome the wood planks. The sun is warm, the breeze is pleasant, and the air smells so clean. I smile up at him, but he's focused on watching his plane get secured. With a shrug, I pull out my cell phone and realize immediately I have no service. Holding it up in the air, I search for bars, but there are none.

Marcus looks over at me and eyes the phone. "Did you need to make a call?"

"No, I..." I slip the phone back in my pocket. "Is there no service on the island?"

"No. But I do have a satellite phone. We aren't completely cut off."

"Oh good. I promised to call Gia when we got here."

Marcus gives me a dimple-forming grin. "Then we'll see that you do."

The young man helps Lucas unload before he turns to us. "The cart is waiting, Mr. Sterling."

"Thank you, Juan." He puts a hand on my lower back. "This is Ms. Hanson, my guest this weekend."

"A pleasure." Juan nods but does not extend a hand. Instead, he gathers up our bags and starts to walk away.

Marcus gestures for me to follow and, as promised, something like a large golf cart waits for us. Lucas gets in next to Juan. Marcus and I climb in the back, and he looks at me with a small smile. "What do you think?"

"It's gorgeous," I answer truthfully, my gaze bouncing around the scenery as we start to move. The air feels heavier as we move away from the water. Thick, flowering succulents swallow up the sides of the road. The floral scent blends with earth and salt, and I breathe in deeply.

"This road goes to the residence and accesses the outbuildings." Marcus waves a hand at the road ahead. "Otherwise, it's all footpaths to get around the island. Juan has this cart and a utility vehicle as well, both electric."

The foliage changes to creeping vines, fluttering ferns, and thin-trunked trees as we turn and head uphill. "Does Juan live here full-time?" I ask.

"He does, and Carmen, his mother, is my housekeeper."

"And Lucas...?" I've become rather curious about him on this trip.

"He handles everything, including my security," Marcus says breezily.

I guess I didn't think about his need for such a thing, but that makes sense. I stay silent as the house comes into view. It's two stories, with beige-tinted stucco siding and a red tiled roof. The front entry has a narrow porch, with two rectangular columns reaching up to the top roof line. A second-story balcony is on either side, and terracotta shutters flank the windows.

The home itself has a sprawling feel without looking like a mansion, and the landscape outside is cared for but blends into the island seamlessly. "It's so pretty," I whisper out loud.

Marcus takes my hand and squeezes it. "I know."

Juan pulls up to the bottom of the front steps, where a

middle-aged woman with ample curves and a small smile waits for us. Her hands are folded in front of her, and her black hair is tied in a tight bun on top of her head.

She takes a step forward as we climb out of the cart. "Mr. Sterling." Her smile grows.

"Carmen. Hello." Marcus takes my hand. "This is Emily Hanson, my guest."

"Of course. Ms. Hanson, welcome." She waves a hand to the front door. "Juan will deliver your things to your room. I have refreshments for you when you're ready."

Marcus leads me up the steps and through the open door. I gape at the large foyer that pours directly into a living room beyond the curved staircase leading up to the second story.

Miles of large, stone tiles cover the floor, making up the stairs as well. The cathedral ceiling has a large ceiling fan lazily pushing the air around. Marcus leads me into the seating area, and I marvel at how the dark wood accents blend with the creamy, plastered walls. An arched doorway connects to a spacious dining room, and large windows with a set of french doors bring the outdoors in.

Marcus escorts me outside, where there is another dining table under a covered portion of the patio. It opens up to comfortable deck chairs and an infinity pool that appears to blend into the sea beyond.

"Wow." That's the only word I'm capable of. This looks more like a high-end resort than a home. I know I shouldn't have expected less from the man who took me to lunch on his yacht, but wow.

"Come, let's call your friend and let her know you made it."

I follow him back inside and we enter a long hallway off

the living room and he opens a door to his office. I study the large monitor on his desk as he retrieves the phone from its charger. "I thought you didn't have an internet connection."

He chuckles. "You can do a lot of work on a computer without the internet."

Marcus hands me the phone and I pull mine from my pocket. It's not something I do anymore—memorize phone numbers—but I find Gia's contact and dial the numbers. I'm disappointed when I get her voicemail. "Hey, Gia. We're here. It's amazing! Marcus has been wonderful." I blush and glance at him. "I'm sorry I missed you. I'll try again later."

Hanging up, I hand the phone back to him and press out a smile. "Thanks."

Marcus offers me a hand. "Let me show you your room. We can freshen up and meet by the pool for those refreshments."

I roll my lips together to suppress my excitement. I can't believe I'm here, with him, on a dream island vacation. "Okay."

# 9

## MARCUS

Emily seems incredibly pleased with her new home. I hold her hand as I lead her upstairs.

"How many bedrooms does it have?" she asks as her head swivels and she's taking in all the little details.

"Five up here. Carmen and Juan have an apartment off the kitchen, and Lucas has the only other garden-level bedroom." I guide her to the second door on the right. Emily steps inside and looks around the room with parted lips and wide eyes. I follow her gaze to the large king-sized bed with a rattan headboard and matching bamboo side tables. The attached seating area has a flat-screen TV on the wall, and she eyes that. "Do you have cable?"

"No, but I have downloaded some movies and television shows if you prefer that type of entertainment."

She glances back at me before moving to the little writing desk tucked under a window and gazes at her ocean view before going to the double doors that open to the balcony.

I follow her outside and step up behind her. This corner of the house is built on a rocky cliff that drops to the ocean below. Though my home is only two stories, it's a good five-story drop to where the waves crash into the rocks below. Given Emily's fear of heights, I thought this was the best room to put her in. "Do you like it?"

She looks down, blowing out a long breath before turning to me. "It's gorgeous."

I place my hands on her hips, feeling the soft fabric of the capri pants she's wearing. The halter-like blouse shows off her swimmer's shoulders and those pretty arms. She looks back at me and those eyes have picked up more greens with the turbulent water behind us.

"Let me show you the rest." I take her to the attached bathroom first. She runs her fingers over the granite counter-tops and picks up a bottle of scented bodywash that sits near the free-standing tub.

"I made sure Carmen supplied you with everything you would need."

She opens the glass door to the generous shower. "It's pretty."

"I'm glad you like it. You should be comfortable." I pause outside the closet. "Emily, here on the island, we enjoy a more casual dress during the day, but I prefer formal attire for our evening meal."

She turns to me with surprised eyes, and the color drains from her face. "Why?"

I shrug. "It's a common tradition in these parts."

"Oh." She glances at the door to the bedroom. "I didn't know. I'm not sure I brought anything 'formal.'"

"I assumed."

That comment has her eyes back on me.

"So I provided that for you." I open the doors to the large walk-in closet, soon to be filled with all of her new clothes. Today, only two dresses hang in here, and I pick up the closest one, a black cocktail dress that sparkles with the silver thread woven into the fabric.

"Oh?" She stares at it like she's never seen such a dress.

I replace it and remove the other, a soft mauve chiffon with a flowy, asymmetrical skirt that will look lovely when we dance.

Emily is speechless, and I rehang the dress.

"I remembered you saying you borrowed dresses from your friend." I look back at her. "Now you have some of your own."

"Marcus..." she whispers. "No. I mean, that's too much."

"Emily." I step closer to her. "Don't be like that. I can afford it. Really, it's the least I'd like to do for you."

"I d-don't know what to say," she sputters.

I frown at her words but recover quickly. "You could say 'thank you,' but it's not your gratitude I'm seeking. It's your happiness."

She stares back at me for a beat, then a slow smile tips her lips and grows. "Thank you."

Satisfied with her response, I wave a hand at the shoe shelving. "And I purchased some appropriate footwear."

I had Carmen select four choices to put out for her, and she takes a look, studying each pair of heels with a little frown. She clutches one pale-colored sandal to her chest. "They're beautiful. I'm sorry, this is a little overwhelming for me."

I move to corner her in the closet. "For one, I sincerely hope you are not filled with sorrow." She raises a brow. I smile at her reassuringly. "It's one thing to apologize, it's another to be sorry. I do hope the overwhelm is in a good way."

Her lips part, but she seems at a loss for words. She replaces the shoe and turns back to me. "It's in a good way."

Pulling her into my arms, I drop a soft kiss on her pretty lips. "I'm glad." I open the door of the closet that leads back into the bedroom.

"Did you bring swimwear? A cover-up?" Should I have put those out as well?

She glances at her suitcase. "I did."

"Very well. I'd like to show you our little beach before it's time to prepare for dinner."

She returns my smile. "That sounds great."

I leave Emily feeling immensely satisfied with how that went and head for my own suite. My rooms are a tad more spacious than the one I put her in—for now. I stride quickly through my own seating area as I strip off my shirt. I need a shower, a change of clothes, and some time to settle the excitement I feel when I'm about to close a deal.

As I wash off this day of travel, I recall Emily's face when she saw our home. She'll be floored by our penthouse back in New York. Perhaps we could honeymoon at the estate in England. I dismiss that thought as I shut off the water. It will be winter, and I despise the wet weather. We can take a late spring holiday there.

In my closet, I choose a pair of black swim trunks with a breezy short-sleeved shirt and, feeling refreshed, I head downstairs. Carmen is already laying out the food when I walk outside. "Thank you," I tell her, ignoring her pursed lips and downcast eyes. Carmen is not happy that I've brought another woman here. Her approval isn't my concern.

Emily greets me at the pool, wearing her bikini, with a silk wrap tied around her waist. I wouldn't call that covering up; rather, two small slips of black fabric that cover her breasts, tied on with strings. I hide my disappointment not because I don't think she looks beautiful, but my staff shouldn't be exposed to all of that. Her wrap is tied low, her belly button on display. She looks like a floozy, and I shake my head. We'll rectify that behavior. "You look lovely." I get up from the table and pull out a chair for her.

"Thank you." She blushes with a grin and takes her seat.

She should feel embarrassed. I sit down across from her, pinching my lip and regarding her suit. My irritation flares a notch when Carmen returns. She eyes Emily before asking me if I'd like her to pour the prosecco.

"No. Thank you." I dismiss her and open the bottle myself. Pouring a glass for Emily, I then hand her the flute.

She lets out a nervous laugh. "I don't think I've ever drunk this much champagne in a day."

"Hmm." I pour my own glass. "Well, we're on vacation." I raise my glass for a toast, then watch her sip her wine as I taste mine as well. "How is your room? Do you have everything you need?"

She swallows with a nod. "Yes. Thank you."

I glance over her bikini top again. "Did you purchase that suit for this trip?" I ask.

Her cheeks get pink again. "No. I borrowed it from Gia."

Well, that explains a lot. "I'm not sure it flatters you."

Her hand flutters to her chest as her lips form a little O. My eyes go to the pendant I gave her, and I relax a notch. "I'm not saying you don't look good, it's just a tad scandalous," I add to relieve the tension I just created and go to her.

I offer my hand and she stands. "In most places, it would be appropriate to wear your sarong like this." I unknot it and raise it to retie it around her chest.

Her cheeks are filled with blood now that she realizes her blunder and she sits back down. "I apologize for offending you," she says tersely.

I clench my teeth at her tone but relax my jaw as I retake my seat. "Not offended. If we were alone, it would be perfect, but I don't need Juan and Lucas ogling my beautiful girlfriend."

Her cheeks don't cool, but her lashes flutter down with a shy smile. "Girlfriend?" She peeks back up at me. "Would you be jealous?"

Jealous? No. It's not like any man would survive trying to take what's mine. "I apologize, Emily. I was raised in a very proper family, and those teachings have carried over into my adult life." I shrug, taking my plate and filling it with food. "I suppose it takes getting to know one another to understand expectations." I glance back at her. "Which is exactly what this weekend is about—getting to know one another."

She bites her lip and looks down without responding. I'm good enough at reading faces to realize she's feeling chastised, which is fine. No one steps into my life completely perfect, and sometimes the learning curve is the most entertaining part of a relationship. "Let's eat. There's so much I want to show you yet."

Emily remains fairly quiet as we finish our lunch. I top off her champagne, hoping to relax her a little. She finally gives me a long look and a small smile. "I've never owned a bikini." She chuckles softly. "I believed Gia when she said all I'd need was a swimsuit and flip-flops for an island vacation."

"Ah." I lean back a little myself. "One might expect that from a lingerie model."

Her brows rise. "Gia does more than model lingerie." Then her eyes narrow. "You sound like you dislike her."

"I don't know her well enough to like or dislike her. I just know she's not my type," I reply, picking up my flute.

"What is your type?"

"I think that should be obvious to you." I tip my glass toward her. "I like beautiful, smart women who blush like a maiden, yet have the strength to deal with a man like me."

She blushes on cue.

I drain my glass. "Are you finished? Would you like to see the beach?"

Her lips tip up. "I would."

Taking her hand, I guide her past the pool and to the stone steps. Tucked in a rocky nook, a waterfall supplies my hot tub and she eyeballs that. "That's the outdoor shower." I wave a hand in its direction by the side of the house. She glances at it, but I keep us moving.

Our feet hit the dirt path that's surrounded by trees and flowering bushes. It's a few more steps before the cove comes into sight below us. Emily stops to take in the view, and I admit, it is a jewel. "The water is shallow and protected here. It's warm and perfect for swimming."

I gesture for her to go ahead of me, and we descend the trail cut into the hillside until we greet the beach. We both remove our shoes and stick our toes into the white powder sand. The sunlight sparkles off the turquoise water as we approach the gentle waves that roll in rhythmically.

Emily shoots me a grin before she walks into the surf

until she's ankle-deep in the water. "This is so amazing, Marcus. I've never seen a beach like this."

I join her in the water and place my arm around her waist. "It is pretty, and the scenery is even more beautiful with you in it."

That has a pretty smile lighting up her face, and her eyes sparkle like the sea as she looks at me. Once again, I'm amazed at my luck in discovering her.

# 10

## EMILY

Blowing out a long breath, I attempt to relax and lean into Marcus's side. I knew my suit was revealing, but I'd hoped for a different reaction from him. Everything has been a little odd since we arrived here. Between the formal dinners, the dresses, and then that conversation at the table, the reality that Marcus is out of my league is really setting in. I'm scared now that, as he gets to know me, he'll truly see I couldn't meet his expectations.

"Come." Marcus tightens his hold on my waist. "Let's walk."

We stick to the wet, packed sand and start down the beach. He points at the large, rocky outcrop that protects one end of the cove. "The boat ramp is on the other side. There is a rugged trail to get over it, but otherwise, the only access to the bay is from the house."

I glance back at the house that sits on the cliffs that guard the other end. "The water appeared so rough from the view of my room."

"Yes," he agrees. "The depth of the water changes, and

there's nothing to break up the waves. The rocks make it dramatic too. This is the safest place to play in the water." He waves a hand at the steep hillside that rises to our right. "I'll show you the other side of the island tomorrow. There's a trail that gives you a bird's-eye view, but the terrain makes it near to impossible to reach the shore without a boat."

"I still can't believe you own an island," I mutter, looking down at my feet in the sand.

He chuckles. "Real estate is real estate. Mine is just surrounded by water." He points down the beach. "This stretch is nearly a mile. If you take the trails and make the full loop, it's a little over three. It's not a huge plot of land."

We stop at the rocky wall between the beach and the boat dock. He shows me the trailhead. "You've already seen the other side, though, and you'd want shoes to do that path." He pulls me into his arms and gives me a gentle kiss. "Would you like to take a dip before we return to the house?"

I glance at the water. "Are there sharks?"

He laughs. "I've never seen one in the bay."

Does that mean he's seen them elsewhere? I'm not afraid of water. I am wary of everything that lives in the ocean.

Marcus leads us back down the beach, stopping midway before removing the breezy, light blue shirt he's wearing. It's the first time I've seen him without a shirt and oh my goodness. His pecs are defined and rock-hard abs disappear with a dark trail of hair into the waistline of his shorts. His shoulders and arms are cut, and it's obvious he isn't skipping out on his workouts. He grins at my appraisal as he drops the shirt on the sand, then tugs at the knot holding up my wrap, letting it fall next to his shirt.

I feel the urge to cover myself, but he grabs my hands and gives my body a long look.

"I thought you said my suit wasn't flattering," I say as heat rushes to my face and floods my belly.

"I thought I clarified there is a time and a place to show skin," he replies, tugging me so our bodies are flush and giving me a kiss that lets me know my bikini did have its desired effect on him. He breaks our kiss, keeping my hands, and starts to walk backward toward the water. "That is a very sexy-looking bikini, and you, Emily, have a very beautiful body."

His feet splash as he hits the surf, and he pulls me in with him. The water isn't freezing, but it's still a shock to my heated skin, and I suck in a sharp breath when I reach waist-deep. He crouches down, letting the water cover his shoulders, but still holding my hands. "Keep coming. It feels amazing once you're used to it. Trust me."

I trust him, take another step, and bend my knees, sinking deeper into the cool water. It is shallow. My feet easily reach the sandy bottom, and I soak myself up to my neck before I stand.

I laugh at myself, and Marcus smiles, standing to his full height and grabbing me around the waist. "You need total immersion."

I open my mouth to ask what he means, but he shows me instead by picking me up and dropping me in a wave. I come up sputtering, grasping my top, which feels like it slipped, and glare at him.

He laughs, lowering his body again and tipping his head back, wetting his hair. He looks back at me with a dimple-forming smile, and my breath catches in my throat. He's simply gorgeous with his hair slicked back, droplets of water clinging to his broad shoulders breaching the surface. He could be a model.

My whole body heats at the sight of him, but I make sure my top is in place before anything. I realize immediately the suit is not made for swimming.

"It feels good. Right?" he asks, moving forward and reaching for my hands.

"It does, though my shocking introduction was rude." I give him a chastising look.

He laughs, pulling me closer to him. His smile fades as he studies my face. "You are so beautiful, Emily."

My stomach swoops, and the air between us changes from playful to electric in a blink. He cups the back of my head and presses his lips to mine, and any chill I'd felt vanishes as I give myself to this kiss. His arms come around me, and I wrap myself around him as our connection deepens; his tongue dances against mine, sparking sensations that explode in my core. His hand drops to my bottom, pressing my body into his, and the friction further heats my growing desire.

The fire inside me ignites, but he pulls back, cupping my cheek with his hand, and he stares into my eyes. My heart rolls in my chest from the searing look he gives me, and I'm more than sure I won't be a virgin when I leave this island.

We play in the surf, stealing kisses, touching, exploring each other. Marcus never attempts to breach the line of my suit, nor do I with his, but I do wonder if I'd stop him if he tried.

I'm wound up and needy when he tells me to lie back. I raise a brow, not fully understanding, but I lean back into the water. His hands come underneath me, supporting me as I sway on the gentle swells. He holds me as I float, keeping his feet in the sand, and guides me through the bay. It doesn't break the intimacy, but it aids in cooling the desire that was beginning to blaze out of control. My gaze goes between the fluffy white clouds against the blue sky and Marcus, who's looking down at me.

He stills, dropping one more kiss on my lips. "It's time to head back."

My disappointment is palpable, but I pull up a smile and right myself in the water. Though I feel like I toured the cove rather thoroughly, Marcus has parked us close to where we dropped our clothes, and we splash out of the water hand in hand.

"Did you have fun?" he asks.

"Yes." I pick up my wrap. "But we didn't bring towels."

"No," he agrees and nods to the house. "There are some in the showers, though."

My wrap clings to my body, and he carries his shirt, grabbing my hand. We start the walk back, the sun drying my skin, and I wish we could have soaked that up, lounging on the beach after our swim. "Can we come back here tomorrow?"

"Of course." He grins at me. "We'll do a proper beach day with towels, a blanket, and a picnic lunch."

My insides melt again. I take one last look at the cove. The late afternoon sun seems to have changed the color of the water as it sinks toward the horizon. "This is so beautiful here."

"Yes. We'll have a spectacular sunset tonight. We should dine outside again, by the pool."

"Okay," I agree, but my stomach sinks a little, remembering expectations. "Which dress was I supposed to wear tonight?"

He looks over at me, dropping his gaze from my face to my feet. "The black one."

I'm grateful for his guidance as we climb the stairs. We stop at the showers and I frown. "Marcus, I didn't bring a change of clothes."

He plucks a woman's robe off a hook and hands it to me. My heart drops with a thought. "Was this Karyn's?"

He studies my face for a beat. "There is nothing left of Karyn here."

Is that grief? But another thought runs over all that. "Do you entertain many women here then?"

His eyes chill a degree. "Only the ones who are special."

I have no idea what to do with that comment.

He sighs. "Carmen probably arranged for this when I mentioned you were joining me."

Now I feel foolish, and I take the robe. "That was thoughtful."

"Are you jealous?"

I look down at my feet as my cheeks warm again. I know he's playing with me for my earlier comment. "Maybe," I whisper.

He tips my face up with a finger to my chin. "Know that when I want something, I'm very focused. As long as I'm with you, I won't want to be with anyone else." He takes my cheeks in his hands. "I'm not a player, Emily. Unless I'm playing for keeps."

My pulse trips into overtime, and I'm not sure if it's from the look in his eyes or the words he's saying.

He smiles and flicks his eyes to the shower stall behind me. "Wash up."

I can hear the water from his tap as I step under the spray in my separate stall. Only a wall of woven palms separates us, and I can't help but picture him naked. I wash out the salt water from my hair and scrub off the sand, knowing I can have a more thorough shower in my room. His tap shuts off before mine, but when I step out in the robe, he's waiting for me, dressed in shorts and a soft cotton T-shirt.

He runs a hand through his wet hair and offers me his other. "Shall we prepare for dinner?"

"We shall," I lightly tease him, taking his hand. We pass the pool, and I'm hoping we'll play in that before the weekend is over, too, and then enter the house together. "Where is your room?" I ask as we climb the stairs.

He cuts me a glance. "At the end of the hall." He deposits me in front of my bedroom door. "Dinner is at six. Meet me a few minutes before in the living room."

I bite my lip, containing my grin. "Okay." I'd still love a more thorough tour of the lower level, but I can find the living room.

He grabs my chin, his eyes narrowing. "Okay is so plebeian. I'm not a fan of that word."

I blink, not sure what to say to that. "All right?"

He brushes a kiss to my lips. "I had such an enjoyable time with you today. Thank you."

"I had a wonderful time too. Thank you."

I slip into my room and lean against the closed door, settling my conflicted emotions. Plebeian? What the hell? I try to explain that away with his admission of a rigid upbringing, but what does he expect? I can't be something I'm not, and is that what his expectations are? Then again, he can't crawl down to my level. That's not my expectation—is it?

# 11

## MARCUS

Emily joins me in the living room wearing the cocktail dress and I inwardly smile. Let the lessons begin. I glance at my watch. "You're late."

"I, umm?" She glances back at the stairs as if they hold her excuse.

I sigh. "Umm, what?"

She blinks and looks back at me. I shake my head. "Come, I have wine chilling outside."

She joins me reluctantly, and I take her hand, guiding her through the doors to the deck. "Are you upset with me?"

"No, not upset. I have an issue with tardiness. It's rude and it irritates me."

"I'm sorry."

"Emily…"

"No. I do feel bad for disappointing you."

I stop and brush my fingers over her cheeks. "Don't be sorry." *Be better.* "You didn't know. It's fine."

Emily looks down, turns her head slightly, then perks up. As I predicted, the sunset is spectacular, and she walks away from me to take it in. She stops at the pool, where the oranges bleed to gold and reflect off its surface as well. Admiring the way the light accents her hair, and her figure in that dress, I pour our glasses before joining her.

"This is spectacular," she murmurs.

I hand her a glass. "I told you it would be beautiful tonight."

"You didn't lie." She gives me a shy smile and tastes the wine as we both watch the sun sink on the horizon, and it seems to sizzle where it greets the sea.

"It is beautiful, but it's even more lovely sharing it with you." I clink my glass to hers. If I thought the sentiment would please her, I'm confused when she frowns and looks down.

"Marcus, I've been thinking." She glances back up at me. "Today has been wonderful, but I'm not sure I'm the woman you should be sharing it with. I don't know about formal dinners, and apparently, I don't speak appropriate English. I'm just me and I—"

"I know who you are," I cut her off. "I like it, appreciate it even."

Her brows furrow. "What? Appreciate how?"

I chuckle softly, looking back at the sinking sun. "When you learned who I was, you wanted to run rather than seduce me with hopes of sinking your claws into my fortune." I glance back down at her. "You were blatantly honest about your past. You never tried to be something else to entice me. You were refreshingly real in a life where I wade through poorly contrived illusions. I appreciate that."

I'm being sincere, but I do need more from my wife. Emily is bright, seems to be a quick learner, and I remind myself we don't have to get it all done in a day.

Her lashes flutter down, and she focuses on the surface of the pool. I touch her arm. "Come. Carmen has prepared a lovely dinner for us."

I lead her back to the table, and Carmen delivers our meal with a platter of breaded Tilapia, a side of rice, and steamed vegetables. It's a more simple affair than our first dinner, and Emily looks relieved. I pour us both more wine. "Emily, I do have a confession."

She blinks and looks back at me curiously.

"I did lie to you."

"Oh?"

"Yes, when I said I live my life without concern for others' opinions. The truth is, in business, people do have expectations of me, and I do prefer to win the deal rather than be a rebel."

She presses out a smile and looks down. "So you have two faces?"

I lean forward to get her focus back on me. "I promise, I will remove the mask for you."

Emily searches my eyes. "Thank you."

I smile at her response and gesture to her plate. "Try the fish. Carmen is a wonderful cook."

She tastes a bite and agrees. "It is good. How long has Carmen worked for you?"

I look out at the darkening ocean. "She's been with me since I built this house. Juan basically grew up here."

"She's a single mom?" Emily asks.

"She is. Her husband was a fisherman who drowned at sea." I glance back at her. "She was widowed far too young."

Emily's eyes fill with compassion. "That's sad."

"It is. However, I do pay both of them well to maintain this place year-round for me."

"Hmm." She swallows and picks up her wine. "But you only come down in the winter months?"

"No. Not necessarily, but perhaps more frequently to escape the cold. I'm not a fan of snow."

She sets down her glass. "I actually like winter. Christmas is my favorite holiday."

Religion has played such a tumultuous role in my life and I have to school my frown. "Really? Are you a Christian?"

Her cheeks pink up a little. "I believe in God, but I've never been to church, so maybe not a good one. Are you?"

I chuckle. "No. I was raised in a protestant family, but no, I don't believe in God, or heaven and hell." I taste my fish and chew thoughtfully. "I've learned man creates his own destiny."

"But isn't that God's intention? You know, free will and all that."

My lips twitch at her naive interpretation. "Sure, if you piece together religion in a way that works for you. You're free to sin, but then you can ask for forgiveness. You have freedom of choice, but if it's the wrong one, you can pray and hope the Almighty grants your wish." I shake my head. "You're either blessed with abundance or forsaken and struggle, but I can promise you, those with abundance didn't gain it by doing good deeds."

She glances around the pool deck. "Is that you? Did you get your abundance by doing bad things?"

I set down my cutlery and lick my lips. She's an inquisitive one. "I inherited my wealth through generations of people who did bad things." I pause, looking back at her. "Then I used it to come here and make more money because I enjoy it. I love the challenge, and I like to win, and I'm sure some of my opponents wouldn't feel they were treated fairly."

Her brow goes up. "You cheated them?"

"No. I was smarter than them."

She digests that as I toy with my wineglass.

"I told you I'd take off the mask for you, so there you have it, that's who I am."

Emily huffs out a little breath. "But I read that you have a foundation and support many charities."

"I do, and like most people in my tax bracket, sometimes if you give money away, you end up making more." I take in her pinched reaction. "It's expected of the wealthy to give back. What charitable things do you participate in?"

She huffs out a little laugh. "I think I'm my own charity right now, but I have volunteered for the animal shelter. It's how I found Bella."

"Ah. Animals. Why don't you volunteer for the soup kitchen at Christmas? I do."

"You do?" she whispers.

"Of course, and the publicity I gain from it puts my company in a good light." I sip my wine as I take in her reaction to that. "You can judge me, but I can guarantee I do more than the lot of you commit to."

"I don't judge you," Emily replies softly, then blows out a breath. "Maybe I judged you. Politically, I lean toward giving more incentives to the working class and less to the rich."

"Yes." I chuckle. "The evil one percent. Right?" I let out a weighted sigh. "Yet you overlooked the evil to have lunch with me on my yacht and come here for the weekend."

"First of all, I didn't know we were going to a yacht..." She shakes her head. "Yes, I wanted to come here. But"—she raises a hand—"it was to spend time with you, not because it was some luxury vacation. I would have been just as happy to spend the weekend with you on the Jersey shore. I'd probably feel more comfortable too."

I laugh and lean forward, clasping her hands with mine. "Which is what I like about you." I give her fingers a squeeze. "All I'm saying is that a man is more than the size of his bank account. We're all human, and ninety percent of the time we put our individual desires before the needs of others, regardless of where we are in life." I release her hands and lean back. "I could have given away my inheritance. It wasn't earned." *Perhaps it was.* "I could have come to America penniless and made something of myself. 'Pull myself up by my bootstraps.' Isn't that what you say? Would that make me a better man in your eyes?"

"No." She glances away. "I'm sorry..." I cringe, and she adjusts. "I apologize, it's just I've never been with someone like you. Maybe I made some assumptions, but I like the man I'm getting to know. I appreciate your honesty."

"I'm enjoying you too." I look at her plate. "Finish your dinner."

Our conversation stalls as we eat. The sky grows dark, Carmen clears our dishes, and we enjoy the rest of the wine by the pool. I point out the stars, brilliant here with so little light noise. Emily gazes at them and gasps when a shooting star lights up the sky. "We should make a wish."

I grin and pull her close to my side. "I wish for many more nights with Emily here with me."

She chuckles and looks down at the pool. The lights have come on and it softly glows in the night. "Let's swim."

"Now?" I raise a brow.

"Yes. Now." She looks up with a smile, but it fades. "I apologize, is it inappropriate to swim at night?"

I tuck a strand of hair behind her ear. "No. I don't think so." I glance at the pool. "It's a little risqué."

She giggles, knowing that I'm teasing. "No, fun. It would be fun."

I grin and look down at her. "Ms. Hanson, if your wish is to swim, it would be my honor to do that with you."

I'm rewarded with a brilliant smile, and I feel like a kid as we jog up the stairs to retrieve our swimsuits. I do like Emily, I muse as I change. The more I learn about her, the more I know she's the one, the woman I've been searching for. Emily is the perfect combination of honest and polite. Intelligent yet naive.

With towels in hand, I collect her at her door. I'm happy to see she's covered up appropriately, should we run into one of my staff on our jaunt to the pool.

It's the first time I've swum at night, but as I playfully grab Emily in the water, and she giggles and squeals, I'm seriously enjoying it. She holds on to my shoulders, smiles lighting up her face, and I can't help but drop a kiss on her lips.

We hold on to each other as our kisses become more and more fervent, and I wonder if tonight is the night. Because once she gives herself to me, she's mine to keep. I wasn't sure it would be this soon, but take your blessings where you find them, and I press her against me so she can feel my growing desire.

She stiffens and leans back. "Marcus, I, umm..."

I let her go, moderately irritated. "You, umm, what?"

She blushes and looks down. "I'm sorry."

Is she trying to piss me off?

"It's just..." She treads water until she finds the bottom with her feet. "I've never been, you know."

"I don't know," I say as I approach her. A slut in a pool? I believe that. As attracted to anyone else? I believe that too. "What?"

Her blush deepens and she looks away. "With a man."

That stops me and leaves me a little speechless. She's a virgin? What lucky star was I born under? This means once I do own her, I'll be the only one she's known, and she'll have no reference, other than her imagination, to tell her what's right or wrong. "Emily, I apologize. I wasn't trying to pressure you. I got lost in the moment, but I told you, I'm a gentleman. I understand the word no."

She shakes her head, still avoiding eye contact. "It's not that. I mean, I don't know." She looks back at me, so beautiful in the starlight. "No one has made me want to... until you."

I'd swear my heart swells, and I'm next to her in one stroke. I pull her into my arms and look down at her. "Emily, you make me want it as well. It's our first night, and we don't have to rush anything. When—if—something happens, it will only because you know it's what you want." I cup her cheek with my hand. "Understand?"

She allows me to hold her closer. Honestly, it's doing nothing to cool my body, but patience is key. I lean back enough to plant a kiss on her forehead. "It's late. Perhaps we should turn in."

She's so fucking precious, perfect, and I already feel she's mine. An overwhelming wave of possessiveness slams into me. It's nothing like I'd felt for the others. I know, now more than ever, I want to keep her, protect her, and show her the world. When I'm through, the words 'I never' will not drop from her lips.

## 12

---

## EMILY

Have I ever felt more mortified in my life? He's not the first man I've explained my situation to. It's not a situation—it's a life choice! But with everyone else, I was putting on the brakes because I didn't want to. With Marcus, tonight under the stars, the way he heated my body with his kisses... I can't say the same. I just felt it would be polite to give him a heads-up.

He put on the brakes. He said all the right things, but now, sitting at my vanity and towel-drying my hair, I wonder if somehow my virginity was a turn-off for him. He dropped me off at my room with a kiss on my cheek. Oh right, and alerting me breakfast is at seven. Who sets that time for breakfast when you're on vacation?

He informed me he had a staff meeting after and would set out a lighter affair if I wanted to wait. I've no idea what that means, but I agreed to that.

I stand and drop the towel, put on my pajamas and leave the bathroom. On the balcony, I breathe in a lungful of salty air with my eyes closed and my head tipped up into the breeze. It's so beautiful here, and I look down at the foamy water as the waves crash into the rocks below. The froth seems to glow in the moonlight, and the sound seems equally violent and soothing at the same time.

Tonight, I swam under the stars with a British billionaire. I frolicked with him in his secluded bay. Fricking came over on his privately owned planes, one he even handily flew himself. It's a lot for a girl like me to swallow in one day.

A part of me knows I'm falling for this man, but there's a niggling doubt in my brain. Like the waves below, he's somehow soothing yet disturbing at the same time. I leave the doors open so I can listen to the sounds of the night and climb under the covers on this luxurious bed.

*Emily Hanson, how did you end up here?*

I smile to myself as sleepiness takes over. Marcus admitted he liked me for my honesty, not my poise. Yes, we come from two different worlds, but he seems content to let me grow into his.

As I drift off, I'm a little relieved I didn't have to face sex tonight, then again, a little disappointed he didn't press. I know if he had, I'd have succumbed because I do want this with Marcus. I'm sure there are parts of him I'd like to change. There are pieces of me he'd like to ignore too, but that's probably every relationship. No one is perfect.

---

AS SOON AS my eyes open, I know the sun is high. I wash up and dress for the day. The living room is empty when I come down the stairs, but food is out on the dining room table.

A light affair includes a bowl of fruit with pastries and a

carafe of hot coffee. There are also fixings for tea, and I wonder if Marcus prefers tea to coffee. I take a seat at the large dining table alone and fill my plate. Now I really wish my phone worked out here. I'd call Gia. She'd know what to tell me. Of course, I can hear her in my head. *"Just do it, Emily."*

Lucas passes the doorway, hesitates, and stops, turning to look at me. "Ms. Hanson."

"Hello." I haven't seen him since we arrived, and I almost forgot he was here at all.

"Are you enjoying your stay?" he asks.

I do believe those are the most words he's ever said to me. "Yes. Thank you."

He leans on the doorjamb, arms folded over his wide chest, and studies me quietly. It's a little unnerving.

"Are you hungry?" I wave a hand at my light affair.

"No."

Okay? "What can I do for you, Mr....?" I don't know his last name. He doesn't offer that information, just stares at me with pale blue eyes. "Do you know where Marcus is?" I ask.

"His office," he answers readily. "I'll let him know you're here." He pushes off the wall and leaves. I breathe. What was that about?

My thoughts turn back to Marcus as I peel off a layer of this flaky pastry. I'm not sure I have the courage to be forward about what I want, but I hope I've dropped enough clues so he'll take the initiative to make a move.

I close my eyes as the buttery bread melts on my tongue. I must be dreaming. That man, this house, the food...

"She's awake."

The sound of Marcus's voice has my eyes snapping open and my cheeks warming. "Good morning."

He looks at his watch with a raised brow. "For a little longer at least. Did you sleep well?"

I did, with dreams of him. "Yes. Do you always get up so early?"

He takes a seat at the table with me. "Do you always sleep so late?"

I glance down at my coffee cup. "On weekends, yes."

He doesn't say anything, and I look back at him to find him staring at me. He finally clears his throat. "Yes. I prefer to get up early. It seems like a waste of time to sleep the day away."

For some reason, my cheeks get hotter, but I force a smile. "I'm excited to spend more time on the beach."

"Good. First, I wanted to take you on the boat and give you a tour of the island."

"Okay." I shake my head. "All right."

He chuckles. "Did you bring any other swimsuits?"

I stare back at him for a beat. "Um, yes. I have a one-piece."

"Hmm. That probably has a better chance of staying on in the water. Doesn't it?"

I shift uncomfortably in my seat, warring between being embarrassed and angry at that comment. "I suppose it does." I don't manage to keep either emotion out of my voice.

"Good. Go change into that and meet me down here in thirty minutes." He rises and comes over to pull out my chair. Honestly, I could have eaten more, but I stand, abandoning my meal.

He doesn't join me on the stairs, and I walk alone to my room. I'm trying to reconcile how I feel about him when he says things like that. He doesn't sugarcoat his feelings.

Maybe I should just be happy he prefers to have me covered and comfortable.

I put on the suit and regard my reflection in a tall mirror. This one has full bottom coverage, and the tank top shows no cleavage at all. My fingers touch the butterfly pendant, and I let go of my petulance. I select a pair of shorts to wear before I scoop my hair into a ponytail. Hopefully, my flip-flops will not offend him. I smirk at the thought and head back down to meet him.

We walk rather than drive down the road to the dock, and the morning is warm already, but the breeze picks up as the water comes into view. "Tomorrow, we'll get an earlier start and I'll show you the trails," Marcus comments as we near the dock. There is a boat, but it's not the same one that was here yesterday. This looks more like a little dinghy I've seen used at the harbor.

"Where is the other boat?" I ask as we approach Juan on the dock.

"I told you, that was a supply boat."

"Oh." That makes sense. It's not like you can take a quick trip to the grocery store here. I glance over at the plane bobbing in the water where we left it.

Juan holds the rope while Marcus helps me into the little rubber craft. Despite the look, it feels rather sturdy, and I relax a little. Marcus hands me a life vest and allows me to get that on before Juan tosses him the rope and we float back, away from the dock. A moment later, a motor comes to life, and with his hand on the lever, Marcus steers us away from the island before turning and taking us parallel to the shore.

I find some handholds and grab on as we rock over the waves. "The water can be a little rougher here on the north and east side," Marcus informs me as we round this end of the island. On this side, the trees and foliage seem to come right up to the water line, and there isn't a beach in sight. They rise up on what looks like a steep slope, and the greenery is so thick it seems to be one living carpet swaying with the breeze.

"The water on this side is deeper. If you're searching for a shark, you might find them over here." He winks at me.

I grip the holds tighter. "Good to know. Why aren't you wearing a life vest?"

He chuckles. "I'm not planning on getting wet."

I look over at him, wearing swim trunks and a blue cotton T-shirt. He looks handsome as ever as he competently steers this craft through the waves. "We're actually both wet," I comment as more spray flies up and hits us.

His smile grows. "True." He glances at me. "You look good wet."

My eyes trail over his torso, where his damp shirt hugs his broad chest. *So do you.* I'm not really brave enough to say that out loud, so I look back at the shoreline. "There's a little beach." I point to it as a sliver of sand comes into sight.

"Yes. It's not really a hospitable place to stop, though. The sand crabs are plentiful and happier left undisturbed."

I wonder what that looks like as we pass by, and soon, we're turning again. It amazes me how each side of the island is so different. This one has little vegetation but rocky cliffs that drop straight into the sea. It's not long before I see the roofline of the house, and I have a sense of where we are. "The island isn't really that big," I comment as we come around the cliffs and, from here, I can see the rocks that lie below my balcony.

Marcus swings the boat a little farther out as we pass the

spot. "It's not, and most of it isn't worth trying to develop, but I like the little pocket I have."

"Yes, it's beautiful."

The little bay comes into view, and it's just as pretty from this angle. We lazily drift by it, both of us quiet and enjoying the view. He swings out again to go around the rocky outcrop that separates the bay from the boat dock. Despite my uncertainty regarding this little boat, I'm a little sad my tour is over. "That was fun," I say as we drift toward the dock where Juan is waiting.

"It was." Marcus smiles at me before gathering the rope and tossing it to Juan. He pulls us closer, securing the boat, then offers me a hand.

With my feet on solid ground, I wait for Marcus to join me. The breeze cools my damp skin, and with the weight of the vest gone, I feel the heat of the sun. Brushing the loose strands of hair off my face, I shield my eyes and look out at the sparkling water. Lost in the view, I startle when Marcus puts an arm around me.

He turns me, glancing down at my flip-flops, and shrugs. "I wanted to show you the trail to the beach from here."

I look over in its direction. "Okay." I remember his comment from yesterday about it being rocky. "Will my shoes work?"

"Those aren't shoes, but yes, I think you'll be fine."

I look at his feet, and he's wearing more of a water shoe, with a thick sole. Marcus takes my hand and leads me toward the trail. "You did bring sturdier shoes, right?"

"Yes." Sneakers.

"Good. You'll be more comfortable on our hike tomorrow."

We start to ascend the trail, and aside from being gravelly and rocky in spots, I'm doing fine in my sandals. We pause at the top, and it's incredibly scenic with the bay below on one side and the wide-open sea on the other. It's breezier up here, and between that and the sun, I've dried off a little, but I do wonder with this humidity if you ever feel completely dry.

Marcus wraps his arms around me, pulling my back to his chest as we both enjoy the view from here.

"I've never been somewhere like this," I whisper.

He kisses my hair. "I'm glad you like it here, Emily. I don't share this place with many people, but I'm happy to share it with you."

I turn in his arms to thank him, but he cups my cheek and gives me the softest kiss that completely melts me. Aside from his occasionally annoying comments, I feel like I'm living in a fairy tale, and this is the perfect setting for a girl to fall in love.

I look back out at the bay, then ruin our moment by asking about Karyn. "Is this where your wife died? Does it hold painful memories for you?"

His eyes cool, and he turns me away from him but continues to hold me close. "Yes. We were on holiday." His sigh flutters my hair. "The truth is, Karyn wasn't being honest with me. I believe she was preparing to leave me." He rests his chin on my head. "Perhaps it was me, not spending enough time with her, or paying enough attention. I'm not sure. No one knows what happened that day, but had she lived, our marriage wasn't going to work. She wasn't the person I was meant to spend the rest of my life with."

He sounds so sad, and my heart goes out to him. "I'm sorry."

"Don't be. To answer your question, I do have memories

of Karyn here. I choose not to lose myself in the painful ones; rather I honor her by remembering the better times we shared."

I lean into him. "I apologize for bringing her up."

"No." He kisses my head again. "It's normal for you to be curious about my past. I wish mine were as unblemished as yours."

I stiffen a little in his arms. Does he mean my virginity? I turn my head to look at him, and he gives me a sad smile. "Let's live in the moment, the present. Today is about you and me." He gazes back at the ocean. "If you waste time watching the wake from a boat rather than looking forward, you might miss what's coming ahead."

I relax back into him, but he releases me, taking my hand again. "The last part of this trail is a little trickier. Let me go ahead."

He didn't lie. There really isn't a trail going down, more like rocky steps, some larger than others. Marcus takes it like a mountain goat with sure feet, turning to help me in spots, and I see why he frowned at my shoe choice. No, Gia. I need more than a bikini and flip-flops on this vacation. I'm a little shaken and 'glowing' again when we reach the bottom of the trail. It turns into the same gravelly surface we started with as we approach the bay. "That was challenging," I mutter as I pull off my sandals and stick my toes in the sand.

Marcus smiles at me. "You did great. You're not a complainer." He takes my hand again. "I like that."

My cheeks warm at the compliment, but something catches my eye and I focus on that. A blanket is spread out in the sand about mid-beach, and I see our picnic has been set up for us. I shake my head, thinking it must be nice to have a staff at your service. Personally, I'm starving, having not finished breakfast.

We reach the blanket and Marcus pulls off his shirt, tucking it under the picnic basket. My mouth dries again at the sight of his physique. He grins at me and gestures for me to sit.

"Let's see what Carmen has in store for us," he says as he opens the basket. "Ah..." He holds up a plastic pitcher and studies it. "Her passion-fruit martinis. You'll love them." He plucks out the clear plastic cups. "Better served in a proper glass, but..."

I shrug. I don't mind that. He continues to dig food out of the bottomless basket, removing an assortment of cheese and meats, crackers and finger sandwiches. Marcus places everything on a wooden platter before pouring our drinks.

I taste the martini, and this drink is chilled, refreshing, and delicious. He raises his cup to toast with me. "To island life."

I grin. "Cheers."

"To the beautiful scenery." He eyes me appraisingly, and I tap my cup to his.

"Dig in." He waves a hand at the platter, then selects a cracker and loads it with cheese. "The sandwiches are crab salad."

"I've never eaten this much seafood—ever," I mention as I taste the sandwich.

"No? Why? Do you like it?"

"Yeah. I mean, I'm kind of a steak and potatoes girl." Really, I'm more of a ramen, mac and cheese girl. "But it's good. I've been enjoying the different flavors."

"Good. I'm glad you like it. I enjoy seafood, but here, it's a staple." He leans back on the blanket, exposing his glorious chest to the sun. Marcus has a golden tint to his skin, and I guess for some reason, I pictured the British as pale, quick to burn, not necessarily tan. I mention it, and he grins. "Perhaps it's the French blood that made it into my ancestry."

"That's interesting. I don't really know what ancestry runs in my blood."

Marcus props himself up on an elbow. "Emily, do you want to learn who your father is?"

I huff out a little laugh. "No. I mean, I doubt he even knows I exist." I set my food aside and hug my knees. "It doesn't really matter—I guess, unless you have kids, but..."

"I don't intend on having children either."

Did I say that? "Why?"

"I was blessed to be an only child, and I know who my ancestors are. Sometimes it's kinder to end a line rather than continue it."

My brows come together as I stare at him. "I'm not sure what you mean."

He smirks and looks away. "I mean, my family has a long history of service to the country, loyalty to the crown. My grandfathers earned many awards and accolades, but I wouldn't call them good people and my father was useless. My mother was basically insane."

I'm a little shocked, but I pull it together and close my mouth. "My mother isn't exactly sane either."

He chuckles as he lies back down. "I got that impression."

A heavy silence settles between us, and I stare out at the aquamarine water in the bay. I'm not sure what to think of his confession. We nibble at the food again. I try the cheese and enjoy the sandwiches, but I'm really loving the martinis.

After I finish my second cup, I'm starting to feel the alcohol even though I can't really taste it.

"Hey." Marcus nudges me. "Are you finished? Would you like to swim?"

"Yes." I look back at the water and laugh. "I love to swim, but I've never really spent time in the ocean."

He stands and reaches for my hand. "Why? You live by one."

"I know, but there wasn't time to run to the beach during school, and I worked during summer break." Now all I do is work and go home. Gia is right. I'm becoming the recluse cat lady.

"I was like that at your age," Marcus admits. "Focused on school, then growing the business. Now I know there is a time to work and a time to play."

I chuckle. "So you were never the playboy billionaire?"

He raises a brow. "No. That would be my partner."

"Heath? I wonder what will happen with him and Gia."

He snorts. "I don't see that relationship working out. They're a little too much alike."

I kind of got that impression too. I shimmy out of my shorts and feel warm as his eyes light up. I realize it's not just his looks I'm attracted to. Maybe it's his work ethic, or that he doesn't hide pieces of his past from me. If we could get him to loosen up from the rigid upbringing, I'm sure we could make this work.

# 13

## MARCUS

Emily joins me in the family room, wearing that flirty dress and looking absolutely lovely.

"Perhaps there is a god and he's delivered the perfect woman to me."

She blushes, and I scoff at the thought. My mother's concept of piety saw us all as sinners who needed to repent and added a whole new level to her instability.

"You look incredible," I add with a smile.

"Thank you." She fidgets with her fingers and looks down. "How did you choose these dresses? They fit like they were made for me."

I gather both of her hands in mine. "I guessed." I move her into a little twirl before gathering her into my arms. I was right, this fabric was made for movement.

"My shoe size?" She peeks up at me.

"Did I get that right too?" I raise a brow before dropping a kiss on her lips. "Come. I had Carmen prepare something different tonight. It's not steak but a pork dish."

"It smells delicious," Emily comments as I take her to the dining room. "We're eating inside?"

"Yes. It's breezy tonight, with a forecast of light showers. I thought we'd be more comfortable inside."

The doors to the deck are still open, and the breeze flutters the gauzy curtains. I pull out Emily's chair, and she takes her seat before I join her. As I fill a plate for her, Emily raises a brow.

"What?"

"Nothing. It's just you always serve me or pour the wine. I'm capable of serving myself."

I regard her and recall her upbringing. "I'm sure you are. I was raised to be a gentleman. Plus, it pleases me to take care of you. Perhaps you've spent so much time taking care of yourself, the sentiment eludes you."

Her cheeks pink up. "No. I mean. Thank you."

I study Emily as she cleans her plate. I'm not sure if it was our full day in the sun that has her appetite up. She has a pretty glow from our time outdoors, and I enjoy that as we eat. I ask her what the best part of our day was, and she bounces between the beach and the boat ride.

"That boat is merely for playing around the island. It doesn't hold enough fuel to make it to another one," I interject casually.

"What happens if something goes wrong with the plane? I mean, you could be stranded here."

"No, I wouldn't. I have the phone to call for help." I give her a wink, which makes her smile.

Emily takes a sip of wine, licking her lips as she sets down the glass. "Can I ask you something?"

"Anything," I reply, curious to know what she's thinking.

"What did you mean when you said that your mother was insane?"

"Ah." I glance over at my mother's little treasures displayed on the dining hutch. "She was very religious. A lady at all times when in public, and demanded that my father and I held up to those social obligations too. However, in private, she was a vicious drunk."

I let Emily absorb that before I continue. "She was very controlling, judgmental, and used the Bible like a weapon."

"Oh." She looks back at her wine. "I'm sorry. My mother also has issues with alcohol. That and really bad judgment in men. When I went to college, she moved to Florida to live with some gambler she met in Atlantic City. Not a successful one," she adds with a sad smile.

"Hmm." I recall her telling me about how often they moved, lived in a commune of all places. "I realize you had a hard childhood, between the lack of money and a stable parent. I can assure you that you could have all the money in the world and still have a shitty upbringing." I raise my glass to her. "We aren't so different, Emily."

She raises her glass too. "Maybe not. It wasn't all bad. I mean, there were times when it was just her and me, and we had fun. I probably make it sound worse than it was. How about you? Do you have any good memories from your childhood?"

For a moment, I don't answer. Did I have any? "My grandfather bought me a pony when I was seven."

"Oh?" Emily perks up. "I've never ridden a horse, but I like to look at them."

I smile, recalling my childhood home. "We had a lovely stable, and I rode that pony every day. I was young, but oh, our adventures. We'd gallop through the fields, leaping over huge obstacles..." I laugh, taking a sip of wine. "By that I mean small hedges and straw bales."

Emily's face lights up as I describe how we battled imaginary warriors, prevailing every time, and how I perceived him as a gallant steed and myself a brilliant knight when I'd ride up to the barn.

She giggles. "That does sound fun."

"It was." I agree with her. "Until we started competing."

"Why? What happened?"

I shrug. "We won."

Her brows furrow. "I don't understand. How was that bad?"

I look down, remembering that day. "I showed everyone our blue ribbon and boasted my pony was the best."

She shakes her head. "And?"

I glance back at her. "And pride is a deadly sin. My penance was his loss."

She frowns. "His loss? How? What happened to your pony?"

"He passed away from an injury."

Her whole face falls into a frown. "That's so sad." Emily reaches over and touches my hand. "That wasn't your fault, though."

I stare at our hands, recalling the incident. *It is your fault when your mother caused the injury to punish you.* I swallow and twist my lips into something of a smile. "It was sad. He is a good memory, though, and a constant reminder that nothing is permanent. It's better to live in the present and not lament on yesterday."

She rolls her lips together and toys with her wineglass. "I never had a pet when I was young. Bella is my first. And it was the first time I think another living being loved me unconditionally."

Ah yes, the cat. I watch her eyes as she speaks and know I can't separate her from that. I need to make arrangements. "Emily, I'm so glad you're enjoying the island. The last two days have been wonderful."

Her fingers brush over her pink cheeks. "They have. Tomorrow is our last day. It feels like it's gone by so fast."

Tomorrow isn't our last day; rather it will be our beginning. "Did you enjoy dinner?"

"I did."

"Good." I stand up. "Stay there."

I leave Emily to find the remote for the sound system in the adjoining living room. Selecting a playlist first, I return to retrieve her.

"What are we doing?" she asks as I hold out my hand for her.

"Would you dance with me?"

She giggles as she takes my hand. "Dance?"

I don't reply as I lead her into the living room, take the remote from my pocket, and press play. The first notes from an old tune by Ray Charles start, and I set down the remote before gathering her in my arms. "Yes, dance."

"'You Don't Know Me'?" She comments on the song and gives me a shy smile.

She is so sweet. "No. Not yet."

Her cheeks get rosier as she takes my hand. "I'm not sure I can dance well like this."

I rest my hand on her lower back. "It doesn't matter. I simply like having you in my arms." I lead us into the first steps. Emily gracefully follows my lead, and when I twirl her, her skirt flares. Her smile grows as I pull her back into my arms and drop a kiss on her lips.

"You're so beautiful, Emily," I whisper in her ear. She leans into me, and I hold her closer. Together, we sway to the end of the song. Silence fills the room, and I can hear the rain has started. Emily is looking up at me, her eyes glittering, her lips slightly parted, inviting me. I cup her head with both hands and give her the kiss she's looking for.

Her arms come around my neck, and I don't back away this time; rather I deepen our kiss. My tongue teases hers, savoring her sweet flavor. My fingers thread into her silky locks, and my hand trails down her spine, resting at the base, and I press her into me.

She attempts to lean away. I fist her hair and change the angle of our kiss. I don't give her room to think or even breathe but let her know exactly what my intentions are.

Footsteps in the room have us pulling apart. Emily places her hand on my chest and looks up at me with wide eyes and glistening lips.

"I apologize, Mr. Sterling." Carmen breezes past us. "It's raining. I felt I should close the doors."

"Thank you, Carmen," I tell her without looking away from Emily. Grabbing her hand in mine, I lean in a little. "Come."

Emily doesn't protest as I escort her to the stairs. We pass the door to her room and go to mine.

"Marcus?" she whispers as I open the door.

"It's fine." I turn on the lights and show her it's an innocent sitting room, no bed. "I just wanted some privacy. Will you share a nightcap with me?"

She looks around the room, and indeed, the wind has picked up outside and the curtains to my balcony are in a frantic dance. I release Emily to close the doors, then go to the sideboard and pick up a bottle of scotch. I turn to her with a raised brow. She predictably blushes and shakes her head. "No to the scotch."

I chuckle. "Trust me."

I take out two chilled glasses from the mini-fridge below, as well as a wedge of lemon. Adding some ice cubes, I then pour the scotch, top it off with the soda, and garnish with a twist of lemon. I hand her the glass with a smile. "Try it."

She takes a tentative sip, then lifts an uncertain shoulder. With my own glass, I walk over to the sofa. "Sit with me."

She takes the seat next to me and sets her glass on the coffee table in front of us. Chewing her lip, she looks around the space nervously before she regards me.

"What's running through your mind, Emily?"

Her blush deepens, and she looks away. "I, um..." She pulls in a deep breath and attempts a smile. "I told you I never have... I mean..." She blows out through pursed lips, fluttering her hair. "With you, last night, I wasn't exactly saying no."

"If you could articulate, perhaps I'd understand any of that." Her eyes widen, and I sigh. "Are you suggesting you want to make love?"

Her gaze drops, and her cheeks are blazing red now. I set down my drink and lean closer to her. "Emily, I promise that I brought you here so we could have some privacy. I wasn't trying to imply"—I glance at my bedroom door—"anything." I touch her chin with my finger and get her eyes back on me. "I told you, I'd never pressure you to do anything you don't want."

She licks her lips nervously as her eyes search mine.

"You said make love, but really, this would just be sex. You don't love me."

I sit back a little on the sofa. "Hmm, love. I think it starts with a seed. If you nurture it, it grows into a beautiful, flowering plant with many roots that can withstand adversity. When does that seed get planted? With the first look? A first kiss?" My lips twitch up. "The first dance?" I casually lay my arm over the back of the sofa and play with a lock of her hair. I read something like that in a poem. I'll tip my hat to that poet now because I can see the change in her eyes.

She's so different from Karyn, who fell into my bed rather easily. Emily is a challenge I have to work for, and I make a promise to myself, I'll put my back into that labor.

"Hey." I get a little closer and let my fingers tease the hem of her skirt that exposes her knee. "Tell me why you waited."

She blinks a couple of times. "I, um, I wanted it to mean something. I wanted it to be special."

I nod, looking down at where her flesh has pebbled under my touch. "You wanted it to be a gift? A beginning? A promise?"

"Yes," she whispers.

I look back into her eyes and know she'll get all three of those wishes. "Are you waiting for marriage?"

"No." She shakes her head. "For the right person."

I palm her knee now, letting my finger brush just slightly under that hemline. She doesn't push my hand away but leans forward, bringing her knees together as she picks up her drink. She takes a nervous sip and glances at me. "How about you? How did you lose your virginity?"

I chuckle. "That's a bold question." I remove my hand and take a drink myself. "Let's see. I was young, fourteen if I recall." I suppress my grin at her expression, but I know it's not a scandalous age for a young man. "She worked in our home and flirted with me often. One day, my parents were out, and I stole a kiss." I smile as if the memory matters. "We made plans to meet later in her room and, being she was a little older than me, she gave me a lesson when I did."

"Oh." Emily takes another shaky sip, but when she leans back, I continue to toy with her hair.

"After that, I pursued several meaningless liaisons. Conquests of sorts. It wasn't until college that I met someone who made me see sex could be more than a pleasurable release."

That has her eyes back on me. "Your first love?"

"Mmm." I shrug. "Maybe. To be honest, love has eluded me. I may have thought so at the time, but obviously it didn't last. It did make me realize I wanted more from a relationship than sex. Perhaps it's also what made me see that relationships need to be nurtured, respected, and controlled if there's the hope for them to flourish."

Emily sets her glass back down. "Controlled?"

"Yes. I do believe relationships work within boundaries." I take another drink and lick my lips. "Say your partner has a cat, and you're possibly allergic, but you accept that—for her."

Emily's eyes light up with curiosity and I continue. "Say that I love to fly little planes, and you're terrified of that, but you join me because it pleases me."

"Or"—she lifts a finger—"it's the only way to get to an island vacation that will please you both."

She's adorable. "Or that." I set my glass down and focus on her, my hand resting back on her knee. "As I became an adult, it changed my perspective on intimacy. I no longer have the goal of conquering the moment, but forging a future." My fingers slip back under the hem of her dress and stroke the soft flesh of her inner thigh. "I don't think our philosophies are so different."

She shifts in her seat. More goose bumps erupt on her skin where I touch and she closes her eyes.

"Kiss me, Emily," I whisper, leaning closer.

Her eyes open slowly, then her lashes flutter down as she leans in and brushes her lips over mine.

# 14

## EMILY

Does he have any idea how his touch lights up my body? How his words stir my heart, or the way his lips feel so perfect on mine?

His fingers curl in my hair and he pulls me closer, deepening our kiss, and I'm melting in his arms. His fingers trail farther up, under my skirt, and the tingles spread over my skin and puddle between my legs.

It's true. I'm not waiting for marriage but for the right man, and nothing about this moment feels wrong. The warmth spreads through my belly and wraps around my heart.

I lean closer to him on the sofa, draping one leg over his lap, giving him more access and, as his hand travels up, my focus narrows.

No one has ever stirred these sensations in my body. Maybe I felt twinges, a little tingle from a kiss. Is this my sign —that he's right for me?

He fists my hair, his tongue dances with mine, and his hand cups my ass, pulling me closer to him. The underlying fear buzzes just below the sensual energy that floods my body. I know your first time hurts. I have an idea of his size, having felt him through his swim trunks, and it intimidates me as much as it stimulates me. I shudder, and I'm not sure if it's the fear or the fact he just grazed his fingers over my center.

*Stop overthinking this, Emily!*

He touches me again, and I know it's not fear. I'm throbbing in places I've never truly recognized before.

His hands grip my hips, maneuvering me so I'm straddling his lap, and his lips never leave mine as I adjust in this new position. I lean back to pull in a breath, and his mouth finds my neck, his teeth scraping over the sensitive flesh. My breasts feel heavy and my clit is needy and I press my whole body into him, trembling under his kisses. Marcus pushes my skirt up to my waist and slips my dress off one shoulder, exposing my breast in a lacey bra, and he pulls down the cup and covers my nipple with his mouth. I wrap my arm around his neck, holding him to me, and gasp when he pulls back, suddenly standing with me in his arms. My legs wrap around his hips, and I look into his bright blue eyes as he carries me across the room.

I feel like a starlet in a romantic movie, and I know we've sealed the deal when we cross the threshold into his bedroom. I lost my shoes somewhere in the tangle on the couch, and I'm barefoot on the rug when he sets me down. His fingers fist the hem of my gown and he starts to lift it up. "You look beautiful in this dress."

I pray the lighting hides the color in my cheeks, and I lift my arms as he whisks the gown over my head. "You're even more beautiful without it."

I stand in my panties and my lopsided bra, which he

quickly relieves me of. I've never been naked with a man before, and I resist the urge to cover my breasts as his face lowers and he takes me in another kiss.

My fingers curl into the fabric of his shirt, and I feel like I should start on those buttons, but I'm uncertain, so I simply greet his kiss, hoping he can feel my desire for this. He backs me up until I hit the edge of the bed, and I sit back, scooting toward the center. He joins me, nipping at my lips, my neck, wherever his lips can reach, and each contact has me begging for more.

He rests back on his heels as he unclasps his cufflinks. His eyes appraise me beneath him, and he starts to unbutton his shirt. For me, it's like slow motion as each inch of skin is exposed. He doesn't say anything, but his eyes speak volumes and I drown in their message. He wants me.

Shucking off his shirt, he lowers to me, touching his lips to mine, and his chest brushes my breasts, and I don't question anything anymore. He doesn't rush anything; rather he wraps his arms around me, pulling our bodies close, and devours me with kiss after kiss. His hand slips between my legs, into my panties, and he starts to strum me like an instrument, the hums from my throat completing the chorus.

"Marcus," I breathe as he focuses on my clit. I start to climb, a brutally beautiful ascent until I find the crest, and the sensation builds in my belly, shoots out through my toes, and lights up my fingertips. I cry out, holding on to him while I fly apart.

He doesn't move his hand, holding me in my orgasm until it becomes uncomfortable before he lifts his head and looks at me. He slides off my panties. His eyes seem to darken, and my insides twist from the intensity of his gaze.

Marcus climbs off the bed, pulling down the duvet and

urging me under the sheets before he steps back. He removes his belt before undoing his slacks. His eyes never leave mine as he exposes himself to me and goes to the bedside table. His throat bobs on a swallow as he removes a small square packet and shows it to me. "Emily, do you want this?"

I realize he's holding a condom, but I know he's not asking about protection. He wants me to tell him I want us.

"Yes." My voice is breathy, but it doesn't waver. I do want him. I do want this, and my eyes meet his briefly before they drop back down to his cock. It's long and thick, straining tight against his belly. He climbs onto the bed and notices my fascination with his manhood. Taking my hand, he runs my fingers along his length. His skin is velvety smooth, and he encourages me to wrap my fist around his width. Together, we run my thumb over the head, spreading the slick fluid that's leaking from him. Marcus brings his hand to my lips and slips his thumb between them. I taste him for the first time, and his eyes close briefly as I suck him in. It bolsters my confidence a notch. I affect him too, and for the first time, I realize why some women enjoy giving head. I merely tasted his thumb and he got that look on his face.

Marcus rips the pack open with his teeth, removes the condom, and rolls it on. I watch every inch of latex as it coats his length and swallow hard. His lips take mine again and he nudges my legs apart, settling his hips between them.

I stiffen a little, but he nips down my neck, squeezes my breast, and holds my eyes as his tongue teases my nipple. I quiver with anticipation. My mind liquifies, all concerns forgotten.

He shifts, taking my head in his hands, nudging my entrance with the head of his cock. "Emily."

I blink my eyes open on his. "You are so beautiful." He

strokes my cheek with his finger. "I don't want to hurt you," he assures me with his gentle touch. "It won't always. I promise."

My heart leaps because that means we'll have more than tonight. That beginning, our promise. "I know."

I prepare for him to enter me slowly, but my eyes pop wide and my whole body tenses when he thrusts into me hard. Whatever lubrication my body prepared for me does nothing to ease the sharp slice of pain. I cry out, but he swallows it with a kiss, holding my head between his hands.

"Fuck, Emily," he breathes against my forehead. "You are so tight."

I match my breath with his as he gives me a second to adjust and accept this foreign object inside me. My breasts brush his chest with every inhale, and then he starts to move.

New splinters of pain radiate from my center and shatter in my heart. I feel like I'm being torn in two, and I press on his arms and try to move away from our contact. He holds me steady, driving into me over and over.

"Emily," he growls, forcing my jaw shut and capturing my lips again. He doesn't slow; rather his hips move at a rate I didn't believe possible. With my knees bent, I drive my heels into the mattress and take every thrust, knowing whatever magic I felt in our foreplay will not be happening now. I squeeze my eyes closed and pray for it to end.

Marcus fists my hair and tugs the roots. "Emily, look at me."

I open my eyes and something changes. It's less painful, or perhaps I'm simply numb. His movement slows, his head tips back, and the look of pure ecstasy on his face has my stomach doing a slow, pleasurable roll.

"Marcus?" I whisper again, and his eyes snap open and

lock on mine. It's both stimulating and unnerving at the same time.

His nostrils flare on an inhale before he drops a kiss to my lips and rests his forehead on mine. "Emily."

We stay like this for a minute before he shifts his weight off me. Stroking my hair off my face, he searches my eyes. "Are you all right?"

Am I? Aside from the pulsing, burning sensation between my legs, I think I'm in a state of shock. "Yes," I tell him, but I'm a little disillusioned. Where was the dramatic end? The explosive finale?

His gaze roams down my body as if assessing for himself whether I'm all right. He drops a light kiss on my lips and rolls away from me. "I need to dispose of the condom. I'll be right back."

He disappears in the bathroom, and I let out a long breath. Gathering the sheet around me, I sit up and look at this room for the first time. It's lit softly by a bedside lamp and, unlike the breezy island feel my room has, this room is darker. Heavy drapes keep out the moonlight, and in the glow from the lamp, I study the artwork on his walls. The paintings seem religious in nature but dark, with angels and demons torturing humans.

A subtle chill runs up my spine, and I turn as Marcus approaches the bed. He shows me a washcloth and pulls down the sheet. "Let's clean you up."

I immediately see the blood staining the sheet, and my cheeks heat as my mortification grows. "I'm so sorry." I start to scoot back.

He puts a hand on my knee. "For what?"

My eyes bounce between his and the stain.

"Emily, stop." He presses on my shoulder. "Lie back."

I slowly comply, and he gently presses the warm cloth between my legs. He focuses on the task before looking back at me. "Can I be honest?"

I stare at him, not sure how to answer.

"I've never had sex with a virgin before."

Oh. My. God. I press my fingers to my cheeks. "Me neither."

He chuckles at my response and finishes cleaning me. Tossing the cloth on the floor, he joins me under the sheet. I silently vow to pick that up before Carmen cleans in here.

"Come here." He opens his arms for me, and I curl up against him. "It's not something you should be embarrassed about, Emily. In fact, I'm rather honored you chose me to be your first."

I don't respond to that either. I'm preoccupied with processing the way he touched me before and what happened after he entered me.

"Are you regretting it now?" he asks when I remain quiet.

I turn to see his face, his eyes trying to read me, and I shake my head. "No."

Marcus brushes my hair back as a small smile plays on his lips. "Good." He gives my forehead a kiss. "Emily, when I look at you, I see more than a beautiful face. I see a woman I want in my life—for a long time, I hope."

He tucks my head under his chin and pulls me close. I wrap an arm around him and hold him back. My heart melts between his words and his warm embrace. Maybe I was disillusioned from reading about sex in romance books, but everything before and after has been perfect.

"Tell me you see that too," Marcus whispers to me.

I close my eyes and relax against him. "I do."

# 15

## MARCUS

I wipe the steam from the mirror with a towel and regard my face in the reflection. It's been called a handsome face by people, and I learned early that good looks can open doors, but paired with a sharp mind, one could rule the world.

Squirting the shaving cream in my palm, I quickly cover my jaw with the thick foam. Today, I feel like I do, and I'm not a god, but I do control the fate of one pretty woman.

After wetting my razor, I drag a line down my cheek, removing the stubble, and I reflect on last night. The way Emily gave herself to me and how she felt in my arms. I'll never forget the feeling of power, knowing I was her first, or the sensation of her tight heat encasing me.

I rinse my face and grin at my reflection. Today, I'll show Emily more of her new home. It's important for her to know where she can go and the areas that are simply dangerous.

In my closet, I select a casual pair of shorts and a white cotton shirt, dressing for comfort for our hike. When I reenter the bedroom, Emily is still sleeping, and I watch her for a moment. As if she can feel my presence, she opens her eyes and leans up on an elbow.

I smile. "Good morning."

"Hi," she replies, her voice husky with sleep.

I think she looks rather enticing, naked in my bed, but I don't have time to linger with that. "I have a short meeting with Lucas before breakfast. Can you be ready to meet me in an hour?" I ask as I approach the bed.

She looks around my room and nods slowly. "Yes."

"I'll see you at seven." I lean down and brush a soft kiss on her lips and leave her before any other ideas bloom in my head. We now have all the time in the world to play, and I need to get these arrangements underway this morning.

Lucas is already in my study when I arrive. "Good morning," I greet him, then round my desk and take my seat.

"Sir."

"This morning, I need you to return to New York. There's some cleanup you need to do for me." I remove an envelope from my top drawer and hand it to him. "The details are in there."

He removes the slip of paper inside and reads it quietly. "A cat?"

I smirk at his only comment. "Yes, a cat."

He gives me a long look before replacing the note in the envelope. "All right. Anything else?"

"Yes. Return on Thursday. I have a charity function this weekend I shouldn't miss."

"Yes, sir. Good luck with the storm."

I turn in my seat to gaze out the window behind me. The morning light is starting to brighten the sky, and the ocean looks calm. "I quite like the storms," I murmur before looking back at him. "Thank you."

Lucas excuses himself to prepare, and I have a fleeting moment of gratitude for his loyal service to me. Of course, I have enough on his background that if he ever turned on me, he'd be spending his life behind bars. It's the rare person who gives you their loyalty freely. Much like Carmen. As sweet a woman as she is, I could also make her life a living hell if she betrayed me. Even good people are capable of doing bad things.

I check the time, noting I still have thirty minutes before breakfast, and leave my study to find her.

Both Juan and Carmen are in the kitchen. Juan is shoveling down his breakfast, and I focus on Carmen. "Lucas will be taking the plane this morning. He won't be returning until Thursday. I assume you will be preparing for the storm today?"

"Yes," Juan answers me, wiping his mouth with a napkin. "I'll get started now."

"Thank you." I lean against the counter. "Could you also reactivate the rest of the security cameras for me?"

"Of course, sir," Juan replies, and Carmen turns her back on me to fuss over the stove.

Juan hops off his stool and leaves the kitchen. I regard Carmen's back. "I realize you disapprove, Carmen."

She turns to me with a frown. "No. She seems very nice. So young."

"And your problem with that is what?"

"It's nothing. It just feels so soon after..."

The hesitancy in her voice irritates me. "After Karyn?"

"What really happened to her?"

A little whisper of anger blows through me. How dare she ask me that? "Karyn drowned, much like your husband did."

A little flash of fear lights her eyes, and I step closer to her. "You need to let that go. Forget it, like I've forgotten what you've done."

She looks at her feet. "Yes, sir."

"Emily is ready for the rest of her wardrobe." I study her face for an indication I need to say more. Satisfied, I turn on my heel. "I know you'll have a busy day. I'll handle lunch myself."

As I leave the kitchen, Emily is right on time. I smile at her, despite the fact she's wearing cut-off denim shorts, frayed at the hem, and a form-fitting tank top. I'll replace her wardrobe soon, and this shit will end. At least she's wearing trainers. "Hello, Emily." I hold out a hand, and she takes it. I give her a look, head to toe. "Did you wear your bathing suit under that?"

"I, umm, no."

I grin to cover my irritation with the ums. "I didn't either." I run my tongue over my bottom lip. "But I was thinking we should take a swim after our hike."

"Oh." She looks back at the stairs. "Should I change?"

"No." I pull her into my arms and kiss her head. "Let's have breakfast."

---

THE MORNING SUN is warm as Emily and I step out the front door. "It's already so humid out," Emily comments.

"Yes. They're predicting rain tonight." I take her hand and we start down the driveway to the road. Instead of heading down toward the docks, we go up and head for the trail. "The generator house." I wave at the first building we pass.

She looks at that, then shields her eyes to glance at the roof. "Is that a satellite dish?"

"It is. For the phone."

"Hmm. I didn't realize they needed a dish to work."

I don't respond to that, but tug her hand to keep us moving.

"It's crazy. I've never been in a home off the grid before, but I don't notice a difference."

I chuckle. "Yes, well, it's one of the reasons I prefer to spend time here in the winter. I don't waste energy on the air-con."

She smiles up at me. "I did notice that. It's not uncomfortable, though. There's always a breeze."

"The house was designed to capture those breezes. The trees provide a shaded environment for most of the day." I shift the pack on my back and point to another structure. "That's the equipment shed, Juan's domain." I squeeze her hand. "He's very territorial and keeps it locked all the time."

She laughs like it's a joke. The road narrows, and I tell her this is it for any vehicles. "It's all on foot from here. This side of the island is untamed and beautiful."

"I think everything I've seen has been beautiful," she says. "I love how the landscape around the house blends perfectly with the island."

"It does. However, Juan sprays for bugs. Out here, they are abundant. We leave this side to the spiders and snakes."

"Snakes?" She looks up at me with concern clouding her eyes.

I could tell her they aren't poisonous, but I don't. There's a reason for our field trip today. Emily needs to see her new boundaries. Anytime my grandfather got a new horse, he'd show him the fence line of its new paddock. It saves them from surprises and sometimes fatal injuries.

We continue up the footpath and pause as we round the southern tip to take in the ocean views. "It feels like there's nothing around for miles."

"There really isn't anything around for miles." I wrap an arm around her. "Or people, which will make our skinny-dip completely private."

She laughs and smacks my chest. "No. There's Lucas and Carmen and—"

"And they can't see the cove from the house."

Her laughter dies and she searches my eyes. "You're serious."

I grab her hand again, leading us around to the east side. "If you're ever up here on your own, stay on the trail." I point to the right. "There are some steep drop-offs and the vegetation is thick. You might not see them before it's too late."

She looks down at the trees and brush, with the ground blanketed with ferns. "That's where the spiders and snakes are?"

I chuckle. "Exactly."

"Okay."

I allow Emily to walk a few paces ahead of me, and I shake my head at her shorts. It's not that they look bad on her. She's a shapely woman. It's that they're slutty. It's an advertisement for a one-time shag, and Emily is anything but that for me.

As we approach the north end, again we stop and take in the views of the dock, the bay below, and the ocean blending into the lighter blue of the sky on the horizon. "God, Marcus. This place is so gorgeous. I wish we didn't have to leave tomorrow."

I wrap my arms around her, pulling her to my chest. "I'm glad you like it."

She leans into me, taking in a deep inhale. "It smells better than the Atlantic."

"Most places do," I agree.

She looks down at the dock. "What are Lucas and Juan doing?"

I glance down there also. "They're preparing the plane. There's a storm predicted to come in tonight."

"A storm?"

I take her hand. "It's just precautionary if the waves get large. Come, let's go for our swim."

Her brows shoot up. "You were serious."

"Emily." I smile at her. "We saw each other naked last night."

"Yes, but it was—"

"Beautiful," I fill in for her.

"Dark," she clarifies.

"Not so dark. Relax. Trust me, it will be refreshing and fun." We both have a sheen of sweat from the humidity. Her forehead is shiny and her chest is dewy. "Come on." I tug her to follow. She lets out a nervous giggle but quiets as she learns this downward trek requires some concentration. It's narrow, steep in spots, and rocky. Together, we navigate down to where we meet the road, and everything opens up and levels out.

As we pass the dock, I catch Juan's eyes and he gives me a subtle nod, letting me know that he's taken care of what I asked. Lucas is watching us as well, and I understand their curiosity around Emily. Their approval isn't a necessity for me, only their compliance.

Emily giggles when she stumbles as we take the path to

the bay. My lips twitch up, and I tug her to continue when she attempts to pause and look out at the turquoise water. It's nearly translucent where it's shallow, and yes, it's pretty, but I'm ready for her to be naked.

As we reach the middle of the beach, I drop my pack in the sand and turn to her with a smile. "Let's cool off."

"Marcus?" she breathes as I tease the hem of her tank top.

I shrug and pull off my shirt. "I'm going in. I'd really love for you to join me." Her jaw drops along with my shorts and I smirk. "Come on, Emily. No one but me can see you here."

Her cheeks pink up, and I turn, walking into the surf. It's not until I've dipped my head back and wet my hair that I see her, gingerly making her way to me. She's covering her breasts with her arms, and she kept on her panties. The fish will be investigating those floating on the current soon.

"Why would you leave your underwear on?" I grin at her as she lowers herself neck-deep in the water.

"I, umm, well, I've never done this." Her cheeks get two shades redder.

Ah, a new first. I pull her into my arms and kiss her, twirling her in the surf as I slide my thumbs under the fabric. "You have a beautiful body, Emily. There's no reason to hide it out here."

She doesn't fight me as I slip them down and off her legs. I fling the panties and she gasps. "Marcus!"

Pulling her closer, I laugh at her shocked expression. "A sacrifice to the sea."

"I would have thought this would be inappropriate behavior."

"Not in private. Everything changed for us last night." Capturing her lips again, I swallow her reply and my hands

roam over her flesh. I'm seriously considering an ocean chris-
tening to our relationship when the plane takes off.

Emily pulls out of my embrace and looks up. "What's
happening?"

I pull her back into my arms. "Lucas is moving the plane.
I told you, a storm is coming tonight."

She watches as the plane gains altitude. "But he's coming
back tomorrow, right?" Her worried eyes search mine.

"Emily. What are you concerned about?"

"Um..." She pushes away from me and I let her go. "My
job, obviously. I need to be back at work on Tuesday."

"Ah. The entry-level, minimum-paying job? Seriously, I
think you could do better."

"Marcus!" She glares at me. "I can't afford to lose this
job. Do you understand the economy? Jobs aren't easy to
come by."

"I understand the economy. Probably better than you do.
I also understand you are a woman who deserves better." I
pull her back to me. "You don't need that job anymore."

She stiffens in my arms. "How can you say that? I'm
barely making it with the money I earn now. I can't be
unemployed."

"I'll take care of you now."

Her jaw drops, but no words come. I close her mouth
with a finger. "I thought we agreed last night that we would
make this work."

"Marcus..." she whispers as her brows draw together and
a little pout forms on her lips.

I cup her chin in my hand. "Was that a lie, Emily?"

Her eyes widen, and she tries to pull back, but I grab her
waist. "No." She shakes her head. "No, it's just..."

"Just what?"

My grip on her tightens and she places her hands on my shoulders. "Marcus, we've only known each other for a couple of weeks. You shouldn't—we couldn't—I wouldn't..."

My fingers dig into the slickened skin of her waist. "We *couldn't* what?"

Emily pulls in a shaky breath. "It's too soon for you to say things like that. I need to be on that plane tomorrow."

I relax my fingers and wrap my arms around her. "Emily, I promise I will get you back to New York." And I will. It just won't be tomorrow. I'm not ready for her to completely freak out. I've been enjoying this day with her, and I don't want it to end in a fight. "All I'm saying is think about it. As my girlfriend, people will start looking at you. It doesn't bother me where you've come from, but others will read into it and judge your intentions for being me. The paparazzi will follow you, take pictures of that shithole you live in, and your life will be splashed all over every gossip rag in America and across the pond."

She stares back at me, and I tuck a wet lock behind her ear.

"I'm only thinking of you. I want to protect you from that kind of backlash."

I drop a kiss on her slightly parted lips, nibble and tease until she relaxes in my embrace and kisses me back. Her lips, salty from the sea, part and our tongues touch in a gentle dance. Her arms loop around my neck, holding me to her, and my hands slide down, over her waist to cup her bottom. She gives herself to me, wrapping her legs around my waist and allowing me to guide us through the waves. My fingers slip lower and tease her tender flesh. "Are you sore?"

"A little," she admits.

I hold her with one hand and slip a finger inside her. She

tips her head back, welcoming my intrusion as my thumb finds her clit. "I want you, Emily."

Her eyes open and lock on mine. I continue my seduction and manipulate her while I think of all the things I have yet to teach her. The thought has me hard, hot in the cool water. "Touch me," I whisper to her, and the good girl she is adjusts to hold on to me with one arm and wraps her fingers around my cock.

Together, in the privacy of this bay, we play with each other. Little mewling noises escape her throat as she draws closer to her climax. It spurs my desire, and I gently pump into her hand, needing more, but wanting her to finish first. She cries out and her pussy spasms under my fingers. I release her to wrap my hand around hers and encourage her to tighten her grip, increase the pace, and bring me to the same place she's coming back from.

I look down at the distorted view of our hands underwater, my breath coming fast, my vision blurring as I swell with her touch. A soft, milky cloud stains the clear water and I groan, tipping my head back and giving myself to her.

## 16

## EMILY

I'm not sure what to think as our feet clear the water, my hand in his. I don't believe I'm capable of thinking clearly after what just happened in that bay. Marcus stops at his pack, opens it, and produces a towel. My cheeks heat as I take it and wrap it around my body. That was my very first skinny-dipping experience and it was amazing!

He's still naked, and the sun glints off the water running rivulets down his skin. My eyes rest on his manhood, relaxed now but still impressive. I've seen pictures of naked men before. I just never thought of a penis as being attractive. I'm attracted to that one.

He tilts my chin with a finger, getting my eyes to rise back up to his. "Do you like what you see?"

"I, umm..."

He tips his head slightly and smirks. "Dry off. I only brought one towel."

Marcus takes a bottle of water from his pack as I pat my body down, still slightly embarrassed to be completely nude on this wide-open beach. I glance over to see his head tipped back as he drinks the water. His throat bobs with his swallow, and I've never seen anything so sexy as Marcus, naked on a beach, drinking water. He caps the bottle and hands it to me. I exchange that for the towel, and I take a hasty sip before wiggling my clothes onto my damp body.

Marcus zips up his pack, and he stands with a lazy smile. "We'll shower outside, then change for lunch."

"Okay." Hand in hand, we start walking down the beach. My mind rolls back to his comments about my job, my home, the paparazzi, and the nerves start to mingle in my belly. What am I doing with this man? I'm not sure a girl like me can survive the life he leads. As far as coming here? No regrets. But the future...? Of course everyone is going to see me as the gold digger, not Cinderella who met the prince at the ball.

We met in a bar!

I glance back at the bay and see the dark clouds on the horizon, and I get even more antsy. We're stranded here now! There is no plane. A storm is coming. "Marcus, this storm isn't a hurricane, is it?"

"No." He squeezes my hand. "Just a tropical storm."

That's still bad, isn't it?

Marcus glances down at me. "Emily, it's fine. They roll through here this time of year. We know how to prepare."

I wonder about that as we climb the stairs and reach the showers. My robe awaits me, and I shake my head. What now? Will we shower together now, or... Nope. Marcus ducks into the other stall and I step into mine. It feels like so much has happened in the last two days, and I let go of Marcus's comments from earlier as I wash the salt and sex from my body. I'm still a little sore, and I wonder what tonight will look like. Will I sleep with him? Or alone? And shit! I'm out of dresses for that formal dinner!

Marcus is already dressed in fresh clothes when I step out in the robe.

"Carmen will collect our things and wash them," he tells me.

"Okay."

He bites his lip, then smiles. "Okay." He takes my hand and as we walk around the house, both Carmen and Juan are securing the shutters over the windows. That's not the only difference. All the furniture on the pool deck is missing the cushions, is stacked away from the pool, and appears to be chained together. Another shiver runs up my spine and I glance at Marcus. "What are they like? These tropical storms?"

He squeezes my hand. "It's nothing really, but the winds can be intense. The rainfall will be heavy. It may cause some flooding."

"Oh?" I glance back at the ocean.

"The house is built on high ground for a reason, Emily. The shutters will protect the windows from any branches or other projectiles that might break the glass. We'll be fine, but..."

"But?" I look back at him.

"But sometimes we lose power. The generators should kick on automatically, but they can be bitchy. I won't risk Juan running around in the storm so I can turn on a light." He grins at me. "If it happens, I believe you'll look beautiful in candlelight."

I stare back at him as I process that. It's kind he won't risk Juan, but I'm not sure I mentioned to Marcus I'm deathly afraid of storms.

Both Carmen and Juan glance at us as we approach the doors to the house. They don't look worried, and I pull in a breath.

"I'm a little scared of storms," I admit.

Marcus looks down at me. "Why?"

I chew my lip, wondering if I should tell him. It's so clear in my memory as if it happened yesterday. The sour taste of fear in my throat, how my body shook, then seized at the sound of the roof being torn off. It was loud, like I was lying on the tracks as a train careened over me. I felt the impact of the debris raining down on the mattress that covered me as I curled up in that tub. The worst part was facing my death alone.

"Emily. Why?" His eyes are roaming over my face and I swallow hard.

"In Oklahoma, we lived in a trailer and there was a tornado," I start cautiously. "It was awful. In the morning, the trailer was gone. The whole trailer park was gone, and it took hours for the rescue team to dig me out."

Marcus stops, his eyes sharp and focused on mine. "Where was your mother?"

"Not home."

With a sigh, he pulls me into his arms and kisses my head. "I promise you, that won't happen tonight." He hugs me tighter. "I will be with you."

I take the comfort his warm hug provides and nod against his chest. "I know. It's not the same, it's just that storms trigger some anxiety for me." Being stranded on an island during a storm heightens that.

"Emily, Carmen is busy, but I'll make us some sandwiches for lunch and we'll have some tea."

"Tea?" I give him a sidelong look as we head up the stairs.

He chuckles. "Yes, tea."

He stops at the door to my room and I remember my lack of dresses. "I, um... how should I dress for lunch?"

He raises a brow. "Comfortably."

"Okay. Well, I did bring some dresses. Will one of those work for your formal dinner?"

He laughs. "Emily." He takes my face in his hands. "Wear whatever you like." He drops a kiss on my lips. "I'll meet you downstairs in thirty minutes. I'll do my best with lunch."

I'm smiling when I slip into my room and close the door behind me. My body feels light from this morning's adventures, and I shake off the anxiety I have about the storm.

My belly swoops at the memory of my orgasm in the cove, and I press my hands to my cheeks, recalling I gave him one as well. Grinning, I open my closet door. Marcus is perf—

My jaw drops as I flick on the light. The walk-in space is full. I mean, completely full. Every shelf is stacked with folded clothes. All the hangers dangle with several dresses. The shoe organizer is loaded, and my suitcase is gone.

I slowly step inside and run my hand over the dresses. Why? My curiosity is only fueled as I pick up one shoe. I know Gia, and I realize what these shoes cost; this pair alone could pay my rent for a month. I look around the space, completely dumbfounded. What did he do?

MARCUS RAISES a brow as he both pours tea and watches as I approach, obviously in a new outfit.

"You look lovely," he comments.

"Where are my things?" I ask, folding my arms over my chest.

"What things?" He tops off the cup before setting down the pot.

"My things. My clothes!" I wave my arms for emphasis.

"Ah. You mean your dime-store knock-offs? Your five-dollar flip-flops?" He chuckles. "Burning, hopefully."

I stare at him with my mouth hanging open. "What?" I finally manage to spit out.

He points at a chair. "Have a seat. I made sandwiches." He picks up a plate and fills it from the platter in the middle of the table. I stare down, noting the crust is cut off and the little triangle sandwiches are perfectly sized.

"No." I shake my head and my insides quiver with a mixture of insecurity and adrenaline. "When did you do this? It had to be before we came here."

"It was," he agrees, taking his seat and picking up his teacup. "You mentioned something about your lack of clothes in a text message. Forgive me for thinking you'd be appreciative of my gesture."

He takes a sip, waiting for me to reply. I'm not sure what to say.

"Marcus, it's too much too soon. Why?"

His eyes roam over the blouse I'm wearing. Sleeveless and white with a laced sweetheart neckline. "Emily, the shorts you wore today, they were ripped at the hem and I could see your ass cheek. Do you want that on the front page of the latest gossip rag? Or highlighted on a social media site, discussed on X?"

My cheeks fall with my heart. "No." I don't want that, but it's making me question if I want him.

"I don't either. Why can't you see I'm only trying to help you?"

"Why can't you see this is wrong?" I lift my hands, palms up. "I'm just Emily Hanson! Yes, I'm young. Yes, I haven't found my career. Yes, I'm surviving on a budget. That's who I am!"

He sets his cup back on the saucer. "Do you want to know what I see?"

I shake my head.

He smirks. "A brave, young woman who had a shitty upbringing. A smart girl who found a way to get an education and grow beyond her past. A beauty that must have had many suitors press but saved herself for the right man to claim her as his own."

That was kind of sweet—no, wait. "Claim?"

"Yes." He runs a finger over the handle of his teacup, focused on that before looking back at me. "It's a romance not often told these days. When a heart holds out for her true love, and a scoundrel like me recognizes it."

Well, what the hell. "Scoundrel?"

He presses his fingers to his lips, suppressing a smile. "My apologies. Honestly, I thought of the wardrobe as a gift, a helpful gesture to bring our worlds together. I see you are displeased. I'll have your things returned."

I run my sweaty palm over the soft cotton shorts and shake my head. "That's not what I meant."

His eyes narrow. "What did you mean?"

I've never handled confrontations well, and I regard my feet as I think of my answer. "Just that I'm not sure I'm good enough for you."

He chuckles softly. "I believe it's the other way around. Please sit and enjoy your lunch."

Sitting down, I cross my legs and try to control my inner trembling. He reaches over and takes my hand. "I understand my world is very different from the one you know. But now that we are together, I'll do everything to help you fit in."

"No. Marcus, we weren't together like that when you did this."

He frowns and his eyes cool. "You're right. I knew what I wanted before we came here. When did you decide, Emily?"

I open my mouth to respond, then close it again. Picking up my teacup with a shaky hand, I take a sip, and it clatters as I set it back on the saucer.

"You're shaky. You should eat something."

I swallow hard but choose a sandwich off the platter. Marcus is quiet as he eats and watches me closely. His unsettling stare doesn't soothe my nerves. I'm not wrong, but somehow, he's turned it around in a way that has me wondering if I'm right.

Marcus finishes his tea and sets down the cup. "I have some work to finish this afternoon. Are you all right on your own?"

I'm sure the weight of my confusion shows on my face. I need some space. "I'm fine. Is it all right if I take a walk while you work?"

He glances out the window. "Of course you can. You are not a prisoner here." He looks back at me. "Do it now if you want to. The winds are picking up. The storm is coming."

# 17

## MARCUS

Emily's response was expected, but a man can always hope his woman will be appreciative of his gifts. I slam my office door with a little too much aggression and round the desk to take a seat. Checking the security cameras on my monitor, I see that Emily was brave and headed outside. I pull up the beach camera, and the waves are getting bigger, but she's keeping a distance from them.

Carrying her shoes, she walks through the sand, and just the sight of her makes me forgive her a little. The blustery wind is blowing her hair around her face, but when she turns to face the ocean, it blows back, giving me a lovely view of her profile, and I remind myself to be patient with her.

Keeping one eye on the surveillance, I make sure she's being safe as I dive into some contracts I need to go over. I message Heath and let him know a storm is coming in and I won't be back until the end of the week. Then I shoot off an email to Mr. Thompson to do a background check on Laura Hanson, Emily's mum. Seriously, the best gift I could give Emily would be to rid her of that woman.

I PACE THE LIVING ROOM, holding a glass of cognac and wondering about Emily. I needed some space from her after lunch, but now I'm wondering if I gave her too much time alone with her thoughts.

A flash of lightning makes it through the shutters, followed by the distant roll of thunder.

"Sir, dinner is prepared, whenever you're ready," Carmen tells me from the shadows of the room.

I glance at my watch and look at the stairs. "Thank you, Carmen."

Pleasingly punctual, Emily descends the stairs. She selected a cream-colored, off-the-shoulder dress that ends mid-thigh. I move to greet her at the bottom of the stairs and frown when I notice she's not wearing shoes.

She follows my gaze, then meets my eyes with a shrug. "I didn't think we'd be going outside."

Is she trying to be a rebel? "No." I reach out my hand. "You're right. It's already started to rain."

In the dining room, I set my glass of cognac on the table. "Would you like wine?"

"Yes, thank you." Her lashes flutter as she looks down. She's not the brave lion she's trying to be. I don't need a lion. I don't need a fucking cat, but that's the sacrifice I'm making to ensure this relationship works.

"It's a simple merlot, but I enjoy the flavor." I hand her a glass.

She thanks me, and I pour for myself before taking a seat. A sharp crack of thunder has her stiffening in her chair. "Emily, I promise this isn't a tornado. If I were concerned, we'd have left today. By morning, the sky will be blue and the sun will be out."

She gives the shuttered doors a wary glance as the wind howls outside. "No, I'm sure it's fine, it's just..."

Carmen brings our dinner to the table, and Emily looks away as it's served. It's a simple affair tonight. Roast pork and baked potato wedges with a bowl of fresh greens.

I serve Emily the salad myself. "Are you still upset about the clothes?"

She runs her hand over the silky fabric of her dress and shakes her head. "No, I..." She closes her eyes and pulls in a deep breath through her nose. "No. But I think we should talk."

I fill my own plate. "All right."

"Being here with you this weekend... this island... it's all been wonderful. I want you to know that, but I'm concerned about what it's going to look like when we go home."

I look up at her. "You should be. That's smart, and it's why I'm taking care of everything."

She shakes her head. "I don't understand what that means."

I set down the salad bowl and lean back in my chair. "It means that going forward, I will take care of you, I will teach you, and when we do return home, you will be prepared for anything the world has to throw at you."

"How?" She raises a brow. "What are you saying? In the next twelve hours, you'll teach me how to dress, change my career, and move me to somewhere more acceptable?"

I chuckle. "No. I assume it will take more than twelve hours to accomplish that."

"Marcus! That doesn't make sense. We leave tomorrow."

She lets out an exasperated sigh. "I was thinking that maybe we shouldn't be public about our relationship, until, you know... we know."

That irritates me. "What don't we know?" When she fails to answer, I pick up my fork and pluck through the greens. "I'm afraid that ship has already sailed. Photographers have pictures of you on my yacht and boarding my plane to come here." I stab an olive and pop it in my mouth before meeting her surprised eyes.

"What?"

"It's already started." I fish out a chunk of cheese and shrug. "People are dying to know who the mystery woman is and articles about Karyn are being resurrected. A waiter from the night of our first date has commented about our romantic dinner, and the media is frothing at the mouth." I glance back at her. "You won't be returning home to the life you knew, but as far as us *knowing*, I think we both have agreed what this is."

Another loud boom shakes the windows and she winces. "Marcus, I do want this to work, but it's so much. I need time. I need—"

"To what?" I pick up my wine. "Go back to the dismal job you hate? You'll miss the commute on the train? Or returning home to eat a boxed meal that's probably shortening your lifespan? What about any of that do you need?" I take a sip and watch her face as she tries to formulate an answer.

"Yes," she finally says. "Yes, I need to go back to all of that because it's my life. A life I worked hard to have, and I'm not giving that up because you have all of this." She waves her hand over the table.

My jaw clenches and I mentally relax it. "I see. So everything you said about us was a lie. It was a good time on a fantasy weekend, but in the end, you really don't want me."

Her eyes pop wide. "No. No, that's not what I'm saying." The rain starts to come down harder and she wraps her arms around herself. "I'm trying to say this is an adjustment, and I need time."

"Emily, my world doesn't afford time. But if you're saying that you prefer the life you had to a life with me, then yes, tomorrow you'll go home. But your life will be without me in it."

Her face falls and the color drains from her cheeks. "Marcus...?"

I stop her with a shake of my head. "If I were to gamble, I'd know when to fold and when to hold. I've already told you how I feel, but if we aren't playing the same game, it's better to end it now."

When she fails to come up with an answer, I nod at her food. "Don't waste Carmen's time. Eat your dinner."

She slowly picks up her fork with a shaky hand, and we eat in silence. It doesn't matter. She's not going home tomorrow. I just want her to have some culpability in this relationship.

No matter how well this house was built, it doesn't stop the noise of the pounding rain or the raging winds. Personally, I like the violent sounds of a storm, but Emily's eyes flit between her food and the doors. I stay silent. I've laid down the gauntlet. Now it's her choice to decide how the next few days look.

She finally lays down her fork and takes a sip of wine. "Marcus, I'm not saying I don't want you in my life. I'm simply trying—"

"Good." I set my napkin on the table. "Because I felt it

before, but after this weekend, I know it. I want you with me."

A rather loud boom of thunder shakes the whole house as the wind blows something into the shutters. Emily physically jumps in her seat, and I go to her. "It's just thunder." I hand her the wineglass. "Have another drink."

She clutches it and gulps half the glass while I rub her back. "I know the thunder scares you. For me, the sound of a storm is like music."

Her brow creases. "What?"

"Yes. Come, I'll show you." I step back so she can get up, then lead her into the living room, where I find the remote for the sound system. With her settled on the couch, I select a song and sit next to her. The first strands of the orchestra begin, gentle and soft. "See. This is the start of the storm. The quiet patter of the first raindrops."

Emily licks her lips but fails to come up with a response, so I lean back and put my arm around her, turning the volume up a little to drown out the sound of the wind. The music picks up in intensity and I nudge her. "Now the storm is building."

She bites her lip and I smile. "The lightning lights up the angry sea." The percussion section punctuates the song. "Thunder."

The crescendo swells and I wave my hand as though I'm the director. "The building, the climb, the cliff." She snuggles closer to me and I tighten my hold on her. The music quiets to a single piano. "The eye, the quiet before the real storm." I squeeze her to my side.

The orchestra explodes. All the instruments join in this grand finale and I look at Emily. "The climax."

She blinks, and I brush my fingers over her cheek. The

song quiets again to just a few notes played on the piano. "The aftermath, the peace, the knowing that the world will be all right." I give her a soft kiss.

The song ends, and I have more to say as her eyes glitter and I see a flash of understanding, but suddenly, all the lights go out. "Well, shit." I seek her hand out in the dark. "Come. We'll go upstairs."

A nervous giggle escapes her. "I can't see anything."

"Trust me. It's not my first walk in the dark." I pull her up, and she wraps her arm around mine. I assist her with the stairs and take her past her room.

Once we are in my seating area, I leave her standing in the dark and make my way to the sideboard, feeling around for the lantern. With a twist of the switch, the room fills with soft light. I hold up the lantern and smile at Emily. "Have a seat. I have some candles in the bedroom."

She lowers herself onto the sofa. I locate a flashlight and leave her with the lantern to find the candles. Thunder rolls in the distance, and I believe the storm is passing as I light two candles in the bedroom and return to Emily with two more.

She watches as I get those lit. "Romantic," she murmurs.

I grin as I look back at her. "I knew you'd be beautiful in candlelight."

She curls her legs up under her and hugs the arm of the sofa. "Marcus, what I was trying to say is that I do want this. It's just scary for me. The clothes, the talk about my job, my apartment. It's a bit overwhelming. I don't know what to think."

I lean back into the cushion and cross my legs, allowing her to keep her distance. "I understand. Let me try to explain. Years ago, I met a young woman. She was a barista at a coffee shop I frequented. Sterling Enterprises had started to gain traction, and the media loved the story of a British billionaire living in New York. I was featured as one of the most eligible bachelors and I didn't mind the attention. In fact, I felt it helped our young company. Elizabeth didn't handle it well, though."

I stand and go back to the sideboard, pouring each of us a small serving of port. "It started innocently." I hand Emily her glass. "We'd have a cup together when her shift ended, and she'd tell me about her plans for her future. She was saving for college, working two jobs. She was honest and sweet, and I fell for her completely. But I didn't warn her about what life would look like with me." I let out a sad chuckle. "I didn't even know exactly what it would look like." Taking a sip of port, I swallow it down, enjoying the subtle burn. "I took her to a business function, and the paparazzi descended on her like flies to shit. They tore apart her outfit, her looks, and dug into her past." I set down my glass and look back at Emily. "People she thought were friends turned on her for their five seconds of fame on camera, debasing her and her motive for being with me."

"I'm so sorry, I—"

"No." I hold up a hand. "No, I didn't know how deeply it was affecting her. I told her to ignore the news. I'd just built this house, and I brought her here to bring some peace and sanity to our lives. In retrospect, I wish I had seen the signs because when she risked her own life, I was completely unprepared."

"Marcus...?" Emily whispers.

I reach over and run a hand over her leg. "It was a long time ago, but if I had helped her more, prepared her, not left her to figure it out on her own, none of that might have happened."

"What happened to her?"

I close my eyes. "I'm not exactly sure. We argued that night, and I didn't realize she had left the house until it was too late."

"Too late for what?" Emily's voice warbles around her words.

"She, well, it was dark. She took the trail up, and my guess is it was slick from a recent rain and she slipped. I don't know. We didn't find her until the next day."

Her eyes grow round and I shake my head. "That's why I warned you about those steep drop-offs."

Emily presses her fingers to her lips and shakes her head. "Marcus, I'm so sorry."

I give her knee a gentle squeeze. "Don't. I just want you to understand why these conversations make me terse. I want you in my life, and I realize your sacrifice is larger than mine. I only want to prepare you for that, so you don't feel like Elizabeth did." I lean forward to pick up my drink. "Honestly, I have so much to offer you in return."

"Do you mean the money? Marcus, my interest in you has nothing to do with your wealth."

I look over at her and smile, nodding at her glass. She picks it up and I touch mine to hers in a toast. "That's one thing that attracts me to you."

She takes a tentative drink, but her eyes seem to search the room for some kind of answer.

"Emily, I told you I have expectations I have to meet publicly, and yes, everything you wear, do, speak could be dissected and discussed on the next morning news show." I take her glass and set it aside. "Personally, I don't care if you wear anything, which is why I have this private space where we can run naked on the beach. But when we're back in New York"—I close my eyes and shake my head—"it all changes, and if you do want this—us—you need to be prepared." I scoot a little closer to her and pull her into my arms. "I hope you choose us."

# 18

---

## EMILY

I lean into Marcus, enjoying his warmth but feeling emotionally scattered by this whole day. Tomorrow we'll go home, get some space from each other and a little perspective. I shudder slightly, wondering what my life will look like now.

Marcus strokes my hair and his touch is comforting, but I can't stop thinking about the story he just told me. It's tragic, but that's two women who have died on this island. Another shiver runs through me as the lightning briefly lights up the room. The thunder booms and I can hear the steady noise of the trees being brutalized by the wind, the crash of the waves on the rocks, and the relentless rain. It doesn't sound like a pretty song to me.

Marcus tips my chin up with two fingers. "Relax, Emily." He gives me a kiss and initially, I resist, but he persists. His lips are magic, nibbling at mine until I give in. Our tongues touch and my stomach dips, the tingles shooting straight to my core.

"You are so beautiful," he whispers before nipping my

earlobe. His fingers brush over my knee and start a slow journey up. I shift, wrapping around him as he takes my lips in another kiss, each one wiping away any concerns or anxiety as I melt in his arms. He presses me back. My skirt rides up and he palms my bottom.

His head comes up, and his eyes burn on mine. "Emily?"

I bite my lip, uncertain how to explain. Marcus did provide me with brand-new lingerie, but I was still angry about the clothes and his comments.

"Are you wearing anything under this dress?" he asks.

My face grows hot, and something flashes in his eyes. It both excites and scares me. Grabbing my dress, he yanks it down and reveals the truth. I didn't wear a bra either.

"This is incredibly naughty, Emily. Are you a naughty girl?" His voice is low as he gazes at my breasts.

I shiver at his tone. "W-what?"

He runs a finger down my chest to my nipple and pinches it. "Let's be clear that formal attire includes panties." He palms my other breast. "But if this is the game you want to play, I'm willing."

My arms are pinned by the dress, and I try to get free, but he stops me. He leans in close, his breath tickling my face. "Good girls get rewarded. Do you know what naughty girls get?"

My breath freezes in my lungs, and I shake my head with a swallow.

"Fucked." He provides the answer with a gentle kiss to my cheek. A confusing mix of fear and anticipation has my heart racing.

"Marcus?"

He responds by turning me away from him. "Knees on the cushion, hands on the armrest."

A shiver runs down my spine as he positions me on the sofa. He settles behind me and pushes up my skirt. His fingers brush between my legs and a low growl escapes him. I close my eyes, embarrassed by how wet I am for him.

Spreading me with a hand on each ass cheek, he blows a cool breath on my heated flesh. My eyes pop open when his mouth covers me completely and he flicks my clit with his tongue.

Oh. This isn't something I've experienced, and the intimacy of the act scatters me a little. I try to pull away, but he holds me to him, sucking me in as he swirls his tongue. The touch is so soft compared to his whiskers that rasp against my tender skin, and the combination is seductive.

My breath quickens with my pulse. The pressure inside me builds, and I gasp when he takes me between his teeth, shaking his head. I'm so close, and I moan my disappointment when he leans back. He doesn't leave me wanting, driving a finger inside me. I press back into his hand, and he slaps my ass. Incredibly, my pussy clenches around his finger while my heart freezes under the sting.

His palm runs over the flesh he just abused. "So naughty. No panties, no bra. It's like you were begging to be punished." He adds a finger and smacks me again. My mind is reeling from the insult and the pleasure he's drawing out with his other hand.

"Marcus?" I breathe, but suddenly his mouth is back, his tongue hits my spot, and I explode.

He stays with me as the aftershocks keep coming, then kisses my bottom. I glance over my shoulder, and he's removing his belt. "Did you want to get fucked, Emily?"

I'm not sure that I did, but I do now. Marcus shoves

down his pants, fisting his cock, and this position we're in feels animalistic and raw. "Answer me." He raises a brow.

"Yes," I squeak out.

Grabbing my hips, he drives into me without mercy. It burns, yet somehow fuels the fire inside me. Fisting my hair, he keeps my head up and wraps his fingers around my throat. "Did you want to get fucked like a little slut?"

He pulls me back to his chest. His hips slap against my bottom. My arms are still pinned to my sides, to where I can do little to participate in this. Every thrust drives me higher and the fear seems to fuel my desire. His hand drops from my throat to my clit, and it's a mindless blur of movement and pressure, pleasure and pain. I feel like a helpless leaf caught in an eddy, and I can only hope to get sucked in or shot out because I can't sustain this.

His grip tightens on my hair. He groans in my ear and I fly apart. Marcus grabs my hips in both hands. I fall forward, clutching the armrest of the sofa, and he comes with a final slap to my ass.

My fingers dig into the soft fabric of the couch, my heart rate unreasonably high, and my breath coming hard. Marcus pulls out, and a wet trickle runs down my thigh. His fingers trail over the hem of my skirt and he pulls it down, covering my bottom before he stands up.

I turn slowly, gingerly adjusting to sit with my legs under me, and I fix the sleeves of my dress. He adjusts his pants, and I'm at a complete loss over what just happened.

"What's wrong?" he asks.

"You hit me."

"I spanked you," he corrects.

I look away. Hit, spanked, whatever. It hurt and it still hurts. Marcus sits down next to me, draping an arm over the back of the sofa, and toys with the ends of my hair. "It took your mind off the storm."

I don't respond to that, but look at the window, and I can still hear the wind. I feel like I just survived a whole different kind of storm.

Marcus sighs. "Emily, what did you think would happen when you came to dinner dressed like that?" He tugs my hair, and I glance over at him. "It's fine with me if you want to play the naughty girl." He looks completely serious, and I'm seriously confused.

"What?"

"Now you know you can set the tone for what our love-making will look like."

I close my eyes and shake my head. I'm not sure I'd call that making love, but I can't deny my body liked it. "Marcus, you didn't use a condom."

"I know. I trust since I'm the only man you've been with, there is no disease to worry about."

"But I'm not on birth control."

"And I'm sterile. I told you I don't intend to have children."

It takes me a minute to digest that. "You had a vasectomy?"

"No." He pulls me closer to his side. "I had an injury when I was young, but I wasn't disappointed by the outcome." Dropping a kiss on my hair, he gives me a little squeeze. "I think the storm is passing. Are you ready to go to bed?"

I'm not sure. He leans forward to blow out the candles and picks up the lantern. "Come with me, Emily."

I take his hand, my legs a little shaky as I stand, and follow him into his bedroom. Setting the lantern on the bedside table, Marcus then pulls down the duvet and watches me in the dim light. I pull my dress up and over my head, then fold it neatly and place it on a nearby chair. It's past time for me to get embarrassed of my nudity with him. Thunder rumbles, and it sounds distant now. Still, I wrap my arms around myself. Marcus is undoing the buttons of his shirt, his exposed skin glowing in the candlelight, and he gestures with a nod for me to get under the covers. I comply without a word as Marcus pulls off his shirt.

"Emily, why are you pouting?"

"I'm not." Or at least I don't think I am. "I'm just confused."

"Why? Because I spanked you?"

No. Because I liked it. I bite my lip as I regard him. "That was only the second time I've had sex, and it was..."

"Amazing?"

"Rough."

He steps out of his pants and sits on the bed. "Can I assume from the way you dressed tonight you enjoyed the first time then?"

I don't say anything, but I notice one of us has underwear on as he joins me under the sheets. He pulls me into his arms, and I rest my cheek on his chest. "Were you angry with me for that?"

"Did I seem angry?"

Kind of.

He kisses my head. "No, Emily. I was turned on."

"Oh." Me too. How?

Running his fingers through my hair, he lifts a lock and sniffs. "Let's say I'm not the kind of man who always finds vanilla interesting." He tightens his arm around me. "Sex should be felt and expressed in the moment, and that moment was very charged, wouldn't you say?"

Charged? "Yes," I whisper against his skin. Is it wrong and naive of me to feel confused? Now, in his arms, his warm skin against mine, I feel safe and cherished even. I close my eyes and chalk it up to my naivete. I'm sure Gia's eyes would be glowing if I told her about that scene. Marcus has taught me a lot about myself in one short weekend. I'm both sad and relieved that we go back to reality tomorrow.

---

I WAKE to a hand roaming over my skin. I'm curled up with my back to Marcus's chest. He holds me close and cups one of my breasts. His fingers roll my nipple with gentle tugs and soft caresses. Warm lips brush my shoulder. He kisses up my neck and my body starts to heat under his attention.

His hand slips down, between my legs, and he gives me a gentle stroke. "Are you sore?"

My lips part to answer him, but I gasp as he grazes over my clit. That part of my anatomy seems to be just fine, and I press into his hand. "Oh, Emily." He sighs against my hair, and he starts to work his magic.

The truth is, I am sore, and I know when he enters me, it's going to hurt. I'm finding I'll take that in exchange for the pleasure he's giving me now as he works both my breasts and my clit. His lips nibble the sensitive skin of my neck and shoulder, causing a collision of sensations to melt in my belly. The pressure builds slowly—not the storm from last night, more of a gentle swell—and I float on the wave, letting it take me higher. My orgasm washes over me, from my toes to the top of my head, and his name leaves my lips as I pulse against his hand.

Marcus presses his erection into my bottom, and I know what he's seeking. I adjust my position to help him. Unlike before, he does not thrust into me hard; rather he nudges my entrance gently and slides in slowly. It's a lazy seduction, teasing, and he takes my hand and encourages me to touch myself. My flesh is slick. My clit is sensitive and very, very aware. Marcus places his hand on my lower belly, pressing down while pushing in, and another wave of pleasure swamps me. He grazes my skin with his teeth and picks up his pace. I'm surprised that even though there's a sting where we meet, he feels so good inside me. Every thrust, every touch, every kiss brings me closer to the edge. "Marcus," I breathe.

"Yes, Emily. Come for me."

His breath is hot on my ear, and I start to quiver, trying to hang on, hold out, feel more, but I slip. He groans, pounding into me harder, digging his fingers into my flesh and holding me tight as I come apart.

His hips jerk, and I keep my eyes squeezed tight. Something about the feeling of him unleashing inside me draws out my orgasm, and I relish every second. My eyes are slow to open when he stills. He stays with me, stroking my skin gently and giving my shoulder soft kisses.

A little smile tips my lips, and I think about his words from last night. Sex should be expressed, and this morning it was loving and beautiful. Maybe I can survive the many faces of Marcus because every time we've been intimate has a different flavor, but they've all been wonderful.

# 19

## MARCUS

One shard of sunlight makes it through the break in the curtains, and I wonder what today will look like as I hold Emily close. It's not just the destruction we'll face in the wake of the storm, but that Emily thinks she's going home.

I run my nose along her shoulder and inhale her sweet scent. It's there, beneath the sweat and the sex, and I silently vow to her everything will be all right.

She stirs in my arms, turning to look at me. I tuck a lock of hair behind her ear. "Good morning, beautiful."

She gives me a shy smile. "Good morning."

Fluffing a pillow, I scoot up to lean against the headboard and pull her to my chest. I'd love to play with her some more, but I know there's too much to do. Emily lies quietly in my arms, looking around the dimly lit room. "Marcus, what is with the artwork in here?"

I chuckle as I look over the paintings in my room. "I brought these back from our home in England. It's a reminder to me of how religion can be seriously skewed. Some see God and angels as saviors. Others see the evil in interfering with anyone's fate." I brush my lips over her hair. "Personally, I'd prefer to be the captain of my own ship."

"It's kind of creepy," she mutters.

"Yes. So was my mother. She purchased this collection." I pull her back into my arms. "Emily, I'm sure there's a mess outside to get started on. There's a robe in the bathroom you are welcome to, but I need to get up. I'll have Carmen set out something for breakfast."

She gives the window a nervous glance. "What do you mean? You'll be cleaning up after the storm? When does Lucas bring the plane back?"

I unravel myself from her and pull on my boxers. "With only Juan and Carmen on the island, I'll be helping with the cleanup." I climb off the bed.

"Wait." Emily sits up. "When are we leaving? I need to pack." She frowns. "Marcus, where are my things? I do appreciate the wardrobe, but I want my clothes back." Most of them are Gia's.

I drop a quick kiss on her forehead. "I'll sort out Lucas and let you know."

I leave her and slip into the bathroom. Emily can pack if she wants, but it will be a waste of her time. Starting up the shower, I drop my shorts and give my face a quick glance in the mirror. I'll skip the shave today. There's too much to get to. I smile to myself as I step under the spray, but my smile fades as the water is cold. Has Juan not handled the generator yet? I do my best with a quick cleanup, dress in jeans and a work shirt, and return to find Emily still in bed. "The solar is being problematic, and the generator is still not on. You might want to wait for a shower."

She blinks but doesn't respond. Is this still about her clothes? I felt we went over that last night. I sit down on the bed to lace up my boots. "Emily, are you still upset about last night?"

She shakes her head. "No."

"Good. Give me a kiss then."

She leans over and obeys, pressing her lips to mine. I give her a smile. "I'm going to go find us some power."

I squeeze her knee under the blanket and stand. I'm sure this is the least of her petulance I'll experience today.

Carmen is already opening the shutters as I come down the stairs.

"Good morning, Mr. Sterling."

"Good morning, Carmen. How does it look out there?"

She returns to her chore. "Not bad. A couple of downed trees, limbs, and leaves everywhere. Juan has already started on that."

"Very well. There is still no power?"

"Juan believes it's a quick fix. He's outside," she replies, turning her back to me. "Is there something specific you'd like me to prepare for Ms. Hanson?"

"No, just set something out for her. I'll go find Juan."

As I go through the doors to the pool deck, I see the devastation immediately. Juan comes around the corner with a chainsaw in his hand. "Mr. Sterling, we had some debris hit a solar panel. I've got the generator working now."

"Good. It was a cold shower this morning."

Juan grins and gestures to a downed tree. "Just starting to clean up now."

"I'll help." I leave him and walk to the equipment shed to grab some gloves. I return to find he has already started, and I help by loading the cut wood in the utility vehicle. The sun gets higher as we finish the third tree, and I look up to see Emily watching me.

Tugging off my gloves, I walk toward her. She has her hair pulled into a ponytail, wearing one of her new, more appropriate outfits. She waves a hand at the pool deck. "This is a mess."

"It is," I agree. "It will take a couple days to put everything back in order."

"A couple days? But we leave today. Right?"

I study her face and wonder when exactly I want to start this fight. "I think I should stay and help."

Her eyes get wider. "What does that mean? I'll go back to New York without you?"

"Emily..." I step closer to her.

"Marcus, I need to get home."

"You won't be going back to New York without me."

Her eyes change from confused to resolved.

She stands a little straighter. "I need to go home today."

Juan starts up the vehicle to move the wood. We both turn to watch him drive off. "Lucas won't be coming today," I say without looking back at her. "It's fine. He'll speak with your employer so they understand the situation."

"What?"

I keep my eyes averted as I continue. "I said you won't be returning without me, and I need to be here."

"Marcus, I need to call my employer, my neighbor. Everyone is expecting me back today."

"The phone needs to charge after the power outage."

"Then how are you contacting Lucas?"

Now I look at her. Seriously, she's pressing me into a corner and it's pissing me off. "I'm sure your place of employment isn't open today. We'll take care of everything tomorrow."

Her mouth hangs open, but she doesn't reply, and I

tuck a strand of hair that escaped her ponytail behind her ear. "Emily, pick up a rake. The sooner this is done, the better."

With narrowed eyes, she glares at me, then sighs. "Fine. Where is the rake?"

I find a rake for her and stuff it into her hand. She takes her frustration with me out on the leaves, and together we load the piles into the cart for Juan to haul off. As the sun gets higher, she slows down and begins to relax. She peers over at me.

"I didn't picture you actually cleaning this yourself."

"Why?" I saunter toward her. "You think a privileged man like myself is incapable of hard labor?"

"No." She looks away. "Maybe."

"Emily." I draw her into my arms. "Sometimes there's a need to delegate, but trust me, where it matters, I do the work myself."

"I like this side of you, Mr. Sterling."

Ah. She's teasing me. "I like all sides of you, Ms. Hanson."

Emily starts to smile, but it fades quickly. "Marcus, what about Bella? I have no way to contact my neighbor."

I smooth out her ponytail. "We'll take care of the cat."

"How?" She tries to pull back.

I hold her tighter. Since she no longer has an apartment, obviously, I've already made arrangements for the cat. "We'll call your neighbor when we can." I drop a quick kiss to her confused lips.

As we finish up, I glance at her. A dusting of dirt is clinging to her damp skin, and I'm sure I'm a mess too. "Let's go down to the beach."

"Now?" She raises a brow.

"Now," I confirm with a laugh. "We'll rinse off in the bay. Naked." I wink.

She blushes. "Marcus?"

I ignore the question mark and grab her hand. "We know we aren't going home today. Let's play while we're still here."

She takes my hand, and the crisis is diverted. She's accepted this part of her fate. There's no reason to escalate it now. She's adorable as she smiles up at me, enticing one out of me as well. That desire to possess her completely wells up inside me, and I wish I didn't have to leave her. It wouldn't look right for me not to show up to my own fundraising event, and Emily is nowhere near ready to be exposed like that. But I will miss her, and I start making plans to lay the groundwork for bringing her home.

---

EMILY COMES DOWN THE STAIRS, fresh from her shower, and she looks beautiful. I close my laptop and stand to greet her, pick her up, and give her a little twirl before dropping a kiss on her lips. "You smell like sunshine."

Her lashes flutter down. "I didn't realize sunshine had a scent. I think you smell the coconut-scented shampoo."

"Maybe." I step back and look her over. "Whatever it is, I like it." I glance at the door as I take her hands. "I still need to help Juan. Are you all right on your own?"

"Yeah." Her eyes go between me and the computer. "What were you working on?"

"A speech for an event later this week."

"What event?" she asks.

"It's a fundraiser for my foundation." I wiggle my fingers at her. "Come, there's something I want to show you."

She obediently takes my hand, and I lead her down the hallway.

"Is the phone working?"

"Not yet. Don't worry, Juan will get everything sorted out." I open the door to the library, and she steps inside with me.

"Oh, Marcus. This is beautiful." She immediately goes to the shelves that line the room and brushes her fingers over the spines of the books. It is a nice room, with a cozy reading nook near the large windows. Karyn decorated this space, and the feeling in here is more feminine than in my study. She chose light colors for the walls and shelving, adding splashes of color between the knickknacks and throw pillows. The collection of books, however, is mine.

Emily takes one off the shelf and shows it to me.

I recognize the title. "Ah. A classic. I realized I hadn't shown you this space before, but you're welcome to use it anytime you want."

"Thank you." She opens the book and flutters through the pages. I stand by the door, watching her closely. This woman stirs something inside me. She has since I first laid eyes on her. That possessive need to protect her hits me again—hard. "I'll be outside if you need me."

She glances over and gives me a smile. "All right."

# 20

## EMILY

Curled up on the sofa, I lay the book on my lap and look up at the clock on the wall. I realize I've been immersed in this story for nearly two hours. Leaving the book on the armrest, I stand and stretch. I'm still perturbed about the change in plans, but like he said, it's not his fault there was a storm. After I accepted that, I enjoyed helping him clean up. I more than enjoyed it when he cleaned me up. A smile tips my lips as I slip out of the library and close the door behind me. The hallway is dark, the only light coming from the windows in the living room at one end. Curiosity creeps in as I look down the hall and wonder what else is down here. I remember Marcus saying Lucas has a room on the ground floor.

I check the door at the end of the hallway, and it's locked. The one across from it opens when I turn the knob, and I'm surprised to see it's a media room—no, like a small theater. I realize I haven't watched a TV show since I got here. I haven't missed that either.

I try the door to his office, and when it opens, light floods the room from the window behind his desk, showing a view of the ocean beyond.

I didn't really take everything in the first time I was here. The furniture is sturdy, mahogany and probably antique. Shelves flank the windows, holding black-and-white photos, and I walk over to study those. The women are wearing long gowns and gloves. The men are in uniform. They aren't smiling, and I wonder if these are the ancestors he accused of doing bad things to grow their wealth.

One photo is of a little boy sitting on the floor at the feet of a man and woman on a sofa. I instantly know it's Marcus from his eyes. They're bigger in this little boy face, but they hold the intensity I've grown to know. This must be his parents, and his mother is a stern-looking woman with black hair and blue eyes. His father is less impressive. Shorter, rounder, with a styled mustache. Marcus obviously takes after his mother.

I move to a large bookshelf on one wall, lined with thick, hardcover books, and I run my finger over those, reading the titles before I turn toward the desk. The bulky-looking phone is cradled on a charger, and I pick it up. Pressing the on button, it lights up and my heart soars.

Thank God.

But the screen changes and requests a passcode. Shit.

I look around the room, having no idea what his code might be. I don't even know his birthdate.

Clutching the phone, I leave to find him. I'm sure he just didn't know the phone had charged. But now I can call my neighbor.

I see Marcus through the doors leading outside. He's shirtless now as he helps Juan remove the pool cover. His muscles bunch with his movements, and tingles run up my spine when I remember how those felt under my hands.

He turns and sees me, his lips curving into a slow smile. My cheeks get warm again, and I step out and hold up the phone. "It's working."

His smile fades. Leaving Juan, he strides over to me. "You went into my study?"

I'm confused by the tone of his voice. "I wanted to check the phone." I hold it out to him. "I need to call my neighbor. I don't know your passcode."

He frowns as he takes the phone from me. "Lucas already contacted your neighbor. Everything is fine."

That doesn't make any sense. "I'm sorry. How?"

He rolls his eyes. "Obviously, I know where you live, Emily."

"And I have more than one neighbor."

"Yes, but you told me her name. Will you relax? I told you I'm taking care of everything."

Did I tell him her name? I take a step back, eyeing the phone. "Still, I could call her and thank her for doing this a little longer."

"Which would be redundant. One of the things you'll learn is that we have people to do that for you."

I stand a little taller. "I don't need people to do that for me."

He ignores me. "If you'd like, I can have my assistant send her a thank you basket."

"What? No. I just want to make a damn phone call!"

Oh. That has his eyes narrowing. "Ladies don't curse."

I take another step back. "Marcus." I hold up my hands as he advances on me, like I could physically stop him. "I apologize. I just wanted to make a phone call."

"And I told you, that's been taken care of." His voice is low and ominous, and my heart starts to race.

What is happening right now? "Please. I just..." I look around the pool deck. Juan is still working but not watching us.

"Emily, go to your room. I'm working, and your rudeness and interruption aren't welcome right now. When I'm through, we can have a civilized discussion."

Civilized? "My room?"

He clutches the phone tighter in his fist. "Go!" he yells.

I leap back, my heart coming to a painful stop in my chest. What the hell happened between this morning and now? His face isn't leaving an option for me to argue. I turn on my heel and run.

---

ON THE BALCONY, I huddle on a lounge chair and stare out at the endless sea. My heart rate has settled. The anger simmers while the fear evens out to a steady hum under my skin.

I'm so confused. All I did was ask to make a phone call. That anger from Marcus wasn't the normal anger you confront in an argument with someone. It came from nowhere. Yes, I was upset that the plane wasn't coming, but I adjusted my attitude. Aside from that, we had a perfect morning. Loving sex, laughing while we cleared the debris, frolicking naked in the bay. What changed?

My heart feels heavy as I listen to the waves crash on the rock below. As much as I want to believe Marcus is perfect, there's too much that conflicts with that. I've enjoyed the fairy tale, a handsome billionaire whisking me away to a fantasy island, being romanced and seduced, but something is seriously off with him.

I frown at the thought because Emily Hanson doesn't appreciate people for their money but for their honesty and authenticity. Unfortunately, I think Marcus is showing me who he is, and I'm not sure I like what I see. I glance back at the ocean and admit I'm afraid.

"Emily."

I flinch at the sound of my name and turn as he comes through the doors, onto the balcony.

"We should talk about what happened earlier."

No. I don't want to talk about it. Logically, I know I didn't do anything wrong. "I just wanted to check on my cat."

"And the cat is fine. I told you that."

I get up off the lounge chair and face him. "Why did you get so angry?"

"Why can't you trust I'll take care of you?" he shoots back. "This is your problem, not mine. You can't accept the fact that someone else can handle things for you."

"Because I don't need you to handle things for me, or Lucas or your fuc—" I snap my mouth closed. "Or your assistant."

His eyes narrow.

I take another step back. "I'm sorry."

"I told you I would help you learn to be my wife." He advances on me.

I hold up a hand. "Wife?"

He stops, closing his eyes and pinching the bridge of his nose. "Girlfriend." Those bright blues pierce into me when he opens them. "With me, you don't have to worry about petty details. I have a staff to take care of that." He takes another step closer. I take another one back.

"I don't need a staff. I just needed to make a phone call."

"Can we stop the bullshit for a minute?" he asks with a raised brow.

I don't know. Why can he cuss but I can't? "What bullshit? What do you mean?" I retreat further.

His lips tip in a sarcastic smile. "I see. You want to test me. You want to draw out this side of me." He cocks his head slightly. "Did you enjoy your last spanking?"

A band of fear tightens around my chest. "No."

"That's not the message I got when you came on my cock." His smile fades and his eyes cool. "I have rules, Emily." He advances and I back up until I'm against the railing of the balcony. Marcus places a hand on either side of my body, caging me in and leaning close. "Rule number one. You do not go into my study unless you're invited."

My pulse skyrockets and my breath comes faster. "I didn't know."

"You do now. Rule number two. You will speak to me properly and not like some back-alley whore."

I swallow hard at the blazing look in his eyes. The waves crash mercilessly against the rocks below me as his lips get closer to my ear. "Rule number three. If I give you an order, you will obey."

My eyes close as his warm breath tickles my ear.

"Turn around," he whispers.

"Marcus, please." I try to lean away from him, but there's nowhere to go.

"Turn. Around."

Fear slithers through me, causing my insides to shake and

my heart to race. When I don't comply, his nose brushes my hair. "That was an order."

Marcus steps back. Placing a hand on my arm, he forces me to obey. My hands grasp the railing and I'm breathing so hard now, I'm possibly entering a full-blown panic attack. "Please," I beg him again.

He slides my shirt up, exposing my lower back, and my shorts with my panties are lowered to expose my bottom. He presses himself against me. "I thought I was clear. Good girls get rewarded. Naughty girls get fucked."

My eyes sting and the first tear leaks out, trailing down my cheek and dropping down to the rocks below. "Marcus?"

His hand slips between my legs, and he starts with a gentle caress. "I don't want to hurt you, Emily. It pains me to do so, which is why I need you to listen." Suddenly, his hand is gone. I suck in a deep breath, but it whooshes out of me when he slaps my ass—hard.

I cry out but it's strangled when his fingers wrap around my throat.

"There's consequences when you disobey orders, Emily."

His grip on me tightens, cutting off my air, and I claw at his hand.

For the first time, it dawns on me that I'm truly in danger. Marcus is not the man I thought he was, and we aren't playing a game right now. I'll do or say anything to make this stop. "I – I want to be good. I'll listen. I promise." His hand rubs my ass cheek to soothe the sting. I blow out a breath and quickly continue. "I didn't know the rules. I'll obey. Please don't do this."

"Do what, Emily?"

"Hurt me."

I can feel his hesitation. Is he listening? "It's not fair to punish me for something I didn't know."

His fingers press deeper into my flesh. "What do you want, Emily?"

I close my eyes. "You. I want you."

Marcus wraps his hand around my throat and pulls me up so my back is flush to his chest. "Do you mean that?"

I swallow hard against his palm. "Yes."

He turns me, his eyes searching mine for lies. My heart pounds against my ribs but I reach up and touch his face. "I apologize for making you angry."

His gaze softens a notch, and he dips his head to claim a kiss. I don't resist but wrap my arms around his neck and press my body into his. He urges my shorts down my thighs until they drop at my feet.

"Tell me that you want this." His voice is low but demanding.

"I do," I whisper.

"Then show me."

I don't really know how. He does like it when I touch him, so I place my hand against his erection. His eyes roll back with the pressure, and he presses into my touch. "That's good, Emily. Turn around."

My muscles tense but this time I obey, turning around to face the sea. My blouse comes off next and he drops it. I watch as it flutters down to land on the rocks below and wonder if that was a message. If it was, it was received. I white-knuckle the stone railing and widen my stance. "Please, Marcus. I need you."

I focus on the horizon as he gropes my breasts, slipping his hand lower to tease my clit. I refuse to enjoy this, but my body betrays me when I get wet from his attention.

"That's a good girl," Marcus purrs from behind me. His finger dips inside me, and my sensitive flesh quivers around his intrusion. He pulls my hips back, rubbing his cock between my folds. A single bird flies by with a shrill cry that matches the one stuck in my throat as he enters me. The splinters of pain from my abused flesh are not masked by my arousal this time.

A whimper escapes me that he mistakes for pleasure. "Oh, Emily," he groans. "You feel so good."

"So good," I manage to say as the colors of the ocean blend with the blue sky.

My mind disengages from the reality of what is happening. I encourage him, pressing back to meet his thrusts with soft sighs and strangled cries. All I need is for him to believe I want this too.

Marcus digs his fingers into my flesh as he pounds into me, his pace quickening with his ragged breath. "Come with me."

I'm not sure how to fake an orgasm but I mask a sob with a moan. It seems to tip him over the edge. His hips jerk, then still.

A breeze blows in from the ocean, cooling my sweat-dampened skin and fluttering the strands of hair not stuck to it. I become aware again of the maniacal chant of the waves below me. Pieces of the world come back to me in little increments. The feel of his hand appraising my aching bottom. The sound of his breath, deep and choppy. The scent of the sea as the spray leaps up for me, never quite making it all the way.

Marcus wraps his arms around me, pulling me up while his cock falls heavily from inside me, and I breathe. His fingers trail over my cheek, past my jaw to my neck as he kisses my hair. "You are perfect, Emily. I know you're the one for me."

I squeeze my eyes closed, fending off building tears. "I feel the same about you."

He turns me around, palming my face and tipping my head for a gentle kiss. "I have work still to do," he says. "Dinner is at six. Be punctual."

I watch as he disappears inside, but I don't follow. I'm still afraid to move.

Speak.

Breathe.

The same bird soars by again, and I focus on it as I attempt to pull my thoughts together. I stand up taller but my knees give out and I sink to the floor, clutching the railing to break my fall. When my ass hits the stone, I curl up into a little ball, holding myself as I completely fall apart.

# 21

## MARCUS

"Explain to me how Emily got inside here."

Carmen is avoiding eye contact, and the guilt is written all over her face. "I was cleaning and I forgot something. I didn't realize she was even downstairs."

"This shit is unacceptable." I glare at her son, who also looks contrite. "When I'm gone, Emily needs to be contained. A fucking locked door would help!"

I stride around my desk and sit, facing both of them on the other side. "I've taken care of you, Carmen." I nod at Juan. "Your son too. Is it too much to ask for a little loyalty and compliance in return?"

"No." Carmen's hand flutters to her chest, clutching the cross she wears every day. "No. I'm so sorry."

"Yes. You are sorry." I tap my fingers on the desk, focusing on that before raising my eyes back to hers. "Go. Prepare dinner. Juan, make sure that fucking shed is locked. Please."

They both scurry from my study, and Carmen's ample ass clears the doorway.

I found her when I was building my home on the island. She worked at a bar and was one step away from being homeless after the death of her husband. I saw it in her eyes when she spoke to me about it. She was easily manipulated into a confession.

I allowed her to taste me more than once. She was younger and definitely more attractive then, but she always knew with her skin color and muddied history, she'd be nothing more than my whore. I did promise her my support, a job, a home. I only ask one thing in return. To fucking do the job I give them!

I suck in a deep breath. It's fine. Mistakes happen. Running my fingers under my nose, I breathe in Emily and my cock stirs. In one way, I regret the way events changed today. Again, perhaps it was better to get this started sooner than later.

I can be giving, and I enjoy the seduction phase of a relationship. However, if she's wife material, some discipline is warranted, and it would be a lie to say I don't enjoy that too. It was an early education, learning what type of woman worked for my personality. The wealthy women of my class think too much of themselves. The blatant whores think too little. But there's a middle line. Emily fits there perfectly.

I close my eyes and picture her face, trying to cover up her fear while defending her petty actions. It was insanely attractive. Training them is rewarding for me. It's like breaking a horse. They buck and fight in the beginning, but when they succumb, the trust and partnership will grow into a rewarding relationship. That's where I see myself ending up with Emily. She's attractive, smart, and I picture her on my arm as Mrs. Sterling as the cameras snap photos of the perfect couple anywhere we show up.

It makes me think of the event this weekend.

Emily is nowhere ready to walk that red carpet, and I pull up my speech on the laptop. Like I give a shit about cancer. My grandfather did die from it, but I didn't spend a minute with him after he was hospitalized for it. That was after my parents' deaths, and we can all be honest. He created the woman who tried to destroy me.

Heath calls and I snatch up my phone, remembering how this day went wrong. Emily has a phone, which I'm sure she's not smart enough to link into my network, but I should probably cover that base too. "Hello, Heath."

"Marcus. Hey. Are you taking Emily to the fundraiser this weekend?"

"No. Why?"

"Oh. I invited Gia."

Well, what the hell. That relationship needs to end. "Emily has decided to extend her vacation down here. She loves the island."

A moment of silence follows that statement. "Really? Hey. Gia has been wondering why she hasn't called her. Is everything going all right there?"

"Better than expected." I shove my hand through my hair. "Tell Gia that we survived the storm and Emily has been thoroughly enjoying her stay."

"Yeah. Well, I think Gia is worried about her. Maybe have Emily give her a call. I'll see you Thursday?"

I grit my teeth. Gia needs to realize she isn't the center of Emily's world anymore. "You will probably see me Friday morning." I close the lid on the laptop. "Next week, I'll be working from here again."

"Jesus. Why?"

I get Heath's concern, but I don't care. "Because I think I've found Mrs. Sterling."

"Marcus." He starts slowly. "It feels like you just buried Mrs. Sterling."

"Heath." I mimic the way he drew out my name. "I could sit with despair and grief, or I could recognize life goes on. Emily is perfect. She's the one."

"Okay." Another beat of silence. "I feel like I've heard you say that before too."

I don't reply for a moment. There's no truthful way around his accusation. "What happened to Sara wasn't my fault."

"I know."

"And Elizabeth..." I close my eyes and shake my head. "She was hurting. I didn't see it."

"I get that," Heath breathes into the phone.

"Karyn..." I swallow hard. "Honestly, I think she chose to die."

"Marcus. I'm not trying to say anything. But you have a pattern. You meet a woman, you get attached, and you lose focus on everything else."

"Not true," I defend myself. "I'm completely prepared for the fundraiser, and I've already gone through our upcoming contracts. I'm not losing focus on that. I'm simply envisioning the future."

"Hey. It's fine. If you found something in Emily, go for it."

Which is exactly what I'm doing. I'm appreciative that he understands.

"But if you're leaving after the weekend, maybe I should fly down. We have an important project to discuss and we won't have time if you're taking off again. Plus, I could use a little island time. Maybe I could stay through next weekend."

My whole body tenses. Emily isn't ready to entertain guests. "I can make myself available this weekend."

"Yeah." I hear the grin in Heath's voice. "I can't."

My lip curls slightly. "Why?"

"It's the last weekend before Gia heads to Europe. Plus, she'll be happy to know I'll have eyes on her friend and confirm she's alive and well."

Rubbing my forehead, where I'm developing a steady headache, I sigh. "We'll figure it out on Friday. See you then."

I hang up, place the phone back on its cradle, and stare at it. One slip-up from Carmen could destroy everything now. I click on the mouse, pulling up my surveillance, and find Emily still in her room. A hard lesson was learned today, but she came around beautifully. My heart trips over the thought and I shake off the feeling.

Next, I check my email and read the one from Lucas. He's making progress in New York, and I respond to his question.

*Just get rid of it all.*

Then I pause, feeling a little guilty.

*Save anything that looks like a personal memento and store it in my apartment.*

The pain in my head is magnifying and I find some pills in my desk. I pop a couple and swallow them dry before I read the next email from Mr. Thompson. The background report on Emily's mother is unsurprising. She's exactly how Emily described her. A self-centered bitch who never had the right to have a child. She also has meager funds in her bank account, which has me seeing a problem in my future. Karyn's mother was like that. Expecting I'd take care of her because I married her fucking daughter.

Those women are like a tumor. Starting small, mostly undetectable until it grows and threatens your very existence. That gives me inspiration, and I add something similar to my speech.

Noting the time, I toggle back to the security images and see Emily hasn't moved. It irritates me a little. She'll be late for dinner. Pushing my chair back, I stand and find my patience. I get it. First lessons are hard. Double-checking that the door is locked, I head up to rouse Emily. The key to being a good disciplinarian is consistency. You can't set expectations and then not follow through with the consequences if they aren't met.

When I shove open her bedroom door, she startles and sits up on the bed as I enter. "What are you doing right now?" I ask.

"I..." She looks around the room, anywhere but at my face.

"Yes. I'm confused too. You should be getting ready for dinner." I go to her closet and select a dress for her, then toss it on the bed. "You have forty-five minutes."

Her gaze sweeps over the dress before landing on me, but she keeps her mouth closed. This isn't my fault. I'm not the one who set the mood the day. "I'll see you downstairs."

I leave her to get ready with an uncomfortable energy buzzing through my veins. What happened? We were fine an hour ago. In my closet, I select a dress shirt and a gray pair of slacks, wondering why people don't understand the concept of taking care of your appearance. In my home, I would have been whipped for being late to dinner or showing up without shoes. Emily has had her grace period.

With one last look in the mirror, I shudder when I see my mother's eyes looking back at me. We. Are. Not. Alike. My vision clears, and it's my own handsome reflection looking back at me. The pills helped, but there is still a dull echo of my headache behind my eyes. My chest feels tight as well, and I rub it with the heel of my hand. This is not me feeling angst about what happened with Emily earlier. We're fine, and if she stays in line, the sooner we can go home together.

That thought eases my mind as I head downstairs for dinner. The vision of Emily and me together in the future is a bright one. It will be a rough week or so, but eventually, she'll understand the lengths I'll go for her and what I need in return.

## 22

---

## EMILY

Marcus slams out of my room, and I stare at the door for several minutes before I peel myself off the bed. Sliding open the drawer on the nightstand table, I take out my phone and power it on. I know it's useless. I've tried a few times before and there is no service, but I search for a network I can link into. Nothing shows up.

I drop the phone on the bed and look at the door before glancing back at the dress at the foot of the bed. So many emotions cycle through me, and I almost feel like I'm the crazy one, but I'm not. What I do know is I'm stranded on an island, far from any other shores, with a man who is wholly capable of hurting me.

I glance at the clock and shudder. I don't have much time, but I need to wash him off me. The shower doesn't comfort me, and I hesitate to put any effort into my appearance, but my fear of upsetting him overrides my bravery.

I promise myself to figure this out, but so many things are bombarding me as I dress.

*"Karyn was going to leave me."*

*"Elizabeth and I fought that night..."*

I smooth the skirt of this dress and stare at myself in the mirror. Did he kill them?

*Survive, Emily.*

I repeat that to myself over and over as I brush out my hair. I'll find a way out of this.

---

MARCUS WAITS in the front living room when I come down the stairs. I lift my chin and meet him in the center of the room.

"Emily. You look lovely."

Anger slithers through me at the thought that sentiment would have made me smile yesterday. He holds out his hand, and I glance up at him as he leads me into the dining room. My nerves are frayed, and I don't know what to do. I have no idea exactly what could set him off. I feel like a member of the bomb squad, figuring out if I should cut the green wire or the red one.

Getting me seated, he pours us some wine, like he does every night. I fold my hands in my lap and look down.

"Emily, why are you pouting? I thought we worked everything out this afternoon."

"I'm not pouting." I squeeze my fingers together so hard it hurts. "Everything is fine."

He lifts a dark brow. "Your body language doesn't reflect that."

I breathe in deep and try to relax on an exhale. "You scared me earlier."

"I know. And you apologized for making me angry. Have you accepted responsibility for that or was it a lie?"

Oh God. Is he insane? I remind myself that all I need to do is get off this island. "It wasn't a lie." He sets the wineglass in front of me before taking his chair at the head of the table. I focus on that rather than looking back at him. "When is Lucas coming with the plane?"

"Thursday," he says breezily. "We should talk about that. I do need to go back for this fundraiser, but you will be staying here."

That has my eyes shooting up to meet his. "What?"

"I know." He lifts a hand. "I'd love to take you to the gala with me. It's not as if I'm taking someone else. You simply aren't ready."

Carmen breezes in and sets out a platter of freshly cooked lobster and a creamy pasta side dish. Her face is a little pinched as she looks at me when she places a small bowl of melted butter by my plate. I'm less worried about that and more concerned about what Marcus just said.

"Thank you, Carmen." He keeps his eyes on me as she leaves us. "Have you had lobster before?"

I shake my head. "What did you mean about me staying here?"

"I mean, you aren't ready to face returning to New York right now." He picks up the tongs to place one of the crustaceans on my plate and another for him. "Eating lobster is a brutal affair, really." He tucks a napkin into his collar. "It's messy but extremely delicious."

I remain silent as he picks up the lobster and, with a quick twist, snaps its shell. I jump a little and those blue eyes send a chill through me as they meet mine again. "Use this fork,"—he holds up one of the utensils—"to remove the tomalley."

I swallow hard as he scrapes off the green paste from the

white flesh. Choosing a different fork, he digs out some of the meat, dips it in the butter, and tastes it. "Hmm. Delicious."

My insides are now a jumbled mess, my nerves quivering in my belly and closing my throat. I pull in another steadying breath. "You can't leave me here."

He washes his bite down with a sip of wine, leveling his gaze on me. "I realize how this could be an insult to you. Trust me, if I could, I would bring you with me. It's just not an option for this particular event."

"I don't care about the event," I grit out. "I want to go home."

He sighs. "Emily, you are home."

My heart slams to a stop inside my chest, and he nods at my plate.

"Try the lobster."

When I fail to move, he reaches over and grabs it, repeating the process of cracking it open and preparing it for me. Digging out a forkful of meat, he dips it in butter and holds the fork to my mouth. "Eat."

Like a baby, I press my lips together and shake my head. He drops the fork, and it clatters on my plate. "This. This is why I can't take you anywhere. What the fuck are you doing right now?"

Quickly realizing I cut the wrong-colored wire, I pick up my fork and taste the meat. The flavor doesn't register as I choke it down. I feel the reality of my situation was pounded into me earlier, but for some reason, it just continues to get more shocking.

Marcus leans back, perhaps relaxing because I some-what complied. I grab my wine and take a shaky sip. I don't believe telling him I want to break up is an option right now. "I'm sorry. I mean, I apologize. I was a little surprised that you wouldn't want me with you at that fundraiser."

"I understand that. Trust me. It feels like there's one every five minutes. We'll have the opportunity to dress you up and show you off soon."

It takes me a second to digest those words. "So you aren't leaving me here forever?"

"No." He lays out his hand on the table, palm up, and I look at it for a beat before putting mine in his. Our fingers intertwine and his lips twitch up. "No. Believe me, I want you with me all the time. This is a transition period, and you get to decide how long it lasts."

His rich, smooth voice rolls over me but doesn't calm me. I stare down at our hands. "Marcus, you're scaring me."

He lets go of my hand. "Then stop pissing me off."

I watch sullenly as he goes back to eating the lobster. I have no appetite, but I look at the one on my plate and wonder if refusing the food would be offensive. Because right now I feel like a little bug and he is the big shoe about to squash me, so I start plucking at the meat.

Marcus takes another sip of wine, setting down his glass, watching me eat. When I put down my fork, he picks it up, gathering another bite and lifting it to my lips. "More."

My lips quiver as they part, and I accept the food, understanding the message fully. Rule number three. If he gives an order, I obey.

---

I ALLOW Marcus to hold my hand as he leads me up the stairs, but my heart skitters at an unhealthy rhythm when we stop at my bedroom door. He turns me to him, stroking my cheek with a finger. "It's a warm evening. I thought we could swim tonight."

He thought what? "Marcus, I'm tired. I think—"

"You are not tired. You're still upset. Don't start with the lies now."

I search his eyes and they've chilled a degree. He cups my chin, brushing a kiss over my lips. I freeze at the contact and he leans back. "We had fun that night, didn't we? Change into a suit. I'll do the same and collect you here."

Reaching around me, he opens the door. I'm scattered. The last thing I want to do is swim with the man, and I duck into the room, closing the door. It's the first time I've noticed there isn't a lock. Pressing my hand to my chest, I take a couple steps back, staring at the doorknob. Now that I'm alone, my breathing is once again bordering on hyperventilating. I spin, going to the bathroom, and see the same thing. There is no way to lock this man out.

I press my back to the wall and sink until my butt hits the floor. Clutching my head in my hands, I push back the tears. Crying won't help me now. I need to think. Is this what happened to his wife? Did she disobey? I can't keep the questions from circling in my head.

"Emily?"

The sound of his voice churns in my stomach, bringing bile to my throat. "I'm changing," I call through the door.

Slowly picking myself off the floor, I go to the closet and start to undress. Flashes of this afternoon flood me and collide with memories of the more tender, intimate moments we've had. How could I have been so blind?

*"I'll take off the mask for you."*

The red flags were there, everywhere!

"Emily?"

His voice is closer. He's in the bathroom.

"Almost ready." I grab a random suit off the shelf. I have several now, but I don't look at my selection, just pull it on. As I step out of the closet, he greets me in the bedroom, and his eyes appraise my choice. I realize I should have paid attention. The neckline of this one-piece plunges and ends just above my belly button, barely covering my breasts. "I'll grab a cover." I step back into the closet. Oh God. I snatch a silk cover. This was not the message I meant to send tonight.

On shaky legs, I go back to the bedroom and look everywhere but the bed. "I'm ready."

I take his hand, and he leads me out to the stairs. "You're doing great, Emily. There's no reason for us to stay in a tangle because we had a disagreement."

Is that what he calls it? A tangle? "Marcus, you can't leave me here."

"Why? I think it's in your best interest. You need to understand that everything I do is to protect you. To protect us."

We step out onto the pool deck, and I don't stop him when he removes my wrap. I follow him down the wide steps, into the water, with one word on repeat in my mind.

Survive.

Marcus pulls me toward the deeper end, and at some point, my feet don't touch the bottom anymore. I pedal my legs as he continues to hold my hand and we approach the end of the infinity pool, where the water flows over the concrete wall and the dark ocean appears to stretch out beneath us. He turns me, pressing me against the edge. "You are so beautiful, Emily." He cages me in with his arms and I fight the flashback of what happened on the balcony earlier.

Leaning in, he kisses my cheek. "I don't want to fight with you."

"I don't want that either," I breathe out.

"Good." He pins me against the wall and kisses me. It's a confusing concoction of sensations that rushes through me. Fear wars with the warmth of his lips. The desire to flee clashes with the innate need to hold on. My muddled brain takes a beat before I realize I'm not only allowing this kiss but letting him deepen it. His fingers dig into the back of my head, changing his angle as his lips slant over mine.

Panic wells up inside me and I push against his chest. He leans back as I suck air into my lungs. I can't do this, even though he's looking at me with that desire in his eyes that melted me before. I press my feet into the wall and launch into the water, giving myself some space from him.

Marcus lets me go but follows me. "What's wrong?"

Treading the water, I try to calm my rapid heart rate. "What do you mean?" I backpedal until my feet find the bottom of the pool.

"I mean, it feels like you're trying to get away from me."

"No." My pulse skyrockets. The edges of the deck are shrouded in inky darkness. The only light comes from the glowing pool and the swath of yellow pouring out of the doors to the house. Where would I go?

I keep walking backward until the upper half of my body is out of the water. His eyes roam all over me. "Are you cold?"

"What?"

He's next to me in one swift stroke of his powerful arms. "You have goose bumps."

Maybe. There is a breeze that's licking my skin, but I'm

not sure I'm feeling anything but fear at the moment. "I'm okay."

He smirks, then surrounds me in a blur of movement, picks me up, and lifts me out of the pool. I'm stiff in his arms and he smiles at me. "Let's enjoy the hot tub."

I blink as the water drips into my eyes and try to focus on his face while holding on to him at the same time. What is he doing? After everything that happened today, he's acting like nothing transpired, carrying me effortlessly and grinning at me like we're lovers enjoying the evening.

Instinctively, I struggle. "I can walk."

"I've got you," he replies. "That first night we swam together, I realized something. You're different from any other woman I've been with. You make me feel things I haven't felt before."

I look up at him, unable to form a response, and we're already at the hot tub. He settles me in the bubbling water and the heat stings my skin. I scoot back quickly as he joins me.

"You're still upset about earlier?" he asks.

I hug myself in the steamy froth and shake my head.

"In part, I think what happened was my fault."

How does he not see it as totally his fault? "I don't understand."

"Carmen. She knew to keep that door locked and she was negligent. I assure you, I corrected her and it won't happen again." He scoots closer to me, pulling my stiff body into his arms, and kisses my hair. "We should let go of what happened earlier and enjoy this evening."

Nope. "Marcus, earlier, you—"

"Corrected you?"

"Hurt me."

"When?"

Oh, for fuck's sake. "Why do you keep your study locked? I don't understand what made you angry."

"Confidentiality. Sterling Enterprises has government contracts, and access to either my laptop or my phone must be limited."

That really doesn't make sense. "Why can't I go home? What do you think you're protecting me from?"

"The media, obviously." He gives me a little squeeze. "You're so young, Emily. I know you don't understand, but trust me. I will put some things in place that will take care of those problems."

I roll my eyes up to the few stars that twinkle through a thin blanket of clouds. What problems? Does all this have to do with that first girl, Elizabeth? My confusion only magnifies as we sit in the bubbling water. Did I overreact earlier? No. He did. I sigh. There is no way I'm letting him leave here without me.

# 23

## MARCUS

The hot water relaxes me a little and I close my eyes, taking in the chorus of the singing insects surrounding us. The scent of the island wafts on the breeze, and I know I'm not a monster for keeping her here. I realize that I need to watch my temper, but she'll learn. Everything will go smoother for both of us if she just obeys.

I continue to hold Emily close, even though everything in her body language is screaming for me to let her go. I drop a kiss on her head and move away. "It's late. Let's go to bed."

Her eyes grow round and her lips part slightly, like she has something to say, but then she snaps them closed. I reach my hand out to her. "Come."

She's slow, but she takes it and I lead her over to where I left the towels. I wrap one around her shoulders. Emily tries to back away, but I tighten my grip and begin the process of drying her off, finishing with a gentle rub to her wet hair.

She pulls on her wrap as I dry myself, watching me warily, and I run my knuckles over her cheek. "Nothing has changed."

Emily looks down. "Everything has changed."

I narrow my eyes. "I won't allow you to speak like that. Come." Snatching her hand again, I feel the trembling in her fingers. It's fine. Sometimes fear is a great motivator. At least she complies, following me inside the house and up the stairs. She hesitates at the door to her room, but I keep walking without letting her go.

As soon as we're over the threshold, I close the door, turn her, and press her into it. When I lean in to give her a kiss, she turns away, and I grab her face, getting her to look back at me.

"Marcus, I..."

"You what?"

"I don't want to sleep here," she answers in a shaky voice.

I quell the ripple of anger that slithers through me. "I said, nothing has changed."

With her lips firmly pressed together, she closes her eyes, but when she opens them, that mix of greens and golds glitter with a new determination. "You're right." Her arms wrap around my neck, and she kisses me.

My cock leaps to attention as she softens in my arms. That coconut scent still clings to her skin, and I breathe her in. My fingers curl in her hair, and I break the kiss by pulling her head back. "What do good girls get?"

"Rewarded?"

"Exactly." I grab her hand and pull her toward the bedroom. Carmen has left a lamp on for me and turned down the bed already. Emily is focused on that, but I turn her toward me and untie her wrap. It drops to the floor, and I glance over that bathing suit again. It's simply scandalous. "Where did you get this?" I ask, running my finger along the plunging neckline.

"From you," she whispers.

"Hmm. We'll need to speak with Marguerite. Imagine if the paparazzi got a random photo of you in this." I start to peel the wet swimsuit from her body.

"W-who is Marguerite?"

"Your personal shopper," I murmur as I expose her breasts. Crouching down, I tug the suit over her legs and pause to take a whiff of her neatly trimmed pubes. We should probably wash off the chlorine. I stand quickly. "Let's rinse off."

Emily studies the large shower stall in the bathroom as I get the water started and remove my trunks. This is something we haven't done before. I smile to myself as the thought forms of what I could show her in there.

I hold the glass door open for her. "Go on. Get in."

She takes a tentative step inside the glass-encased enclosure and tips her face into the spray. She's so fucking gorgeous, and she has no idea of the power she has over me.

I follow her and grab the body wash. "Hold out your hands."

Emily pushes the wet hair off her face before holding out both of her hands, and I squeeze the gel into them. I frown, realizing it's my scent, not hers. As soon as I'm back, the separate bedrooms will end. "Wash me."

That has her eyes searching, but I don't move or speak. I wait for her to obey. Slowly, she places her hands and starts to create some suds, rubbing little circles on my skin. Well, my pecs will be clean. "Everywhere," I prod, moving her hands down to my stomach. She tentatively complies, avoiding going any lower. I give her a break and spin around. "Get my back."

When she finally gets that area soaped up, I turn back to her. "We still have my legs."

Emily glances down briefly before looking back at me.

"Yes, you should probably kneel."

The word has my half-erect cock perking up and rising to full mast as she lowers herself and starts to wash my legs. It's a teasing torture when she soaps up my calves and thighs but avoids everything else. "Emily. What's the problem? You've touched me before."

With a determined set of her jaw, she takes my cock in her soapy hands and starts to work me like I taught her. The suds coat my balls, and she gives them a gentle massage too. I wrap my fingers around hers and encourage more pressure. "That's so good," I praise her. "Don't stop."

Emily finds a rhythm, and I grip a handful of her wet locks. I picture sliding my width between her sweet lips, the soap her saliva coating me, and the droplets on her cheeks her tears. The fantasy pushes me further, and a groan escapes my throat.

I widen my stance to brace for the inevitable. The pressure builds and the base of my spine tingles. I tug on her hair, pulling her head back, and her gaze locks on mine without missing a beat.

"I'm going to come."

Her eyes widen but she doesn't slow the pace. Her fingers grip me tighter, and with a low growl, I let go. Emily covers the head of my cock with her hand and I spill my seed into her palm.

It takes me a minute to calm down as she washes the evidence from both of us. I look down on this beautiful creature and this feeling tugs inside my chest. We're going to be fine. She's already mine, and her compliance deserves a reward.

I offer her a hand to stand. Grabbing a bar of unscented soap, I roll it in my hands, preparing to return the favor. I start with her neck and massage the suds down to her breasts. Those pink nipples harden under my touch. Her eyes are closed. Droplets of water cling to her long lashes and her lips are so soft.

My hand glides down, and I give her pubes a teasing touch. Her lashes flutter up, and there's something different in the way she looks at me now. Perhaps it's the innocence I've stolen from her. She's not the curious little virgin she was before. Emily knows exactly what I'm going to give her.

I take a knee to wash her legs, and I linger to inhale her scent. I can almost taste her arousal, and I slide my hands up her thighs, brushing my thumbs over the junction where her legs end and her pussy throbs.

"I want this too," I whisper against her skin. My finger glides over her pussy and she's slick, not from soap, and I slip inside her. Pumping gently, I cover her with my mouth and nibble at her ripening flesh.

She exhales a shuddering breath when I suck her clit between my lips. I work her between my fingers and mouth, giving her that reward. Training can be challenging. The ebb and flow of discipline and kindness. Pain and pleasure. It's the give and take when teaching someone boundaries. Now Emily is taking the pleasure, and she floods my tongue as I give her more.

Her breath comes faster, little whimpers escape her, and she braces her hands on the tile wall. Her body stiffens and I take her to the brink, relishing her soft cries and the way she spasms around my finger.

I hold her like this until she tries to move away, and I stand. Her cheeks are flushed, and I wipe my chin before dropping a kiss on her parted lips. "Let's go to bed."

## 24

### EMILY

Back in the safety of my room this morning, I brush up my hair and clip it. Last night was a nightmare, but at least nothing happened after we went to bed. Still, I'm a zombie because every time he moved, I twitched. I'm not sure I slept at all.

I have no idea how I'm going to do this, but I need to convince Marcus to let me go back to New York with him. I can play the good girl and get rewarded. Then I can run for my life.

As soon as I'm home, I'm going straight to the police. This is basically kidnapping, and I'm not going to stay silent about it. How's that going to look for his precious reputation?

I flip on the light in the closet and reach for a pair of shoes. My heart drops. The shelf that held my purse is empty.

No. I know I left it there. I do a full spin, checking every shelf, but it's nowhere. It can't be gone. It has my phone, my wallet, and the passport Marcus helped me obtain.

He can't do this to me. I bite back fresh tears, and a

trickle of anger clashes with the disbelief. The idea of trying to sweet-talk my way out of this evaporates.

I find Marcus in the living room, waiting for me. He gives me that charming smile. "I thought we'd have breakfast outside. It's a lovely morning."

All the bravado I felt marching down those stairs starts to drain. "Where is my purse?" I ask in a shaky voice.

He raises a brow. "Seriously, Emily, I can't be responsible for keeping track of every little thing for you."

I straighten my spine a notch. "It has my ID, my passport, and my credit cards."

"Which we should cut up. I noticed you're a little overextended on those." He holds out a hand for me. "Come."

"What?" How would he be able to know that?

He wiggles his fingers impatiently at me, and I stare at his hand. The anger is still simmering, but the fear is growing. I take his hand and follow him outside. He pulls out a chair for me, and I watch him closely as he takes his seat.

"Marcus, it's Tuesday."

"I'm aware." He unfolds his napkin with a snap and places it on his lap.

"It's just that I need to call my boss."

His blue eyes stay leveled on mine. "After today, you'll no longer have a boss. It's taken care of."

My heart drops and I hold up a hand. "Wait. What does that mean?"

"I told you, now that you're with me, you don't need that job. So I had Lucas send a resignation letter for you."

"What?" I take a few breaths for that to sink in and shake my head. "Marcus, the idea you can keep me here is insane. People will notice I'm gone."

Carmen comes out to serve breakfast, and he waits until she's back inside before looking at me. "Who?"

I shift uncomfortably in my chair. "My coworkers. Gia. My mother." And that's about it, except for my cat. "My neighbors."

"Your mother?" He snorts and serves me some eggs. "Gia knows where you are, and your coworkers understand the reason you quit. You have me now."

"I, what?"

"Your neighbors realize you are moving out. You already told me you aren't close to any of them. I'm sure they won't miss you."

"I'm…" I close my mouth at the chilling look he gives me.

"Everyone in New York, the world even, will know exactly why you made these hasty decisions. After a brief but romantic affair with me, you chose to stay here to plan our wedding. Your mother will probably be thrilled."

When I fail to respond, he continues. "I know. I would have rather waited too. Do something around the holidays, perhaps. But things escalated that I couldn't foresee. I believe now we should just get it done."

I swallow hard, my mind racing and my heart pounding. What escalated? Me? "I don't recall you asking me to marry you."

"Emily." He sighs. "I told you I would put things in place to make your return to New York easier. The media will love it between the whirlwind romance and a hasty wedding."

I'm back where I was last night; afraid to cut the wrong wire. "Marcus, that's, um… a lot." I take a sip of my orange juice, trying to think. "Can I ask you something?"

"Of course."

"Why would you want to marry me?"

He sets down his silverware. "Why would you even question that? I think I've made it abundantly clear what my intentions were the moment I brought you here. You told me you wanted this too."

"When?"

His nostrils flare on an inhale. "When you chose me to be your lover. You said you wanted a promise of forever. Now you have one."

The tension is rising at this table, and I take a bite to try to alleviate it some. I mean, I thought we were talking about dating, not a lifetime commitment to a madman. "I know. It's just, you never asked the question, and maybe we should wait a little longer and get to know each other a bit more."

A small smile tips his lips. "I see. How long do you want to stay here? A month? Six? How much time do you need to accept that you'll be my wife?"

"Umm..."

His smile fades. "At least long enough for that sound to stop leaving your lips. Emily, when you meet the people in my world and fail to articulate, everyone is going to think you're uneducated. That isn't true. You're far from ignorant. Act like it."

I roll my lips together and pull in a breath, ignoring that and going back to his last point. "Are you saying I won't go back to New York until I marry you?"

He leans back, crossing his arms over his chest. "I'm saying, when we return together, you will be Mrs. Sterling. When you return depends on how long it takes you to accept that."

I press my hand to my stomach, suddenly feeling a little nauseous. A breeze blows in from the ocean, cooling my damp forehead, and I look out at the water. This beautiful island has somehow become my nightmare.

Marcus resumes eating his food. I try to choke some down as well while my brain plays over possibilities to get away. He signals he's done when his fork clatters on his plate. "Emily, I've already made arrangements to return here on Monday. I'll only be gone a few days. Carmen and Juan will see to your needs, and I've asked Lucas to stay here and make sure everyone behaves. I'm doing everything I can to make sure this relationship is a success."

I blink and look up at him. I think I have an idea of what happens when his relationships aren't successful. "I want that too," I manage to say. "Why Lucas?"

He lifts a shoulder. "I trust Lucas to keep you safe."

Safe from what? Another shiver of fear runs through me. Sucking more air into my lungs, I try to quiet the shaking of my insides. "All right. What about Bella?"

He leans his forearms on the table, his eyes bright. "She's taken care of. Seriously, how much do I have to do to prove that I want you?"

I don't know, but those words have fifty thoughts racing through my mind. What did he mean? She's taken care of. In the light of the man I'm seeing now, that could be really bad for her.

---

I PLACE my hands on the railing, watching the plane as it lands and disappears behind the rocky cliffs toward the dock. The last couple of days have been me walking through a minefield. I'm so confused by everything. I'm scared to death of setting off the bomb, but since that day, all he's given me is gentle touches. That is as long as I'm a good girl. If I try to back away, that's when the threats start. I'm learning the pattern and what won't get me hurt.

Today, my anxiety is skyrocketing. One week ago, I came here for a long, romantic weekend. Now I'm not completely sure I'm ever going home.

Marcus enters my room, and I meet him at the balcony doors. He looks handsome as ever. Did his good looks dazzle me? His liar's charm? It's like swallowing a large pill. Am I that stupid?

He smiles at me, holding out a hand. "Come. I have a gift for you."

I don't want his gifts, but I step into the room. "You're really leaving me?"

He rolls his eyes. "Emily, it's only a couple of days. As much as I'd like to spend every minute with you, you do realize I travel often. You'll need to learn to be less dependent on me."

My jaw tenses as I bite back my thoughts. I don't want to be dependent. I want to be free! He wiggles those fingers, and I resist an eye roll, stepping in and taking his hand. "Lucas flew the plane in, but he's staying here?" I ask.

"Yes. I don't require a copilot for the short jump to Tortola."

How short is that? I recall it wasn't a long flight in the seaplane, but I also remember the expanse of water that lay between the two islands.

I take his hand and we head downstairs. As soon as we hit the bottom step, the front door opens and Lucas walks in, holding a small crate. My heart leaps and I look at Marcus.

He smiles. "I brought the cat home."

"Oh my God!" I run to Lucas and grab the crate, set it on

the floor, then open it. My large, fluffy kitty is inside and gives me a sleepy look.

"I gave her a tranq to help with travel anxiety," Lucas mentions as I pull her out.

"You drugged her?" I hug her to my chest and glare at him.

"It helped." His eyes go between me and my cat before turning to Marcus. "Sir, Juan is loading your luggage now."

"Yes." Marcus comes over to me and strokes my hair. "Give me a minute to say goodbye."

Lucas disappears out the front door, and I look up into Marcus's striking blue eyes. He smiles. "Are you pleased?"

I hold Bella tighter to my body. Am I pleased? Yes. Thank God he didn't hurt her or give her away. The look in his eyes has my blood stilling in my veins. He actually believes he did something nice for me.

"I'm glad. I didn't want to separate you from the only living being that you felt loved you unconditionally." He cups my cheek, his thumb tracing it. "I want this relationship to work and for you to see I'll make every effort to ensure it does." Marcus brushes his lips over mine, Bella pressed between us.

I pull back, hugging her tighter. "Thank you."

I catch the flash of disapproval in his eyes before he nods at Bella. "Maybe keep her in your room. I'm not comfortable with her having free run of the house."

"Okay." I glance over at the open doors to the pool deck. I'm not comfortable with that either.

Marcus snorts. "Okay. Come here and give me a proper kiss goodbye."

I breathe through the tightening in my chest, shift Bella into a one-arm hold, and step closer to him. He cups the back of my head, pulling me closer, and I close my eyes. His warm lips brush over mine again. Marcus breaks the kiss, running his thumb over my bottom lip. "I'll miss you too."

Did I say that I'd miss him?

Lucas comes in carrying a bag and holds it up. "The cat's supplies."

"What?" Marcus eyes the bag.

"Food, bowls, litter box. Where do you want it?"

Marcus rolls his eyes before looking at me. "Why you want a creature that shits in the house is beyond me." He turns to Lucas. "Put it in Emily's room."

I bury my nose in Bella's soft fur and peek up at Marcus. His lips twitch up slightly.

"Enjoy your pet. When I return, I expect you'll have gotten over this petulance and give me a warm greeting."

I open my mouth, but I'm at a loss for words.

Juan comes through the door. "Sir, we're all set."

Marcus keeps his eyes on me, picking up a lock of my hair and rubbing it between his fingers. "Goodbye."

"Goodbye," I whisper back.

He pulls me back into his arms, squishing Bella between us and resting his cheek on top of my head. "We're going to be all right."

I nod, but I don't have anything to say back. He lets me go with a last long look, then turns to join Juan. I wait until the door closes behind them before going to the stairs, but I catch Carmen watching me from the kitchen doorway.

"She's a pretty cat."

I swallow. "She is. Thank you."

"It was very generous of Mr. Sterling to allow you to keep her."

My pulse trips into a frantic beat. Does she know what

he's doing to me? She has to. Who put all those clothes in my closet? Took my purse and my phone? If I'm not in my room, I'm with Marcus most of the time. She knows. I get my feet moving and jog up the stairs, kissing Bella when we reach my room. "We'll be okay."

Lucas comes out of my bathroom as I step into the bedroom. "I thought with the tile floor, that would be the best place for the litter box."

"Okay." I look past him at the bathroom door. "That's fine."

Lucas might not be taller than Marcus, but he's broader. A wall of muscle with short-cropped hair and chilling, crystal blue eyes. I'm certain I've never seen him smile, his lips always turned down and his square jaw tight. Today, he's wearing light blue jeans and a T-shirt that stretches over his wide chest. His biceps flex as he crosses his arms and eyes Bella.

"I wouldn't let her out of this room. She wouldn't survive outside."

I rub one of her clawless feet. "I know."

"You might want to stick close to the house as well."

Those words send another shiver through me. Are we talking about my survival? I swallow hard. "I didn't want to stay." Would he help me if I asked?

He takes a step closer to me and I suck in a deep breath, but his eyes go to the corner ceiling of my room. I follow his gaze, and it's the first time I notice it. A little orb-shaped device is placed there.

"There's no audio," Lucas tells me. "But he watches."

Oh. My. God. Is that a camera?

"This house has ears, and if you try anything, it will be reported. Be careful."

Another shot of fear slams into me. I was right.

"Let me know if you need anything," Lucas says as he walks to the door.

I have nothing to say back. My heart is pounding with the realization that Marcus has been watching me this whole time. When the door closes, I set Bella on the bed and go inside the bathroom. My eyes roam over the ceiling, and yes, there is another device in here. Jesus. I look away and see that Lucas has filled the litter box and set out a bowl of water. Another sits on the counter by Bella's food.

Back in the bedroom, I lie down next to my cat. She's still lethargic, purring softly as she naps. Stretching out next to her, I let the sound relax me a notch, but then I hear the plane take off and I close my eyes.

There has to be a way out of this.

# 25

## MARCUS

The wheels of the plane touch the runway in a smooth landing. I rub my temples, and Christ, these headaches have been frequently annoying. The drugs I have aren't helping. I'm not a stranger to migraines, but these are becoming persistent, and I make a note to see a physician before I go back to the island.

Leaving Emily wasn't the easiest choice. We needed more time, a better understanding of what we have together. I know she's afraid, confused, but I did my best to show her over the last couple of days how much I care.

I think it was a fatal flaw with Karyn. I should have spent more time showing her how I felt. I believe in the training method. Add pressure to get results, back off to reward the effort. Emily is sensitive, though, and I chalk it up to her innocence. Elizabeth was similar, and I know I can't allow what happened to her to repeat itself with Emily. But I believe she is stronger than that. Smarter. My mind wanders to how sweet she is, how she feels in my arms, the scent of her skin. I could breathe her in all day, and soon I'll have the opportunity to do just that.

My car waits for me on the runway, and I adjust my tie as I walk to it. It's odd not having Lucas with me, but another young man from our private security company opens the car door for me.

I thank him, sliding into the back seat. "Steven, I'll be working from home today."

"It's Stephan," he corrects me, and I raise a brow. Really? Because that's a New York accent I'm hearing. Not European or a Bronx-raised Russian mobster.

"Fine. Stephan. Home first."

I haven't missed this city, but my penthouse apartment overlooks the park and I enjoy the view. It gives me a sense that something can grow in this hostile environment.

Stephan walks with me to the elevator when we park in the garage. He joins me for the ride up as well. "Security has already cleared the residence, sir."

"Thank you," I mutter. It's a condition of my life. The notoriety lines my pockets but chews away at my sanity. "Are you staying next door?"

"Yes, sir."

Lucas has a separate apartment next to mine, and Stephan heads there as we step off the elevator. As soon as I'm in my penthouse, I remove my suit jacket and loosen my tie. Pulling my phone out, I call my assistant, Melissa.

"Mr. Sterling. You're back."

"I am." I head into the open kitchen and grab a bottle of scotch. "I need you to get me an appointment with Dr. Johnson for tomorrow."

"Routine or medical?"

I pour my drink and roll my eyes. "Medical."

"All right. Anything else?"

Probably. I'm having a hard time pulling my thoughts together through the pain. "Is everything ready for Saturday night?"

"Yes. Also, Mr. Carrington wanted me to ask you to call him when you checked in."

Heath can wait. "All right. Thank you, Melissa." I feel like I'm forgetting something. "I'll see you tomorrow."

Ending the call, I pick up my tumbler and walk over to the wall of windows. Some days I feel like a god up here, staring down at the petty people going about their mundane lives.

That makes me think of Emily. That's what I forgot. I need to call Melissa back so she can issue a press release. It's time to announce I'm engaged.

———

THERE'S a feeling of vulnerability when wearing a paper gown, talking to the doctor in his crisp white coat. He makes a note on his tablet and continues to question me. "How frequent have they become?"

"Daily," I admit.

"Hmm. Are you experiencing increased stress? Any changes in diet?"

"No, and no."

He glances up at me. "Mr. Sterling, I'm going to suggest an MRI just to rule out anything serious. I can prescribe you something stronger today, but we'll need to continue to monitor your bloodwork."

"That's fine." The only reason I'm here is for some stronger drugs.

"Okay." He pats my shoulder. I stiffen a little and he drops his hand. "Let's get you to radiology." He makes another note, then looks back at me. "Oh, by the way, congratulations. I read that you are engaged."

That makes me relax a notch. "I am. Thank you."

He steps out and a tech comes in with a wheelchair. "I can walk." I hop off the table.

"Hospital procedure," he replies.

This is also a humbling experience. I'd sooner take my own life than be reduced to an invalid. I stare straight ahead as we pass others in the hallway. I'm wheeled to radiology, placed in the metal tube, and I go over my speech for the event as they scan my brain.

Back in the exam room, I dress and wait for the doctor to return. My patience is thin as half of my day is being wasted.

He finally returns, wearing a grim look. "Mr. Sterling, we have the results of your MRI."

The world starts to fall away as he shows me an image. Some words get through, like tumor, inoperable, and biopsy.

"I'd like to get you scheduled for the procedure right away. We can make a plan when we know what we're dealing with."

I stare back at him, unable to pull together a response, and shake my head to clear the fog. "I'm traveling on Monday. I'll have to call your office."

The doctor frowns. "Marcus, this is something I need you to take seriously."

Oh. Now I'm Marcus? "Listen, Derek." I slip his given name in to show we are not friends. "Are you sure this is even my scan? It's been a few headaches. Otherwise, I feel fine."

"I'm sure. From the size of the tumor and the onset of

your symptoms, I'd say it's aggressive. This is why you don't want to wait."

"But you've already deemed it inoperable?"

"Because of its location."

Then what is the point, really. "If I do nothing, how long do I have?"

His brow rises. "I can't answer that right now. If it's benign, it's possible we could manage your symptoms for years."

"And if it's not?"

"It's possible with radiation and chemo we could shrink it enough to buy you some time." He starts to scribble on my chart. "We have a great oncology team here. Once we know more, we can put a plan into place for you."

The doctor continues to go over new medications, and I half-listen to the instructions. My mind is on Emily and our suddenly shortened future together. "Would I lose my hair?"

He hands me a handful of paperwork. "Some medications do cause hair loss, but we will probably have to shave a good portion for the biopsy."

I have the mental image of my grandfather shrinking into a worthless shell of a man. I can't do that. "I'll be in touch," I assure him so he'll leave.

Stephan meets me outside. "Where to, sir?"

"The office."

My mind is still organizing everything I've just learned, and I barely register getting in the car. The drive to our office building is short, but the traffic is heavy. We move at a snail's pace, and I ponder my options. Stephan pulls into the employee parking garage and gets out to open my door. "What time should I collect you?"

I hardly spare him a glance. "I'll call you."

Pulling myself together, I straighten my tie and collect my thoughts as the elevator takes me up to the executive floor, and I stop by Melissa's desk. "Is Heath in his office?"

"Yes, sir."

I've known Heath since I was eighteen. He's edging close to being the longest relationship I've ever had in my life. We started this company with his ideas and my money. He's happy to let me run the business while he focuses on creativity. This is evident when I step into his office. His desk is littered with papers, but he's hunched over the drawing board, studying some schematics.

"Hello."

His head whips up, then he smiles. "Well, look what the cat dragged in."

"Hmm." I step up behind him to peek at his work. I'm an intelligent man, but not in this arena. I have no idea what he's concocting here. "Electric car?"

"Battery. They'll need to improve for the industry to really take off." He hops off his stool. "As of now, they can't compete with a gas-powered vehicle."

Which is funny, since his family made their fortune in oil. Heath's way of rebelling was to find a way to put them out of business.

"So." He gives me a look from head to toe. "You did it."

"Did what?"

"Asked her to marry you."

"Ah. I did."

Heath shakes his head and walks over to his desk, snatching up his phone. "Gia is climbing the walls. She says this is not like Emily. She won't answer her calls or texts, emails, nothing. Emily has been ghosting her."

Gia's name sounds like nails on a chalkboard. "Maybe

she didn't see her as such a close friend after all. Honestly, she didn't really talk about her after we left New York."

Heath looks at me with a raised brow. "Maybe. It sounds to me like they've stuck together like glue since college."

I huff out an irritated laugh. "You mean the two minutes Gia spent getting an education?" I wave a hand. "The thing is, Emily's phone won't connect on the island. She probably has no idea Gia was trying to get hold of her."

"Why?"

"The phone? It's dated. I'll get her a new one."

Heath leans a hip on his desk. "You okay?"

No, I'm not *okay*. I'm fucking dying. "I'm fine, just a little headache. We need to make some different arrangements for next week. Is it possible we could go over what you need now?"

"No." He pushes off the desk. "It's a whole presentation I want to give you, and I have plans tonight." He wiggles his eyebrows.

It doesn't pull a smile out of me. "Fine. I can make time for you over the weekend."

Heath shakes his head. "I can't. It's Gia's last weekend before she leaves for Europe."

I let out an irritated sigh. The way I left things with Emily, I'm certain she isn't ready to entertain a guest. "Whatever, Heath." I pinch the bridge of my nose and squeeze my eyes closed. This conversation is making things worse.

"Are you all right?" Heath asks again.

"I'm fine." I wave a hand. "I'll see you tomorrow night."

"Sure," he replies by dragging out the word. I can read the questions in his eyes, but I don't have answers for him right now. I need to make some serious decisions.

I'd hoped for more time with Emily on the island, to let

her adjust to the idea of saying 'I do.' What I choose to do could seriously hinder that if I need to be here for treatment. Time feels like it's not an option.

I enter my office and breathe. Unlike Heath's disorganized space, my desktop is pristinely clean, orderly, the only way I can function. I drop into my chair to fire up the computer. Even though I should be digging into things I've delayed, I pull up the security cameras and find Emily. It seems she's pretty much grounded herself to her bedroom. On the bed with the fluff ball, she's reading. Her expression shifts from a little frown to a small smile, and I know she's immersed in her story.

I keep that screen open as I delve into my work, glancing at her from time to time. She stays pretty stationary, occasionally futzing with her hair. The cat rolls to its back and she gives it a belly scratch. With the camera feed, I don't feel like we're so far apart.

Emily sits up and looks directly at the camera. It's the first time she's done that, and it almost feels like she can see me too. Something in my chest stirs. Emily doesn't understand yet what a precious gift I'm about to give her. My heart.

Bella stretches and I lay down my book. She's recovering from her trip and settling in. It seems wrong to keep her locked in my bedroom, but honestly, it's nearly the size of my apartment, and I didn't let her outside there either. It slowly dawns on me that I've kept her captive, much like I am now. I wonder if she has the same desire to be free.

Thunder rumbles in the distance, and I glance outside. A dark cloud sits on the horizon, but I don't need to feed into that anxiety. What I need is a plan.

Dinnertime is approaching, and I feed my cat before I head downstairs. I was informed that the meal schedule would remain the same, and knowing that I'm being watched is motive enough to stick to it.

Carmen is waiting in the dining room when I come down. Her smile seems insincere.

"I made steak for you tonight."

"Oh?" I take my seat at the table. "Thank you."

"Mr. Sterling mentioned it was a dish you preferred."

Over veal? One hundred percent. That should have

been my first red flag. I've minimized my contact with both her and Juan. That goes for Lucas too. I haven't seen him since he brought Bella to me.

I eat alone, and the ticking of the grandfather clock is my only company as I consider my options. I can't swim away. I think about the small boat Marcus and I took around the island, but I haven't seen it since that day.

Carmen reappears just as I finish my wine. She starts to clear the table. "Was everything to your liking?"

"It was. Thank you." I stand up and glance out the window. "I'm going to take a little stroll before I turn in."

Carmen follows my gaze with a frown. "Don't go far. It's going to rain."

"I won't," I assure her and head out through the open doors to the pool deck. The clouds have socked in this little island, hanging low, dark and gray. The road is empty as I head in the direction of the generator house. I'm disappointed when the first drops of rain start, and I know I should turn around, but something catches my eye. The door to the equipment shed is slightly ajar.

I chew my bottom lip. This feels a little too good to be true. Juan must have left it unlocked, which means he could be coming back. I can't pass up this opportunity to look.

My pulse quickens as I approach the shed. The rain starts falling harder. I push the wet hair out of my eyes and breathe through my nerves. With a trembling hand, I reach for the handle on the metal door and push it open.

The light inside comes from a single bulb, casting the edges in shadows. The two utility vehicles take up most of the space, and I move between those and see the dinghy on a small trailer. Hope swells in my chest, but it's quickly squashed. The odds that I could hook it up, grab my cat, and get it down to the water without being seen are slim.

I look around the rest of the shed and eye the two jet skis, some shelving holding multiple tools, and I wonder if I could use one as a weapon. I move closer to inspect them further, but I notice a table that's loaded with computer equipment. The monitor glows with a soft blue light, and my heart rate triples. It's working. My first thought is contact with the outside world. I know Marcus said there wasn't an internet connection, but I'm doubting everything he ever told me. I take a tentative step forward.

"What are you doing?"

I nearly leap out of my skin, slamming my heart back into my chest with my hand. Lucas is standing in the shadows with his arms over his chest.

"N-nothing."

"Nothing?" He steps into the light. "What were you thinking?"

My gaze bounces over to the dingy. "I was just taking a walk."

"Mr. Sterling wouldn't be happy with you snooping around in here." He takes two steps forward. I back up toward the door. The rain is falling hard now, and a loud crack of thunder quickly follows a flash of lightning. My anxiety increases another ten notches, and I stumble over the threshold.

"Emily, wait."

I don't wait. I turn and run. He's going to tell Marcus and I'm doomed.

"Emily!"

His voice spurs me forward, my legs pumping as I burst

up the trail. Puddles have already started to form and I splash through them, my only thought to survive.

I round the bend and head north. His feet are slapping the wet earth behind me.

"Emily! Stop!"

He sounds too close, but I don't stop. Instead, a new blast of fear has me running faster. The rain is coming down in sheets now and I can't see far ahead. I'm not going to be able to outrun him. I need to hide. I look to the right and I leap off the trail into the brush and make it all of two strides when my ankle rolls and my feet come out from under me. I land on my ass, and between the mud and the wet undergrowth, I might as well be on a slick slide. I grasp anything to stop my descent down the hillside, but the ferns simply slip through my hands.

"Emily!" Lucas yells over the rain.

Another flash of lightning brightens the sky and I see exactly where I'm headed. Straight down to the rocky coast below. I flip to my stomach, reach out, and grab the trunk of a small tree, wrapping my arms around it. I desperately try to get my feet under me, but they slide uselessly in the mud.

I stop struggling, my breath coming hard and fast, my heart trying to break free from my ribs.

"Emily."

I raise my eyes and see Lucas's legs a few feet above me, but something else catches my attention. A large, green snake is slithering toward me. My scream sticks in my throat. I don't have the lung capacity through the crippling fear to get it out.

"Don't move," Lucas tells me, but I'm hardly listening, too focused on the flicking forked tongue that's coming closer. If I let go of this tree...

Suddenly, Lucas's hand appears, fisting the snake behind its head, and in a flash, he flings it away from us.

I peek up at him, and he's shaking his head. "What the fuck?"

He glances back up toward the trail. "Emily, listen to me. If I try to pull you up from here, we're both going down."

I swallow hard. Maybe that's my escape. Death.

"I'm going back for some rope. You okay? Can you hang on?"

"I think so," I whisper.

He starts to back up carefully. "Don't let go of that tree."

*Don't leave me here!* The thought screams in my head, but I don't voice it out loud. The rain is still coming down, but the canopy of leaves somewhat shelters me under these trees.

I don't see Lucas anymore, and I start to shiver. My eyes search the undergrowth, looking for spiders, snakes, lizards— what was I trying to do? Get myself killed? I know now more than ever I want to live.

Clinging to the tree, I start to shake harder and my teeth chatter. I try a few more times to get my knees under me, but it's useless. The rain is slowing, the storm is passing, and I rub my forehead on my arm, wiping the wet hair from my eyes.

"Emily."

I crane my neck at the sound of my name, but I don't see him. "I'm here!" I cry out.

Suddenly, I see his feet again and I look up. He has a rope tied around his waist, tethering him to a tree near the trail, and he tosses the end to me.

"One hand. Wrap it around your wrist several times."

I shake my head. "I... I can't let go."

"One hand," he repeats and tears heat my cheeks.

Tightening my hold on the tree with one arm, I shakily reach for the rope. Fisting it, I do what he said and wrap it around my wrist several times.

He nods. "Hold on. Let go of the tree and grab it with your other hand. Try to plant your feet."

A sob escapes me as the reality hits me. If I let go of this tree, I'm probably going to die. "I'm scared."

"I know." His voice is deep and calm. "Let's do it on three. One. Two..."

I'm not sure I hear him say three, but I grip the rope tight and let go of the trunk. I immediately start to slide and the nylon tightens painfully around my wrist. My other hand wraps around the rope and I stop. I glance up at him. He's literally my lifeline at the moment.

"Okay." He starts to pull. "Use your feet, Emily."

I hold on for dear life and do what he says, moving one agonizing inch at a time closer to him. He pulls harder and I feel like my hand will be torn from my body as the rope tightens, but I move a little farther.

Lucas loses his footing and lands with a thump on the wet ground. I slide back, but he holds the rope firm. "It's okay. I'm not going anywhere."

With his knees bent and his legs slightly spread, he appears closer, and I start to pull myself toward him while he holds the rope steady. "That's it. Help me out."

We work together until I'm able to grab his calf. Lucas clutches my shirt and tugs me up. He gets his hands under my armpits and drags me onto his lap. My arms come around his neck, and I hold on.

We're both panting now, and we take a minute to catch

our breath. He gently strokes the wet hair plastered to my head. "I'm going to pull us up to the trail. Can you hang on?"

With my eyes squeezed closed, I nod against his chest. He keeps one arm around me, and I don't look, but I feel the movement and he inches us up the hill. I don't open my eyes again until he hauls me up and sets my butt on flat ground.

Lucas scoots back until he joins me. "What the hell, Emily?"

We both take a moment to breathe in the fact we're alive before he looks over at me. His eyes travel the length of me. "You're a fucking mess."

I glance down at myself. I'm covered in mud and the scratches on my legs have bloody rivulets cutting through the dirt. "I know."

He sighs as he unwraps the rope from my wrist. His finger grazes over the torn flesh. "Fuck." He shoves to his feet. "Stay here."

I'm pretty sure I'm not capable of moving. He releases the rope from the tree, coils it up, and tosses that over his shoulder. Squatting down, he gets an arm around my back and the other under my knees and scoops me up.

"That was fucked up, Ms. Hanson. Where did you think you could run to?"

I don't know. I wasn't thinking.

"What were you hoping to find in the shed?"

I don't answer that either.

He bounces me in his arms, shifting my weight as he heads down the trail. "I think it's time for you to accept that you can't escape this island."

"I think I can walk now."

He tightens his grip. "You hurt your ankle. Just relax."

I stop struggling, but I don't relax. I haven't figured out how dangerous this guy is. He just saved my life, but... "Are you going to hurt me?"

"Why would I do that?"

I don't know. In fact, I don't know anything anymore. "I just want to go home."

It's getting dark, and the lights of the house are almost welcoming. Lucas carries me through the french doors into the living room, where we greet two pairs of wide eyes.

"Oh my goodness. What happened?" Carmen rushes forward.

"She slipped on the trail." He looks at Juan. "Shut off the cameras."

Juan doesn't move and Lucas snaps, "Now!"

That has Juan scurrying down the hall, and Lucas heads for the stairs with me still in his arms.

"He's going to see this," Carmen says nervously.

"I'll delete it."

Lucas adjusts my weight again, and I say nothing as he totes me up the stairs. He doesn't stop as he enters my bedroom and kicks the door closed behind him. Bella leaps off the bed and stretches before following us into the bathroom, and Lucas sets me down on the edge of the tub.

Glancing at the camera in the corner of the ceiling, he frowns. "We need to get you out of those wet clothes and clean you up before I do first aid."

The loss of his body heat has me shivering again, and I wrap my arms around myself. "I'm fine."

He snorts. "You're pretty far from fine," he says and flips on the water to fill the tub. "Get out of those clothes."

I'm not doing that with him here. "I can wash myself. You can go."

"Yeah. Okay. I need to change too. Clean up, and I'll be back to help with that ankle."

I blow out a long breath as he leaves. Checking the water, I shut off the tap and begin the process of removing my wet clothes. Tears sting my eyes as the pain shoots up past my knee when I attempt to stand. I'm more than a mess, and the scrapes and scratches sting as I settle into the bath. Blood and mud stain the water a rusty hue. Nothing is life-threatening though, and I run the washcloth over my skin, exposing my injuries. Aside from my ankle, my wrist is the worst. Deep rope burns have rubbed my skin raw. The terror I felt when I let go of that tree sends a shiver through me despite the warmth of the water.

There's a knock at the bathroom door. Bella meows, and I call out, "Just a minute."

I'm shaking as I pull myself out of the tub and reach for a robe. I wrestle it on, tighten the belt, and then collapse on the toilet stool. Lucas did save my life. I'm not sure that buys my trust, but he's the only one here who has recognized the danger I'm in. "Come in."

Lucas enters wearing clean sweatpants, a white T-shirt and holding a first aid kit. Bella escapes out the open door and he kneels in front of me. His fingers gently palpate my ankle. "This needs to be wrapped. I brought up an ice pack for you."

"Thank you."

"Tonight was a fuck-up, Emily. You wouldn't have been the first person to die sliding off that cliff."

"Do you mean Elizabeth?"

His eyes snap up to meet mine.

"Did you know her?" I ask. How long has he worked for Marcus?

He shakes his head. "She was just another one I couldn't save."

My lips part, but fear freezes the words in my throat. Was her death even accidental?

# 27

## MARCUS

The audience is quiet as I read over the last lines of my speech. With a shake of my head, I continue. "These tumors can start small, sometimes undetectable until they grow and threaten your very existence. This is why preventive health-care is important and should be accessible to everyone." I pause for the applause. "In the end, we all benefit from finding the cure. Individually and as a society. Thank you for coming tonight to support this charity."

I step back from the podium while the guests put their hands together. Gia is sitting with Heath at the nearest table. She claps with everyone else, but I can see she wants a piece of me.

The host of our event replaces me on the stage. A comedian whose name doesn't stick with me, but he gets the crowd laughing as I return to our table. I take a seat next to Heath, and Gia leans over. "Nice speech."

"Thank you." I hold eye contact, irritated and wishing she were anywhere else.

I had a reprieve when they arrived, staying busy backstage, then through dinner, but she's not backing off now.

"We need to talk."

I take a sip of water and nod. "About what?"

"About Emily," she hisses.

Heath lays a hand on her arm. "Not now."

He gives me an apologetic look and I shrug. "Heath is right. It's a conversation we shouldn't have at the table. Would you care to join me on the veranda?"

Our event is being held in this rotating restaurant high above Manhattan, but there is an observation deck that's open when weather permits.

She glances at the doors, then at Heath.

He eyes both of us. "Just bring her back in one piece."

That's funny. As if I'd kill the woman with nearly five hundred witnesses. Our host is announcing the band, which is perfect timing, and I stand. "Let's go get your questions answered."

The sky is mostly clear and a few stars make their presence known, but the light of the city mostly drowns them out. I step up to the high cement wall and lean against it while Gia hugs the doorway.

The band strikes up, and I watch as couples take to the dance floor before focusing on her. "So talk."

Tonight, she's wearing a form-fitting, metallic silver dress that reaches the floor. I won't deny Gia has a lovely shape. I'm also so happy she won't be dressing Emily anymore. Her breasts are barely covered.

She places her hands on her hips and blows out a breath. "Why hasn't she called me?"

"I told Heath her phone isn't working on the island."

Her eyes narrow. "She could use yours."

"She could. But she never asked to." I cross my arms over my chest. "Why is it so hard to believe she's happy where she is? I realize things happened quickly, but Emily has agreed to marry me, and now she's busy planning that."

"No." She points a finger at me but doesn't come closer. "That isn't Emily." She starts to pace but stays by the doors. "Emily doesn't do anything without talking to me."

"Maybe she's grown beyond the person who needs someone to validate her every move." I hold my posture as I stare her down.

She turns to confront me. "No. That's not what our friendship is."

"No?" I raise a brow. "I can only speak to what my fiancée has told me. She felt lost in your shadow, yet strived to be noticed, and when she was, I believe she blossomed and doesn't need you any longer."

Gia's eyes grow round. "What?"

"Gia." I push off the wall and take a step forward. "I see it, and you know it. You're just a snowflake in a business that will eat you alive. You'll evaporate before you make any impact, while Emily will carry my name. My fame. And as Mrs. Sterling, she'll have everything, while you smile in your underwear. That's what really pisses you off."

"No." She shakes her head and clings closer to the doors.

"Yes." I tilt my head slightly, regarding her. "You felt above her, tossing her some clothes, dragging her to high-end events, drowning her with your success. In my eyes, you're nothing but a little slut that—"

"Hey. Everything all right out here?"

Heath steps out to join us, putting an arm around Gia while she stares at me, apparently surprised by my words.

"What did you just call me?"

I don't feel the need to answer that. She heard me. "When I return, I'll let Emily know that you are concerned." I move to go back inside.

"No. You just called me a slut!"

"What?" Heath's eyes bounce from her to me.

I smile at both of them. "Emily might have mentioned the number of suitors in your life. It was an educated assumption."

"Christ. Marcus, stop," Heath snaps.

I'd be happy to, but Gia is all puffed up now that she has backup. "You are such an arrogant bastard," she hisses, getting in my face. "If you do anything to hurt Emily, I will cut off your balls."

"Enough." Heath pulls her back a step. She wrenches her arm from his grasp and stomps through the doors. I keep my eyes on her for a moment before looking at Heath.

"I apologize. I shouldn't have called your date a slut."

He chuckles, running a hand over his too-long hair. "Yeah. Why do I get the feeling I'm the one who will be paying for that comment?"

Probably because he is. It's not my problem. I rub my forehead. The drugs are wearing off and I'm ready to leave this party. I did my part and Heath can take over from here. "I'm actually not feeling well, and I let that woman get under my skin. I'll go make my round of handshakes, and then I'm going to cut out early."

Heath rolls his eyes but says nothing as he follows me inside.

Unfortunately, there are a lot of hands to shake. People are aware of my engagement, and everyone wants to congratulate me. Several have questions about Emily, which I answer proudly.

Yes, she's young but very intelligent and motivated.

No. Her family isn't wealthy. She's also not materialistic.

"And what about the fact Karyn hasn't even been gone a year yet?" Mrs. Carrington asks.

I look at Heath's mother calmly. I do hate this woman. It's obvious she's made more than one trip to the open bar this evening. Her glassy eyes shine with glee, thinking she got one in on me.

"Marianne, are you insinuating I didn't mourn for her long enough?"

She gives me a condescending smile. "No. I'm sure you grieved. It's funny, you love that Cinderella story. Take the handmaid and turn her into a princess. Or wait, Karyn was a waitress, and this girl, what does she do?"

"What are you implying?" I ask, trying not to let my irritation show.

"It's unfortunate you didn't marry Sara. At least her family was worthy of yours."

"Marianne, that's enough." Mr. Carrington puts a hand on her arm.

I roll my lips together to suppress the anger. "Actually, my family thought she was a worthless American and that I could do better." I wave a hand at both of them. "New money doesn't impress descendants of royalty. Heath didn't make an impression either." I glance over at him in the corner, probably trying to calm down Gia. "Maybe he should have married Sara."

I hit my mark, but she comes back at me. "And maybe then she'd still be alive."

"Yes. Well, as always, it was lovely to see both of you tonight. Thank you again for your generous donation."

I turn to leave them, but Heath's father walks with me. "Marcus, excuse Marianne. She's just—"

"A bitch. I know."

Seriously, I could say anything to this man, and he'd allow it. He was so desperately happy to have any connection to me, my name, my family. Since I've become a part of their lives, he clings like a parasite whenever I'm around.

"She can be," he agrees. "She shouldn't have brought Sara up."

"No. She shouldn't have."

I met Sara in college through Heath. His family was friends with hers. The truth is, Sara did not die by my hands. Rather, much like my pony, she was a lesson from my mother. Where pride killed the little horse, Sara's issue was my lust. The only good thing that came from her death was that it spurred me to face my parents. My mom can be sure that today, I indulge in more than seven deadly sins.

"Don't worry about it, Henry." I head for his son. "I'm just going to say good night to Heath and then I'm heading home." I check my phone to make sure Stephan has the car ready.

Gia is obviously still pissed at me. If looks could kill, I'd be a pile of ash right now.

"You two enjoy the evening." I shake hands with Heath and his father while ignoring Gia completely.

"I'll see you Wednesday," Heath reminds me.

"Right." Good Lord. Emily and I will need to have a conversation before that happens.

Stephan greets me at the door and escorts me to the waiting car. My head is pounding now, and I lie back against the seat and close my eyes. Sara's bright smile greets me. I can picture how the morning sun lit her face, her blue eyes glittering as she worried her bottom lip with her teeth.

*"Your mother is going to hate me."*

*"My mother hates everyone. Don't feel special."*

*"How did she take the news of our engagement?"*

*"Poorly."* I drop a kiss on her forehead. *"It doesn't matter. The woman can't dictate every part of my life."*

Sara was the first girl I fell hard for. She would have made the perfect wife. What I forgot was the fact my mother was insane. How? I don't know. The woman had my pony put down in front of me. She took a hammer to my balls when she learned I'd impregnated the maid. I shouldn't have been shocked by the lengths she'd go to ensure I didn't marry someone she felt was beneath us.

"Sir, we're here."

Thank Christ. I shake off the uncomfortable thoughts, happy to be home. One thing Mummy can't do is tell me whom I can or can't marry.

The lights in the penthouse increase my headache, and I go straight for the scotch. Downing a couple of pills, I head for my study and open the safe. Tucked inside is the ring box, and I remove it. This isn't sentimental to me because my grandmother wore it, but it was passed on to me for the day I chose a wife. I didn't give it to Karyn. Maybe I always knew she wouldn't be my forever.

Taking a seat at the desk, I fire up my computer and make some notes. For one, Emily and I need to move up this wedding date. It won't be a proper church ceremony, but I'll have Lucas order what I need. After that, I envision at least a week, if not two, celebrating our honeymoon on *The Temptress*. That should give me enough time to make a decision about my diagnosis and decide if Emily is ready to come back to New York.

My visions of the future have me missing her and I pull up the camera feed, but all the screens are blank. I run through all of them, then reboot my computer. Still nothing. I temper my anxiety with another shot of scotch and grab my phone. When Lucas doesn't answer, I check the weather and see a small storm passed over the island this evening. Disappointed, I shut down the computer. I'm sure Lucas will have everything working by morning.

# 28

## EMILY

Lucas brushes his thumb over my calf while he meets my gaze with icy blue eyes. I suppress another shiver. I'm not sure if I should say anything at all, but I ask anyway. "Did Marcus kill Elizabeth?"

He takes a bandage from the kit and starts to wrap my ankle. "Elizabeth, like you, thought she had somewhere to run. She was wrong."

I bite my lip, digesting that as he finishes with the bandage and begins to apply ointment to the scrapes on my legs. His touch is gentle, and I could be wrong about him, but there are things I need to know. "Did he kill Karyn?"

"Karyn was plotting to leave him." He lifts one shoulder. "She confessed to the wrong person."

Who? Was it him?

Lucas applies butterfly bandages to one especially deep cut. His application is practiced. "You've done this before," I comment.

"In the military. Sometimes you can't wait all day for a medic."

I recall Marcus talking about his ability to fly. "You were in the Air Force?"

"Marines."

He moves to my wrist and winces at the sight of my torn flesh. "This is going to sting." He applies more ointment, and he's right. I hiss through the pain. That wound is covered in gauze before he bandages it as well. "Marcus is going to be pissed."

Fear slithers down my spine. I know what almost happened the last time I made him angry. I'm not sure I can talk myself out of this one. "You scared me. I panicked and ran. I'm sorry."

He moves to my elbow next, eyeing the wound there before digging into his supplies. "I know you're scared, Emily, but you need to accept there is no way off this island right now."

His voice is calm and soothing. Would he help me? "Why couldn't you save the other women?"

He applies a large Band-Aid to my elbow and pats down the sticky edges. "I think we're almost done."

He didn't answer my question. Lucas stands, setting the kit on a counter. He begins to roll up the sleeve of my robe, checking for any other wounds. I don't even see it, but I feel the sting and I jerk my arm away. "What are you doing?"

He stares back at me with a syringe in his hand. "It's for the pain and it will help you sleep."

I rub my upper arm and glare at him. "I'm not in that much pain."

"Come on." He pulls me to my feet. "Let's get you to bed."

Putting weight on my foot is agony and I almost collapse. Lucas puts an arm around me and supports me while we leave the bathroom. I'm already feeling the effects of the drug by the time we reach my bed. He tosses the covers aside. I sit down on the edge and blink my sleepy eyes. "How can you work for him if you know what he is?"

Lucas doesn't answer, putting an arm under my legs and adjusting me to lie back on the bed.

"You had an honorable career and now you're doing this?"

He pulls the covers over me. "Maybe you overestimate how honorable it is to be a soldier."

My lips press into a frown. "You could save me. You can call the police."

"The police can't help you either."

"Why?"

Lucas brushes the damp hair from my face. "Because he owns them too." He taps my chin. "I'm turning the cameras back on. Go to sleep."

---

MORNING HITS me like a ton of bricks. I hurt everywhere. Bella threads between my legs as I hobble to the bathroom to feed her. Memories of last night come back to me. I don't recall falling asleep, but I remember the last thing Lucas said to me. Marcus owns the police—and apparently Lucas too.

I contemplate that as Bella crunches on her kibble and I brush out my tangled hair. Lucas was kind and took care of me after the fall, but will he tell Marcus, or will this be our little secret?

There's a lot to consider from what I learned last night, but one thing is clear. Marcus was involved in the deaths of both his young girlfriend and his wife.

My pulse leaps when I hear a knock. No one has bothered me here since Marcus left. I limp into the bedroom, still in the robe I slept in, and the door opens before I reach it. It's Lucas carrying a tray with my breakfast.

I give the camera a nervous glance.

"It's okay. I shut them off," he says and sets the tray on the coffee table of my small seating area.

"Can't we just leave them off?"

His lips twitch in a smirk. "How is the ankle?"

I hobble over to him and sit down on the loveseat. "It's doable."

"Good. I brought you something for the pain."

I shake my head. "If you try to inject me again—"

"Aspirin," he cuts me off and gestures to the pills next to the orange juice.

Still feeling wary, I pick up the tablets and wash them down with the juice. Lucas sits in the adjacent chair, watching me with those icy eyes.

"You're staying?" I ask.

"We need to redress the bandage on your wrist."

I set down my glass. It's true. That one would be hard for me to do on my own. "Okay."

My breakfast is a 'simple affair' this morning. Yogurt topped with granola and a bowl of fruit with a croissant on the side. I pick up the fork and spear a piece of melon. "Why are you helping me now when you won't actually save my life?"

He pins me with a chilling look, then shakes his head. "I am doing my job, which includes saving your life."

"But you're hiding this from Marcus. Why, if it's your job?"

His eyes soften a notch. "To protect you. Whether you believe it or not, I do care if you live."

My eyes water and I blink against the tears. "Then why won't you help me?"

Lucas gazes past me at the window where the island breeze flutters a gauzy curtain. "You all fall for it."

What?

"I watched you do it." Those icy blues are back on me. "A pretty girl living on a shoestring caught the attention of a billionaire. You came here willingly. What were you hoping for?"

Love? "The point is that I'm not staying here willingly." I set the fork aside. "I didn't see who Marcus really was until I came here, but you knew, and you let it happen."

Lucas doesn't respond to that but moves to sit next to me. He begins to unbandage my wrist. "My hands are tied, Emily," he finally says. "My job was to make sure that you were safe while he was away. In some respect, I fucked that up." His finger grazes over the bruises forming around my raw skin. "Let me get the medical kit."

I stay silent as he retreats to the bathroom. Any hope I had in believing he'd be my ally is dwindling. He returns with Bella on his heels. She has no reason to trust him. He drugged her too.

Lucas sits next to me and applies the balm to my wound. "There was no other way to pull you out without causing you pain."

"You should have just let me fall." I pout.

His eyes snap up to mine. "Why would you say that?"

I shrug. "At least this nightmare would have ended for me. Don't act like you care if I live or die now."

Lucas refocuses on bandaging my wrist. "You don't

understand." His gentle fingers wrap the gauze. "If I tried to get you off this island, he'd kill both of us. It's not an option."

I'm shocked into silence as he tops off my dressing with tape. There must be something I can do to get away from here. "If we did get off the island, we could go to the police. They'd protect us."

"You don't understand the scope Marcus has. The local authorities are in his pocket. There's nowhere we could run or hide where he wouldn't find you."

A dreadful feeling of hopelessness swamps me. "He said I can't leave here unless I marry him."

His jaw tightens. "Then marry him."

I'd rather die, but I know that's not true. My only hope to get free is to go home. Lucas slides off the sofa to kneel in front of me, and he starts to unwind the bandage on my ankle. I jerk my foot back. "I can do that."

"Let me help you."

"I've been asking you to."

He gives his head a little shake. "Emily, the only way either of us will ever be free of Marcus is if he stops breathing."

I blink several times as I look down at him. I knew things were bad when he left me here, but how on earth did I wind up in this situation? It's insane that the first time I have given a relationship a chance, it's with a psychopath.

"What does Marcus have on you that makes you afraid of him?" I ask in a small voice.

For a moment he doesn't answer but focuses on rebandaging my ankle. Then he finally says, "It's not fear. I owe him."

Wait. That doesn't make sense.

Lucas raises his gaze to meet mine. "I chose one prison

over another but if I do my job, I'm free. Do you understand?"

No. Not really. "Were you in prison?"

He rubs his hands over the fresh dressing. "How does that feel?"

"Fine." I'm no longer concerned about my ankle. Who is this man taking care of me?

Lucas stands only to take a seat on the chair. Bella jumps in his lap and starts to purr. The seconds tick by as he regards me with those icy blue eyes. I stare back at him, attempting to comprehend any of this.

"I think I can help you." He finally breaks the silence. "Not here, but when we go back to New York."

The temperature in the room seems to drop, and I rub my arms. "How?"

I'm afraid of the answer, because he just said the only way I'd be free is if Marcus is dead.

"You don't need to know, but you will know when it's over and you can thank me later."

"Lucas..." I start off slowly. "What do you mean? I can't be a part of anything... illegal."

"You won't be a part of anything."

That icy feeling further chills my blood. "Why would you? I mean..."

"I thought about what I just said." He strokes my cat thoughtfully. "This isn't the life I want anymore. I can help us both."

My brain is conjuring a thousand possible scenarios, and each of them ends up with Marcus no longer alive. Could I live with that? The idea scrapes against my morals, but will I live if he does?

Lucas begins to clean up the first aid supplies. "In the

meantime, you keep doing what you're doing. Let Marcus believe that you want this relationship too. If getting married is the path back to New York, walk down that aisle." His gaze locks with mine. "Don't do anything to make him suspicious. I'll be as invisible to you as I was before."

Something in the way he said that sounds like an accusation. "You weren't invisible to me."

His lips twitch up slightly, and he sets the kit on the table next to my tray. "I can't keep shutting off the cameras. Carmen will bring the rest of your meals. You need to rest that ankle and take it easy for a couple of days."

"Wait." I stand and wobble a little until I find my balance. "I'm scared." Not just about my current situation, but also what I think he's proposing.

"You should be scared," he says with one last chilly look before turning away from me.

He walks out my door and I'm stunned, nearly to the point of numb. I need Gia. What would she say? But I can hear her voice in my head.

She'd tell me to survive.

# 29

## MARCUS

The sun is hot, and my shirt is already sticking to my skin as I approach my plane at the airport. One of the mechanics greets me with a handshake.

"Is everything in order?" I ask him.

"Yep. We didn't find any issues, Mr. Sterling."

"Thank you." I press out a smile for him and climb aboard. With Emily's ring in my pocket, that excitement starts to thrum through me at the thought of seeing her again. Receiving this diagnosis has given me some perspective. It's uncertain how much time Emily and I will have together, but I'm planning on making the most of every moment.

I go through my routine checks before taking off. Visions of how our life is going to look fill my head as I fly over the sparkling blue water. We'll have our wedding at home, and I've alerted the crew on my yacht that we'll be arriving on Friday.

My island comes into view and my excitement builds. I hit the water with smooth precision, like I've done a hundred times before. As I float toward the dock, I see Juan already waiting for me.

He greets me, grabbing the rope. "Lucas kept Emily with the cart. She's still limping."

That's just perfect. I'm not only being robbed of my warm welcome, but I'll have a lame bride to boot.

Lucas informed me that she hurt herself this weekend when I briefed him on my plans for this week. He mentioned that he's asked her to stay in her room. I should have just locked her in that room.

Emily is in the vehicle and Lucas is leaning against it. He says something to her I can't hear, and she turns to look at me. The first thing I notice is she's wearing a pretty, yellow sundress. That was thoughtful. Her hair is down, hanging in soft waves and fluttering around her face in the breeze. I smile as I get closer and then frown when she struggles to get out of the cart.

I take in her bandaged wrist and wrapped ankle as well as the pout on her lips.

"I thought we discussed a warm greeting for when I arrived."

She takes a tentative step toward me and I pull her into my arms, laying the sweetest kiss on her rosy lips. "You are a lovely sight after a shitty weekend." I glance down at her ankle. "Come. We'll get you back to the house."

Juan joins us, Lucas takes the wheel, and I help Emily in the vehicle. "Tell me what happened."

Her frown deepens. "I slipped."

"Where?" I pick up her arm and check out her bandaged elbow.

"On the trail. I fell into some brush."

"Hmm." Vague. "I told you to be careful on those trails. Why were you out in the rain?"

She meets my eyes with a shrug. "It wasn't raining when I went out."

That makes sense. The storms can roll in fast and grow violent quickly. We pull up to the house and I help her inside, immediately taking her upstairs. She pauses at her door, but I keep her moving to our room. "I realize you chose to sleep there while I was away, but we aren't doing that anymore."

Going straight to the sofa, I sit down and pull her into my lap, taking that kiss I've been waiting for. When I let her up for air, I brush my thumb over her bottom lip. "Other than taking a spill, how was your weekend?"

"Oh." She looks around the room nervously. "It was fine."

"I know you were worried about being here alone, but I'm home now. Here, I got something for you."

I shift her off my lap to remove the ring box from my pocket. Her eyes are on that, and they grow wide when I open it.

"I know." I pull it out so she can have a closer look. Several diamonds surround a large ruby. "It's been in my family for centuries," I tell her as I pick up her hand. "Do you like it?" I don't wait for her to answer as I slide it on her ring finger. How could she not like it? It's perfect.

"Marcus?"

"Hmm?"

"It's so..."

"Beautiful?"

"Big."

I chuckle. "It is. It looks good on you." She tries to pull

her hand back, but I hold it, placing a kiss on her knuckles, and I brush a finger over the bandage on her wrist. "Now, do you want to tell me what really happened the other night?"

Emily looks down at her hand. "I slipped off the trail. It was so steep, and Lucas had to throw a rope down to pull me up."

I stare at her in disbelief. "That must have been terrifying."

She nods. "It was."

It would seem Lucas left out a few details when he briefed me. That sensation of unease stirs in my gut. The feeling I get when someone is lying to me. I brush Emily's hair over her shoulder. "I'm so grateful you're all right."

I wrap my arms around her, and she doesn't resist, resting her cheek on my chest. On a deep inhale, I breathe in her sweet scent. "I don't know what I'd do if anything happened to you."

The weight of this day, my diagnosis, and our uncertain future are heavy. All I need is a dose of Emily. I stand and offer her my hand. "Come here."

She's slow, but she stands and allows me to lead her back to the bedroom. Tipping her head back, I kiss her hard and she startles when I start to pull off her dress.

"Shh. I know you're hurt. I just want to hold you."

She gives me a wary glance as I drop the dress to the floor. "I see we're braless again," I say, appraising her naked breasts.

"That dress has built-in support."

I smirk at that and take her hand, leading her to the bed. "Just lie down with me."

She sits on the edge of the bed, and I keep my eyes on hers as I strip down to my boxers. I could use a shower to wash off the travel, but I'm tired and what I really need is Emily in my arms. Climbing on the bed behind her, I pull her close and run my nose over her shoulder. My cock stirs, but I close my eyes and let the tension slowly leave my body as I relax against hers. "I need you, Emily." She stiffens and I sigh. "I need you in my life." I reach around to toy with the ring on her finger. "I want to get married tomorrow."

"Tomorrow?"

"I don't want to spend another day without you by my side, and as Mrs. Sterling, I'm assured you'll be mine until death parts us."

Emily is quiet for a moment before she asks, "How do you plan on getting married here?"

"Basically, we'll say some vows, fill out the paperwork, and file it on our way home."

"Home?" she whispers.

"Home." I don't mention which home. I feel a need to return to London. My home. Not knowing how long I have, I might not have a chance later. There are demons there I need to lay to rest. I look at one of the paintings on the wall and think of my mother. Did she do this to me? Cut my time short with Emily as an act of vengeance from the grave?

She's quiet for a spell and I relax a little more, wondering if she dozed off. I'm starting to, but I stir when she asks, "Where will we live in New York?"

I'm not sure Emily and I will make it back to New York, but I humor her. "I have a penthouse apartment near the park. You'll love it."

Emily turns in my arms and searches my eyes. "What about my apartment? I need to pack, and—"

I shake my head. "Lucas already did. Honestly, there

wasn't much worth keeping. He packed some personal mementos he thought you'd want to keep."

"Lucas went through my stuff?"

"I thought we already had this conversation. We have people to handle those things."

She pouts, and I give her a quick kiss. "Stop worrying about everything. I paid off your lease, all of your credit cards, and the stupid student loan with that incredibly high interest rate."

Her eyes widen before she puts her back to me again. I kiss her shoulder and pull her closer. "You've been a good girl, Emily. Relax. You have me to take care of everything now."

## 30

## EMILY

Marcus falls asleep and I lie awake in his arms. I'm afraid to move and I hardly breathe. Other than lazily cupping my breast, he hasn't tried anything more. His muscled arm holds me close and his chest hair tickles my back.

My insides have been a jumbled mess since my conversation with Lucas. There must be another way. I didn't see him again until this morning, and he just reminded me to play along. The last thing I want to do is trigger Marcus.

I've barely said four words to Carmen, even though she's the one who delivered my meals. She didn't have much to say to me either. There was no lack of politeness, but suspicion and disapproval were evident in the way she looked at me.

Marcus finally stirs. Propping up on an elbow, he kisses my cheek. "It's getting late. Go change for dinner. I'll clean up too."

He doesn't have to ask twice. I slip off the bed and back into my dress.

Marcus drops a kiss on my lips as he heads to the bathroom. "Dress nice. We're celebrating tonight."

I gingerly make my way to the hall and brace myself on the wall as I hobble to my room. My ankle still hurts when I put weight on it. Bella is on my bed and I sit down next to her. "I'm engaged."

She closes her eyes and purrs as I scratch her chin. Her pleasure doesn't mirror my mood. Tomorrow? I guess that's better than next week but it's all so crazy. I look back at Bella. "It will only be a few days until we're home."

In the bathroom, I give myself a quick sink bath and reflect on the afternoon as the ring catches my eyes. He gave me an heirloom, and I'm sure it's worth millions from the size of the stones. It feels weighted and awkward on my finger.

In the closet, I select a simple, black sheath dress and slip it on as I regard my reflection in the full-length mirror. I assure my reflection that I'm strong enough to do this. All I need to do is survive.

The knock on my door makes me jump and I hurry to answer it. His eyes roam over me and a slow smile tips his lips until he sees my bare feet.

"I can't get my foot in a shoe," I whisper.

He offers me his arm. "So it looks like I'll have a barefoot bride. Let's have the ceremony on the beach."

Right. Where his last wife died. Taking his arm, I shake my head. "I don't think I can make it to the beach. Maybe by the pool."

"Then by the pool it is."

When we hit the bottom stair, Lucas comes in the front door. He looks over at both of us, then gives Marcus a curt nod and breezes past us.

My stomach churns. I know—or I think I know—what Lucas is planning, and I can't believe I'm in the middle of this or even considering being an accomplice to it.

Marcus raises a brow. "Are you all right? You're pale."

"No, I'm fine. My ankle hurts, that's all."

He lets it go and gets me seated at the table. Giving me his charming smile, he removes a bottle of champagne from the ice bucket. He pops the cork and fills both flutes before handing one to me. "To my beautiful bride-to-be."

I clink mine against his, taste the bubbling liquid, and glance out at the ocean as the sun sinks closer to the horizon.

Marcus eyes me curiously. "What are you thinking?"

"Nothing." I set down my flute.

"You know, you can be honest with me." Marcus tips his head. "Something is going on in that pretty head of yours."

I breathe through my nerves. "I was wondering what my life would look like in New York now."

He chuckles. "Obviously different from what it looked like before. What are you concerned about?"

Obviously, whether or not I'll be locked in a high tower. "My, umm... I don't have my passport."

"I do." He takes another sip of champagne and raises a brow at my dropped jaw.

"You took my purse?"

"Which I put in my safe. Carmen and Juan are probably trustworthy, but why take chances?"

He looks completely serious, and I press my lips together as I formulate my next question. "Is that how you knew about my credit card accounts?"

Marcus sighs and sets down his drink. "Emily, when I decided to marry you, of course I had you investigated. It's fine. A few blemishes on your credit report won't cause much concern. You're young, fresh out of school. It's to be expected. In fact, we'll spin that to the press."

"The press?"

"I told you they'd be looking into you. I simply control the narrative so I can be ahead of the story." He waves a hand. "Really, aside from your mother, you have no skeletons in your closet, but we can handle that too. You broke free of that abusive relationship and made it on your own. The public will love that story."

I bite my lip hard. He sounds so breezy and calm, like all of this should make sense, but it doesn't. I may have never had a serious relationship, but I'm sure they don't look like this. Or do they when you fall into a relationship with a British billionaire? I shake my head. "Marcus," I start off cautiously, "you realize taking my things without telling me is wrong. Right?"

His eyes cool a degree. "What are you doing right now?"

I'm not sure, but it keeps bubbling out. "You hit me."

"When?"

"On my balcony."

He barely suppresses an eye roll. "I spanked you. You enjoyed it the night before. That's kink, not abuse."

Oh my God. "You never proposed to me, and you left me here against my will." I hiss out those last words.

Marcus slams his hand down on the table. "No. I explained to you why I chose to leave you here. That was to protect you, and I can offer you more as my wife than I could as my girlfriend. What did you think we'd do? Live together without a commitment?"

"Umm."

"And shit like that. I can't set you loose in my world when you can't even articulate a full sentence."

I can't explain why, at this point, I let words like that make me feel less. I shake my head. "Maybe I'm not the right person for you."

He sighs. "Emily, you're perfect. I understand you're young and inexperienced. I can forgive these accusations. You asked me for a promise, for forever, you told me this is what you wanted. Why can't you see everything I've done has been for you, for us?"

Carmen arrives to serve us. She glances at my ring. "Congratulations, Ms. Hanson."

I simply stare back at her, and she offers Marcus a small smile. "Did you need anything else?"

"No, Carmen. Thank you."

He glances at me. "Eat. I have a surprise for you after dinner."

The fight inside me wanes and I pick up my fork, reminding myself to survive. There's nothing I could say that he won't talk circles around.

As soon as I lay my napkin on the table, Marcus stands, holding out his hand. "This is a new beginning for us, Emily." He leads me inside the house and up the stairs.

I pause by my door. "I should check on Bella."

He tugs me to keep moving. "She's a cat. She's fine."

I give up and follow him to his bedroom. Marcus takes me straight to the closet, opens the door, and waves a hand. "What do you think?"

All of his things are on one side of the massive closet and mine take up the other. When I fail to answer, he goes to my dresses, running a hand over them. "Here it is." He selects one, a silky white full-length gown. "Your wedding dress." He holds it out to me. "Do you like it?"

I know better than to give the wrong answer. "It's beautiful."

"You're beautiful." He leans in to give me a kiss, and I clutch the dress to my chest as he deepens it. I pull away.

He raises a brow. "What's wrong?"

*Don't make him angry.* "My ankle still hurts."

Marcus drops his eyes to my injured leg and nods. "I'm aware of that."

"I think it's bad luck to sleep together the night before the wedding," I add.

"And I think you make your own luck." He takes the dress from me and hangs it back up. "Emily, I considered your ankle." Marcus steps closer, reaching around to unzip my dress. "So I thought we'd try something new."

"What?"

He slides the straps off my shoulders and the dress puddles around my feet. Removing my bra, he steps back and looks at me with heated eyes. "I want to feel these"—he touches my lips—"on my cock."

A small gasp escapes me and I step back. "I've never..."

"I assumed." With his hands on my shoulders, he steps me back farther until I hit the padded bench at the foot of his bed. "I believe you enjoyed it when I kissed you here." He brushes a finger between my legs. "Making love is a game of improvisations. You can pleasure me in more than one way too." He presses me down with his hands until my butt hits the bench. "Give back, Emily. I'll teach you what I like."

He continues to watch me as he removes his shirt, followed by his belt and his pants. Oh, God. This is happening. I close my eyes and briefly recall there was a time not long ago that I wanted to try this with him. Now the thought repulses me.

His palms cup each side of my head. "Open your eyes, Emily."

Yep. The boxer briefs are gone too, and I stare at the erection in front of my face. I'm pinned between a rock and a hard cock. I'm certain that no is the wrong answer.

He tips my head back. "Look at me."

The tone of his command sends a shudder through me, and I slowly lift my gaze to meet his. His eyes still hold heat, but there's a glint of something animalistic that frightens me.

He nudges my knee with his leg. "Spread them."

I hesitate and he shakes his head. "Emily," he purrs. "I'm not marrying a woman who's reluctant to please me."

My pulse skitters. No marriage means no New York and equals zero hope for freedom. I know I can survive a blow job, and I spread my legs for him.

He steps closer, fisting his length, and he pumps it slowly in front of me. Something unwelcome stirs inside me. The memory of the first time I watched him touch himself. I was mesmerized by his body, his good looks, and my foolish belief that he cared.

Marcus massages my head gently with his other hand. "Are you ready?"

His rich voice rolls over me, seeping into my insides, and my brain shuts down. I can do this.

"Just open your mouth."

My eyes shoot up to his, and he nods as my lips part. "Wider." He slips the tip into my mouth, urging me to take more. "That's good, Emily. Like that. Give me your hand."

I raise up my hand and he fists it around the base of his cock. "Squeeze, like this." He guides me to grip him harder with his hand over mine, then to give him little pumps as he urges my lips to my fingers. With a hand on the back of my head, he encourages me to bob, gently giving me a rhythm. "That's so pretty, baby. Use your tongue, suck me like a stick of candy."

I wouldn't say it tastes sweet, but clean, with a scent of his soap and an undercurrent of musk. He lets go of my hand and allows me to figure it out.

"I need more, love. Suck."

He cups my head and presses in deeper, and I gag as he hits the back of my tongue. He groans his approval and does it again. I fist him tighter, more to hold him at bay, but it seems to encourage him. "That's it. Swallow me down." And like a command, I swallow the saliva building in my mouth. Marcus holds my head steady and starts to pump harder. I give up, holding his cock in one hand, grabbing his leg with the other. I choke and sputter when he hits my throat. My eyes water, drool coats my chin, and my jaw starts to ache. I look up at him, and his eyes are nearly glowing as he watches me take him.

His head tips back. A low growl leaves him and a salty flavor coats my tongue. He holds me down on him while he jerks in my mouth, and I close my eyes. When he finally pulls out, he puts a finger to my chin, closing my mouth. "Swallow it."

I obey, swallowing down the thick, viscous texture, and he smiles, eyes glittering with approval.

"Lovely," he purrs. "Do you know what good girls get?"

He holds out his hands for me and helps me stand. In a swift movement, he lifts me onto the bed. In another blur, my panties are gone and my legs spread. Marcus runs his nose through my pubic hair. "Rewarded," he whispers against my thigh, followed by a lick of his tongue. Uncontrollable pleasure floods my belly and I squeeze my eyes closed, not wanting to feel anything yet feeling everything as he flicks my clit. Marcus took his time, learning me, how to please me, and my body hasn't forgotten. My breasts are suddenly heavy, my nipples alert and needy, and I cup them both. He growls against my flesh and starts with slow circles, avoiding my clit but building anticipation. I'm so close when he sucks me between his lips and begins to tap me rhythmically with the tip of his tongue, right where I need him. I press into his mouth, silently begging for more pressure.

He holds my hips down and continues the torture until my thighs are trembling around his ears. When he sucks me in again, my orgasm rips through me almost painfully. I tremble and grasp my breast harder as a cry leaves my throat. Marcus holds me in it, through every aftershock, making me twitch and moan beneath him.

He finally lifts his head, and I look down to meet his eyes. Wiping his lips with his fingers, he grins. "Delicious."

I'm not capable of words as he climbs on the bed, still catching my breath. Marcus pulls me into his arms and kisses my head. "I missed you, Emily."

He cuddles me with my back to his chest. One tear leaks out of my eye. How did I respond like that? "I missed you too."

---

I WAKE to the sound of moaning and glance at the clock. It's 4:00 a.m. and I'm alone in bed. "Marcus?"

Something shatters, followed by a thud, and it's coming from the bathroom. I roll to my side and see the light on under the door. "Marcus?" I call for him again. Slowly, I climb out of bed and approach the bathroom. I give the door a tentative knock. "Marcus?"

He still fails to answer, and I try the knob, finding it unlocked. As I crack it open, I find him naked on his knees, his head against a cabinet and pills scattered on the floor around him. "Marcus!"

The pain in my ankle is forgotten as I rush over to him. I crouch down and place my hand on his shoulder. "What happened?"

He lifts his head, and my heart stutters at the pain in his eyes. "Get out," he growls.

I shake my head. "Let me help you."

Marcus closes his eyes and clenches his jaw, pulling in a sharp breath through his nostrils. "Need two. Two pills."

Eyeing the mess on the floor, I spot the shattered glass and spilled water. "Did you fall?"

"Two," he grits out.

I'm spurred into action and pluck two pills off the floor. He opens his mouth.

"You need water."

He shakes his head, and I can see the agony he's in, so I stick both pills through his lips. His throat works to swallow them dry, then he lets go of the counter, falling back on the floor and holding his head.

I have no idea what is happening or how to help him. I pick up the pill bottle, but I don't know the name of whatever he's taking. "Marcus, I don't know how to help you. Should I get Lucas?"

"Give. Me. A. Minute."

It's more than a minute that I sit on the floor with him

while he remains on his back. He rips at his hair and tries to suppress moans through tightly pressed lips.

I rub his leg, knowing I'm not really helping, but letting him know I'm here. The ring on my finger catches my eyes, and I look back at his face. I absolutely do not want to marry this man, but it hurts to see him in this much pain. "Marcus, I think we need to get you to a doctor."

His eyes open and focus on me, so bright blue against the red rims. He drops his hands. "No. The pills are helping."

"What are they?"

"For migraines," he mutters, rolling to his side.

I've never had one, but I've heard they can be awful, crippling even. Marcus pushes himself up, his muscled arms shaky, and I reach to help him.

"Stop, Emily. I can do this."

I'm not sure I'd be any help anyway. I stay on the floor as he gets his legs under him before reaching for my hand. Certain that would find us both back on the floor, I gingerly put some weight on my foot and I'm able to get myself up as well. Wrapping my arm around his, we support each other as he staggers and I limp back to the bedroom.

Marcus falls heavily into bed, and I gently cover him up. He pats the side next to him, and I go around to join him. "Maybe we should postpone the wedding," I whisper.

"No. I'll be fine in an hour or so." He rolls his head to look at me. "I forgot to take them before bed. I was distracted."

"Maybe I should go clean up the floor."

"No." He lays his hand on mine. "Stay with me."

I settle against my pillow and stare at the dark ceiling. A fan pushes the air coming in through the open windows with a steady whir. I focus on it while he holds me until his breathing evens out, his body relaxed, and I'm sure he's back to sleep.

How is it possible to feel compassion for someone who has ruined me? Hot tears leak out of my eyes for me as so many emotions are warring in my body. Somewhere along the line, I've lost myself. I'm going crazy.

# 31

## MARCUS

I wake to an empty bed, which pisses me off, but then I see it's already nine o'clock. With a sigh, I rub my head. It's better, just a dull, steady throb compared to the paralyzing pain I'd felt earlier. Seriously, I believe I blacked out for a second.

That has me thinking about Emily, her concern, and how she cared for me. That feeling in my chest stirs again. She is the perfect woman. I set the boundaries for her, and now I believe she would have thrived within them.

Realizing I'm wasting daylight, I climb out of bed to get this day started. The bathroom floor is clean, the broken glass in the wastebasket, and I'd bet that it wasn't Carmen who took care of this. It makes me smile.

After a shower and a shave, I dress and leave to find my bride. I pause by her old bedroom and knock on the door before opening it. She wasn't a hard find, sitting on the bed with her cat.

"Have you had breakfast?"

Emily shakes her head. Why does she look sad? Because of last night?

"Come. Carmen is probably confused by our absence. Let's get something to eat."

She unravels herself from the cat and joins me.

"I was thinking of a sunset ceremony," I tell her as we go downstairs. She seems steadier on her bad ankle this morning.

"That's fine," she mutters.

"You don't sound fine with it."

She sighs. "It doesn't matter. Whatever you want."

Carmen bustles out of the kitchen. "Mr. Sterling?"

"It's my fault, Carmen. Could you just throw something together for us? We'll eat outside," I add as I glance at the pool deck.

"Of course." She disappears again and I lead Emily outdoors.

I pull out a chair for her and glance at her wrapped ankle. I shudder to think what could have happened to her. "I have a couple things to get on today. Rest your leg after breakfast, and then we'll start preparing."

"Ok—all right."

Nice fix. "I do apologize that we aren't having a proper wedding."

Emily nods slowly and gives the ocean a wistful look.

I sigh. "Are you upset about that?"

"No." She faces me. "It's fine. How are you feeling this morning?"

It was a nightmare to have her see me like that. "Much better, thank you."

She studies me carefully. "Do you get those migraines often?"

"More often lately." I need to decide if I'm going to explain that to her.

Carmen returns with our breakfast and Emily selects a muffin. Her hair is down today and flutters back with the breeze. It's lightened some with her time in the sun, and her skin has picked up some color too.

She's quiet as we work through our meal. When she finally drains the rest of her tea, I ask her if she's finished.

Emily peeks up at me with those eyes, more green than gold this morning. I love how the color changes with her moods. "Yes." She places her napkin by her plate.

"Good. Let me help you upstairs." I offer my hand. "I have a few things I need to work on this morning."

"Is it all right if I spend some time with Bella?"

"That's fine. It'll be a couple of hours. We can have lunch together at two, then we'll get ready." I can't suppress my grin. "I have an idea. I'll surprise you."

Why did that comment make her look like she wants to cry? I tweak her chin. "Smile for me."

Emily obeys, pressing out a small smile, and I drop a kiss on her lips. My steps should feel lighter as I head back down the stairs. Emily has behaved beautifully since I've been home, but how she did while I was away, that's still a mystery I need to solve.

---

IN MY STUDY, I spend an hour on the phone with my lawyer, making the necessary changes to my will. Originally, I had left everything to Heath. I owe him so much. Now, I've only left him with the business, but I added that if in the event Emily and I perish at the same time, everything will revert back and go to him. In the aftermath of our accidental death, it would look wrong that Emily wasn't my beneficiary.

It's a decision I came to terms with last night. After our honeymoon, Emily and I will visit London. I'll show her my childhood home while I put things in order there. After that, I'm not sure. Perhaps I should return to New York or maybe we'll come back here. It will depend on how I'm feeling by that point.

I call in my staff and go over my plans for the day. They've all received instructions before now, and they assure me everything is being taken care of. As I dismiss Carmen and Juan, I glance at Lucas. "Could you stay, please."

His expression doesn't change as he sits back down and waits for them to leave. When the door closes behind them, I give him a tight-lipped smile. "I would like you to officiate the ceremony."

He blinks and looks away. "I'm not ordained."

"No, you are. I took care of it for you. It was between you and Juan." I chuckle at the thought. "You were the obvious choice."

His nostrils flare on an inhale as he looks back at me. "Fine. Was there anything else, sir?"

"Yes. Emily and I will not be returning to New York. I'm planning to take her on a honeymoon and your presence isn't required there."

The skin around his eyes tightens slightly, and for a moment, we stay in a little stare-off. It's not that Lucas has ever been warm toward me, but I feel lately he's been breaking some protocols around courtesy. Has he forgotten that I own him?

I lean back in my chair. "Let's go over what happened the night Emily was injured."

Lucas folds his hands together and looks down. "I told you. She went for a walk. It started raining, so I went searching for her." He glances back at me. "It's a good thing I did. Where she went off the trail was a dangerous spot."

"Hmm." Why do I still smell like something is missing from this story? "I'm grateful to you for helping her."

He holds my gaze. "I knew what you'd do if I let anything happen to your fiancée."

"Yes, that's true. You'd be dead." The problem with Lucas is we are in somewhat of a stalemate. While I could destroy him, he could make my life uncomfortable too. This is the first time I feel like he's not being honest with me. His story around the cameras, Emily slipping off a perfectly flat trail, and the way she pales whenever he's in the room. Something happened between these two while I was away, and somehow, I get the sense he's hiding something.

"Lucas, why don't you pour me a glass of scotch. Feel free to have one yourself. We'll celebrate my wedding day."

He glances at my liquor cabinet before standing to fulfill my request. Lucas is a proud bloke and I know it irritates him to be given meaningless tasks. He doesn't question my order as he pours and hands a glass off to me.

I raise it up. "To me finding the perfect woman."

He sits back down across from me and takes a sip, but his jaw is tight and his eyes are cold. I taste the scotch and regard the amber liquid as I swallow. "Emily is a pretty girl. Not movie-star beautiful, but there's a sweet innocence about her that attracts me. So honest. She couldn't lie if she tried."

I question the twitch in his right eye, but my printer goes off, receiving the fax from my lawyer. I reach back to remove the paper. "I made changes to my will today. I need you to sign as my witness." I hand him the paper.

He takes it from me, reading it before looking back up. "You're leaving her everything?"

"Who else would I leave my wealth to? If anything happens to me, I'll know Emily is taken care of for life." I set down my glass, keeping my hands wrapped around it. "Don't worry. There's still a provision for you and Carmen as long as you stick to the non-disclosure agreement.

"I don't recall you changing your will when you married Karyn," Lucas remarks.

I raise a brow. That isn't his business. "At the time, I wasn't concerned about dying."

He eyes me for a beat before picking up the pen and signing the document. "Was there anything else, sir?"

"No." I force a smile as I take the papers from him. "Go help Juan with the preparations."

Lucas steps out, and I make a quick call to Heath and let him know I'll be there to meet him on Wednesday. "We'll burn the midnight oil like we used to in the old days."

"You don't have to come over with Lucas," Heath assures me.

"No. I have something to take care of there anyway." I want to get my marriage license filed as soon as possible.

I check my watch as we hang up and head out to find Carmen. As expected, she's preparing lunch in the kitchen. "We're having a casual day. Could you serve that on the balcony of my suite?"

She glances at me. "Because you don't want Ms. Hanson to see the preparations outside?"

"No." Outside, Lucas and Juan are preparing the deck. "I'd like it to be a surprise." I turn to leave but grab the door-jamb and stop, looking back at Carmen. "Tell me what really happened the night Emily was injured."

She looks instantly guilty. "I don't know. She went for a walk after dinner. It started to rain right after she left. I'm not sure why she continued."

"Hmm. So you told Lucas she was missing and he went looking for her?"

She starts to wring her hands. "He was working on the security system in the shed. Maybe he saw her pass him."

"Maybe." The door to the shed would have to be open if that happened. "Carmen, if something happened between Emily and Lucas, you'd tell me, right?"

Her frown deepens and she shifts on her feet. "I didn't see anything happen."

My jaw clenches. They're all keeping something from me. "If you do, you let me know."

I leave her, and the questions are growing as I jog up the stairs. With a rap of my knuckles on her door, I push it open but don't see her right away. I find her with the cat sitting out on her balcony.

Emily turns to look at me and sets down her book. "Is it already two?"

"It's a little past two."

She swallows, swinging her legs off the lounge. "I'm sorry. I wasn't watching the time."

"Don't be sorry." I give her a gentle reminder. "We have a change in plans anyway. We're dining in our suite."

"Oh." She scoops up that cat and brings it inside. "Why?"

"I just wanted time alone with you. Come."

She places the cat down on the bed and limps toward me. I give her my arm and help her back to our room, leaving the door open so Carmen can come in. I lead Emily to the balcony, and she steps out and looks around. Traversing the entire side of my suite, it has incredible ocean views, plus a little slice of island. She hobbles to the railing. "I've never been out here before."

I wave my hand at the small table, perfect for two. "We'll eat here." Even though it's afternoon, my balcony is covered and, between the shade and the breeze, it's quite comfortable.

Carmen arrives with a large platter and Juan follows her with a tray holding champagne and orange juice. Emily is quiet while we're served, watching Carmen prepare the mimosas.

I wait until I hear the door close behind them and pick up my flute. "Cheers."

Emily obediently taps her glass to mine and takes a sip. Then two. I thought the alcohol might help calm her nerves.

"So what's the surprise?" she asks.

"Finish your lunch first." I nod at her plate.

She cuts into the fish Carmen prepared and tastes it.

"Good?" I ask her and she nods.

I relax a little and start on my meal. Emily asks how my headache is. I give her a long look, still unwilling to talk about my diagnosis. "It's better." I pour us both more champagne, topping it off with a dollop of orange juice. "I do want to thank you for trying to help me this morning. I'm sure finding me like that was shocking."

She presses her lips together and nods. "It looked very painful."

I huff out a laugh. It's the worst pain I've ever experienced. "It was."

"I worked with a girl who had migraines and she used acupuncture to help."

"Hmm." If only that were the treatment plan I'd be facing. "I'll look into that."

I'm getting antsy by the time Emily finishes her drink, but I hold up the bottle and ask if she wants more.

She licks her lips and shakes her head. "No."

I set it back down and stand to pull out her chair. I'm excited to get on with this day. Emily is going to be beautiful, relaxed, and compliant.

"What are we doing now?"

"Your surprise." I take her hand and lead her back to the bedroom. Her little gimp falters, and I slip an arm around her to get her over the threshold. "Wait here." I point at the bed and she stares at it with wide eyes. I don't linger on her expression. I know the girl loves having sex with me, but that's not my intention this afternoon.

In the bathroom, I start to fill the tub. I find the bubble bath and other fragrances Carmen had purchased for her and add those. She also left me a bowl of petals from one of the flowering plants. It's not rose petals, but they are pink and smell good. I toss those into the frothy water and go back to my bride.

She's sitting nervously on the edge of the bed, and I offer her a hand. "Come. It's ready."

In the bathroom, she looks sufficiently surprised. "Marcus?"

"Here." I urge her to sit on the lip of the tub. I kneel in front of her and start to remove the ACE bandage on her ankle. Running a finger over the swollen, bruised flesh, I shake my head. "You rolled it pretty good." I begin to un-bandage her wrist, and if I was surprised by the state of her ankle, I'm seriously taken aback by this. "Emily?" The rope burns are angry, and her skin is raw. She pulls her hand away, and I regard the rest of her more minor injuries. Some scrapes and scratches on her legs, what looks like rug burn on her elbow. "I'm still trying to picture exactly how you slipped off the trail. Were you not looking where you were going?"

"No. I mean, I don't know."

"Hmm." I pull Emily up to stand. "How did Lucas know where you were?"

"I-I'm not sure."

And the lies start. I will get to the bottom of this—later.

Her skin pebbles with goose bumps as I start to undress her. She looks everywhere but at me.

"Emily, what's wrong? I just wanted to spoil you a little." She allows me to help her into the tub, covering her breasts with her arms. I pull off my shirt, and she's sitting stiff as a board in the water. Picking up the loofa, I wet it and sponge her chest. "Lie back. Relax. I realize this is another new first for you. I wanted to do something special for you today."

She blinks, averting her gaze and color flooding her cheeks. I know I'm not giving her the wedding she deserves. I simply want to pamper her a little.

"What do you think of the flower petals?"

"They're nice," she admits, sinking lower into the water.

"Hmm." I sniff her neck. "They smell nice too. Like you."

She still doesn't say anything but closes her eyes and relaxes back as I start to wash her. I'm careful around her sore spots and admire her breasts that bob in the bubbles. "Do you take bubble baths often?" I ask, sliding the loofa up her inner thigh.

"No," she breathes.

She doesn't flinch when I wash between her legs, and

forgoing the loofa, I hand-wash her here. Her hips shift at my touch, but not in a bad way. Emily likes her orgasms, but she won't get one now. It should be a slow burn to the wedding night.

Sliding my hand up her belly, I play with each breast, toying with her pink nipples until they're ripe and ready, then stop.

I smile at the little frown that forms, and she opens her eyes.

"Let's do your hair."

I urge her to sit up and use the spray nozzle to wet her hair before grabbing the shampoo. It has an island-like scent, and I inhale deeply as I lather her hair. With her head tipped back, she looks like she's enjoying the gentle massage I give her scalp. "Does that feel good?"

"Hmm," she replies, and that's a good enough answer for me. I give her a good rinse before adding the conditioner. I've done this a time or two before and I know that has to sit a minute. Piling her wet hair on top of her head, I run my fingers over her exposed neck, her shoulder, and the soft skin of her back. "So beautiful," I murmur. And all mine.

I spend the next minute massaging out the tension from her. She remains quiet, but I know she's enjoying the attention. After I rinse her again, I sweep her hair over her shoulder and turn her face to steal a kiss. "Lie back and relax. I'm going to take a shower."

Taking one more look at her as I stand, I see her eyes are closed, her forehead is smooth, and her lips relaxed. Mission accomplished.

I don't waste time, taking a quick rinse, afraid her water will cool and she'll get chilled. I'm fast to dry off and tuck the towel around my waist before going back to her. "Emily? Let's get you out now."

Her lashes flutter as she opens her eyes and slowly sits up.

I'm careful getting her out of the tub and linger while I dry off her body. "Sit, let me wrap your ankle."

With her towel wrapped around her, she perches on the edge of the tub and watches as I tend to her. I add some ointment before rebandaging her wrist. I look up at her, loving the curiosity mixed with a touch of confusion in her eyes. I miss how she looked at me before—with trust. I want to get us back there. "Let me get your robe."

Together, we get the robe on her, and she looks up at me with shiny eyes. I'm lost in the greens, the gold flecks, and take advantage of her soft lips and kiss her again, a little longer, a little deeper, with a lot less resistance from her.

# 32

---

# EMILY

Marcus wraps his arms around me, deepening our kiss, and my brain is liquefied. I don't know which way is up or down anymore. What's wrong or right. I'm frozen somewhere between fear and confusion.

He pulls away, looking down at me with hunger darkening his eyes, and his lips tip up. "Come. We still have work to do."

He leads me to the vanity and urges me to sit on the bench, digs through drawers, and finds a hairbrush. He starts working it through my hair and I'm speechless. I feel like I should stop him, tell him I can do this, but I don't. I stay quiet when he pulls out the hairdryer, turns it on, and I lean into the warm air as he dries my hair.

Our eyes meet in the mirror when he sets the tools aside, and his lips twitch. "You know, I understand why you told Lucas you were afraid and why you would ask him for help."

The fear creeps back in. Lucas told him all of that?

"I... I didn't."

"Be honest. I told you I understand. I thought when I

brought your cat here, you knew I had your best interest at heart. Now I realize what you were really thinking. That you were abused and trapped." He shakes his head. "Now that you know the truth, what I need to know is if he took advantage of you when you were in such a fragile state."

My eyes flick back to his, my pulse skyrocketing. "No."

Marcus crouches down behind me and rests his chin on my shoulder. "Good. I can forgive you for this." He reaches around and fingers my ring. "Everything changes for us now. Don't disappoint me."

My breath comes short with my heart pounding and I try to read his eyes. What did Lucas tell him? "I won't."

He kisses my cheek and stands with his hands on my shoulder. "If I could have, I would have hired you a team to pamper you today, do your hair and makeup. Make you feel beautiful."

He's giving me whiplash and I'm unable to form words.

"To me, you're beautiful without the fancy hair or makeup." He brings a couple of locks over my shoulder to frame my face. "You're perfect just the way you are. Leave your hair down." He strokes my cheek. "And go light on the makeup."

Still afraid to speak, I simply nod.

He drops a kiss on my head. "Go, try on your dress. I'm going to shave and get ready."

I wait for him to leave before I stand on shaky legs and duck in the closet. Closing the door, I lean against it and try to calm myself. I can't make head or tail of Marcus, but one thing's for sure. I can't trust Lucas. Why would he say anything? Maybe he was lying about helping me, and in some sense, that's a relief. I knew last night, when I sat with Marcus in the bathroom, that I couldn't be a part of hurting anyone. I fill my lungs with a deep breath. What I need to do now is get home, and to do that, I need to behave.

I take the gown off the hanger and caress the silky fabric. It feels light as air and flows through my fingers like water. It fits perfectly, and I step out to regard myself in the full-length mirror. The dress accents my curves without feeling tight. One slit up the side gives me room to move, and I turn to admire the back. The white color accents my bronze skin, and I shake my head. If this were a fairy tale, the dress would be something I'd choose. Simple, classic, beautiful.

I jump when Marcus steps up behind me. "Ah. My bare-foot bride." He grins at me in the mirror, still in a towel, and gives me an appraising look. "You look lovely."

I turn to look up at him, and he brushes my cheek with the back of his fingers. "Go on. Finish up in the bathroom. I'll meet you in the sitting room."

He passes me and starts going through his clothes in the closet. I stare at his wide shoulders and muscled back. The towel is low on his narrow hips, and I wonder how God made such a flawless body with such a scary mind. I shake off the thought and slip back into the bathroom. As I add a touch of mascara, Marcus's words reverberate in my head. Did I misunderstand everything? He kept me here to protect me? Was it kink? He did bring Bella to me. Was everything Lucas said to me a lie? Letting me believe he killed Karyn? I'm so confused, and in some ways, I want to be wrong and for this to be right.

I regard my reflection with my hair down, the humidity enhancing my natural waves. My eyes seem brighter with the color my face has picked up from the sun. I don't look abused, other than the evidence of my self-abuse from trying to run away. Maybe I am going crazy.

Marcus is having a drink when I find him in the other room. He sets down the glass and offers me his arm. "It's almost time. I have another surprise for you."

I link my arm with his. The fabric of his suit is almost as soft as my dress. He looks incredibly handsome, his dark hair combed back, his face clean-shaven, and his blue eyes hold no malice as he gazes down at me. Together, we leave the room and head for the stairs. I try to walk without a limp, and he shortens his stride to accommodate me.

My nerves amp up as we approach the doors to the pool deck. I give Marcus a nervous glance and he smiles. "Relax. I took care of everything."

We step outside and the first colors of the sunset are lighting the sky. It's pretty, but not what I'm focused on. Somehow Marcus has turned the deck into a garden. There are so many flowering pots, and a trellis dressed in green vines with little white blooms mingled in. Ribbons form an aisle and while Carmen and Juan stand to the side, Lucas appears to be waiting for me at the end, wearing a suit. His pale blue eyes bore into me, a stern expression on his face. I glare back at him, knowing what I do now.

Marcus squeezes my arm. "Do you like it?"

I'm stunned. "When did you do all of this?"

"I started making the arrangements after I released the press statement that we were engaged last week."

My mouth falls open. Press statement? I glance back at Lucas. "There isn't a pastor, or..."

"Lucas has agreed to officiate our wedding."

"Lucas?" I look between the two of them. "Can he do that?"

"He can and he's happy to." Marcus squeezes my arm and nods at Carmen, who starts the music with the remote in her hand. It's not a wedding march but some piano music that reminds me of the calm before the storm.

My heart starts to race, and my confusion only gets worse as I hold on to Marcus. His stride is relaxed but confident, and his familiar scent wraps around me in an almost comforting way.

Lucas watches us approach, his face expressionless, and I'm questioning everything.

We stop and Marcus turns to face me. I look into his bright blue eyes. His gaze roams over my face and a small smile tips his lips.

The music stops and Lucas clears his throat. "We are gathered here today to witness and celebrate the marriage of Emily Hanson to Marcus Sterling."

My stomach drops and the blood rushing in my ears drowns out most of his words as he leads us through the vows. Everything seems blurred, but I snap back to focus as Marcus smiles at me, with sincerity in his eyes, as he promises to love me. A word he's never said. To cherish me in sickness or in health, till death do us part.

A shiver runs down my spine as he removes the ruby ring and slips the wedding band on before replacing it.

My voice quivers as I repeat my vows, promising to love and obey. I glance at Lucas, and he gives me a little nod as he prompts me to say, "Till death do us part."

Oh, God. I swallow hard and repeat the line. Such simple, traditional vows have never sounded so ominous.

I'm handed a ring. It's black, not gold, with an intricate design of intertwined circles carved into it. I slide it on Marcus's finger with a shaky hand. He covers mine with his, and I hear Lucas announce he can kiss his bride. I feel naked and exposed as Marcus kisses me in front of everyone.

My emotions whirl inside me as Marcus breaks the kiss, and Carmen and Juan politely clap. I turn to see Juan snapping photos with his phone. Marcus squeezes my hand. "Smile for me."

---

THE SUN HAS SET and it's dark as we finish dinner. Our table is cleared and Marcus flips through the photos Juan took of the ceremony. I stare off into the distance, reconciling this new reality.

Marcus touches my hand. "Later, after we're back in the city, we'll plan a huge reception party."

I glance back at him. He's removed the jacket and tie, his sleeves rolled up, exposing his forearms, and I hate how handsome he looks. "All right."

"That night, I'll get you that team of people and make you feel so pampered."

I blink and look away again. For me, as weddings go, today would have been perfect if it weren't for the man I married. "When do we leave for New York?"

"After the honeymoon."

"Honeymoon?" I glance back at him. I open my mouth to ask where, but his phone rings.

He checks the screen. "Christ. I'm sorry. I need to take this."

I'm surprised when he leaves the table and goes inside to answer the phone. Picking up my glass, I take another sip of wine, and I'm startled when Lucas crouches down by my chair.

Carefully setting down my glass, I turn to him, anger bubbling inside me. He betrayed me. "What?"

His eyes narrow on mine. "Why would you tell him anything?"

"What? I—"

"Now he's suspicious. You've ruined everything."

"No." I start to shake my head. "You're the one—"

"Lucas?" Marcus's deep voice startles both of us.

Lucas stands and clears his throat. "I was congratulating the bride."

His eyes go from Lucas to me. "Really?"

"Yes. Congratulations to both of you. Was there anything else you needed tonight, sir?"

"No." Marcus keeps his eyes on my face. Lucas places his hands behind his back, and I don't miss his middle finger lifting as he walks away. I pull in a shaky breath and focus on Marcus. "Honestly, all he said was congratulations."

"Really? Why do you look shaken?" he asks.

I touch my fingers to my cheek. "I don't know."

"Are you afraid of him, Emily?"

"No." I don't know. "He didn't hurt me. All he did was help treat my injuries and bring me a couple of meals."

"Meals?" Marcus lifts a brow.

"He was just checking on me."

"Ah. Did you two have conversations when he brought you those meals?"

I lick my lips nervously. "Not really." My insides are trembling and I feel like a witness lying on the stand. "Nothing happened, Marcus."

"All right." He stands and reaches for my hand. "Let's take this celebration somewhere more private."

I'm shaky as I take his hand. He leads me through the house and up the stairs. I pause at my door. "I-I forgot to feed my cat."

"I'll ask Carmen to do that for you." He tugs me past it. We enter his sitting room and he leads me to the sofa. "Here, sit."

I lower myself and he goes to the sideboard where a fresh bottle of champagne waits on ice.

I stay quiet as he pops the cork. He hands me a full flute and sits next to me, lifting his glass to tap against mine.

"To new beginnings."

I dutifully drink to his toast. He sips as well and sets his flute on the sofa table.

"Um... where are we going on a honeymoon?"

He licks his lips. His eyes focus on mine. "*Um*. I thought we could take *The Temptress* around the islands for a week, maybe two."

My cheeks warm at his subtle reprimand. "I'm sorry." *Shit!* "I apologize."

His lips twitch up. "Emily, it doesn't matter anymore. Just be yourself. That's who I fell in love with."

"You never said you loved me," I whisper.

He's quiet for a beat, then shakes his head. "Why would I do everything I have if I didn't love you?" He takes my glass from my hand and sets it down before shifting to face me. "I didn't ask you for the words because I knew how you felt. The words don't matter. It's the actions that count."

My mouth hangs open, and I close it before I say something stupid. I don't love him, but he confuses me. "Marcus—"

He puts a finger to my lips. "Wait. There's something I need to tell you." He drops his hand. "I believe honesty is important in a marriage. Do you agree?"

"Yes." I would, but somehow, I'm afraid of the direction this conversation is going.

"Good. This isn't easy for me." He pauses and runs his fingers through his hair, messing it a little. "Last week, I saw a doctor about my headaches." He looks back at me, licks his lips and forms a sad smile. "I was diagnosed with a brain tumor. Basically, I'm dying."

My eyes roam over him, and I'm thinking that isn't possible. He looks so strong, so handsome, but my mind leaps back to him on the bathroom floor, writhing in pain. "Marcus?"

"It's all right. It's not like I'm dying today. It's just that I've decided not to have treatment."

My heart constricts. "Why?"

He leans back, pulling me with him so his head is on the armrest and I'm on his chest. He wraps his arms around me and holds me tight. "It's not operable. I don't know if it's benign or not, but the only way to find out is to drill a hole in my head. Worse than that, they want to cut my head open and try to remove some of it, which would only buy me more time. The treatments alone could kill me before the tumor will."

"No." I try to shift in his arms.

He holds me tighter. "I don't need your opinion, only your understanding. I do apologize. I know you wanted to wait for the wedding, but that's why I rushed everything. With the time I have left, I wanted it to be with you."

I push on his chest, and this time he loosens his hold. His eyes are bright but sincere, and my heart is breaking. Was I wrong about everything? "Marcus, those treatments could save you. I'd be with you all the way. You must at least try—"

"Shh," he hushes me. "It's my life. My decision. And you will be with me to the end. That's the only thing that makes any of this bearable."

Tears sting my eyes, and he cups my cheek. "Don't. Today I feel good, and this is a horrible conversation for our wedding night." He tips his head to the side. "I just couldn't live with this secret. I needed you to know."

My lips part because I want to argue for him to do something to save himself, but he lifts his head and kisses me. His arm holds me tight and his fingers thread through my hair, holding me to him, and I don't fight it. His confession only complicates things for me more.

He breaks the kiss, palming my face and running his thumb over my bottom lip. "Don't be sad, Emily. Be mine. Tonight and for however many more days we have." He shifts me off him and gets to his feet, pulling me up. "Come. We skipped a tradition."

# 33

---

## MARCUS

Emily is still looking at me with watery eyes. I shake my head and scoop her up, bridal style. She squeaks and I grin as I carry her over the threshold to our bedroom. Setting her down, I turn her to our full-length mirror and our eyes meet in the reflection.

Her brow furrows. "What are we doing?"

"Looking at what a beautiful bride you are," I respond, running my hands down her arms. I had my reasons for disclosing my condition to her tonight. If Emily is having any lingering doubts, I know the compassionate side of her will even her out.

She appraises herself in the mirror, and I brush her hair to the side to kiss her neck. "Today, I'm a very lucky man."

With a finger, I tease the dip of this dress in the back and trail my touch down her spine until I get to the zipper. "Seeing you in this dress, it's been driving me crazy." I love the way her toned back causes a little divot where her spine lies, the gentle curve before it reaches her ass. I slowly expose that, and she trembles a little, but I know it's not all fear. Slipping the straps over her shoulders, I admire her swimmer's muscles and the miles of smooth skin. Emily only has one mole, on her right shoulder, and I kiss it before I slide the dress off her body. Her breasts are exposed, and she's wearing a slip of silk underwear.

Taking in the length of her, I ignore the wrapped ankle. At any other time, I would have put her over my knee, spanked the shit out of her, and taught her running from me wasn't an option. Times are different now. She has nowhere to run. We'll never walk down that red carpet together. There's no reason to train her to be perfect, and maybe she is perfect just the way she is.

"You. Are. A. Goddess," I whisper in her ear.

She tries to turn away. I put my hands on her shoulders. "No. Look at yourself."

She blinks, her eyes meeting mine as I slide my hands down to her breasts, cupping them. "Your breasts are perfect. One handful each." I massage them before focusing on her nipples. "These are just like soft, pink rose buds."

I toy with those until they lengthen, tighten, and beg for more. Her lips part with a small sigh and I know she's heating up. I glide down her tummy to the swell of her lower belly. "I love the contours of your stomach. Strong, then soft. It's like your personality. That's something I find attractive too."

"Marcus."

She shifts her weight to her good foot, but I'm far from finished. I slip my hands into her panties. Her pubes tickle my finger, and I adjust to hold her hip with one hand while the other continues to explore. "You smell so good when you're aroused, like wildflowers after the rain." I test my theory, slipping my finger through her folds, and yes, she's not unaffected. Her little gasp confirms that, and I slip a finger inside her. "I love how your cheeks flush when you want me. Look how pretty you are."

I gather the wetness pooling and drag it to her clit. That blush deepens and her eyes brighten. Oh, Emily. Does she have any idea how lovely she is? Her lashes flutter down and with my lips by her ear, I whisper, "Keep your eyes open. Watch me make you come."

I play with her, teasing her clit until it swells, moving between that and driving inside her sweet, wet pussy. Moving my hand from her hip, I hold her with my forearm between her breasts, my hand lying gently under her neck. Her chest rises and falls as her breaths quicken. She keeps trying to close her eyes, fighting to keep them open.

"That's it, love. Watch." I apply more pressure. Her little nub hardens and I gentle my touch, dragging out her pleasure.

"Marcus," she breathes.

"Emily. Tell me what you want."

A strangled noise escapes her throat. It vibrates against my palm. She's so fucking beautiful as I hold her like this. Vulnerable. Mine.

I add some teasing touches, drawing her out further, bringing her to the brink. She twitches against my finger; so close. "Watch," I order as her head tips back and her eyes close. She lifts her eyelids halfway, and I press hard on her needy flesh. Emily shudders in my hold. "Watch yourself come."

A little moan escapes her, but she sees through hooded eyes as she breaks apart for me.

I lighten my touch. Her chest is heaving. Her face, neck, all the way to her breasts flush. A damp layer of sweat amplifies her glow. "See how beautiful you are? That's what I see, Emily."

I rest my chin on her shoulder. "You can't deny you want this—me—us. I know your mind went to dark places, but trust me, all I care about is you."

She blinks and meets my eyes in the mirror. "Marcus, I..."

I grasp her chin, holding her gently. "Stop denying what you feel."

I only give her a few seconds to consider that before I wrap my arms around her, picking her up and taking her to the bed. Setting her down gently, I step back and start on my shirt buttons. "I've missed you. I promise, I'll be gentle."

Her eyes are still hooded, her breath uneven, and I excuse her for not responding as I whip off my shirt. "I need to be inside you, to feel us together." I toe off my shoes as I start on my belt. She stays seated on the bed, watching me undress. I love the way my body entices her, and I drop my pants along with my boxers. My cock has been ready and throbbing, and I grab it as I step closer to her. "Tell me you want this too."

Her eyes dart between my hand and my eyes, and she finally scoots back on the bed. I follow her like a panther stalking its prey. When she's too slow, I grab her legs and adjust her on the mattress. She gasps, but her legs fall open for me.

I climb over her, grasp her head, and kiss her, soft, teasing, pulling her out, sucking her in. Emily starts to greet my lips. Her fingers thread through my hair, and I taste her last sip of champagne on my tongue.

Lifting my head, I search her eyes. "Are you all right? Your ankle?"

She bites her lip and nods. I adjust to line up with her, press in slowly, and I fill her fully. Her head drops back and her eyes close. The animal in me wants to take from her, but the need to show her I care outweighs the repercussions of the beast. I move slowly, grinding my teeth to hold back and watching her face for signs of pain.

When her hands come to my hips, pressing me, asking for more, I relax. Propping on an elbow, I grab one of her breasts, plumping her flesh as my pace picks up. Her eyes open on mine, her pupils taking over the greens and golds.

"Oh, Emily." I groan. "You feel so good." Too good. My stomach clenches as I hold back. Slipping my hand down, I find her spot and tease as I pump harder. She cries out, but I don't believe it's pain. She wants us together as much as I do, and that place in my chest aches again. I drive into her harder, trying to rub her in the same rhythm, but I'm losing focus. "Emily!" I shout. I'm so close, and I need her with me.

She cries out my name, her knees crushing my hips, and my balls draw up. My whole body tenses and my orgasm shoots up my spine, pouring into her.

---

EMILY FACES me as I stroke her hair. Our skin cools and I pull the duvet up over us. Tonight, we consummated our promise. Mine that I will always be with her, and hers that she will never leave me. "Do you remember when you asked me if I'd ever loved before?"

She nods slowly, her eyes growing wary.

My mind wanders to memories of Sara. "I was in love with a woman."

"Karyn?"

"No. I did believe Karyn was the one. You know? I believed it, but I was wrong." Emily doesn't respond to that, so I continue. "When I was in university, I met a girl, Sara. She was brilliant in every way. Sweet, fun, and she found ways to pull me out of my shell. I fell in love with her and asked her to marry me."

Emily's brows draw together. "What happened?"

I tuck a lock of hair behind her ear. "She died."

Emily leans away and that familiar suspicion fills her eyes. "How?"

"She was on holiday with her family in France. Sara was on a boat with her brother when it exploded." It doesn't bring forth the same emotions to say it out loud as it used to. "She was murdered."

"Marcus?"

"I know. You're wondering why every woman I've been with hasn't survived me. You aren't the first." I shift to my back and focus on the ceiling. "Both Elizabeth's and Karyn's deaths were investigated. They were deemed accidental, and I was never a suspect." It pays to have friends in law enforcement around here. I roll my head to look at her. "If anyone was a suspect in Karyn's death, it was Lucas."

If she put any trust into that man while I was away, it's better for her to know who he really is. "The FBI spent a lot of time questioning him. He didn't have an alibi from the time I left her on the beach to the moment I asked him to go check on her."

"Lucas is the one who found Karyn?"

"Yes." I soak in her disbelief. "I don't believe he was involved, but he does have a criminal record."

"What?"

"It's true. I hired him anyway. He had all the qualifications I wanted, and when he was arrested, I hired him a good attorney. The courts charged him but acquitted him for lack of evidence."

She swallows hard and looks away, but not before I see the questions in her eyes.

"Enough about that. I do know who killed Sara."

Emily looks back at me. "Who?"

"My mother." I wait for that information to sink in before I move on. "Not personally. I think she hired someone. She felt the need to control every aspect of my life. I was never free until she died." I glance over at one of the paintings on my wall. A terrified human is in the claws of a winged demon. "It worked out in the end. My mother lived by the sword and died by the sword." I blink and look back at Emily. "She should have followed the scripture she shoved down everyone else's throats."

Emily studies me quietly before she sucks in a shaky breath. "Marcus, I'm so sorry."

"I feel sorrow around Sara's death too, and I know it's not a good topic to discuss lying here, with you, but I want you to know me. I need you to understand why I've gone to such lengths to keep you safe and I want you to trust me again." I wrap an arm around her and pull her close. "Because I love you, Emily."

She relaxes in my arms with her cheek on my chest, but she doesn't give back the words. I kiss the top of her head.

"I was thinking. I know you were upset about your job. How about you help with the foundation? It would be volunteer work, but I think you'd find it rewarding."

Emily lifts her head to look at me. "Like at the soup kitchen?"

"If you'd like."

One of her brows goes up. "For publicity?"

I chuckle. "It would be good publicity, but I believe you'd do it because you have a kind heart."

Her eyes widen a little as they search mine, and I run my thumb over her bottom lip.

"Is it possible you could find it in your heart to forgive me for what you thought I did?"

Emily pulls her head back. "Marcus, you hurt me. Everything you did hurt me."

Christ! Bend, Emily. "Because you didn't understand. What are you doing right now? You walked down the aisle with me of your own free will. You signed Emily Sterling on the license. You came up here with me, made love with me. Are you saying you've changed your mind?"

She looks away. "No."

I touch her cheek for her to face me, and she still appears reluctant. "I can't promise I won't ever hurt you"—I tap her chest—"here. Couples who are together for a lifetime fight, they get angry, and have different points of view. Then they work through that, and the bond gets stronger."

She licks her lips, but I see a flash of defeat in her eyes. "Come here." I pull her back into my arms. "I cannot envision a future without you. Please try to see that too." I kiss her, teasing her lips until she relaxes and kisses me back. She always softens with sex. Perhaps I'll have to pleasure her into compliance. The thought has my cock stirring again. I roll onto my back and pull her to lie over me.

"What are you doing?" she asks breathlessly.

"Putting you on top."

## 34

## EMILY

At the bottom of the stairs, Marcus pulls me into his arms and kisses me passionately, like he's saying goodbye, even though he'll only be gone for a few hours. He leans back and runs a finger over my lips. "Be good for me." He winks. "Stay close to the house. No one is here to save you if you slip off a trail."

Is he teasing me? "I will."

"Good. When I come back with Heath, use those muscles that make you smile. You're Mrs. Sterling now." He taps his carrier bag. "I'll get the paperwork filed for our marriage license today so we don't have to deal with it on Friday."

I glance down at the leather case by his side. "All right."

I'm still on the fence about being Mrs. Sterling. Yesterday was complicated. Last night was... confusing. I can't imagine explaining to Gia how many orgasms he gave me. What could I say? An incredibly sexy billionaire seduced and whisked me away to a lovely tropical island. Then I was trapped here and held hostage by my own fear as

Marcus orchestrated this whole wedding, promised me the world, and professed his love. All the while, I was plotting to get away from him. Who on earth would believe me? I don't even know what's real anymore.

He drops one last kiss on my lips. "We'll be back before dinner."

I force a smile for him and wait until he's through the front door with Juan before I turn toward the stairs.

"Emily."

I freeze with my foot on the bottom step and look behind me.

"Over here."

I peek around the corner, and Lucas is leaning against the wall. "Come here."

My pulse kicks up a notch and my eyes search the ceiling.

"It's a blind spot," Lucas answers my unspoken question. "Stay close to the wall."

I go to him, but I feel like I'm breaking some law. "What?" I whisper-hiss.

He places his hands on my arms and whispers in my ear, "What did you say to Marcus?"

"Nothing." I push back. "Why did you tell him I asked for help?"

"I didn't."

Is he lying? I swallow hard and search his eyes, but I can't tell. "Listen, whatever you were planning, I don't want your help. I'll figure this out on my own."

"He's not taking you back to New York."

"I know." I mean, I understand that there's the honeymoon first. "I might have misunderstood everything. But everything is different now. He's sick."

"Emily, you aren't thinking clearly." He drops his hands from my arms. "He's gaslighting you, pitting us against each other. I'm seriously concerned for you now that he suspects something."

That shuts me up, but then I recall he was the one questioned about Karyn's death. What am I supposed to believe?

I start to shake my head, but Juan's voice echoes in the foyer. "Lucas?"

I'm suddenly twirled around with my back to the wall. The message in his eyes is clear. Be quiet.

"I'm coming." Lucas lets go of my shoulders and walks away to greet Juan. I stay plastered to the wall until the door closes behind them. I close my eyes and take several deep breaths.

"Mrs. Sterling. Did you need something?"

My eyes fly open and Carmen is in the doorway to the kitchen. I shake my head. "No." Pushing off the wall, I turn gingerly and head back for the stairs. "I'm going to read in my room." Oh my God. What did she see? How would I explain that moment to Marcus?

She turns and disappears into the kitchen, and I hurry on my aching ankle up the steps. My heart is skittering unhealthily in my chest as I limp down the hall and slip inside my room. Bella comes over to greet me, arching her back and purring as she rubs on my leg.

"I know. I'm sorry." I make my way to the bathroom. No one would believe Bella ever missed a meal, but she did last night and is incredibly vocal about it this morning.

My hands are still a little shaky as I pour the kibble into her bowl. Lucas said Carmen and Juan wouldn't say anything, but what would Carmen think if she saw us like that? Would she tell him?

I lean on the counter and look in the mirror, but it's Gia's face I imagine, and I start to tell her everything, from the top. I feel a flash of guilt as I recall conspiring with Lucas to help get me free. "I don't know which one is manipulating me anymore."

Gia doesn't answer because she isn't here. I blow out a breath and push off the counter. This afternoon, when Heath gets here, I'll get his phone, call her, and we'll talk. Gia is neither inexperienced nor naive. She'll help me see things straight.

Returning to the bedroom, I glance around, and it dawns on me that none of my things are in here any longer. "Bella, I'll be back," I call out to her as if she cares. I can still hear her crunching on her breakfast.

In Marcus's room, I take stock of my clothes hanging in the closet. Nothing in here is mine. I wonder what Lucas decided was worth keeping when he packed up my apartment. That irks me. He helped Marcus unravel my life. Why did I ever trust him?

My thoughts confuse me further. I turn and go through his side of the closet. Aside from clothes, cufflinks, and ties, nothing gives me any insight into this man.

Leaving the closet, I step inside the bathroom and open the medicine cabinet. Everything is organized and neat, and I pick up his bottle of pills. What I wouldn't give to be able to Google this drug. Is it simply for pain? Are they for the tumor?

I lower to sit on the vanity bench and set the pills on the counter. What am I going to do? If Marcus is telling the truth, I'm plotting to run from a dying man who loves me and tell the world he's a monster. I'd ruin whatever life he has left.

If Lucas is telling the truth, then I have every reason to believe my life is in danger.

A noise in the other room has me on my feet, and my heart leaps out of my chest. I'm not doing anything wrong. I peek in the bedroom and Carmen catches sight of me.

"Oh, I'm so sorry, ma'am. I didn't know you were here."

She looks as flustered as I do, and again I wonder if she saw Lucas with me. I stand a little straighter. "What do you need, Carmen?"

"I was going to tidy up. Did you want me to come back?"

"No." I have never come across Carmen cleaning, but the evidence is clear daily. I wonder if the woman sleeps. "I was thinking I would read out by the pool this morning, but I don't know where my book is."

"Oh. I placed it in your nightstand drawer." She picks up her cleaning supplies. "I'll start in the bathroom. When I'm finished, I can prepare some refreshments for you."

I look over at the nightstand. "All I need is some water."

"There's bottled water in the refrigerator," she mentions, passing me to go into the bathroom. I wait until I hear her clanking around in there and go to Marcus's nightstand first. Pulling open the drawer, I see more condoms and shake my head. There's a watch I've never seen him wear and a metal box. I attempt to lift the lid, but it's locked. Curiously, there's no keyhole, but a black glass button that I press. It lights up and turns red. Giving up on that, I shut the door and go around the bed to get my book.

I'm three steps out of the room when I remember my clothes are here. I quickly backtrack and slip into the closet, grabbing a bathing suit and a cover. I get out before I see Carmen again and hurry back to my room to change.

Bella is sunning herself on the bed, full and happy now

with her breakfast. Marcus did bring her to me, but now I worry about the honeymoon. Will we take her on the yacht? As I change, I note Marcus has not invited her into his room. In fact, I don't think he likes her at all.

I try to detangle my anxiety, concern, and mixed feelings as I go downstairs and pad barefoot into the kitchen. I've never been inside here. It's huge. A large island takes up the center, and with plenty of counter space and a plethora of cabinets, it looks more like a commercial kitchen than a homey one. Everything sparkles, from the stainless steel appliances to the stone-tiled floor. I pass the deep double sinks, running my fingers over the granite counter, and I pause to look at a magnetic strip on the mosaic backsplash, displaying a set of kitchen knives. An assortment of different-sized skillets also hangs on pegs, flanking the knives and ending on a wall-mounted wine rack.

"Did you need something, Mrs. Sterling?"

I whirl around to see Juan, shirtless with his jeans riding low on his hips. With my palm flat against my chest, I try not to look as embarrassed as I feel. "No. I mean, I was just getting some water."

"I apologize for startling you." He opens the Sub-Zero refrigerator and pulls out a bottle of water. "I thought you were my mother."

Taking the bottle from him, I try for a smile. "I believe she's upstairs."

He grabs some water also, twisting off the top and leaning on the counter. "It's good to see you making yourself at home. I just cleaned the pool. Is that where you're headed?"

"Yes." My cheeks heat as I realize I'm in a bathing suit and a short crochet cover.

Juan nods, then takes a sip from his bottle. I appraise him quietly. He's lean but muscled from his work outside. His face is youthful, no hint of stubble. This is the first time he's really spoken to me, and I realize I don't know anything about him or his mother. "How old are you, Juan?"

A slow grin tips his lips. "I'll be twenty in December."

Twenty? "How long have you lived here?"

He sets down his water. "Since I was twelve."

Nearly half of his life. "What about school? Isn't it lonely?"

"I can read." He shrugs. "I teach myself. Mama and I visit other islands when the house isn't open."

That makes me curious. "Really? How?"

He looks surprised by my question. "The supply boat or sometimes an air taxi."

"Hmm." I didn't realize air taxis existed.

"What in the world are you doing?" Carmen shrieks as she enters the kitchen. "Juan? Has everyone in this house lost their minds?"

I feel the urge to raise my hand but simply stare at her. With a hand on her hip, she points at Juan. "Are you finished working?"

"No."

"Then go." She points that finger at the door. "And put a shirt on when you come into this house."

Juan gives her a cheeky grin, grabs his water, and exits. Carmen turns to me. "I apologize, Mrs. Sterling. I'm sure he didn't mean to offend you."

"I wasn't offended." But my mind is circling around what she said. Did she see Lucas with me?

"Please, Mrs. Sterling, go enjoy the pool. I'll bring out your refreshments."

I don't really feel the need for 'refreshments,' but I nod and leave the room. Juan isn't in sight when I step outside. I choose a lounge in the shade and open my book, but I'm too distracted to read. My thoughts continue to bounce around in my head. I need to take a step in one direction or the other, but I feel stuck in the middle.

# 35

## MARCUS

Lucas is quiet as he flies the plane. I'm a little pensive myself. I hadn't even reached the dock when Carmen notified me Lucas was engaging with Emily again. I wonder if I should bring it up but decide against it. Today, Lucas is officially fired. In the end, my plan will save me from another uncomfortable situation and there's no reason for Lucas to suspect anything now.

I glance over at him and ponder how he thought he could steal my bride from me. He'd know I'd never allow it. Lucas has no issues with killing a person, but now I'm wondering if that includes me. "When Emily and I depart for our honeymoon, I have something you need to take care of."

"What's that, sir?"

"I want you to make her friend, Gia, go away. After that, I need Emily's mother to disappear."

For a beat, he says nothing and I study his profile. Is he conflicted?

"The girl, Gia, is in Europe?" he finally asks.

"Yes. Paris," I confirm.

"The mother is in Florida?"

"She is. I'll send you the background check I received on her."

I'm again greeted with silence before he nods. "When do you expect to return to New York?"

"Emily and I will depart on Friday and probably stay aboard *The Temptress* a week or two, weather permitting." I don't miss his grip on the control column tightening or the way his jaw clenches.

"Gia's should look accidental," I add. "Her mother is a wanderer. Just make sure her body is disposed of. People will wonder if she simply took off and started a new life."

I'm merely toying with Lucas now, reminding him who he is and what he'll do for me. When he fails to respond, I prod, "Is there a problem?"

"No, sir."

To think that a week ago, I would have believed him. I end the conversation as Lucas prepares to land and don't speak again until we are secured to the dock. "Did you arrange for a car?"

"Yes, sir." He gestures toward an airplane hangar. "It's waiting out back."

"Good. We can take care of our errands before Heath arrives."

As promised, a car is waiting in the parking lot. Lucas opens the back door for me before climbing in the passenger seat. It's a short drive to the government building and I make quick work of getting our marriage license filed.

Lucas waits patiently for me as I talk with the clerk. In this part of the world, a little extra money will help get things expedited. Returning to Lucas, I press out a tight-lipped smile. "There's a tavern next door. Let's go have a drink to celebrate my marriage while we wait for Heath."

He raises a brow. "Why don't we just wait at the airport lounge?"

That would be the regular thing to do. "Today, I'm feeling like trying something different. Something local."

"Sir, I'm not sure trying something local is in your best interest. It isn't safe."

"But that's why I have you." I start walking. Lucas knows he can't dictate where I go. He simply must follow—like a dog. It's unfortunate that today he's the hound you know you need to put down. The pet that has become unstable, unreliable, and dangerous. Lucas falls in stride with me, taking a few steps ahead to open the door. He gives the pedestrians and traffic a quick look before I step out.

As soon as I'm back in the heat of the sunshine, I take a right and head for the alley.

"Sir, I think it's safer to stick to the street." He takes hurried strides to catch up with me.

"This is shorter," I reply nonchalantly. "The tavern is just on the other side."

The alley is empty, except for three men near the end. One is leaning against the wall, enjoying a cigarette. The other two are seated in rickety wooden chairs and it would appear they're employees from one of these establishments enjoying a smoke break.

Lucas puffs up next to me. Usually, that's all he needs to do to scare off the average man. He comes around to my other side, putting his body between mine and the strangers. Predictable. The truth is, I am known on this island. I'm not the only wealthy person who frequents this area, but I tend to donate a lot of money to causes that support the population. It keeps me in a good light with the citizens, but today, dressed in slacks and a short-sleeved button-down, I do look like the average tourist.

"Sir, I have an uneasy feeling about this. Let's circle back."

I eye the men. The smoker drops his cigarette and crushes it with his boot. "They look like harmless locals. I'm sure it's fine."

The men avoid eye contact as we pass. It would seem Lucas's imagined crisis is averted until two of them leap up behind us. A gun is pressed to my head. Another is nudging Lucas's back.

"No need for a ruckus. Just give me your wallet," the man behind me says.

I turn slightly to see my assailant. His dark skin high-lights his yellow teeth as he sneers at me. Catching eyes with Lucas, I shake my head slightly and reach inside my pocket for my wallet.

"And the wedding ring," this bloke says, and damn, he's taking it a little far. I glance at my hand, reluctant to remove the ring.

"Now!" he hisses.

Well, what the fuck? I slide off the ring and hand it to him. With a gun at his back, I can see Lucas assessing the situation. He has a weapon too, but the odds of him saving me are slim. He wouldn't have time to draw it before being shot himself. The third man approaches Lucas. He's nose to nose with him before he flicks out his blade. In a flash of movement, Lucas slams his elbow into the man behind him, spinning his body and reaching for his gun. He doesn't have the chance to aim when the knife sinks into his side. The weapon discharges, ricocheting off the brick wall next to me, and Lucas is quickly disarmed. While he made a valiant effort, he must know he's going to die, but Lucas isn't going down without a fight. He turns on the gun-wielding thief, blocking his arm and punching him hard. As soon as he turns to the one with the knife, he's struck with the barrel of a gun on the back of the head. That has him going to his knees, and Lucas looks up in time to receive a foot to his chin, sending him sprawling back on the asphalt. His body jerks as another gunshot echoes in the alley. That pisses me off. This was meant to be done quietly. I glare at the man next to me.

"The money is in here?" He waves the wallet.

"Yes."

"Then we're out." He gestures for his comrades to go.

"Wait, my ring."

He pockets it with a smile and turns to run. I can already hear sirens approaching. This is a shitshow. I run over to Lucas. My fingers press to his neck, and my pulse amps up as I still feel his.

"Fuck!" I scream at him. He moans, pressing his hand to his abdomen, and blood gushes through his fingers. I brush his hand away and notice the red pool forming beneath him. "You shouldn't have touched my wife," I spit out.

He doesn't react. Instead, he appears to have lost consciousness. I stay by his side, the sound of the sirens getting closer. "Bleed, fucker."

I place my hands on his wound when the police car pulls into the alley, sirens off and lights flashing. I raise my bloodied hands up as the officers get out with their weapons drawn. "We were robbed!" I call out to them. "He's been shot."

THE HARD HEELS of my shoes tap out my annoyance as I pace the linoleum floor in the waiting room. Two officers are waiting for me and I hold a finger up to them as I press the phone to my ear.

Heath finally answers. "Where are you?"

"There was an incident. Lucas and I were mugged in an alley. He's been shot."

"What?"

I stop and sit down in one of the metal-framed chairs, pressing my hand to my forehead. "He's in surgery. We're at the hospital."

"Are you all right? I can come to you."

"No. I'm fine. There's nothing you can do. Go back with the plane. I'll be in touch." I glance up and see Tony Benson, the chief of police, making his way toward me. "Heath, I have to go. It's going to be chaotic around here for the next couple days. Whatever you want to do with the proposal, I trust your instincts."

He sighs. "It's not that I question the project. It's how we're going to fund it."

I close my eyes. That's why he's been hounding me. He wants me to personally invest. "We'll work it out, Heath. I can't deal with this right now." I stand as Benson approaches. "I'll call you later."

Hanging up with Heath, I pocket my phone and face Benson. I glance at the two waiting officers, still a distance away, and focus back on him. "This was a fuckup."

"I know," he replies in a hushed voice. "Any word yet?"

"No, but if he lives, I expect you to finish it."

"And I will," he consoles me. "Lucas Tate knows too much about the arrangement between us."

That gives me some assurance, and I sigh. "I'd hoped to

get back tonight, but"—I glance out at the darkening sky and shrug—"it looks like I'll be staying overnight."

"We need to take your statement. I've arranged for a private office here. I'll be with you."

"Fine." Fuck. I need to call home. With a glance at my watch, I see it's been hours that Lucas has been in surgery. He should have been dead on arrival. "Can you get any more information about how Lucas is doing?"

Benson nods. "I'll see what I can do. Let's get the rest over with."

My eyes narrow as two suits approach the nurses' station, completely out of place in this little hospital. I glance at Benson, and he's noticed them too. It's like you can almost smell the Feds. Why are they here? "Find out what that's about first."

Benson leaves me and engages in a conversation with them. I attempt to look unconcerned, reading nonsense on my phone while occasionally glancing over at them. Benson finally gestures for me to come over. Whatever anxiety I feel about the feds' presence, I mask it as I approach them. "What's going on?"

"I'm Agent Simms." One man extends a hand to me. "Lucas Tate was an American citizen murdered on foreign soil. That makes us part of the investigation."

Benson calls over his officers and ushers all of us to this private room. Two words are giving me courage. Was and murdered. Lucas didn't survive.

---

IT'S a grueling hour of answering questions before everyone is satisfied. "Obviously, Mr. Sterling is one of our valued citizens," Benson notes. "That's why I'll be handling this investigation personally."

Mr. Simms nods and looks at me. "Did you feel you were targeted, or were you randomly approached?"

I lift a shoulder. "It felt random. I think it was simply a robbery until my security man retaliated. After they shot him, they all ran. It happened so fast."

Simms nods and looks at his notes. "You gave us a description, but it's rather vague. Would you agree to sit with a sketch artist?"

"Yes. If you can arrange it soon. I'd like to get back to my wife."

"Sometimes details become clearer after a day or two. We'll get that arranged."

Benson steps in. "I can handle that." He looks at me. "We'll bring someone out to you."

The Feds stand and Simms eyes me. "You were lucky to walk away unscathed."

I shake my head. "I'm still trying to absorb that a man I worked with so closely died while saving me."

"The smart thing to do would have been to eliminate any witnesses," Simms adds.

"Yes. I didn't get the feeling these men were the brightest of blokes." I catch Benson's eyes. That is a true statement. This is why it's always better to handle these situations on your own. I simply felt with my limited time, I'd rather spend it enjoying Emily than skirting an investigation into me. My feelings for her are causing me to make rash decisions. "I'd like to call my wife. I'm sure she's getting concerned. Are we finished?"

"For now." Simms sticks out a hand for me to shake. I

stand and take it, glancing at his rather silent partner, to whom I've not been introduced.

"Thank you." I pull out my phone. "Could I have some privacy now?"

My request is granted as the men file out of the room. I sit back down and dial Carmen. She answers right away. "Mr. Sterling? Did you learn more?"

"He's dead. Please get the satellite phone and call me back. I need to speak with Emily."

## 36

---

## EMILY

Bella lies curled in my lap and my book is at my side as I watch the colors bleed from the sky and the first stars appear. Marcus didn't come home. Heath isn't here, and I could see Carmen's concern at dinner. She told me something must have delayed them and that they wouldn't fly the plane at night. That makes sense as the sky darkens and the ocean appears black as ink.

I startle at the knock on my door, and my first thought as I shove Bella off me is that they're back. I know they aren't. I've been listening for the plane to come all day. Carmen greets me when I open the door, holding up the bulky satellite phone. "Mr. Sterling is calling for you."

She hands me the phone, and I stare at it curiously. A part of me still feels like it's a crime to be in its presence. "Thank you."

She closes the door, and I place the phone to my ear. "Marcus?"

"Oh, Emily. It's good to hear your voice."

He sounds shaken, and I have a sinking feeling. "What's wrong?"

"I'm at the hospital. The day grew too late for me to return to you. I'll need to stay here until morning."

Another layer of dread covers me like a blanket. "Hospital?" I swallow hard. "Did you, um... did you have another episode?"

"No. No, it's not me. Lucas and I were attacked in an alley. He... ah... he didn't survive."

"Lucas?" I'm so confused. "What do you mean he didn't..." My voice trails off as I realize exactly what he means. Lucas is dead?

"Yes, love. In his attempt to protect me, he perished. I'm having a hard time with all of it."

Clutching the phone to my ear, I slowly sit down on the bed and some piece of my heart shatters. He's gone? "Marcus..." My voice cracks and I try again. "Are you all right?"

"I am, except there's this whole investigation going on. I hope to have it all wrapped up tonight so I can come home to you tomorrow."

I don't know what to say as one tear rolls down my cheek. It's not possible. How could Lucas be gone? "What happened?"

Marcus sighs. "I'll explain everything tomorrow."

I press a hand to my chest. Lucas isn't coming back? "Is Heath with you?"

"No. I asked him to return to New York."

My heart sinks and that thin thread of security snaps. Heath isn't coming, I still have no way to call Gia, and Lucas...

"I realized something today." Marcus's voice is low and wavers a little. "I could have died too, and the only person I was thinking about was you. We did the right thing, moving forward with this wedding. Time is relative and life is unpredictable. I love you."

I close my eyes as a small part of me still wants that to be true. "Marcus..." I choke up. I still can't return those words. "I'm glad you're all right." It's all I can give him.

"I just wanted you to know how important you are to me, but I need to go. Return the phone to Carmen and I'll see you in the morning."

We say our goodbyes and the screen on the phone goes dark. I quickly press a button, not ready to be disconnected from the outside again, but it requests the passcode.

I drop the phone on the bed and cradle my face in my hands. Lucas is dead and I'm feeling more and more isolated.

I finally leave the bedroom to seek out Carmen. Most of the lights are off in the house, but a glow comes from the kitchen doorway, and that's where I find both Carmen and Juan. Their heads are together and their voices are low.

"Mother, why would you do that?" Juan whispers.

"Everything I do is for you. For us," she hisses back.

Juan swipes his hair off his forehead and catches sight of me in the doorway. "Mrs. Sterling?"

That has Carmen looking over at me too. "Are you all right, ma'am? Can I get you anything?"

"Marcus wanted me to give this back to you." I hold out the phone. "Did he tell you?"

Carmen takes it from my hand. "About Lucas? Yes. It's such a shock."

Juan shakes his head and turns away. Carmen regards her son for a moment, then looks back at me. "We are just so relieved that Mr. Sterling wasn't harmed."

I swallow through my tight throat. "Yes."

She gives the phone to Juan. "Put this away." Then she steps closer to me and rubs my arm. "Come on, let's get you back upstairs. We'll all know more in the morning."

I keep my mouth shut and allow her to lead me back upstairs. I'm scared, confused, grieving for Lucas, for Marcus, for me.

"I could bring you some tea. It might help you relax," Carmen offers.

I stop at my bedroom door. "I need to get Bella."

"Oh, ma'am, Mr. Sterling is allergic to cat hair. I don't think it's a good idea to bring her into your room."

He's what? I never knew that. I still don't feel like Marcus's suite is my room, and I hesitate to go there.

"Mrs. Sterling, I'll take care of Bella in the morning when I clean her litter box." With her arm still around me, she urges me farther down the hall.

As soon as I'm in the room, I close the door and lean on it. I don't want tea, but I do want a drink. I push off the door, go to the sideboard and pour myself a healthy serving of Marcus's scotch.

A gentle breeze blows in through the balcony doors, fluttering the gauzy drapes. A host of stars twinkles in the sky, and I sit down on the floor.

Everything I learned last night plays in my mind. Lucas was on trial for murder. Did he kill Karyn? Was I running from an innocent man into the arms of a killer? Or was Marcus manipulating both of us because he had suspicions? Was that entire story a lie? How will I ever know now?

I take a large sip, then sputter as it fries my esophagus and burns in my belly. I have no idea how people enjoy this stuff, but I need to numb out everything around me and I drink some more.

When the glass is empty, I pour some more and stare into the darkness. It seems vast and endless, and I feel so alone.

---

MY HEAD IS POUNDING and my mouth is dry. I smack my lips and slowly open my eyes. Sunlight pours in from the balcony doors and I'm on the floor. The bottle of scotch is half-empty and the glass is toppled over next to me. I sit up slowly, still in the same dress I was wearing yesterday.

My pulse is a thrumming, rhythmic beat roaring in my ears, but beyond that, there's another noise.

The plane.

Shit! I snatch up the bottle along with the glass and leap to my feet. A wave of dizziness causes me to stumble, but I hold it together and place everything back on the sideboard.

I rush for the bathroom, but in the height of my panic, it hits me. Lucas is gone. Something he said to me whispers in my mind. If Marcus knew he was helping me, he'd kill us both.

I slam my hand against my chest, where my heart sinks like a stone. Did Marcus kill him?

It's not possible. Marcus said the police were investigating and he was participating. Then again, Lucas said that my husband basically owns the police. I'm not sure what to think as I enter the bathroom. My reflection shows a pale and disheveled woman, and I don't know what happened, but I can imagine Marcus's reaction if he finds me like this.

I pop two aspirin and splash water on my face before I brush my teeth. This makes me gag, but I press a hand to my stomach and breathe until the nausea passes. I need to fix my hair, change my clothes. I don't have time because I can no longer hear the plane's motor.

My heart is pounding like I've run a marathon as I change into fresh clothes, and now the question is, would he expect me to wait here or meet him downstairs?

My ankle has improved some over the last couple of days. Perhaps it's my adrenaline that propels me down the hall with hardly a gimp. I pass my bedroom and hope Carmen took care of Bella, but I don't check.

As I reach the top of the stairs, the front door is opening and Marcus steps in before Juan. I start down and he looks up with a shake of his head. "I'll come to you." Marcus shifts his carrier bag on his shoulder. He appears weary as he climbs the steps, and when he reaches the landing, he wraps his arms around me. "Emily."

Marcus holds me for a long moment before he whispers, "Let's go to our room."

He remains quiet as we go back down the hall, but my questions start the second he closes the door. "What happened?"

He shakes his head, walking past me. He drops his bag on the floor and collapses on the sofa. "It was awful."

Marcus recounts everything in detail from the time they were robbed to when he learned Lucas had passed in surgery. I sit down next to him, torn now between wanting to comfort him and asking if he killed Lucas.

Obviously, I wouldn't, so I take his hand and he squeezes my fingers.

"It was tragic. I've known Lucas for so long." He shakes his head again. "It's simply unbelievable."

My eyes water, and he strokes my cheek with his thumb. "It's all right, Emily. I made it back to you."

"I know. It's just so wrong. I can't believe he's dead."

"Yes." Marcus stands abruptly. "Well, you didn't really know him long. We'll just be happy I survived. Carmen tells me you missed breakfast."

I'm confused by the sudden change of topics. "I-I overslept."

Marcus stands and heads into the bedroom. "Where did you sleep?"

Well, hell. I follow him in and gaze over at the still made bed. "I fell asleep on the sofa."

"Hmm." He turns to study me. "Why?"

My nerves amp up. "I don't know."

With a swipe of his hand over his hair, he lets it go and enters the bathroom. "I need out of these clothes and a long shower. Then we should sort out some food for you."

"I can fix myself something to eat while you shower."

Marcus stops, turning in the doorway. "Emily, Carmen mentioned you skipped lunch yesterday."

What the hell? Does she tell him everything? That familiar feeling of fear squirms in my belly, and I press a hand to my stomach. She saw me with Lucas.

"Wait for me. We'll go down to eat together."

"All right." I manage to keep my voice steady and he closes the door. I blow out a long breath. My suspicions are mounting and I'm starting to wonder how long I'm going to survive Marcus.

## 37

## MARCUS

Christ. Does she think I don't notice? Does she believe I don't know? I rip off my shirt and drop it in the trash bin. She should have been waiting by the door, leaping into my arms with tears of relief. I start up the shower and glance at my reflection in the mirror. Yesterday was one fuckup after another, but at least the man was kind enough to die.

I get in the shower and wash off everything that happened in the last twenty-four hours. Today, Emily and I will start fresh with nothing standing between us.

My phone rings before I'm even finished drying myself. I fish it out of my pants pocket and frown when I see who it is.

"Hello, Heath."

"Hey. I was just checking if you were back on your island."

"I am. How about you? Did you fly home yesterday?"

"No. I kept the plane here. I thought perhaps you and Emily would want to go back to New York after everything that happened."

He thought that—why? "No. Emily and I are leaving for our honeymoon as planned."

A long stretch of silence follows my response, and I realize I never told him we were married. "We had a private ceremony on Tuesday," I add casually.

"Jesus. Marcus? What are you doing?" he says with an exaggerated sigh. "You've known this woman for two weeks."

"It's been more like a month." I know that still sounds like it's too soon. "I knew what I wanted and things happened that had me expediting our nuptials."

"What things?"

My irritation is starting to match his. "It's personal."

"Marcus, at some point, we need you back in the office."

He doesn't really. "If I retired tomorrow, no one would miss me and the company would be fine." I chuck the towel with my pants into the laundry hamper and step into my closet. "Heath, my bride is a little distraught that I almost died yesterday. I need to go. We'll figure everything out when I return. Go home."

He starts another argument, but I hang up on him. Heath may be the only person I call a friend, but honestly, sometimes he's simply annoying.

Selecting a fresh shirt and a pair of khaki shorts, I head out to find Emily. She's obediently waiting for me in my sitting room. "Come, love. Let's feed you."

"I'm fine, really," she says as she stands.

"Are you? You look a little pale." That predictably brings some color to her cheeks. It's not like I didn't notice my scotch bottle took a good hit and the used glass on the side-board. Was it her grief for Lucas or concern for me that drove her to the bottle? It doesn't matter. He's gone.

None of it is my concern now. I hold out my hand for her

and smile, pulling her into a hug when she slips her fingers through mine. "I'm so glad we found each other, Emily. You are the only calm in the storm that is my life right now."

Carmen meets us as soon as we come down the stairs. Her eyes roam over Emily before she focuses on me. "Mr. Sterling, we were all so shocked by what happened yesterday, and we are so grateful you weren't harmed."

I glance at Emily, hoping she's taking notes on what the right words would sound like. "Thank you, Carmen. We'll be by the pool."

Carmen bustles out of the room, and I guide Emily outside. Getting her seated, I sit next to her at the table and look out at the view. "It's funny, when you've faced death, everything looks brighter, smells fresher, things become clearer."

I've personally felt that every time I've taken a life. Even though I didn't personally kill Lucas, it feels the same. That rush of power, the feeling you're a god amongst men. I glance back at Emily. "Let's talk about our future."

She looks back at me, lips tipped down, her eyes sad. "After what happened yesterday, I think we should skip the honeymoon and return to New York."

"Why?" Why can't she be happy I'm alive? "Yesterday didn't turn out well for Lucas, but it was an eye-opener for me. I want to live every day I have left—with you. I want to be buried in you, steeped in your essence, and show you how I feel, so when my time comes, you'll understand." I pinch my bottom lip and regard her surprised expression before I drop my hand. "Don't look back, Emily. Let's look forward and enjoy the time we have left."

Emily doesn't get the chance to respond before Carmen shows up with food. A bowl of assorted berries, complimentary cream, and croissants. I take a strawberry and dip it in cream. Holding it to her lips, I wait patiently for her to make the right choice. She opens her mouth for me and I press the berry through her lips. "Now, do you want to tell me why you got drunk and passed out in the sitting room last night?"

She chews slowly, I'm sure to delay answering me.

"I can understand if you were worried about me, but I don't approve of you drinking in excess. I have a personal issue with alcoholics."

She swallows and looks away. "I'm not an alcoholic."

"Then see to it that you refrain from doing that again."

She pouts, and I dip another berry in cream.

"I think we still need some time alone. I was thinking about taking you to London."

That has her eyes growing wider.

"Think of it as an extension of our honeymoon."

Instead of looking excited, she deflates a little. I sigh and hold up the berry for her, pressing it to her lips until she takes it. It's erotic the way she licks the juices and cream from her lips. I may be a dying man, but my cock doesn't know that. "Maybe we should leave here sooner than later." I'm ready to get her away from any unpleasant memories she gathered on this island and spend time giving her new ones.

"Marcus, a man just died. I don't think we should be focusing on a honeymoon right now. Let's go home."

My eyes narrow. "He was my employee, not my friend. What was he to you?"

When she fails to respond, I nod. "Nothing. I understand you don't feel well this morning, which is basically your own fault." I slide her orange juice closer to her. "Here, hydrate."

Emily sips her juice, a little more contrite now. My

phone rings and I take it from my pocket and read the screen. "This is the police, probably regarding the investigation. Excuse me, and please eat something."

I hit accept as I push back my chair to stand. I wait until I'm inside before I speak. "Mr. Benson, what can I do for you?"

"Sir, I had some disturbing information this morning from one of my contacts at the hospital."

"The hospital? What?"

He breathes into the phone. "I-I don't believe Lucas Tate is dead."

That can't be possible. I rub my forehead. "Explain."

"I believe the feds lied. Mr. Tate was transferred out of the hospital while you were giving your statement."

"To where?"

"There's no record of this transfer, only what this man witnessed, but the coroner didn't receive a body and there's no autopsy scheduled."

Son of a bitch. "Find him," I growl. "What about the men you hired?"

"They are out of the islands. They didn't leave any evidence behind," he assures me.

No. They just stole my ring and didn't finish the job. I start to pace the room while pinching the bridge of my nose. This is why you do things yourself!

"There's more," Tony continues.

I huff, "Please, go on."

"Your partner, Heath Carrington, was just seen at the station speaking with Agent Simms."

What? "I just spoke to Heath. He said..." He told me he was still in the islands. What the fuck?

"He was with a young woman, long dark hair, green eyes."

Fucking Gia.

"They want to set up another meeting, but Mr. Sterling, is there a chance they are gathering evidence on you?"

"For what?" I'm seeing red now. "I didn't kill the man. The only link to me in this is you," I hiss into the phone. "So you tell me. Is there a problem?"

"Sir, no. Of course I wouldn't say anything, but is it possible Mr. Carrington or Mr. Tate could?"

Heath doesn't know anything, but why the hell did he omit the fact he has Gia with him? If Lucas is talking, he has to know his business with me will be exposed, and I imagine that would land him with a life sentence. No. I cover my tracks. If one bleeds, we all do.

"I pay you well, Mr. Benson. That supplementary income would be cut off if anything happened to me. Find out what the fuck is going on."

"Sir, I will do what I can."

"No. Do what I've asked and most importantly, find Lucas Tate and finish the job!" I hang up on him before he can piss me off further and walk off the angry energy that has amped up in my body. First my diagnosis, Lucas and Emily, then this? I feel like the walls are closing in around me and it's getting harder to breathe. I try to shake off the headache, but even though the pills are helping, it's a constant dull ache that's driving me slowly insane.

Pulling in deep breaths, I calm my heart as my feet traverse the floor. It'll be fine. It's always been all right. It always works out in the end.

I look up and stop moving when I see Emily standing in

the doorway. Jesus. How long has she been there? "What do you need, Emily?"

## 38

## EMILY

I stare back at Marcus, unable to comprehend what I just heard. Taking a step back, I shake my head. "I was curious. Did they find out anything about the men who robbed you?"

His jaw twitches as he pockets his phone. "No." He strides toward me. "Did you finish your breakfast?"

"Yes." I wrap my arms around myself. What did he mean by *'find' Lucas*? Is he lost? Is he alive? Oh, God. What did he mean by *'finish the job'*?

"What's wrong, Emily?" He tips his head, his eyes roaming over my face. "I realize yesterday's events were upsetting. Again, I apologize for the ring. We'll get a new one."

I'm not sure I can survive how hard my heart is beating now. "The ring isn't important."

"Exactly." He steps in front of me. "The important thing is that I survived and I'm here to talk about it. That's what we should focus on." Marcus rubs my arms. "I have some issues to iron out. Why don't you go upstairs and choose what you'd like to take on our honeymoon? I'll see that Carmen gets us both packed tonight."

I keep my mouth shut and obey, climbing the stairs and stopping to check on Bella. As soon as I open the door, I spot Carmen coming out of the bathroom with a trash bag in her hand.

"Mrs. Sterling, Bella is fine. I fed her earlier and freshened the litter box. I promise to take good care of her while you're away."

At least one of us knows the plan for my cat. "Thank you."

Carmen holds up the bag. "Well, I should get this disposed of."

"Like my suitcase?" It just spills out of my mouth, but... "Do you know where it is?"

She gives the camera a nervous look. "No. Mr. Sterling has already purchased you new luggage. It's in your closet."

I sense her discomfort with this conversation and see the fear building in her eyes. She's as afraid as I am.

"Was there anything else, Mrs. Sterling?"

"No."

As she leaves the room, I walk over to the balcony door and step outside. It's a beautiful day. The sun is shining and the sky is blue, fading to gray toward the horizon. The ocean looks endless and I feel lost and out of options. No one is looking for me and I need to do something to save myself.

Despite it being a warm day, I'm chilled to the bone. Flexing my ankle, I know it's getting better, but I'm nowhere near ready to run from anyone. "What would you do, Gia?" I whisper to the breeze and collapse on one of the lounges. Bella comes out to join me in the sun and curls up on my legs. I start to mentally go through every moment since I set foot on this island. All the red flags were there. Now I'm wondering if I'll ever leave this place. Or will I go on this honeymoon and be tossed overboard? Just another wife who accidentally drowned.

I'm not sure how long I stare out at the ocean, winding myself up. I need to do something, I just have no idea what... And then it hits me. The plane.

I can't fly it, but it has a radio. Right? I glance down at my wrapped ankle and know this is going to be quite a hike for me, but I can't sit here and wait to die.

Edging Bella off my lap, I slowly get up and go back inside. As quietly as possible, I open the door and glance down the hallway. My heart is pounding, but it's do-or-die time.

I peek down the stairs and see no one. Marcus is probably in his study. I could go right out the front door, but if Juan is working outside, it's a good possibility he'd see me. My best bet is to go by way of the beach.

I make it across the living room to the doors to the deck without being noticed and breathe. The anxiety might kill me before Marcus can. My ankle is already complaining when I reach the stone steps and head down to the beach, but my adrenaline pushes me forward.

The breeze is stronger as I hit the sand, blowing back my hair and stealing my breath as it rapidly leaves my lungs. The waves are bigger today, the water choppy, and I wonder if another storm is on the way. There isn't a cloud in the sky to indicate that, and I shove away the thought. There is a storm coming. It's called Hurricane Emily, and it will either save me or end me.

I'm so angry at myself for not thinking about this before, and I use that to press on.

It takes me forever to hobble through the sand and reach the trail over to the dock. I'm completely out of breath now, but I continue, carefully navigating the rocks in my bare feet. I pause at the crest and wipe the sweat from my eyes. The plane is in sight, and no one else is. I'm almost there.

Going down is equally hard, and my leg is throbbing. I'm not sure I totally thought this through, but what was I going to do? Sit there and wait for something to happen?

I'm dragging my foot as I reach the dock. I don't look back but focus on my goal. It's bobbing gently in the water, secured by ropes like it's waiting for me. My heart pounds harder, my breath comes short, and I stop beside the plane. My courage starts to wane. I don't even know how to open the door.

Balancing on one leg, I reach for what looks like a handle and the plane slips out of reach. I scramble back. Damnit! Eyeballing it like it's my enemy, I realize I'll need to step out onto the ski, somehow hold on, and open the door.

Sometimes you need to face your fear and just do what needs to be done to survive. I grab the rope and try to move the plane closer. It's harder than it seems, and I send a silent prayer out to the universe for strength.

# 39

## MARCUS

I hit redial, and Heath's phone goes to voicemail for the fifteenth time. What the fuck! "Heath, you need to call me. ASAP!"

Tapping my fingers on the desk, I check my messages again and still there is nothing new. I'm completely in the dark and I need some answers—now!

With my recent luck, Gia is probably on a warpath to get her friend back. Heath is aiding and abetting her and Lucas is fucking missing. I saw the man bleed. What kind of idiot doesn't aim for the heart?

Tossing the phone on the desk, I pull up the feed for the security cameras, and wouldn't you know it. Emily is not packing like I requested. She's sneaking around the house. What did you hear, Emily?

That was completely my fault. To think she'd follow a simple order, like finishing her breakfast, was foolish. I watch her tiptoe out the doors to the pool deck and switch to the outdoor cameras.

I lean in on my forearms as she takes the stairs to the

beach trail. What is she doing? For one thing, she shouldn't be romping around on her ankle like that. It's irritating to see her being so negligent.

I'm ready to go after her, but I take a steadying breath. There's nowhere for her to go and she knows it. Maybe she just wanted to stick her toes in the water one more time before we're gone in the morning. It's all the other events that have me riled up.

I question that as she hits the sand and starts walking like a lame girl on a mission. This is simply ridiculous. I don't have time right now to go chasing after her. Then again, who knows how long it will take for anyone to get back to me.

My heart rate slows when I see her take the trail over to the dock. What the fuck? The plane? What does she think? That she'll be able to fly away from me, or... Or the radio. Oh, Emily.

I push back my chair and stand. The odds she'd even be able to get on the plane are slim, but I need to intervene before she hurts herself. Slamming out of my study, I wonder where the fuck my trusty staff is as I encounter no one in the house. I'm out the front door and down the steps in a heartbeat. My feet pound on the dirt road. I'm angry, seriously pissed by the time I reach the dock. I pause to watch her attempt to balance on the plane's float while struggling with the door.

"Emily!" I roar.

She startles, then slips and disappears into the water.

"Emily!" I move, sprinting down the dock, but slow when I see her head pop up. She's in a bit of a pickle now. She struggles to hold on to the plane and decipher how she'll get back on the dock.

"What were you doing?" I stand with my hands on my hips, looking down at her.

She blinks the water from her eyes, the drops mixing with some tears. Crying isn't getting her out of this one.

Her lips move, but no words come out, and I shake my head. "What? You're sorry? Because right now you are looking sorry," I snap.

Her eyes get rounder, but a spark lights her eyes. She pushes off the plane and dives under the water.

Son of a bitch! I kick off my shoes and she pops up, filling her lungs and preparing to swim away. I run alongside her until I'm clear enough to dive in. My little Emily might be a swimmer, but so the fuck am I.

I'm on her in three strokes, wrapping an arm around her, and she starts to struggle. I grab her hair and wrench her head back. "Stop!"

There are moments in your life when you could seriously kill someone. I'm having one right now. Using my free arm, I get us to the steps at the end of the dock and keep a hold on her as I haul myself up, dragging her with me. She's slick as she tries to squirm out of my grasp, and I drop her on the wooden planks with a thud. "What the fuck?"

It takes her a moment to catch her breath while avoiding eye contact with me. I kick her sore ankle with my bare foot. "Answer me!"

Emily grabs her leg and raises her eyes to meet mine. At least now she has something to cry about.

"What were you thinking?"

"P-please d-don't hurt m-me," she stutters out through trembling lips.

"How about you don't hurt me," I growl. "Do you have any idea of the heart attack I had right now?"

She shakes her head and looks down. I'm so thoroughly pissed I can hardly see straight. I'm dripping wet, glaring at my equally drenched bride. "Do you want to get on the plane? Hmm? You could have just asked."

I grab her mercilessly by her hair and start dragging her in the direction of the plane. She claws at my hand and tries to get her feet under her.

"What did you want? Did you want to learn how to fly? Do you want to take a little ride? What were you thinking!" I stop by the plane and drop her.

"No. No. I was just..."

"You were just what? Out for a walk? Do you remember what happened the last time you took a walk on your own? Lucas isn't here to save you now," I spit at her.

Her tears are falling at a good rate now. I snarl and look down at my feet. What a fucking mess.

It's a struggle to get my wet feet into my leather loafers while she huddles with her tears. "This is your fault," I tell her in a calmer voice. "If you could simply follow orders, you'd be packing for our honeymoon." I hold out a hand for her, and when she refuses to take it, I no longer resemble calm. I grab her under her armpits and haul her up, toss her over my shoulder and give her ass a hard smack. Christ! "I'm not the one who starts these little wars, Emily."

Her whimpers go ignored as I march toward the road. "Do you think I wanted to go for a swim in my clothes today?" I huff and adjust her weight.

Emily attempts to struggle, and I pinch her swollen ankle. "Stop." I tighten my grip on her legs. Thank Christ she does. I'm winded as I climb the stairs to the front door. She should be happy for the lift, but she's an ungrateful little bitch, just like the rest of them.

I keep hold of her as I stomp inside. Carmen gasps when she sees us. I'm sure we do appear a mess as we drip on the floor.

"What happened?"

"Stay out of it, Carmen," I growl at her and haul Emily upstairs. I don't drop her until we're in our suite. Her butt bounces on the sofa, and she has the audacity to glare up at me.

"What do you want to say, Emily?" I strip off my wet shirt and toss it on the floor. "Do you want to explain why my bride of two fucking days was trying to leave me?"

Her eyes go from angry to wary in a beat. She should be worried.

"Get up." I wiggle my fingers at her. She shakes her head and looks away.

"Get the fuck up now!" God, she is pushing every limit. I grab her hand and haul her to her feet. "We need to get out of these wet clothes. Move." I shove her toward the bathroom.

"Marcus, please..."

"Please. Yes, Emily, please just do what you're told." I give her another encouraging push, and she stumbles a little. I'm seeing red by the time I get her in the bathroom. "Strip," I order her as I remove the belt from my pants.

When she fails to comply, I let it fly with a satisfying smack to her lower back. "Try again. Remove your clothes."

I think she's seeing clearly now as she undoes the button of her shorts with shaky hands. I curl the belt around my knuckles, preparing for the next strike. I wait calmly until she stands before me in her underwear, trembling with her arms wrapped around her.

"I believe those are wet also." I indicate with my eyes to her panties and bra.

I don't think the waterworks have stopped since we left the dock. They seriously piss me off. I didn't ask for this today.

As soon as the bra hits the floor, I hold up a finger and twirl it. "Turn around."

Emily shakes her head, trying to cover her nudity.

I step closer. "Turn. Around."

She slowly complies, shaking even harder. The only thing on her body is the stupid ankle bandage, which is sagging by this point and giving her no support. I look away from that and appraise the red mark on her back. "Put your hands on the wall."

"Marcus, please... I didn't do anything," she whines, and it turns my stomach.

"Except drag me away from my work and ruin our day." I move nearer so she can feel my breath on her skin. "Why?"

"I was j-just..."

"What did you want with the plane, Emily?"

Her silence wins her another slap of the belt. "What did you want to do? Because we both know you hate to fly."

"Marcus, I was scared."

My fist tightens around the leather. "Of what?"

She turns, and I narrow my eyes in warning. One she doesn't heed. "I want to go home."

"And you think acting like this will get you there quicker?"

Her eyes dart around the room like she'll find something or someone to save her. "No, I just thought—"

"That you'd try to call someone to pick you up?" With a flick of my wrist, I hit the front of her thigh. "What were you going to say? Help me, I'm being held prisoner in paradise by my wealthy husband, who's done nothing but love me." I mimic her little voice.

She swallows hard, trying to shield herself with her hands. "Were you involved with what happened to Lucas?"

Oh, she is pushing it. "Do you mean was I there with a gun to my head when he was shot? Yes."

Emily searches my eyes, and I know she wants to say more, but the cat's got her tongue.

"Come here. We aren't done."

"Marcus, please..."

I shake my head and step up to her. "You keep saying that. What are you pleading for? Forgiveness? Do you want to say you're sorry?" When she doesn't come up with an answer, I wrap the belt around her neck, taking the end through the buckle and tightening the noose. "Kneel."

"No." Her fingers fly to the belt, slipping between it and her neck.

"You want to be sorry? Act like it and kneel." I press a hand on her shoulder, encouraging her down. For a split second, I think she's going to do it. Be a good little girl and finally do what she's told. But something flashes in her eyes, and instead of behaving, she grabs the belt and tugs, attempting to run at the same time. It's a war she can't win, and I haul back, flinging her off her feet.

I'm on her in a heartbeat, grabbing her shoulders and giving her a hard shake. "Is this what you want, Emily?" I feel that rush of power and I forcibly push her down, hover over her, getting high on the scent of her fear. "Karyn wanted to leave me," I snarl in her face. "Do you know what happened to her?"

Emily freezes beneath me, and I give her body some of

my weight. "Elizabeth tried to run. That didn't work out for her either." I lean closer and gather her tears on my tongue. "I fell in love with you, Emily. That was my mistake," I whisper against her cheek. "But this entire time, you've been lying to me about how you feel."

I spread her legs with my knees, and she starts to struggle again. I hold her head down with the belt. She can choke off her own air. "It could have been beautiful, whatever time we had left. I would have loved you, cared for you, given you anything you desired." I lean back to look at her clawing at the belt. "I would have killed for you, but it was all lies."

Emily starts to shake her head, like she can deny this shit now.

"I had a plan for us, baby. You've ruined everything. Why? Is this what you want? To see who has the power here and that you are nothing but a little mouse that I can take out and play with when I want? Hmm?" I let go of the belt, grabbing her by the shoulders again. "That wasn't what I wanted with you!"

I'm near tears now. Fucking stupid. I thought she was the one! The one I could love, and she'd love me back. We could have been perfect together. "Why couldn't you just be my wife!" I haul her up and slam her down. Her head bounces on the tile with a sickening thud. Her pretty eyes roll back and close.

"Emily?" I shake her. "Wake up. We aren't finished." She doesn't move, and I slap her cheek. "Wake up!"

Her head turns with my slap, and I see the blood starting to pool underneath her. Shit. What have I done? "No. No, Emily, not like this."

I place a hand on her chest, but she isn't breathing. "Baby, come on, love."

I sit back on my butt and pull her into my arms. Stroking her hair off her face, I cradle her. "Come on. We weren't through. I just needed you to see..." I look away from her. "Me."

I cup the back of her head and my hand is quickly covered in blood. It's smearing my chest and belly, dripping onto my jeans. I fucking killed her.

I realize the warmth on my face is my own tears, and I rub my cheek on her hair. "No, baby. We weren't supposed to go like this," I tell her gently. "Not so soon." Maybe we couldn't have forever in life, but we would in death, and she's ruined everything.

I had it all planned. I know she's afraid of flying, so I'd put her to sleep first. The rush I'd get from witnessing my end wouldn't be her fear. I would have done anything for her.

I look down at her, taking in all the details of her face. The curve of her cheek, that plump bottom lip, and I so want to see her eyes. "I did fall in love with you, Emily." I hold her tighter and struggle to get up. My feet slip in the blood and I go down on a knee but keep her in my arms. There's only one thing I'm certain of now. I'm not living without her.

I take her body into the bedroom, lay her out on the bed, and adjust her head on the pillow. She looks like she's sleeping, and I lower my head to brush my lips over hers. My chest hurts. I remember this pain from when Sara died. It's the feeling of my heart breaking, and I promised myself I'd never experience it again.

My vision of the future dims. The Feds are looking at me, I have another dead wife, and I'm dying. I won't end my time being investigated, tried in court, and having the public scrutinize my life. "We didn't have to end like this," I whisper to my sleeping bride.

I look away and one of my mother's paintings catches my eye. It's one of angels watching a human being tortured. They don't intervene. They never do. If I believed in the beings, I'd imagine they scoff at our plight. Take entertainment from our pain.

I look back at Emily, knowing I have to say goodbye. Lowering my head, I let my lips brush over hers, and they still feel warm, plump, and soft. "I love you," I tell her, but it doesn't matter anymore. She's gone. Emily can't hear my words or respond. It's simply over.

I take a moment to collect myself before giving Emily one last look, and I go to the side table and remove the metal box. With a press of my thumb, it opens, and I remove the pistol. I know I'm dying today, but it won't be with a bullet to the brain. Too easy, too fast. I want to laugh in death's face when I go. But there are two others I can't leave behind. Tweedledee and Tweedledum will have to go.

I check the ammunition before heading out to find them. The world is crashing down on me. It started with Lucas's botched murder. If people only knew that I'd rid the world of one more monster, they might understand. Carmen herself is a killer. Like me, she'd do anything for the ones she loves, but she knows too much. I can't have her start talking when I'm gone. Even Agent Simms said it. Don't leave witnesses behind.

Carmen is predictably in the kitchen when I stroll in. She turns and gasps at the sight of me. "You killed her?"

I raise the gun, and her hands fly up in defense.

"No, Marcus." She starts shaking her head. "I love you. I would never say anything."

The sound of the shot ricochets off the walls and I watch her go down. I'm not shocked by her declaration. In fact, I can't help but wonder now if she sabotaged my marriage to Karyn as well as with Emily. I didn't kill them. She did.

Juan bursts into the kitchen. He sees his mother before me and drops to his knees beside her. "Mama!"

I take a step closer, getting his attention before I shoot. He collapses over her body, and for a moment, I take in the beauty of the scene. At least they got to go together.

I step closer and Carmen's eyes are open and sightless, but I check for a pulse. Juan's back lifts as he takes gulps of air, like a fish out of water. He won't last long, but I end his suffering by placing my hand over his nose and mouth. He's a fighter, this kid, but he joins his mother and I'm resolved as I stand with one last look around the kitchen. None of it matters as I turn to leave. As much as I'll miss this home and regret it never became one I could share with my wife, I'm dying. It's better to go on my own time rather than wait for nature to take its course.

I pass the stairs, briefly pondering if I should put on a shirt, but then I'd need a shower. I can't see Emily again. I've already said goodbye. Outside, I lower to sit on the porch steps and take a moment to collect myself and my thoughts. It's not easy to walk away from my home. Maybe it would be better if I torch the whole place.

The seed is planted and it's perfect. There would be nothing left behind. I glance back and wince at the thought of ruining my creation, but then again, I can't picture anyone else claiming this spot as their own.

Determined, I stand and head for the generator house.

# 40

---

## EMILY

My lungs fill with air on a gulp, and my eyes pop open, and I whimper as pain slices like a knife to my skull. My vision is blurred, but I know I'm in bed, in Marcus's room. Why? I reach up and gingerly touch my head. My hair is wet and tacky, and I look at my hand covered in blood.

I have no idea what happened to me, and I try to sit up, pushing the covers aside. With a sniff, I look around the room and my eyes focus on the bloodstained pillow. I try to pull up my last memory, but everything is fuzzy and it's hard to think with the pounding pain in my skull. I scoot my legs over to dangle off the bed and my bedraggled leg bandage catches my eye. I tip my head and study that as a memory trickles in. Marcus. I was trying to get on the plane and he showed up. He was angry. Hurting me.

A burst of panic has my feet on the floor, but the second I stand, my head spins and I collapse.

I lie face down. My breath comes in ragged pants as my head threatens to explode. I'm confused and extremely weak, but I manage to push up to my hands and knees. With my head bowed, blood trickles down my cheek, onto the white carpet, and I start to crawl. I'm aware that I'm naked, but I feel a bone-deep need to get out of this house.

I make it to the hallway, then to the top of the stairs, and I know I need to get to my feet. Using the banister, I pull myself up, and my head screams in protest as my vision blurs again. With no support, my ankle threatens to give out, and I shift my weight to my good leg. It's clear I'm not running anywhere, but I cling to the banister and maneuver down the stairs sideways.

The door beckons me as I reach the foyer, but another thought hits me. I need a weapon, and with a glance to my right, I can see the front room is empty and the kitchen is just beyond.

I stumble across the tiled floor with a zombie-like gait. Blood trails down my arm and drips off my fingers onto the floor. I chant in my head one word. Survive.

I pause at the threshold and through my foggy brain, I wonder if Carmen is in here, and I hold on to the doorframe and peek inside. It's empty and I breathe.

On shaky legs, I stumble to the center island. It stands between me and the knives on the wall. I use the counter for balance and edge my way around. At the corner, I freeze. On the floor in front of me is Juan, sprawled over his mother in a large pool of blood.

The horror is real, but I'm incapable of reacting. No scream leaves my lips. I don't run toward them or away. I simply stare at their bodies and shut down.

Where is Marcus?

Something catches my eyes near Juan's body, and I focus on that with a tip of my head. A gun? So much better than a knife. I'm fighting gravity as I crouch down to pick it up. It's heavier than I expected, and I've never held one before. The only thing I know is where the trigger is.

I glance around the room, trying to decide which way to go. Out the back? Through the front? And when I get outside, where do I go? Hide somewhere and wait for him to find me? I need help!

The equipment shed. There's a computer in there, and with the gun, I could shoot off the lock. It would seem I have a newfound strength as I limp back through to the foyer, passing the stairs and my own trail of blood. I reach the door and pull it open, stumbling onto the porch. I wince at the sunlight and take a deep breath. I'm not sure I have what it takes to go much farther.

Clutching the rail, I start down the steps, but the hair on the back of my neck rises. A sound to my right has me turning, and the air around me shifts. Marcus is shirtless, covered in blood and holding a gasoline can in his hand. My heart stops beating as those blue eyes meet mine. He drops the can and stares back at me like he's seeing a ghost.

"Emily?"

The sound of my name restarts my heart, and I clutch the gun in both hands, raising it up and pointing it at him.

"Emily? I thought—"

His words are cut off by the sharp pop that explodes from my hand. Marcus clutches his neck, blood quickly oozing through his fingers. His eyes grow wide and lock on mine as he drops to his knees. A gurgling noise comes from his throat, and he reaches his hand out toward me before collapsing to his side on the grass.

Panic, fear, white-hot rage, all my emotions boil over so fast, and I scream. It echoes back to me from the hillside, and

I slowly sink to the ground. I scoot on my butt until my back hits the wall, and I clutch the gun in front of me.

For a long time, I stare sightlessly in front of me. The island birds chirp out their songs, punctuated by an occasional whistle. Fluffy white clouds float against the blue sky, and in the distance, the waves crash on the rocks below. I close my eyes, so tired now, and give my brain over to the sounds of the island. I still need help, but there's no one left to hurt me now and the warmth of my tears is noticed but ignored. I don't have anything left to get me to the shed.

I might have fallen asleep, maybe not, but the next thing I'm aware of is the sound of a steady thumping. It seems out of place here, and I look up as it draws nearer.

A helicopter flies over the house, and I open my mouth to scream, but only a gargled sound leaves my throat. I can't see it anymore, but it's still loud and then it appears again as it circles around. Did they see me?

It hovers and then starts to lower, and I know somewhere inside me I should feel relief, but I'm numb. I close my eyes again and rest my head back against the wall. The thumping noise quiets and I start to drift into the blissful darkness.

"Emily? Emily Hanson?"

It's a man's voice and I hum in response but stay behind my eyelids until fingers brush the back of my hands. I tighten my grip on the gun as my eyes fly open.

The man kneeling in front of me raises his hands at his sides. "I'm Agent Simms. I'm here to help you."

My eyes narrow on him, but he is wearing a ball cap that has the letters FBI on it.

"Emily, can you give me the gun?"

I look down at the weapon in my hands, slightly shocked it's still there, and I drop it between us.

Agent Simms flinches slightly, then picks it up gingerly. I notice two other men. One is next to Marcus. The other is on a radio. He comes over to take the weapon from Agent Simms.

"She needs a medevac, now!" he barks and glances over at the man with Marcus, who stands and shakes his head.

My heart curls in on itself. He's dead? He's really dead.

"Emily, is there anyone else in the house?"

I look back at him and nod.

"Okay."

"I think they're dead," I add.

He blows out a breath. "Okay. Where are they?"

"The kitchen."

He looks up at the guy who's joined us on the porch. He draws his weapon and heads through the open front door.

"Emily?" Agent Simms gets my eyes back on him. "Did you shoot them?"

"No," I whisper and glance over at Marcus, sprawled on his back and unmoving. Something cracks—my wall of defense, I don't know what—but I start to tremble, and it quickly becomes uncontrollable shakes.

The agent sits down next to me, putting an arm around my shoulders. "It's all right." He gently touches my hair in an attempt to view my wound. I wince and lean away.

He drops his hand. "Help is on the way. It's going to be okay."

---

I DON'T RECALL the flight over here, but I remember Gia running to me as they wheeled me on a gurney to an ambulance. I glance over at her now, curled up in a chair and fast

CALDWELL

asleep. Since I first saw her, I've wrapped her presence around me like a warm blanket, and she hasn't left my side unless she's been forced to.

I haven't been able to talk much about what happened, and I'm still fuzzy about parts. I remember Marcus coming after me on the dock, but I have no idea what happened to my head. The doctor tells me that's normal. The memories may or may not come back.

Gia stirs when my hospital room door opens and a nurse peeks in. "Oh, good, you're awake. The FBI is here to speak with you."

"Okay." My voice is weak, but my anxiety grows.

Gia pats my hand. "Honey, it's all right. Heath couldn't hold them off forever."

I don't respond. I know Heath has been here for Gia the whole time, and I'm grateful that he's been protecting me. But the truth is, I killed a man. I'm a murderer.

Agent Simms enters with another man he introduces as Chief Benson with the local police.

"We just need to take your statement, Ms. Hanson," Agent Simms says and glances at Gia.

"What? I'm not getting out of this chair," she snaps at his unspoken request.

"That's all right, Ms. Cincetti. I'm only going to ask you not to interrupt." He focuses back on me. "Let's start with what happened the day of the murders."

A shiver runs through me, but I lift my chin. "It started way before that day."

For the next thirty minutes, I recount everything that happened, well, almost everything that happened after I agreed to go to the island with him. I tearfully get through the day after the storm, and the day he left me there. I mention Lucas, but I skip the details about his plan to help me. I don't know why. He's dead. Or I think he is, but I tell them about the phone call I overheard.

Chief Benson shifts on his feet, drawing my attention to him. He's scowling at me, and I shrink in on myself.

"Emily, Mr. Carrington mentioned that Marcus told him you two got married. Is that true?" Simms asks.

"Oh." Did I skip that part? "Um, yes. I don't think it's legal, though."

"The marriage certificate was signed and filed," Captain Benson says. "It appears very legal and binding."

How do I explain? "Marcus said I could go home if I married him."

"Are you saying you were forced to marry him?" Benson asks.

I nod, the tears I've held back leaking from my eyes.

"Then explain this."

He shows me pictures on his phone. A news article with me smiling next to Marcus with the floral trellis behind us.

"Do you know what I think, Mrs. Sterling?" Chief Benson steps closer to my bedside. "I think you married Mr. Sterling with the full intention of getting your hands on his wealth. In less than two weeks, you folded up your life in New York. How did you break your lease and resign from your job when you say you had no contact with the outside world?"

"I didn't—"

"Stop." Gia holds up a hand. "Emily, don't say another word until Heath gets that lawyer."

I wrap my arms around myself, wishing I could disappear, but I'm done talking. Lucas made it clear that Marcus had the authorities in his pocket. He was wrong about one thing, though. Marcus isn't breathing, and I'm still not safe.

## 41

## EMILY

Propped up against my pillows, I stare at the aerial footage of Marcus's island on the television. My heart feels like lead.

"Marcus Sterling was honored today in London, where he was buried with his family at the Sterling estate," a female newscaster reports. "The investigation continues as to what happened on Sterling Key. Carmen and Juan Diaz were found brutally murdered inside the home, and it's still a question as to who pulled the trigger."

The picture changes to the woman standing in front of swaying palm trees in front of the very hospital I'm in. "Emily Sterling is recovering from surgery, and sources say she is expected to be released soon. In the wake of her husband's murder, she has inherited what is estimated to be over a billion dollars."

I run my hand over my bandaged head and glare at the television as hate and angst churn in my belly. I didn't know about the will.

"As the only survivor of the carnage on that remote island, Mrs. Sterling is the prime suspect. However, the authorities have not commented as to whether she will be charged—"

"Emily! Turn that off." Gia enters with a coffee in one hand and a muffin in the other. Stomping over to my tray, she sets everything down and shuts off the TV. "You need to stop watching that shit."

"Why? How else am I going to learn what's going on?"

Gia huffs. "It's going to be fine. Heath has hired the best lawyer for you and Agent Simms still believes your story."

"Yes, well, the FBI isn't in charge of the murder investigation, so—" I shrug. What's the point? I was finally able to find freedom, only to face jail time.

Gia gathers up my hands and gets me to look at her. "Heath has some good news. You're going home. He's making the arrangements now."

"W-what?" I wasn't expecting to hear that. "How?"

"I don't know. Agent Simms is on his way up to speak to you. Your lawyer is with him." She picks up my muffin. "Here, eat something."

I take the muffin, but my appetite has waned. "I don't have a home," I mutter.

"Honey, we'll take care of you." Her phone rings and she checks it, ignoring the call.

I raise a brow. "Was that my mother again?"

"Yes. I'll call her later."

Gia, my vigilant watchdog, is protecting me again. I spoke to my mom once after my surgery. Her first question was if I inherited any money. I've refused to talk to her again. I can't deal with her and everything else that is happening.

The door opens and Heath precedes Agent Simms and Mr. Brown, my new lawyer. I'm not sure what would have happened without Heath. He's one hundred percent shown up for me.

Mr. Brown hangs back as Simms approaches the end of my bed. "Good morning, Emily."

I only nod in response, not trusting my voice, and wait for him to explain.

His lips twitch up. "It seems you're heading home today."

I'm still absorbing that. "W-what changed?"

"Lucas Tate came forward and corroborated your story."

I stare back before blinking several times. "He's alive?"

"He is. We placed him in protective custody due to questions surrounding his shooting. Mr. Tate has been recovering from his injuries, but we were finally able to get a formal statement."

I press a hand to my chest with a long exhale. "That's why you came to the island?"

"That and Ms. Cincetti approached us, claiming you had been kidnapped."

My eyes widen and I turn to Gia. "You did that?"

"The police here were being uncooperative, so yes. I'd have stormed the White House if I had to."

I squeeze her hand. God, I love her.

"On that note, some interesting information was revealed in our interview with Mr. Tate. It has opened an investigation into Captain Benson and his department," Simms continues. "Plus, we're going to reopen the case on Karyn Sterling as well."

I don't know what to say. It sounds like Lucas told them everything. Perhaps he did end up saving me.

"Em." Heath gets my attention. "I've scheduled a plane for this afternoon. You'll be back in New York tonight."

So many emotions rise up in me at once, and tears spring to my eyes. Lucas is alive, I'm going home, and... "Wait. So I won't be charged with Marcus's murder?"

"Through the joint investigation, your statement and Mr. Tate's, it's been determined you killed him in self-defense. Since you found the bodies of Carmen Diaz and her son before you went outside, we are speculating that Marcus shot them and was then planning to burn down the house."

I blow out another breath, recalling the gas can, and I swallow through my tight throat. If I hadn't woken up, it's possible I could have died in a fire.

"We'll be in touch when you're back and settled in," Agent Simms assures me with a kind smile.

As soon as the door closes behind him, the tears start. I don't know if it's relief, grief, or pure overwhelm. "Could I please have a moment alone?" I ask the room as a whole.

Heath leaves with Mr. Brown, but Gia stays, climbing on the bed with me and pulling me into a hug. I bury my face in her hair and the floodgates open. Sobs rack my body, and a long, painful wail rips from my throat. I shake in her arms while she rubs my back and lets me cry it out.

---

"TO THINK NOT LONG AGO I was terrified of flying," I mutter to Gia.

I'm curled up next to her on a bench-like sofa in the back of Heath's private plane.

She gives me a squeeze. "It's all going to be fine now."

It's not really over. "I don't have an apartment or a job. He left me with nothing."

"Except a billion dollars," Gia points out.

"Which is not in my bank account." Christ. I don't even know where my things are. I don't have a driver's license or a passport. Marcus told me he closed all of my credit cards.

There's a constant stab of pain in my heart every time I think about him. I have no idea what spurred me to pull the trigger on that gun. It's as though I wasn't really present. The doctors were amazed I was even walking around and talking with the injury I had, but the bloody trail I left supported my story as far as Agent Simms was concerned.

"Sweetie, Heath and I discussed this. He has plenty of room at his house. We'll stay with him until we figure it out."

I glance up at her. I haven't asked too many questions, but what the hell is going on with her and Heath? The last time I saw her before I left, she was brushing him off and heading for Europe. That hits me with a new layer of guilt. "I'm sorry you missed your trip to France. You didn't have to stay."

One penciled brow shoots up. "Are you kidding me? There will always be other opportunities, but there's only one Emily."

I rest my head back in her lap. "When did you and Heath get so serious?"

"I don't know." Her fingers brush back and forth over my arm. "After the gala, I knew Marcus was doing something nefarious. I couldn't reach you, my messages were ignored. I was really scared. Heath said he'd check on you when he came out, and I convinced him to bring me too."

"The gala? You were there?"

"Oh, I was there all right. I should have pushed him over that wall."

I'm not sure what that's about, but I don't ask.

"Anyway, Heath's been so awesome about everything,

especially when he learned I was right. Are we serious? I don't know, but I'm forever grateful for him."

I am too. Heath handled everything for Marcus's funeral. We've had several conversations regarding the will. He received everything related to the business, and I ended up with Marcus's personal wealth, properties, investments, and his family estate. It's overwhelming to even think about. Heath has promised to help me navigate everything. He's been so kind, patient, and incredibly attentive to Gia while she's been completely focused on me.

"As soon as I can, I promise to find my own place," I murmur sleepily.

Gia pats my arm. "There's no rush, Em. Let's focus on getting you all healed up first."

I close my eyes and the pain medication always wants to pull me under, but it doesn't stop the dreams. Marcus refuses to leave me in death. I feel him around me all the time. Maybe with some time and space, I'll feel like myself again, but I fear I'm forever changed.

## 42

## ONE YEAR LATER

The comfort of these leather seats does nothing to settle my nerves. My driver sits patiently in traffic while my mother rattles on in my ear. "Emily, all I'm saying is you already own the property in Palm Beach. Just let me live there."

I blow out an irritated breath. I've been selling off the residential properties, and what hasn't sold, I have a property management company handle them. "Mom, I'll see what I can do." Honestly, with the allowance I give her, she should be able to find something herself. Maybe not a mansion in Palm Beach.

We're moving again, and after a few blocks, we pull up in front of the apartment building. "I need to go. I'll call you later."

It's been nearly a year since I returned to New York. I left here a girl full of optimism and opportunities. I'll never be that girl again, but I'm working on redefining myself, and one of my goals is to come to terms with my mom.

Stephan, my bodyguard, opens the door for me, and I

slide on my sunglasses before stepping out. It happens less all the time, but in the beginning, the media was watching for me. Then, my anxiety bubbled constantly under the surface. It was horrifying for me to be recognized on the street, called out to, photographed, questioned.

I learned two things. Dress for success whenever you leave the house, which I achieved today in the off-white linen pantsuit. Also, don't do anything that would cause a headline to pop up later that day.

Stephan opens the door for me and I step into the cool lobby. My heels tap on the marble floor as we cross to the elevators. I just finished my session with Dr. Lynn and I feel exhausted. I would say that therapy is helping, but sometimes I feel like she rips me apart and then sends me home to piece myself back together again.

The elevator doors open directly to the foyer of my penthouse apartment. I chose this place for two reasons. It has security and wonderful views of a city I no longer participate in. I can watch life happen outside and feel secure that I'm not all alone in the world, but my anxiety still keeps me a prisoner within these walls.

I stride through the foyer and into the open front room where I'm greeted by the natural light pouring in through a wall of windows. Melissa is seated at my large dining table, with her blond hair tied in a tight knot at the nap of her neck, scribbling on a notepad beside her computer.

She looks up at me as Stephan closes the door, and shuts down her laptop. "I was just finishing up, Mrs. Sterling," she says and starts to straighten her makeshift workspace on my table.

When Heath assigned Melissa to me as a personal assistant, I knew she had worked for Marcus. It was awkward, but she's been a godsend. She knew way more about Marcus Sterling and his life than I did.

"I have everything ready for the annual gala next weekend. All you need to do is show up."

"All right." Not happening. Gia is begging me to go. She's attending with Heath, but it's a fundraiser for domestic violence and I don't want to be the poster child for every charity I choose to donate to.

I step around the breakfast bar, set down my purse on the counter, and select a wineglass from the rack.

Melissa stands with her notepad in hand. "The governor invited you to a dinner to thank you for the generous donation you made to the democratic party."

One thing I have enjoyed doing with Marcus's money is giving it away. "And I respectfully decline." I grab a bottle of merlot. "Anything else?"

"No," she replies with a concerned smile. "Your mail is on the table. Have a good night."

"Thank you, Melissa."

I don't watch her leave as I give myself a heavy pour of wine and grab my phone from my bag. I don't go very far without it these days. Moving over to the couch, I set everything down and pull my journal out from the sofa table drawer.

It's something my therapist suggested. Writing down my thoughts has brought some clarity to my time on the island and even helped recover some new memories.

For some reason, I've made all my entries letters to Marcus. I think it helps me say all the things I was too frightened to say to him at the time. I roll my lips together and click my pen several times before writing down today's date.

*Dear Marcus,*

*It's one year to the date that you died and my life will never be the same. I put your precious island on the market and I already have a few buyers interested. If I could, I would burn the place to the ground, but I won't.*

I pause, rereading those words. There's still a piece of me left there. My innocence. Therapy has helped me understand how Marcus manipulated me. His cycle of emotional abuse started before he ever hurt me. Studies of people like Marcus show that they target certain personalities. It still makes me angry that I was one of those people. Naive, unsuspecting, trusting. I'm not sure it was completely all those things that made me a sucker. It was a thirst I had to be loved.

I put my pen back to paper.

*I buried Emily Hanson with you. Emily Sterling is nothing like her. I'm getting stronger and smarter every day.*

It was Heath who convinced me to keep the name Sterling. The scandal around Marcus after my story came out was hurting the business. The polls showed more people were sympathetic to me than speculating I was a murderer. After everything Heath has done for me, I agreed. Honestly, in some respects, it makes life easier. Marcus was right. His name does offer me more protection and the power to make things happen.

My phone rings and I sigh when I see Gia's name. Setting the journal aside, I pick up my wine, then answer the call. "Hello, Gia."

"Hey, how was your session today?"

"Good." I take a large sip of wine. "We discussed my mommy issues, then my daddy issues." Dr. Lynn loves to point out that my upbringing without a father could have led me to look for a masculine authority in my life. "Seriously, I have so many issues."

"Em, that isn't true. You were a victim in a terrifying situation."

Hmm. "Did you know I have a victim personality?"

"He was manipulating you." Gia groans. "Anyone could have found themselves in that situation."

"You wouldn't have."

"Well..."

Exactly. I take another fortifying sip. "You know, I felt bad for him when he told me he was dying."

"Because you're a caring person! You need to stop beating yourself up."

It's because I'm a fool. "When do you get back?" I attempt to change the subject.

"Friday. Did you decide if you're going to the gala?"

"I'm not going."

"Why?" she whines.

I take another drink rather than going into my reasons. Gia has no idea what it feels like when other people look at me. It's one reason I rarely leave my home. I'm either pitied or accused. A lot of details didn't become public, which is fine, but some people still believe I killed Marcus for the money.

"Em, you have to go. You're the one who organized it."

I did. Working with the foundation is one thing I have been able to do, mostly from home with the help of Melissa. "Heath is fine with being the representative and taking the limelight. I don't need to be there."

"Emily?" She sighs heavily into the phone. "All right. Friday night, it's you, me, and Thai takeout."

"That I can show up for. I'll buy." I inwardly laugh at that. A year ago, I was taking her hand-me-downs and letting her pay for dinner. How life has changed. "I'll see you Friday."

I pick up my wine and down the rest as I stare out the window. Anxiety and depression can be the result of several things. Emotional trauma, physical trauma—I've experienced both. Along with the money Marcus left me, I have a host of new problems. It doesn't help that I feel completely alone. On that note, where is Bella? Normally, she'll hide when others are around, but she tends to join me when they're gone.

"Bell?" I stand up from the couch and start my search for her.

She's not in her normal spots, on my bed, or sleeping in the laundry room. My concern grows as I come back into the front room. It's open here. There are not many places to hide. The hall to the back of the apartment is dark. There are a few rooms down there I never use. There is one I've started turning into a library. It's the only thing I took from the island home. Marcus's collection of books.

Most of them are still boxed while the shelving is being finished, and I keep that door closed during the day. Maybe I forgot. I flip on the light and the hall illuminates. I hate the anxiety that bubbles up inside me. There is nothing to fear here. The door to the library is closed, but I was inside there earlier. Did I lock her in? With me in my head all the time, it's completely possible. I open the door and freeze.

He's seated in my corner nook reading a book with my cat on his lap, casually stroking her fur, and his eyes rise to mine. Those light blues send a jolt to my heart. "Lucas?"

"Hello, Emily."

For a moment, I'm frozen in shock, then my heart starts to pound with a solid thump. "What are you doing here?"

Lucas sets down the book, still petting Bella. "She's a good cat. So sweet, trusting."

"Umm..." I look at her and she seems content to stay on his lap, but the initial shock is wearing off. "No. How did you get in here?"

A small smile plays on his lips as he looks down at Bella. "I wanted to see with my own eyes that you are okay."

That's not an answer. "You broke into my home?"

He's leaner than before and it shows in his face. His blond hair is a little longer, but those eyes haven't changed.

"It's hard to get near you when you manage to venture out." He picks Bella up and sets her on the floor.

"You've tried?" Has he been watching me? "You could have knocked."

Lucas stands, and even though he's lost some muscle mass, he's still a powerful-looking man. A confusing mix of fear mingles with something like relief to see him.

He takes a step toward me. "Emily, I just wanted to check in with you."

"Why?" My brain snaps back online. "How?" I ask instead. "How did you get into my home?"

He smirks, stepping closer to me. "Your security is average. I could help you with that."

That irks me. "By putting cameras in my bedroom?"

"Stop. At the time, I was only doing my job."

"Working for a madman." I take a calming inhale. Lucas might be the only reason I'm not sitting in prison right now. "I should thank you for telling the FBI what happened."

He nods and takes another step closer. "I couldn't let you go down for killing Marcus."

I wince as I always do when I'm reminded of what I've done. "He almost killed me first."

"I know."

I press my lips together, tears stinging my eyes. "Why didn't you reach out before?"

"I was kept in protective custody until they finished the investigation into Karyn and Elizabeth's deaths. There's more. They suspect Marcus in the deaths of his parents and a woman named Sara Monroe, whom he dated in college. But I wasn't a witness in those crimes."

This isn't news to me. Agent Simms has kept me informed about the investigations. He's been incredibly supportive this last year. For a moment, I regard Lucas and then shake my head.

"I know you've been helpful, but breaking into my home is... illegal. I think you should go. I won't call the police."

He huffs. "The police? Look, at first, I wasn't planning on ever contacting you." He puts his hands in his jeans pockets and shifts his weight. "But then I couldn't stop thinking about you."

I've thought about him too, but that isn't the point right now. "Fine. Let's meet sometime, somewhere public. You are scaring me right now."

"I'm not here to hurt you."

"Good. I still need you to go."

"Hmm." He looks around the half-finished room. "I should probably thank you as well," he says, ignoring my request.

"For what?"

"When you killed Marcus, you freed me too."

I never understood how or why he worked for Marcus.

"In a way, you became my savior," he says.

How do I respond to that? You're welcome? "Lucas, whatever happened between you and Marcus, I know you aren't a bad guy, and I do appreciate your help, but I need you to leave."

He steps closer, cocking his head. "I never admitted to being a good guy." He chuckles. "You came out pretty well from that whole ordeal too, didn't you?"

My pulse skitters and I move closer to the door. "W-what do you mean?"

He meets my gaze again. "I mean you're set for life now." He takes a step closer. "You were compensated well for everything you had to endure."

I shake my head. "What do you want? Money?"

"No." His voice is low.

Fear tightens around my heart like a fist and my lungs seem to shrink. "What then?"

He closes the space between us, reaching behind me to shut the door. "You."

My back hits the wall and I'm paralyzed, incapable of speaking or moving.

"You don't have to be afraid of me, Emily." He leans in closer. "I made you a promise on that island. I've decided it's time to follow through."

I look up into those crystal blues. "What promise?"

"I said when it was all over, I'd come back for you." He

tucks my hair behind my ear. "We started something on that island, and it's time for us to finish it." His finger trails down my cheek. I close my eyes as his hand slides into my hair, cupping my head, and he kisses me.

The End

# THANK YOU FOR READING

Did you enjoy reading *The One*? Please consider leaving a review on Amazon. Your review will help other readers to discover the novel.

# ACKNOWLEDGMENTS

I have to acknowledge my husband first and foremost. He's been my greatest supporter, picking me up when I'm falling down, encouraging me, and inspiring me to do better.

My Aunt Cathie, who – bless her heart – reads all of my books and is my biggest cheerleader.

Adina, I could never thank you enough for all the work you do to help these stories come to life!

Jane, you're amazing. Without you, these stories I've written would be tucked in a desk drawer. I adore you, and your blunt honesty has made me step up and face challenges I'd have otherwise stepped away from and never pressed forward.

I have a global support team, and I appreciate every one of you for helping make these books a reality. I thank you, the reader, who took a chance and read these stories. I hope you enjoyed them as much as I loved writing them.

# ABOUT THE AUTHOR

I live in the foothills of the Colorado Rockies, and I love my dogs, horses, and of course, a good book.

When I'm not roaming around the mountains, I'm searching for the perfect beach!

Aside from my love of romance books, I like thrillers, action, and adventure with a touch of mystery. Perhaps I try to stuff all this into my stories.

I enjoy creating new worlds in my imagination and writing them down to share with everyone. If you'd like to learn more about me, what books are on the horizon, or take a glimpse at what I already have published, visit my website.

Sign up for my newsletter and receive current information on new books, free giveaways and more!

Please visit T.A. on her website:
www.tacaldwellauthor.com

# ALSO BY T.A. CALDWELL

**Inkubator Books Titles**

The One

---

**Other Titles by T. A. Caldwell**

*Near Future Sci-Fi Romance*

**The Donovan Tales Series**

Sanshain - Book 1

Deception - Book 2

Home - Book 3

Expectations - Book 4

Complicated - Book 5

Secrets - Book 6

*Dark Romance*

**The Testa Affairs Series**

Choices

Consequences

*Women's Fiction Romance*

Paradise

Printed in Dunstable, United Kingdom

68815880R00211